GARRY COLQUHOUN KEMP

The Windfall Chameleon

Elaine
with best wishes
Garry

ISBN: 1-4699-4828-1
ISBN-13: 9781469948287

For Sally

PROLOGUE

June 2011

"This gives me very little pleasure, but it's what my 'employers' insisted on," Youssef said with an icy smile as he put a bullet into Ferguson's left knee.

The scream came not from the old man, but from the girl who was cowering in a corner of the office. She pointed a shaking, accusing finger:

"The earth is given into the hand of the wicked."

"Book of Job," Youssef acknowledged benignly. "It won't help."

"Let her go," Ferguson gritted between clenched teeth, clutching with both hands at his shattered leg, "She'll keep quiet."

"True," Youssef agreed, and he shot the woman once in the forehead. Her entire head snapped back against the wall. "But there's nothing like being quite sure." As his victim slid to the floor, leaving a red trail down the pine paneling, he turned his attention to Ferguson's other knee.

The office was fairly large, but not extravagantly so. It was furnished with quiet good taste, the sort of taste that usually only the very wealthy can afford when they hire an eminent decorator. Ralph Ferguson was just such a wealthy man, and he was also blessed with an innate sense of style, so the decorator had not been forced to overcome unwelcome suggestions. The result was the impression of an executive who was both successful and down-to-earth, useful assets in the business world that Ferguson inhabited. Fergoil, modestly named for its owner and founder, was fast becoming a force to be reckoned with in the petroleum industry, driven by the ambition and skill—some would have added ruthlessness—of its sole proprietor.

Youssef looked down impassively at Ferguson. The man was hunched on the Persian carpet, curled into an agonized ball as he tried to ease the excruciating pain of his injuries. Blood smirched the oriental rug and the legs of Ferguson's expensive oiled teak desk. The man emitted a subdued mewling sound, a noise which Youssef recognized from many years familiarity with other people's pain as an attempt to appear courageous.

Appear to whom? Youssef frequently wondered. *Does he really think I'll be impressed with his bravery? Enough to let him live?* It made little difference. It had been ordained by superiors that Ferguson should die, and so he would. Still, Youssef lingered a little longer before putting a bullet through Ferguson's forehead. He liked to observe his victims' behavior. There was often something new to learn. As usual at such times, he had a momentary flash of his childhood. He understood pain and misery.

Emergency services, Fire Department, and police personnel were desperately tugging at the rubble of buildings which had never been designed to withstand this kind of onslaught. Some of the workers, delving through the shattered remains of what had once been imposing corporate statements, took a moment to wonder why building codes had not been more stringent. No matter now. The dead and injured were here, uninterested in the politics of big business.

Four hours or so after the tornado had struck, the members of Unit Four were still pulling victims from the business complex. They were elated: so far they had discovered thirteen survivors—some of them severely injured, it was true, but alive— and the group was on a high. Thad Baker, the unit leader, eased a door transom carefully away.

"There are two people here," he said calmly. "Let's try to get 'em out." His colleagues went immediately to work, hauling beams and the pathetic slabs of wallboard from which the building had been built. The brick facing blocks of the outer structure had been largely thrown aside, so it was only a matter of minutes before the two bodies had been pulled clear of what, judging by the remains of expensive furnishings, had evidently been a senior executive's office. Gently they were laid on a flat part of the remaining floor. A distinguished-looking elderly man, Baker saw, and a youngish woman. Both bodies were badly mangled, but Baker automatically checked for signs of life, knowing it to be useless. No pulse, no breathing, no hope for these two, he realized, seeing yet another pair of bodies among the many which had already been pulled from the wreckage of several buildings. *Jesus, what a night*, he thought, *so many dead, so many hurt.* Not for the first time, he considered taking his wife's advice to leave the department and take up a less stressful job—insurance sales, say— but he knew he wouldn't.

"Let's get the ambulance people," he said. Then, after another look at the victims, the blood being washed from their upturned faces by the rain which continued to fall after the passage of the main storm, "Oh, my God! And the police. "

Chapter 1
June 2011

Beneath the spreading branches of the venerable Council Oak, five men and two women stood. They were there to look over the ground to decide what was needed for the ceremonies of the following day. The sun was setting, yet instead of the usual red-gold of the evening, the atmosphere had a faint greenish cast.

"Storm comin'," one of the men said through his chewing tobacco, and the others nodded agreement. "Be a bad one, I reckon," the man went on. "Maybe we better be leaving. Don't want to get caught here if it turns out real bad."

One of the women laughed, her head thrown back, her black hair glistening in the curious light. "You scared, Billy? Don't you remember why this is our oak, huh? Old Dode'd be laughing at you if he were here." Dode McIntosh had been the last hereditary chief of the Creek Indian Nation, a feisty man, proud of his Creek/Scottish heritage, and much given to wearing a kilt. Billy looked a little shame-faced, and turned away toward the white house which stood across the road and faced the small Creek-dedicated Stickball Park, so that his embarrassment was hidden.

"Yeah, sure, of course. But times've changed since those days, and the lay of the land, too. All that building," he gestured to the west, toward the river, the oil refineries and beyond, "could've upset the balance that nature put here. Don't want to press our luck, huh?" He started toward his Dodge Ram pickup. "Me, anyway." He adjusted his Stetson, with the tall feather in its beaded hatband, opened the truck door and slid inside. "See you guys tomorrow." The starter whirred, the engine caught, and Billy was on his way.

"Jolene," one of the other men said, "Billy's got a point, y'know. Jes' look at that sky now." He pointed, not west this time like Billy, but more southwest. There was a great towering line of clouds approaching, deep green clouds with shades of indigo and yellow, so tall and bulky they looked as though they might collapse under their own weight. Lightning flashed its warning from within the depths of the vapor, and the air seemed to be holding its breath in trepidation. "Yep, think I'll be goin', too." The others, except for Jolene, weren't far behind.

The storm, as such storms usually do, had boiled up from the southwest. Television meteorologists kept "a close watch on it," and promised to keep their viewers up to date—as long, of course, as they stayed "tuned to this station." Cool air from the north was meeting "warm, moist air being drawn up from the Gulf." There were upper level disturbances and unstable conditions, probability of severe thunderstorms, the chance of strong and damaging winds, areas of low and high pressure, an unpredictable jet stream, the likelihood of heavy rain and hail, with the concomitant flash floods and temperatures as high as the mid-nineties. In short, the storm season along "Tornado Alley" was proceeding normally.

In Oklahoma City, Roger Maitland, of TV Channel 1, regarded his array of Vipir, Nexrad, Doppler, and Extended Area radars, as well as the latest satellite feeds. *It looks*, he thought, *like the first of the year's tornadoes is on its way.* A warning buzzer: The National Oceanographic and Atmospheric Administration was reporting a massive wall cloud approaching the Oklahoma City area roughly along the line of Interstate Highway 44. Wall clouds were often the bearers of savage storms, and Maitland had time to reflect that I-44 almost seemed to be devised for the purpose of smoothing the path of such storms through the heart of Oklahoma. *Ice and snow in the winter, too,* he thought. *Maybe I should move to Caracas.* He peered at his monitors. The screens were mostly various shades of red, a sure sign of danger. A disembodied voice from the National Weather Service was announcing a tornado watch for most of the eastern half of Oklahoma, as well as the adjoining areas of Kansas, Missouri, and Arkansas. *They're a bit slow,* Maitland thought, *they should be issuing a warning rather than a watch. People ought to be hearing the sound of the sirens.* Much as he deplored the fact, he understood that there were some potential Channel 1 viewers who might not be glued to their sets, and the sirens were an important way of alerting them to possibly dangerous conditions. For a moment, he wondered about those who were hearing impaired: what good were the sirens to them?

Maitland's immediate superior, immaculately clad and soothingly urbane, was on camera exhorting his audience to take appropriate precautions. "So far it's a tornado watch," he told them, his honest face registering warm concern for the audience's welfare, "but everything points to it becoming a warning any time." He gestured to the "green screen" behind him, representing all parts of the viewing area. The information displayed was predominately in red. "Take cover as these storms approach. Go to a storm cellar, if you have one, or an inside room. At the very least stay away from windows and doors. If you have no alternative, get into a bathtub and cover yourself with a mattress. This is a very dangerous storm." A piece of paper was handed to him from off-camera. "The National Weather Service has now upgraded the tornado watch to a warning for the entire Channel 1 viewing area. A tornado is reported to have touched down in Moore, just to the southwest of Oklahoma City, and is heading towards...." The viewers' screens went blank.

A little to that same southwest of the city, three young men stepped into the street from The Garden Gnome Bar and Grille. They were cheerful, following the announcement that "good ol' Ken" had been given a promotion at his office. They were actually far too cheerful for any one of them to be driving, but they were saved the problem. A roaring, massive black column swirled toward them, picking up debris as it came, tearing the roofs off buildings, flattening street lights, demolishing an entire block of apartments, and flinging good ol' Ken's beloved pickup truck into a creek a hundred and fifty yards away. The three stood stock still for a moment and then, without a word, about-turned in the green night into the tavern, which was completely untouched. The twister ground on, ripping out Channel 1's broadcast tower as it went.

As the evening progressed, the storms came thick and fast. It was later established that more than twenty tornadoes had touched down in central and northeastern Oklahoma. Most of them, mercifully, missed inhabited areas, although several caused severe damage to farm buildings and livestock, as well as the crops which had been ripening so well. And, eventually, the storm, having ripped through Bristow and Sapulpa, hit Tulsa.

The Creek Indians, having been uprooted, even more ruthlessly than Channel 1's television tower, from their ancestral home in the southeast of the country by greedy white men wanting their fertile lands, found themselves (those members who survived a brutal trek) deposited in what is now Tulsa, Oklahoma. Their traditional lands having been stolen for cultivation by slaves, they were graciously permitted to select their own area in this strange, relatively barren region, and picked a hillside to the east of the Arkansas River. There, they declared, the lie of the land meant that tornadoes would not strike the ancient tree which they designated their Council Oak—the place where they rekindled their Council fire and held their ceremonies. The Council Oak is still their hallowed meeting place and, so far, they have been proven right about tornadoes. Jolene had elected to watch from beneath the ancient tree's branches, close to the stylized fire sculpture, and silently thanked her ancestors for their wisdom. She lit a cigarette and took in the churning clouds and the constant flicker of lightning. The sound of thunder was almost continuous, though still distant. The Tulsa of today had grown so much and had become so spread out that many of its newer areas, particularly to the south, not conceived of by those early migrants, were now subject to storm damage. So it was on the night of May 22nd. And Jolene finally decided to go home.

The tornado, which had continued its course northeast, roughly along the line of I-44, struck at 51st and Riverside—having skipped over West Tulsa and Jenks—and demolished a service station, a shopping strip mall, and a handful of other small businesses. The roaring funnel cloud, later designated an EF5 tornado, then bounced back into the sky, before descending again a little to the southeast, where it destroyed a number of relatively new corporate buildings. Among these was the headquarters of Fergoil.

Youssef replaced the bulky pistol in the camera pocket of his "photographer's safari vest," smoothed back his hair, and left the bodies in the sixth-floor office, taking the elevator to the basement. The silence of the building did not in the least disturb him: he had chosen the hour for his "business meeting" with some care. Night was the preferred time for his operations, as a memorial to the one who had died in the night nearly four decades previously. He had already collected a selection of materials from various unconnected sources and seen to their placement in an empty basement closet. He was mentally, and with some irony, quoting Psalm 110—"He shall judge among the Heathen, He shall fill the places with the dead bodies: He shall wound the heads over many countries"—as he set the timer. Maybe the girl's Biblical reference had influenced him. Distant thunder rumbled. It was merely a few moments' work to complete his preparations, remembering a night so many years ago when he had set his first fire.

First: hook up the timer, a cheap alarm clock, to a considerable charge created from fireworks. The Fourth of July celebrations were still nearly two months away, but already fireworks stands were springing up everywhere, and it could hardly have been easier to buy quantities of perfectly legal explosives without even an eyebrow being lifted in surprise. Then soak the bags of wood chips in gasoline and place them almost touching the pyrotechnics. Finally, snake the combustible fuses to the cans of gasoline he had already stored in the air-conditioning ducts. The forced draft would do the rest. It never crossed his mind that there might be others in the building, and it would have made no difference if it had. Later he would have phone calls to make.

It was amazing how easy it had been to persuade Ferguson to meet him so late. Greed, of course. The notion of a new method of profit from oil had been irresistible. Youssef smirked at the weakness.

Footsteps. Youssef heard them approaching at a leisurely pace as he was preparing to pour the gasoline and immediately realized that he had miscalculated the timetable of the elderly security guard. It didn't cause him concern; he still had his pistol, there wouldn't be much left of the guard when the night was over, and the security video system had already been erased and disabled. They, together with fire detectors and smoke alarms, had been turned off earlier in the day by a "security specialist on a routine inspection." Youssef was a well-practiced master of disguise. He waited.

"One bullet in each," Detective Paul Ziplich told his lieutenant. "Execution-style, it seems. Probably large caliber, but Ballistics should have more by the morning. The M.E. estimates death at between seven and eleven p.m., but he says it's difficult, what with the rain and everything, to be sure until he can do a thorough post mortem. Not before four, though, he says, and the storm struck at a little after eleven, so it had to be before then. Then there's the security guard. Anyway, he should have something more concrete in the morning." Lieutenant Malcolm shook his leonine head gloomily and clicked his ballpoint pen open and shut. As if the drive-by shootings and the turf wars between the Crips, the Bloods and other street gangs weren't enough.

"It's already morning," he pointed out, taking a gingerly sip at a Styrofoam cup of ancient coffee from amid the papers on his battered desk. "What about evidence at the scene? Any hope of prints, fibers? Security videos? You know what we need."

"Doubtful. There's been pouring rain—still is—and the building was almost entirely destroyed." Ziplich was regarding his soiled clothing with some sadness. "Parts of it are all over the place, mixed in with bits from the offices on both the southeast and the north. The security cameras had been tampered with, so they give us nothing. We'll try, of course, but"...Ziplich shrugged, and attempted to brush off a smear from his linen-blend jacket. He succeeded in turning it into a longer smear.

"Yeah. You got someone keeping the place secured? There may be company papers, security camera tapes, something that could give us a clue about, I dunno, anyone who might have a grudge against," he put down the polystyrene cup and consulted the brief report in front of him, "this Ralph Ferguson."

"We're on it, but I've got to tell you that there are papers being whipped around everywhere, and we don't know yet which ones come from which buildings, or how many have just been blown away.

They could end up in Miami, for all we know. Mostly it's just rubble. It'll take weeks, at the very least."

Malcolm nodded and rubbed his lined face wearily. "Okay, Zee. Make sure that your guys have the scene sealed off, then go get some rest. I've got a feeling that's something we're all going to need."

Ziplich left, and Malcolm rubbed his eyes again. He glanced at his watch. 6.23 a.m. It had been a long night, and he wouldn't see bed for many hours. With a sigh, he picked up his phone and speed-dialed home. Eleanor would understand why he had woken her up: she was a cop's wife, and she always understood. Malcolm himself was sometimes less sure, and this was such a moment. Until, that is, his wife's voice, warm with sleep, answered him with a quiet "I know you must be exhausted, darling, but you're the one man who can do your job. There's nobody else who can come close, so if you need to stay, I understand. I love you." *That* was why he was here.

The Medical Examiner turned his bloodhound gaze on Ziplich. "The best estimate I can give you is between five and ten. Certainly not earlier, and it's most unlikely to have been after, say, ten. The condition of the bodies..."

"Yeah," broke in the detective with a look of distaste. "I really don't want to know the grisly details, Sam. You know how my stomach is."

"For a homicide detective, you're real squeamish, Zee, y'know that?"

"I just want to get the bastards, Sam, I'm not a ghoul like you." He wiped a hand across his stubbled cheek.

"If it wasn't for us 'ghouls' you'd never solve anything, buddy," Sam told him cheerfully.

"I know, I know. So. What about the weapon?"

"Not my area, Zee. The bullets have been extracted,"—Ziplich winced—"and sent to Ballistics. Check with them."

"Okay. When did you send 'em over?"

"Hour ago, hour and a half, maybe."

"So they should have something soon?"

"I guess. Ask 'em."

They had.

"It's a Webley, British, World War One vintage," Steve Jacobs told Ziplich. He flourished one of the deformed bullets in front of Ziplich's unwilling face. " Point four-five-five caliber. Makes a big hole, 'specially if coming out. Not a lot of these lying around in Tulsa. Probably a wartime souvenir, but who knows? Nothing we have in the database matches, so this is a new weapon to us. You got any ideas?"

Ziplich gave a negative shake of his blond head. "Wish I had. I don't have a clue why anyone would want to waste Ferguson. I've spent a bit of time checking on him, with a whole lot more to go, but he seems to have been a pillar of the community. Lived here forty or so years, philanthropist, donated to museums, Street School, churches, and synagogues, Habitat for Humanity, you name it."

Jacobs scratched his chin. "Where'd he live before Tulsa? Maybe it's an old feud, a payback from the past. For instance, where did his money come from?"

"Oil."

"And how did he get into that? The days of Waite Phillips are long gone." Jacobs pulled a cigarette pack from the pocket of his white coat, regarded it lovingly, and put it back. He'd promised his wife to quit.

"You've got a point, Steve. No more wildcat drilling, no more gushers. Nowadays it all comes from the Middle East."

Jacobs straightened some papers on his desk. "And you have to pay for it. How did he do that to begin with?"

"Maybe," Ziplich said slowly, noticing a dead fly on the window ledge, wondering if it would become a candidate for autopsy, "we should look at his incorporation papers."

"Definitely an execution," the M.E. said. He'd now had suffi-cient time to confirm his initial findings. "One bullet to each head. The guard, though, got it through the heart. Hazard of the business, I suppose. And something else: the man Ferguson's legs were both shot in the knees. There are no other signs of torture—you know, cigarette burns" (here he inhaled from a non-filter Camel) "that kind of thing— but the damage was done before the fatal shot was fired, so I can only assume that the aim was to 'encourage' one, or both of them, to give information of some kind."

"Who to?" Ziplich wanted to know, wondering how a doctor could smoke with such equanimity.

"To whom?" the examiner responded automatically. His father had been an English teacher. "Well, I have no means of knowing. You're the detective, so that's your job. Nor, before you ask," he went on through a plume of smoke, "do I have the remotest idea what the information might be, or why they—if it was more than one person— didn't work on the woman as well." He drew another nicotine breath. "In the few instances of this kind of case I've seen before, not to mention all the books and movies about this sort of thing, they usually threaten to hurt the woman in the hopes that the man will break in order to save her from more agony."

"Maybe they did threaten, and he told them what they wanted."

The M.E. looked unconvinced. "Maybe."

"I don't get this at all," Ziplich muttered. "The guy was a model citizen, as they say. You know, good works, donations to all the right causes, charitable foundations, the whole nine yards. Up to now, I haven't turned up any obvious enemies. It's early days, of course, but everybody seemed to like him, as far as I can tell. I just hope that the papers that were scattered all over the place can be recovered."

"Have you got anything on the woman?" The examiner stubbed his cigarette, then disrobed a stick of nicotine chewing gum taken from a pocket, and slipped it into his mouth.

Ziplich shook his head again. "Not much, really. She's English—well, British anyway—and she's been living with him for about a year. Came here in 2008, moved in with him a year or so ago. Had a Green Card from having worked in New York for a multinational in the mid-nineties, went home, came back. Don't know why, yet. We've asked London for help, but it takes time, and anyway, they're six hours ahead of us."

"Disgruntled ex-boyfriend?" The M.E. was shrugging his jacket on.

"Can't rule it out, but it looks to me more deliberate than that."
Ziplich stood up. "Thanks, Doc. Let me know if you find anything
useful."

"Sure."

Ziplich left.

Ralph Arthur Ferguson. Age 76 Born Laramie, Wyoming, July
23, 1934. Educated local school system, graduated top of his class 1952.
Drafted into the army, served nine months in Korea, reaching the
rank of First Lieutenant. Honorable discharge at the end of his service. Attended Columbia University on a full academic scholarship,
then Harvard Business School. Graduated there third in his class.
Joined Clark, Jenson, and Co., a small accounting firm in Rochester,
New York, before moving to Oklahoma and buying up a minor oil
and gasoline company, Windfall, in 1974. *Just about the time of the big
OPEC crisis*, Ziplich mused. *Remarkable timing. Now where, I wonder,
did he find the money to acquire even a small oil company?* He gazed at the
computer screen, seeking inspiration, and finding none.

"Paul? Supper's ready." Carol, his wife, the best cook Ziplich
could even imagine, was not to be denied. Fact was, he wouldn't
dream of denying her anything. As he was shutting down the computer, he reflected yet again on his amazing good fortune in marry-
ing her. She'd been the most popular girl in his years at the University
of Colorado—spectacularly beautiful, intelligent, and funny. She'd
been her high school valedictorian, having completed her studies
with an astronomical average, and had been immediately snapped up
after college by a law firm in her hometown of Tulsa. Yet she had
chosen him, a moderate student with what was usually described as
a nerdy personality, and their marriage—now in its fifth year—had
been blissful. Their only regret was that, as yet, they lacked the children for which they both so deeply wished.

"Coming, Hon." The computer assured him that it was now safe
to turn it off. Ziplich went toward the enticing aroma of Italian.

Spaghetti Bolognese, his favorite, with that extra touch they'd
learned from a restaurant in Bologna the year they'd vacationed in
Europe; a dash of vodka in the sauce just before it was served over al

dente pasta. Carol had opened a bottle of Chianti Classico, but she hadn't poured it. "Gentlemen pour the wine," she would say her father had told her, "and ladies are happy to have them do so." Carol's father, gone now, rest his soul, had been raised in French West Africa during the war, and when his family had moved to America he had brought some of the Old World courtesies with him. Thus "ladies" and "gentlemen" rather than "men" and "women." Her mother was still alive, a victim of Alzheimer's, living in a church-run home. Ever the gentleman, Ziplich poured the wine while Carol served the spaghetti. He raised his glass to his wife.

"To your gorgeous eyes," he said, "not to mention your gorgeous cooking." Carol giggled and blew him a kiss. She'd slipped an apron over the white blouse and dark skirt that she had worn to the office, and to Ziplich's eyes she was the world's most desirable woman.

The meal, crowned with another of Carol's masterpieces, a perfect crème brulee, put Ziplich in a contemplative frame of mind. Over a cup of French Market coffee, he said to Carol, "Do you know anything about Fergoil?"

Carol tasted her own coffee. "Of course. They're one of our best clients. Why?"

"Because Ralph Ferguson is dead."

"Oh, God!" Carol put her cup down. "Heart attack?"

"No."

"The tornado, then?"

"Again, no. He and his girlfriend were murdered."

"Ralph has a girl friend?"

"Had."

"I can't believe it. Who'd want to do such a thing? Ralph is—was—one of Tulsa's most..." Carol broke off for a moment. Then: "He's such a nice man. Always polite, always looking out for others. His foundations..."

"Exactly. But he wasn't just murdered, he was executed. And tortured first."

Carol's face was the picture of horror. "Oh, God, how awful. A gang? The mob? And who was the girl?"

Ziplich peered into his near-empty cup. "Name of Rachel Taylor. British. Lived in Tulsa for a few years, her second time in the States, but we don't know yet exactly why she came here, and we haven't any record of her working in Oklahoma, so there's the question of what she lived on. Ferguson, of course, had plenty of money, so it may turn out that he was supporting her, but nothing's sure yet."

Carol freshened their coffees and stood up from the table, collected the dishes, took them into their trendy little kitchen, and loaded the stainless steel dishwasher. "Where did she live?" she asked through the open door. Ziplich picked up the two mugs and went into the kitchen too, leaning against a granite counter top.

"With Ferguson for the last year, more or less. Apparently she had a small place in Brookside before that, and I've got a couple of guys checking it all out. Probably have more in the morning. All we really know about her comes from the INS. Her passport was found in Ferguson's house in Maple Ridge—what a house, by the way, which we've scarcely started to check out, let alone the extensive grounds—when we went there. So we were able to get some background when we got on to Immigration about the Green Card she carried. That was in her wallet, along with the usual credit cards and stuff, together with quite a bit of money."

Her cleanup completed, Carol took her coffee from her husband, and they went into the living room of their small but pleasant second-story apartment. They had chosen the location because they liked the view it afforded of the park and the river just across Riverside Drive. Since the building of the low-water dam, the Arkansas at this point was no longer just a stretch of mud and weeds with a few trickles here and there, but actually looked like a river. A pair of swans often cruised majestically, but tonight they had apparently chosen to be away from the danger zone of storms; the rain and a faint electrical smell persisted. From the apartment, the power station and refineries—one of the latter being Fergoil, Ziplich mused—on the far bank were scarcely visible. Usually at night their lights sparkled on the water, so the couple had arranged their chairs near the window. Ziplich sank into his La-Z-Boy recliner and tilted it back a notch.

"It's been quite a long day, what with the storm and everything. It makes it so difficult to piece things together when the potential evidence has been picked up and scattered over several counties. But I need to get more on Ferguson and his company. Was he having business problems? He always seemed affluent, ever since I can remember, but you never know until you start searching. My real question is, where did he find the money to get started?"

"Talked to his accountants?" Carol had perched on her own antique sewing chair and was sipping her coffee. There would be no sewing tonight—but then there never was.

"Not yet. Going there in the morning. They do know we're coming, though, so they should have the information available when we get there. What's more, there's an official request coming to your firm to acquire any information about Fergoil that may be pertinent to the murder investigation. Shouldn't be a problem, should it?"

Carol shook her head. "We certainly wouldn't put any obstacles in the way of the inquiries, that's for sure." *Unless that jerk of a director starts being officious,* she thought.

"That's what I told the lieutenant." Ziplich yawned. "That great dinner of yours doesn't exactly help a guy to stay bright and alert, y'know."

"Ready for bed? You've been going better than eighteen hours."

"Can't yet. I've gotta spent a bit more computer time on this thing, see if there's any little item that can shed light on a,"—he yawned again—"on a motive."

Ziplich's cellphone trilled, so he stood and strolled across the room to where his smudged jacket was draped over a chair back, and pulled the instrument out. "Ziplich. Oh yeah, hi Benny, watcha got? What? You sure? What the hell? Yeah, okay, Benny. Add it to all the mess we got to deal with first thing tomorrow. Thanks. See ya." Ziplich put the phone back in his pocket.

"What is it, Paul?"

"It seems that Ralph Ferguson wasn't Ralph Ferguson at all."

Greyhound sat at his kitchen table, a glass of Pinot Noir close to hand, and viewed with disfavor the report in his email of Rachel Taylor's death. He'd have to inform his superiors that this, as he saw it, gratuitous killing would do nothing but make their task more difficult than it had already proven. Now that his cutout contact in America had been removed he would have to make direct communication with some other operative, and he viewed that as dangerous. He had not had the chance to meet Youssef in many years, but he was well aware of the high regard in which he was held by the JUA council, an opinion he had good reason to share. Now, of course, the police would be all over the case; perhaps the FBI or Homeland Security would be charging in, as well, unless...Well, maybe he could put in a word or two that would help in holding them off. Time was running short now, but when the American thing was taken care of, it really wouldn't matter what the Americans discovered—they could be safely ignored.

Checking his watch, to be certain what the local time would be in the countries he was about to contact, he returned his attention to his laptop, hooked again into the Internet, and started the careful business of composing an apparently innocent message. Not all of its hidden content was complimentary to Youssef, which distressed him but was necessary. Then he would have to send fresh instructions to someone in the United States, and he was uneasy about that. He had, at that point, no fallback agent, and was by no means certain that a suitable one would be available with sufficient speed. Still, it seemed there was no alternative. He sipped at his wine and rolled his shirtsleeve cuffs back. This would be quite a long keyboard session.

Chapter 2
June 2011

It was quiet and comfortable in the tiny Colton Arms. Whenever Grayson went there for a pint, which was virtually every weekday evening, he congratulated himself on having found one of the very few pubs in London without background music or a jukebox, a flashing slot-machine, a television, or (the most threatening of all) *Live Entertainment*. Tucking his elderly briefcase under his tweed-jacketed arm, he approached the bar, a distance of some three paces from the door. It was Millie on duty there this evening amid the dark carved wood, and she had his pint up and waiting a moment after he reached her.

"Evening, Millie."

"Evening, Dan. Chilly out?"

"Not really. Damp, though."

"Never know it was spring, would you?"

"This is England, Millie. It's always November. Not like the weather in 'The Darling Buds of May.'"

Millie shook her golden locks, with the gray parting, sorrowfully. "That's one of the things they mean by fiction, Dan."

"Indeed." He laid his money, correct to the penny, on the counter. "Thanks, love. Sorry, but work to do tonight."

Millie was pressing the keys of the old manual cash register—no programmed touch-screens here—and the money drawer slid open

"I saw the briefcase and guessed as much." She counted the cash in and pushed the drawer shut. "Let me know if I can add anything." Millie was one of "the company's" more discreet sources. The pub's location near the company's office made it a place sometimes designated as a meeting place to those who had stories to tell or information to sell, and Millie was skilled as a watcher who alerted the office to their arrival. Grayson and his colleagues, most of whom preferred trendier sports or cocktail bars, inhabited a nondescript building which was generally believed to be an annex of either the nearby Queen's Club sports complex or Charing Cross Hospital, but certainly not the unacknowledged offspring of Century House.

"More Secret than Service," some wit had once remarked. "Doesn't it make you proud?"

"Well, there's not many in yet," Millie added, "so you've plenty of choice where to sit. That table near the other fireplace, maybe?" The "other" fireplace contained an electric fire with simulated coals, and a light intended to give the impression of flames. It gave no heat today, but it did offer a sort of ersatz cozy ambience which Grayson found curiously comforting.

He took his pint of Old Speckled Hen and headed towards the fireplace, nodding his thanks again to Millie amid the subdued hum of conversation of the few other customers. Once he'd had the first, much appreciated, pull at his beer, Grayson removed the jacket of his gray Harris tweed suit and hung it on the back of his chair. Then he sat down, opened his battered briefcase, and took out the bulky folder it contained.

Taylor, Rachel Naomi. Exact date and place of birth uncertain. Adoptive father: Aaron Joseph Taylor (dec. June 12, 1991) Adoptive mother: Sarah Elizabeth, nee Benson (dec. Jan. 24, 1988) Educated: Haringey Primary and Finchley Grammar Schools, London University. Graduated 1994, BA (Hons).The attached photograph showed a dark-haired young woman; not pretty, but rather striking, with light eyes in this black and white picture—gray or blue, perhaps, Grayson surmised—a straight nose and a determined chin.

Well, her record proves she wasn't stupid, at any rate, Grayson thought. *Wonder why the Yanks are so interested in her. Still, a murder case involving a foreigner does tend to bring out the old curiosity.* He went back to his perusal.

Two pints and a scotch later, he thought he might be beginning to have the answer. Taylor, it appeared, had at one time enjoyed a relationship with an Irishman suspected of having Nationalist sympathies. Since the "peace process" in Northern Ireland seemed to be holding for the time being, there was always the chance that sympathizers had moved on to other fields. Or, and Grayson felt this to be far more likely, they had taken great care to go into deep cover. He sipped at his beer, thinking of the fanaticism he'd seen in the past among many IRA operatives and the equally vicious "Loyalists" who opposed them. Nothing would surprise him where any of them was concerned. Still, he had no reason, other than an uneasy feeling, to believe that Taylor's boyfriend was more than simply that—an Irish boyfriend. He determined to get his secretary to do a complete check in the morning. He glanced at his watch: half past eight already. Well, time for a quick curry and the Tube back to Willesden. *Work on this till two, say, have a zizz, and finish the rest back at the office in the morning. America was, let's see, five hours behind—no, it'd be six in Oklahoma.* So if he had this all written up by lunch, he could get it secure-faxed to them for eight in the morning, their time.

Grayson stuffed the papers back in the briefcase, drained what was left of the scotch, and edged through the now-crowded bar to the door, giving Millie a wave as he stepped outside. It had started raining.

❖ ❖ ❖

"Did you see the television, then, Jimmy?"

"It hasn't moved, y'pillock. Still there on the cabinet."

"Very droll. Extremely humorous. The news, Jimmy, the news. About Ferguson."

"What about him? The job got done, we know that. What else is there?"

"There's investigations."

Jimmy Riordan—although his passport said Malone—shirt-sleeved and, as usual, slightly unkempt, looked up indolently from the sofa where he lounged over his Bushmills Irish whiskey at Tobin (whose own passport bore the name O'Neill), his expression one of faint irritation. "Of course there's bloody investigations, man. There's always investigations after a prominent man dies suddenly. What'd you expect? They'll not find anything to connect us."

"Jimmy, do you not pay any attention to anything at all?" The smaller man was agitated. "The building didn't burn."

A comfortable suite at one of the several Sheratons in New York City. A well-stocked minibar, and there were always room service and the main bar downstairs. Riordan and Tobin had been celebrating the success of the first part of their mission, confirmed by a cryptic telephone call the previous night, and were prepared to begin phase two the following morning. Now Riordan jerked upright from the couch where he had been enjoying that pre-lunch whiskey, some of which spilled onto his rumpled check shirt.

"What d'you mean, didn't burn?"

"A storm. One of those tornadoes, with rain and blasting winds, Jimmy. It tore up the building and several others, and killed a number of people. But the building didn't burn, I'm telling you. The rain, I suppose. Stuff has been scattered all over the place. But two bodies were found with bullets to the head, and one kneecapped. I just saw it on the news. Ferguson and the girl. And a security guard, too. So now they know it's not an accident."

Riordan quietly pronounced a number of extreme profanities. "He wasn't told to hurt the girl. The Committee will go bloody spare. Who the fock does he think he is?" The phone rang and Riordan snatched up the receiver. "Yes?" He listened intently for a few seconds, then: "We've just seen the fruits of your work, you eejut. Get out now. Don't come here, ye stupid son-of-a-bitch. We'll deal with youse later. Got that? We'll be leaving immediately." He slammed the phone down again. "Colum, pack the bags and call a taxi. We've got a change of plan."

Small, dapper Tobin gave vent to a rare display of anger. "'Tis all wasted, Jimmy, all wasted. The days, the months, the years of preparation. All I had to do was go and get it, get the money. 'Twould've been so simple. We've been at it for all that time — me and that Bernadette girl—they were ready and waiting for the audit, and 'tis all lost because of that fule not doing his job right." He banged his fist on the coffee table, spilling the rest of the drink that Riordan had put there when the phone rang. "Wait till I see him. He probably thinks I'm just some stupid little Irishman to be ignored or laughed at." He was flexing his fingers now, and Riordan remembered the sound of a Protestant neck snapping under that grip...

Youssef had also to ring his own superiors to explain the new developments They, too, were relying on the money, and they had a deadline. Time was becoming short.

❖ ❖ ❖

Grayson traipsed through the rain, chicken vindaloo—excellent though it had been—wreaking havoc with his digestion. He'd stopped off at the Lily Tandoori in the hope that the rain would ease, but when he came out it was pelting down, and by the time he reached West Kensington Underground station, he was soaked. His immaculate trousers, usually creased to a knife-edge, were now shapeless and clung to his legs with a soggy embrace. His jacket was heavy on his thin shoulders, and his carefully groomed hair hung lank and dripping, displaying the scalp that he so assiduously covered up each morning with his "creative combing." The tube train was crowded and smelt of wet cloth, the passengers sullen, the graffiti even uglier than usual, and there was the inevitable wailing child. It was almost a relief when, after changes to two more trains, he eventually emerged into the rain and the gray, litter-strewn streets of Willesden, turned left, and walked in the downpour the few streets which led to where his Desirable Residence crouched in a row of identical 1930s semi-detached. It had been all right when Janet was with him: she'd been so houseproud, such a wonderful cook, a magician of a gardener in the miniscule patches front and back. Somehow she had transformed a humdrum suburban blob into an attractive modern home with an air of traditional welcome and comfort. It had always been such a joy to find her waiting for him when he got back from his work, wherever that might have taken him. When Janet announced they were going to be parents, he had been ecstatic, convinced that their decision that he would be the breadwinner, she the traditional wife and mother with a little writing sideline, had been justified, even though that sideline actually earned as much as he did. But there had been complications with the pregnancy. In the end, he had lost both his wife and the baby boy. They had even decided on a name: Patrick. To this day, that name affected Grayson, but he was ashamed to admit to himself that he had to look at her picture to remember exactly what Janet had looked like.

And yet he had fallen in love with her years ago when they were both students at Oxford, he at Magdalen and she at Corpus Christi. They met on the train from London on the way to their first year as undergrads and had never looked either back or at anyone else. When they graduated, both decided to pursue further studies. Oddly, since she had absolutely no background in it, Janet had chosen music and eventually became a respected critic for a provincial newspaper before she and Grayson married. He, in his turn, selected political science, intending to follow a career in the diplomatic service. In the event, he had been recruited by the Firm.

That had been a real surprise to him. He'd been enjoying a pint of bitter at The Bear, a favorite pub of students, as he waited for Janet to arrive. They'd arranged to have dinner together, one of their weekly rituals, and Grayson had even splashed some Burberry cologne on—a rare extravagance. A short, man, clad in a tweed jacket of a singularly poisonous shade of purple and holding a glass of what Grayson took to be whisky, approached the table.

"Mind if I sit here?" He indicated a vacant chair.

Grayson nonchalantly waved his beer mug; he didn't like the current trend to "thin glasses." "Of course not."

"Waiting for someone?" the man suggested, which Grayson regarded as a bit of an intrusion. He was about to give a rather sharp retort, when the man added, "Janet, perhaps?" By now Grayson was becoming quite annoyed with the presumption of this fellow, but once again his answer was forestalled. "You see," went on his unwelcome companion, "we've been keeping a bit of an eye on you."

"Have you really?" Grayson snarled rudely. "And who the hell might 'we' be, anyway? Some organ of a future police state? Go away before I go looking for a copper."

"Yes, well, I rather outrank a 'copper,' so that might not prove your best choice," was the rejoinder. "And Janet will be a few minutes late. I really want to have a little chat with you about your future prospects in the diplomatic service. Yes, we know about your ambitions, and I'm authorized to make you a proposition."

Grayson had immediately realized what was being offered. He'd heard of such things, but had always taken such tales with a large pinch of salt. *Good Lord,* he thought, *I'm going to become a spy.* He had never regretted that decision to serve his country—even though not, it turned out, as an actual spy—with little expectation of recognition. Oh, a knighthood, maybe, when he was pensioned off. At least the job, particularly with the solicitous help of his greatly treasured secretary, had preserved his sanity when Janet was abruptly taken from him. He turned through the gate, frowned faintly at the now weedy garden, and fumbled for the front door key.

"No available seats at all?' Riordan repeated incredulously. "What about Business Class or even First? There must be something."

"I'm very sorry, sir," the American Airlines agent told him. Her nametag identified her as Carmen Alvarez, an extremely pretty young woman whom Riordan assumed to be Mexican or Puerto Rican, though she had no accent to confirm that. "The flight is completely full. There's a lot of official traffic right now, with the Middle East situation and everything, there've been lots of flight cutbacks, and we just started the vacation season, too, you see. You might try standby, but there's a long list already."

"What about other flights? Other airlines? Other airports, for that matter?"

"I'll check for you sir, but it's late for flights to Europe. This was our last flight for today from JFK and," she was tapping at her computer, "you haven't enough time to reach La Guardia to get our last departure from there either. As for other carriers," her hands flew over the keys as she gazed at her screen, "well, there is one from Newark on Virgin Atlantic." Riordan's craggy face expressed hope. "But it's been delayed due to mechanical problems. Won't leave until tomorrow morning. Passengers are being put up overnight at the Holiday Inn at Newark. There are, though, some seats available in their Upper Class. I could get two of those for you gentlemen, if you like. It would get you to London tomorrow in time to catch"—her hands were flickering over the keyboard again—"Lufthansa to Frankfurt. You'd arrive there late, but at least you'd be there."

"What about your morning flights to London or Frankfurt." Riordan's only real interest in Frankfurt was its use to confuse possible surveillance, not that any was anticipated.

"You'd get in much later."

The line of passengers behind Riordan and Tobin was beginning to get restive, and the last thing the two required was a lot of people who might remember them. It was bad enough that Carmen Alvarez had spent so much time with them, but then she saw so many people every day that they probably all blurred into a general mist of faces.

"All right then," Riordan grudgingly agreed, "let's make it the Newark one."

"Thank you, sir. I'll have to cancel out your tickets for your original flight."

"And apply the balance to these new ones, will ye?"

"I'm sorry, sir, they're restricted tickets: no refund or change permitted." He was thinking about The Committee's reaction; more money spent, yet nothing coming in. They wouldn't be happy, since their entire strategy had hinged on this assignment.

"You mean we just flush that money away? That's not right at all."

Carmen was holding her irritation with this man under tight control. *What did these two guys expect, when they show up days before their scheduled flight and try to change everything without prior warning? A vote of thanks from the airline?* She smiled her professional smile and said: "It is unfortunate, sir, but that is the restricted ticket you purchased. The conditions are clearly set out here," she pointed to the fine print on the tickets, "and that's what you agreed to. Afraid there's nothing I can do to alter it." She caught the look on Riordan's face. "But you might try contacting the airline offices after you get back, and see if they can do anything to help."

There was a pause. Riordan looked toward Tobin and saw only an expression of bewilderment. "Oh, all right," he muttered, "go ahead and book 'em."

"Okay, sir. Now, I'll need your passports and a major credit card."

They had left the Sheraton without much trouble, except for a delay in the vast lobby as they waited while a crowd of noisy businessmen, too full of convention hospitality to be aware of any inconvenience they might cause, checked out ahead of them. The cab Tobin had ordered was waiting, and it took them through some of the uglier areas of New York—which meant very ugly indeed—and out to JFK Airport. The surly driver, whose ID proclaimed him to be Abdul Fawzi, scowled at them suspiciously in the mirror through the steel mesh which separated him from dangerous passengers, and the grubby interior of the vehicle smelt faintly of sweat, vomit, and Lysol. The two men had been almost glad to pay the exorbitant fare just to get out of the thing. Now they waited, new tickets safely tucked into inner pockets, for the shuttle bus, "limousine" they called it here, to Newark.

Just about that time Grayson, cozy in warm, dry pajamas and dressing gown, finally leaned back in his worn but comfortable armchair, the one ugly piece of furniture Janet had tolerated, and pinched the corners of his eyes between thumb and second finger. The cup of coffee he'd made in the kitchen after he got home had long since gone as cold as the wet clothes he'd dumped on the bathroom floor. He was pretty sure now that he was right as to why the Americans were expressing interest in Rachel Taylor. He'd finish it up in the morning when he got to his office. He set his laptop on the coffee table, stood up, and went over to the sideboard to pour himself a generous Lagavulin. Sipping at it, he went upstairs and rummaged in his wardrobe for a decent suit—have to take the wet one to the cleaners on his way in—selected a crisp white shirt from his chest of drawers, clean socks, underpants and a handkerchief. Tie? He decided on the Lagos Yacht Club one he'd bought years ago at that shop in Sicilian Avenue. Not entitled to it, of course, but he liked it. Clean his teeth: the mirror showed the face of a man who had seen many things he would have preferred not to. Slightly prominent ("beaky," he'd have said himself) nose, lines around the gray eyes, and a steadily retreating hairline. How could his secretary look at him the way he'd sometimes caught her doing? And she both young and beautiful. Sometimes he had fantasies.... Well. He'd shower and shave when he got up. In the bedroom, he looked at the big queen-sized bed he and Janet had bought together, and felt the usual emptiness. He slipped between the cool covers and had that familiar sense of longing for a lost embrace. Lost, or maybe just dreamt. Or unbidden thoughts of his secretary...

There was a faint "click" from somewhere downstairs. Grayson had never experienced an attack at home, but he remembered all too well an occasion at a hotel in Prague. While not alarmed, he was most certainly prepared. With great care, having turned out the bedroom light, he eased the door open and gazed into the gloom of the upstairs landing. Nothing. Grayson padded silently across the landing, hands already in the "attack" position and carefully peered around the corner of the staircase to the downstairs hallway. There was the slightest movement of a shadow, and Grayson felt his pulse increase, then relax. Crossing the hall between the dining and living rooms was the neighbors' cat. Grayson had forgotten, yet again, to lock the kitchen window. He shooed the cat out, latched the window and went back to bed where he dreamed of the day he survived a bomb attack on his car in Bruges. Waking up sweating, he stared for a long time into the darkness.

Youssef flew First Class, of course, on the flights from Tulsa. After all, he wasn't paying for them. He always flew First Class, always stayed at good hotels, always dined at the best restaurants, always wore the finest tailoring—unless the job dictated something to blend into a particular environment. And always traveled light. It had never happened that he'd had to make what he thought of as an unexpectedly swift exit, but he was at all times prepared to do so. This last one had been no swifter than usual. Not a panic departure, by any means. The gun was in Mohawk Lake, unlikely to be found for years, except by pure accident, and naturally it had no fingerprints and no identifying numbers. In the old days he'd have taken it with him, but now the airport security procedures, while by no means foolproof, simply made concealment more trouble than it was worth when the job had been done. Worth it coming in, yes, since you wanted to avoid someone local identifying you as a purchaser. Also, he liked to use something unusual, as he had here, to give the police a little extra to confuse them if necessary. It was annoying that the building hadn't burned down the way it was supposed to, but he had no control over the weather, so no one could blame him for that. He thought for a minute of the reaction from the man, Riordan. He was shaken, no doubt about it. *Let's hope he won't do anything stupid. No, probably not, oaf though he may be. The stupid one was that Tobin. He might have hidden talents, but they weren't immediately obvious. Why had Riordan brought him along? No matter, that was his problem.* Youssef's other carefully worded call—making no mention of Rachel Taylor—to a very private number in the eastern Mediterranean had not been well received, so he readily accepted the cocktail the flight attendant brought him. He leaned back, sipping, and idly wondered what Malone's and O'Neill's real names were.

So. Dallas. Then Denver, Kansas City, St. Louis, Chicago, Atlanta, and Newark, each leg under a different name, since he had no lack of identification. It took time and patience, but he had plenty of both. Then to London, Brussels, Rome, Cairo—which he was interested to see following the regime change there—and Athens. Soon he would be home. Revised plans could then be made, and shortly after that the operation would restart. Youssef's smile was inward and cruel as he thought of the surprises in store for the enemy. *Oh, yes, they would pay dearly for all those years....*

When the laughing, jeering commandos had finished their filthy work, they had patted young Youssef on the head, and placed the infant brother they had torn from his mother's breast in his shaking arms. "Take care, Sonny," they had said in their guttural version of his language, "or maybe we'll come back and see what fun *you* can offer. Just now, you're a bit too small, but in a few years, who knows? And the baby, too." More laughter, and the five faded into the night, leaving Youssef clutching his little brother and gazing in mesmerized disbelief at his mother's blood-drenched body.

Maybe she isn't really badly hurt, he had thought. *Maybe, if I wash her carefully and try to get her into bed...*But he knew. He'd already seen too much killing in what had once been his pleasant town; Qantara, the only home he could remember. Even at the age of eight, he readily understood that his people were considered dirt by some, interlopers, fit only to be subdued or disposed of. He would remember those five faces, he swore silently to the small bundle mewling in his arms. *And I'll teach you, too, little one,* he promised. *We shall have our vengeance on them and all the rest of their kind.*

Nobody had come to the little family's assistance, despite the shrieks of both the woman and her small boy. The neighbors were all too cowed and afraid for themselves to offer any help until the marauders had gone. Then, finally, the people whose faces had peered fearfully from behind the edges of drawn curtains dared to creep into the desert-silent street and to the open door of the victims' tiny house. Youssef screamed at them to go away; their help was too late, too timorous. Still clutching his brother in his trembling arms, his decision was already made. He would go to his uncle's home in Ramallah, near Jerusalem. He would walk, accepting help from no one, until he was once again with family. Only then could he relax his guard. He had no idea of how to care for the baby, but he knew with total certainty that he would manage. He would steal, cheat, lie, even kill if necessary, but he would survive. And he would avenge.

Youssef wasted no time. He drove his cringing, pathetic neighbors furiously away, while they displayed no vestige of resistance. The boy was unsurprised; they were a spineless lot at the best of times.

"Now we go, Yakob," he breathed. He took a bottle of lamp oil from a shelf in the sparse kitchen, scattered it about, struck a match, and set the room afire. Within moments, the dried-out wood inside the old building had caught and began to blaze. "Goodbye, Mother," he whispered. "God guard you in your sleep, and us in our journey." Then he had turned abruptly and, tiny brother in his arms, taken to the road. That had been 1973, one day into the Yom Kippur war.

❖　❖　❖

In Tel Aviv, a young woman pushing a stroller walked towards a bustling shopping mall. The rocket barrage from Hamas didn't reach this far, and the atmosphere was calm and relaxed. True, there were plenty of armed security personnel of one sort or another always around, but they'd become so much a part of daily life that few people even noticed them. The bundled-up child in the push-chair lolled, apparently asleep. When she was almost in the center of the crowded mall, the woman said, very clearly, "Allahu Akbar," and pressed a switch.

It was Chief Simmons of the Tulsa Fire Department. Ziplich had been dragged from a dreamless sleep by the telephone next to his side of the bed. It was still only nine-twenty-five, but he had been sleeping the sleep of the totally exhausted. "Yeah, Chief," he managed.

"We've found something you guys ought to know about," Simmons told him.

"Something?" Ziplich was trying to pry open his eyes.

"Evidence of arson in the Fergoil building."

"But the building," Ziplich was awake now, "didn't burn, it was destroyed by the tornado."

"Right. But it would have burned if the storm hadn't blown everything to hell and gone. We found traces of flammable substances and ignitable materials in the wreckage."

Ziplich mentally cursed the official language. "You mean a bomb?"

"No. Gasoline and a triggering mechanism hooked up, originally, to a timer. A small charge to set off the initial fire—just fireworks, looks like. It was all in a closet and the HVAC ducts, tucked away, but if it had worked, the whole place would have been an inferno—you know what these buildings are made like, building codes or not. I suppose your guys were looking for victims, so that's how they missed it."

"What's your best guess?"

"You're the detective," the chief replied, echoing the medical examiner, "but if that fire had really taken hold, I doubt your three bodies could have been identified as murder victims, or even identified at all. They'd have been ash, nothing more."

"An attempt to cover up the crime," Ziplich said.

"Seems like it to me, although the arson itself would likely have been discovered."

"Thanks, chief. Try to keep the media out of it. I'll get back with you in the morning." *My God*, he thought as he hung up the receiver, *the morning is going to need eighty hours.* He was asleep again within seconds.

The Holiday Inn was pleasant enough. Riordan and Tobin booked in, had a bearable supper in the restaurant, drinks in the bar—"Just one, Colum," Riordan warned, then totally ignored his own advice—and went to bed. It would be a long day's travel tomorrow, and they had to get their report ready. That could be prepared during the flight to London, and committed to memory. Nothing on paper, the Committee had instructed. The "peace process" in Northern Ireland had been in place so long by now that security precautions had been greatly relaxed, and the Committee was determined to allow no hint of its intentions to seep out. "We'll have no WikiLeaks here," was the word, and the two men took that very seriously.

News media were now reporting a suicide bombing in Israel. Apparently, a young woman had rigged a doll to look like a child, stuffed it with explosives, and detonated it in the Azriely Shopping Mall in Tel Aviv, leaving at least eighty-three people dead and hundreds injured. Damage to the huge buildings which housed the mall was said to be "very extensive," and there were comparisons to the 9/11 outrage in New York. Telephone messages had been made to the effect that Islamic Jihad claimed responsibility. In only a few minutes, Islamic Jihad had issued a denial. Youssef's comrades were at work.

The roundabout route Youssef had chosen got him to Newark too late to make his connection. The flight from Tulsa had been delayed as a result of the storm and that from Atlanta was delayed as well, with no explanation, and he was thoroughly irritated by the time he finally arrived. That irritation might have made him careless. He booked in at the Hilton, and immediately sought a pay phone to arrange a London flight for the morning. He was in luck: a Virgin Atlantic flight, itself delayed, would be departing at 8.00a.m. He booked a window seat in, naturally, Upper Class. Youssef went to the

Hilton bar and ordered a vodka martini, "stirred, not shaken." Too late, he realized, to his own surprise and shame, that he was trying to impress an elegantly dressed and extremely pretty young woman sitting a few tables from him. She looked up, smiled, and drew a small Ruger from her purse.

Youssef was on the floor before the sound of the shot, furious with himself for being so naive. It didn't matter. A small, dapper man who had entered the room—evidently clearly visible to the woman as a reflection in the mirror over the bar—dropped slowly to his knees, then fell face down on the expensive wood floor. The girl tossed the gun aside.

"That shit" she said with quiet calm, "deserved more pain, but I haven't got the time."

She strolled without haste out of the room with absolutely no hint of interference. Youssef observed it all with professional admiration and departed for his own room before official investigations could begin. He'd be on the surveillance tapes, of course, but by the time they had been examined he anticipated being in Egypt. Things were going well there, too, he reflected.

The rain had stopped, but the sky remained overcast, with the threat of more precipitation. Grayson, armed with both umbrella and raincoat, dropped off his creased and still sodden suit at the dry cleaners on his way to the tube station. He asked if they really could *dry* clean it, and received a blank look by way of response. At the tube station he fished out his Oyster travel card, boarded the train, and endured another dreary trip into Central London. One good thing, there was no longer any smoking on the London Underground. When he was a small child, many years ago, he had almost choked on the clouds of smoke when his parents couldn't find room in a non-smoking carriage. Even now, he wondered whether he'd sustained any damage from second-hand smoke, but his annual checkup had never revealed any problem.

From Baron's Court station to the office took five minutes or so, and Grayson quite enjoyed the walk through the cemetery short cut. There was a sense of continuity, of calm, which he always found rather soothing, given the nature of his work. Highgate Cemetery had the same effect on him, weedy though it was, and he sometimes went there just for the atmosphere. Arrived at his building, it was time again to show another card, this time his identification as a physiotherapist, to the amiable but discreetly armed guard at the entrance—a Desert Storm veteran, with a grizzled head, shrapnel in his back, and a photographic memory for faces. There were security cameras all over the place, but what might be less-expected by un-welcome intruders was the system of steel shutters which could be deployed in an instant to seal off all entrances. It had never yet been used. Grayson wondered briefly if the thing actually worked, then took the lift to his fifth-floor office. On the way up he wondered why Americans called lifts "elevators." *To elevate means to raise up,* he mused, *but you can 'lift' either up or down.* He supposed he was obsessing on this American request about Rachel Taylor. And didn't Americans call the ground floor the first floor? At that rate, his office would be on the sixth floor: a handsome promotion. He had the briefcase firm-ly in his left hand, the umbrella in his right, the raincoat draped over one shoulder. Probably be bright sunshine and thirty degrees when I leave, he thought, amused by his own conversion from Fahrenheit to Celsius—although he did still think of that as Centigrade.

LaDonna, his beloved secretary—well, his shared secretary, to be totally accurate, since she also looked after John Bloom and Jacko Perkins—was filing her nails. Grayson was slightly surprised that she had any nails left, the amount of time she seemed to spend on them, although he would have readily agreed that she was always immacu-late. She greeted him with her usual wide smile, a vast expanse of bril-liant teeth in her dark face. LaDonna was the most efficient woman Grayson had ever known—Janet excepted, of course, he reminded himself—and one of the most even-tempered, too. He often thought that, following Janet's death, without her he'd just have jacked the whole thing in and gone to live on the beach at Torremolinos. As it was, he had the hopeless yearning of the middle-aged man for the unattainable beauty.

"Morning, Boss." She was dressed in a white sweater and dark skirt, and looked very cheerful.

"Morning, 'Donna. How is't today?"

"Is't super. No rain. What's more, no panics. So far," she added with the caution born of experience.

"I hate to disabuse you, dear heart, but I believe the panic is about to set in. Is the computer network actually working today?"

"As of now, yes."

"Then be prepared for much work. Better file your nails down to the quick." LaDonna stuck out her pink tongue as Grayson went into the cell which was dignified by the name of his office. He had made very little attempt to make the place anything other than it was—a workspace. Apart from a coat rack and a photo of Janet, it had few personal touches. Several of his colleagues had spent considerable time and money "personalizing" their offices. When, inevitably, they had to move because of promotion, overseas assignment or any of countless other reasons, there were always bitter complaints about the inconvenience of transferring their possessions. Grayson merely took what he was given and thus minimized his disruption. On the other hand, the surface of his standard-issue metal desk was the definition of chaos.

He set to work, and it was soon pretty clear. With the hours he'd spent last night and the confirmation of the computer information now gleaned, slowly, from a series of highly classified sources, Grayson realized that Rachel Taylor had presented a potential danger. Not a danger to the general public, either here or in the U.S. No, a danger to interests in the Middle East. Perhaps the name could have been picked up earlier. No, *should* have been. It was staring at anyone who'd been looking in the right direction. Aaron Joseph Taylor, her father. Except he wasn't Taylor, not originally, anyway. He had been Teicher, a Polish refugee from World War Two. And a Zionist. He remarried very late in life, his first wife having been sent to one of Hitler's camps, never to be heard of again. Rachel, adopted when he was in his seventies, was known to have spent time in Israel in her teenage years, possibly at a kibbutz. What seemed most likely was that she had been recruited to find funding. Israel had spent—and was still spending—a vast amount of money, much of it from American do-nors, in holding down the Palestinian resistance. Possibly, then, one of the Intifada groups had singled her out for elimination, especially if she was close—as she evidently had been—to a very wealthy source. *Poor old Ferguson, Grayson thought, trapped by a woman less than half your age, and dead as a result.*

There remained the question of her ability to enter the United States, which was quite rigorous in its screening process. Or so it ap-peared, until Grayson laboriously uncovered a series of gaffes and oversights on the part of the Immigration and Naturalization Ser-vice. Still, it did seem that Rachel's initial arrival in the U.S. was legal, working as she did for an international company, AllGlobeProduct-Co, manufacturing soaps, cosmetics, packaged foods, videotapes, and a whole variety of apparently unrelated items. She had been a product manager. Grayson wasn't quite sure what that entailed, but it was clearly something fairly senior, as it had enabled her to acquire her Green Card.

A good cover, Grayson told himself. *And once she had a Green Card, she was free to come and go as she pleased. Thank God she wasn't connected to terrorists on the other side; just think of the damage she could have caused.* Then he thought, too, of the carnage of 9/11. *Oh Jesus. Supposing she was playing a double game.*

Suddenly, the details he'd been almost ready to send to those people in Oklahoma seemed more complicated.

"LaDonna!" She was at the door in moments. "Time to put those elegantly filed fingers to work, my dearest." Grayson felt that a little sweet talk coaxed extra effort from the secretary. She was quite aware of it, and allowed him his small vanity. She was desperately in love with Grayson, and would have swum the English Channel in January for him. He, even in the depths of his misery when Janet had died, had been unfailingly gentle and thoughtful toward her, when many would have been inclined to lash out blindly. "What we need is to find a connection between Rachel Taylor," he brandished some of the file papers, "and one, make that any, of the Palestinian groups, no matter how tenuous. Can you do that?" He well knew that her computer skills far exceeded his own, and her security clearance was almost at the same level.

"If there's anything known, I'll find it. If there isn't," she smiled, "I can always invent it."

"Remind me," Grayson said, "to put you over my knee and spank you."

"Promises, promises." And she was gone.

She found nothing. Nothing, that is, regarding Palestinians. What she did find was confirmation of a relationship with one Michael Nolan, a carpenter in Kilburn once suspected of having ties to the Provisional Irish Republican Army—the Provos. They had been what is sometimes known as an "item." No firm evidence had ever surfaced about Nolan's affiliation, if any, but there were grounds for suspicion. And if Nolan, originally from South Armagh, were suspect, Rachel Taylor must be suspect as well. The problem now was that, since "The Troubles" were currently in abeyance, there was no real reason to suppose that there was any connection between Nolan, the Provos, and the death of Taylor, let alone Ferguson. LaDonna reported all this to Grayson.

"Shit," he muttered "'Scuse the language, 'Donna, but this is, not to put too fine a point on it, a bloody nuisance. I was hoping for some crazed anti-everybody Middle Easterner." LaDonna smiled indulgently. One thing she knew for sure about her man was that he most certainly was no racist. "D'you suppose that Taylor crossed the Provos at some time, and they finally caught up with her?"

"There's nothing to tell us so. On the other hand, there's nothing to the contrary, either."

"What do I tell the Yanks, then?"

LaDonna examined her flawless cuticles. "You're the boss."

"But you're the research expert."

"Well, if you really want my opinion, tell 'em what you know for sure, but imply that there's room for further inquiry. That way, you'll be, as I believe Americans are wont to say, covering your ass."

Grayson laughed, his eyes crinkling in the way that his secretary thought made him look like a mischievous schoolboy. "LaDonna, you've been listening to me too long."

She looked at him, head slightly tilted. "I could never listen to you too long."

The hotel security tapes of the incident in the Hilton bar proved to be corrupted.

"What the hell does 'corrupted' mean?" the hospitality manager had screamed.

"It means," soothed a mohair-clad professional, "that we can't recognize faces here."

Youssef had no knowledge of his good fortune with the surveillance system but he had seen, with satisfaction, the early television reports of the Tel Aviv bombing. That would stir up more public sentiment. He then took the hotel shuttle bus to the airport terminal, and caught sight of the two men after he had checked in his suitcase and was nearing the security line. Riordan, tall, bulky, slightly disheveled—too many drinks last night, he surmised—and Tobin, shorter, neat in a curiously old-fashioned way. Looks like an accountant, he thought. It struck him then. That's exactly what he is—the accountant. It's his job to siphon the funds out of Fergoil. That's why the fire was necessary, to destroy evidence. Everything will be frozen after a killing, while after an accident, the company would have tried to keep functioning as normally as possible. His superiors had merely ordered him to follow any instructions Riordan and Tobin gave him and report back when the job had been completed, which he had done. He'd given very little thought however, to the end purpose: the leader had briefly explained that this was all good for the cause, and would result in huge financial benefits. Youssef was content that what he did was part of the larger plan, and accepted that. The fact that he also stood to increase his own considerable fortune was an added incentive. But he also had an instinctive dislike of Riordan. *That man,* he had thought early on in the enterprise, *is going to be trouble.*

He turned slightly away, so that his back was half to the two Irishmen. He realized that he'd been lax in not altering his appearance enough for this leg of his journey. *Wait for the flight to leave. Don't want to have any contact with them. 'Deal with you later,' that Riordan had said. We'll see who does the dealing. For the moment, cancel your ticket, aban-*

don it, doesn't matter. What's that budget carrier to Brussels? CityBird or something. Is it still going? Doesn't matter either. The one thing that's certain is that I'm not going into any security area with them.

Tobin had seen him and cracked his knuckles thoughtfully. Despite his small stature, he was immensely strong—a trait he had developed assiduously under the careful tutelage of his companion ever since the day of their first meeting. *I'd like to get my hands on you, Youssef or whoever you are.* he thought, but said nothing to Riordan, who was seriously hung-over and liable to make a scene at the least provocation. O'Niell watched from the corner of his eye. Yes, that was him, all right. His appearance was altered a little—ah, the horn-rimmed glasses, that was it. Was it coincidence that brought him here? Yes, had to be, since they hadn't known themselves that this was where or when they'd be leaving. What was no coincidence was that he had turned away so abruptly. *He saw us,* Tobin realized, *and now he's trying to disappear. Jimmy warned him when he rang. So. Is he afraid of us? Not likely. Afraid of repercussions because the operation went wrong? Almost certainly. Running for home? No doubt of it. So, what do I do? Find out where he's going, I suppose.*

Newark Airport, once a relatively calm alternative to the ghastly chaos of LaGuardia and Kennedy, was now almost as bad. The crowds were thick, service at the cafes and shops was, for the most part, just as friendly as in New York, and the security checks were just as slow and just as inefficient. Armed officers were much in evidence, but it looked as if many of them were too overweight to pose a serious threat to a dedicated terrorist.

"Jimmy, boyo. I've to go to the lavatory. Keep me place for me, I'll be back in a moment or two."

Riordan regarded him through a haze. "You'll not be long?"

"Not at all. Look, the line goes on forever. It'll be another twenty minutes before we're at the security gate. Just hold on, I'll be back." He was gone before the befuddled Riordan could protest, noting that, as usual, Youssef was expensively dressed. *Probably with our money,* he seethed.

Youssef saw Tobin gesticulating at Riordan, but wasn't certain what that meant. Was he trying to placate a drunk, persuade him to behave, what? But then the little man left the lurching figure of his companion. *I've been made*, he realized. *They're going to want explanations and I'm not going to give them, not to those two. To my principals, yes. To these two louts, no.*

He went into the nearest men's room, entered a stall, and waited, assuming he would be followed, and peering through the gaps between the toilet's doors and walls so conveniently required by a society seemingly obsessed with the belief that unspeakable things—drugs, homosexuality, who knew?—might go on behind impenetrable doors. So he saw Tobin, who was familiar with his extravagant tastes, come in, looking around. He carefully allowed a slight view of his shoes to be visible under the door of the cubicle, in the expectation that the sheer quality of them would draw Tobin's attention. He was right. The man, fingers flexing, approached the stall with some caution—but not enough. A swift whipping back of the door, a hand to the throat, the glint of a knife, and it was done.

He closed the door quietly and left the restroom, and the terminal. His trip home had been slightly postponed. It was a pity that he'd had to leave the knife, a cleverly made ceramic piece that the scanners couldn't see, but the blood would have been difficult to clean away unobserved in the crowded restroom. He paused for a fraction of a moment. No gloves. He hadn't worn gloves. There would be prints, then, but he dared not turn back. It was time to find another route out. It had to be Canada.

Riordan reached the security checkpoint and Tobin had not returned. His head still throbbing and his mouth dry, he turned his bleary eyes on the agent who was signaling him to come ahead. For a moment he hesitated, then decided to go through; he could wait for Colum on the other side, and then go on to the departure gate. Better yet, he thought, there might be a bar in the waiting area where he could find the hair of the dog. He stepped forward.

Charlie Tidwell, an avionics salesman from Wichita, was in urgent need of a toilet. He entered the men's restroom and was disappointed to see that all the cubicle doors were closed. No, wait, one was just slightly ajar. Lugging his bulky document case, he made for the door and pushed it open. Someone was sitting inside and he started to apologize, then stopped, horrified. The figure in front of him did not have his trousers down. What he did have was a knife in his chest. There wasn't much blood—the knife was stanching the wound—but Tidwell, a Vietnam veteran, knew a dead man when he saw one. Several other men, standing at the urinals, were startled when a balding, slightly chubby guy holding a large briefcase yelled, "Somebody get the police!" Most of them just stared at him as if he were deranged. "The police, dammit! The police! Right now!"

The decidedly messy notes that Grayson finally produced were transformed by LaDonna into a concise and coherent report, with the information arranged in logical order. She presented the final draft to Grayson, who marveled yet again at her abilities.

"It's another of your jewels, 'Donna," he told her, and she smiled with pleasure. "Now, we have to send it to some chap in America with the improbable name of Ziplich."

"America's a big place," LaDonna pointed out. "Could you be a little more precise, please?"

It was Grayson's turn to smile. "Sorry, yes. Tulsa, Oklahoma. Here, I've got the full name, official address, fax number, and all the rest here." He passed her a typically confusing piece of paper, certain that LaDonna would be able to make sense of it.

This she duly did, then asked him: "Do you want to send a brief covering note, too?"

"Better, I suppose." He scribbled a few sentences—faster than trying to type, as she had long since understood—and gave her those as well. Then he checked the time on the clock that lurked amid the shambles of paper covering his desk. LaDonna was doing some marveling of her own, by no means for the first time. How was it that her man—for thus she considered him, rather hopelessly—so fastidious about his personal appearance could not keep a desk tidy? Grayson went on: "It's twenty-five past twelve—lunchtime, by the way. That'll be six twenty-five in the morning over there. Let's take a break and send this when we get back." He often tried to engineer a few minutes with her away from the office, and was constantly surprised when she always readily agreed.

Lunch in the canteen wasn't bad; quite good, in fact. One of the advantages of eating here was the low, subsidized cost, another was the consistently decent quality. The disadvantage was that the designer of the place, while making it reasonably attractive—no yellow plastic tables or pale blue walls—had failed to take adequate sound-deadening measures, and the din was usually pretty bad. Perhaps it was a way of encouraging the staff not to linger over their meals. If so, it worked rather well. Today, Grayson and LaDonna were back in the office a little after one. Grayson, comfortably full of steak and kidney pudding, decided to send the fax to Ziplich now. That way, it should be waiting for him when he got in, unless he were an early riser. As it happened, he was.

❖   ❖   ❖

"Ladies and gentlemen, we apologize for the delay." A muffled groan came from the travelers in the waiting area. "We'll be boarding just as soon possible. Thank you for your patience." Several disgruntled passengers approached the desk to demand an explanation of this further delay to a flight that should have departed yesterday, but the agent was unable to enlighten them. "I'm afraid I have no details at this time. As soon as I can give you more information, rest assured that I'll do so." So they perforce rested, though not necessarily assured. Any assurance they might have had would disappear with the arrival of the police.

Riordan, having found no alcohol available, had to resort to coffee as he waited for Tobin to reappear. He'd been on the second cup when the time had come to go to the departure gate. Now he was in a quandary and, as his head cleared a little, he strove to make some sort of decision. Should he stay here, where he could observe passengers as they emerged from the security area, or should he go to the gate and wait there? Where the hell was Colum? The wait for security clearance had been long, but not this long, and he should be here by now. Ah. Was that him now? But it wasn't, just someone who looked a bit like him. Riordan decided to wait a few more minutes then, if Tobin didn't turn up, he'd go to the departure gate. After all, they always wanted you there much sooner than necessary. He took another gulp of coffee. It tasted terrible.

Two security men had come at the run. Tidwell silently pushed the stall door open—he'd been keeping it closed and standing in front of it to keep the inquisitive at bay. One of the police felt for a pulse, knowing full well from the glazed eyes there wouldn't be one. The other ushered all the onlookers out, except for Tidwell and the man who'd rushed to call them. The officer who had tried for the pulse, "Melendez" his name badge said, looked at Tidwell, who had completely forgotten his need for the bathroom.

"You find him?"

"Yes."

"When?'

"Three, four minutes ago. Just pushed open the door and there he was."

"Know him?"

"Good God, no! Soon as I saw him I yelled for someone to get the police."

"'Sright," confirmed the one who had done so. "I seen him headin' fast for the john, an' heard him shout. Thought he was crazy for a moment, then I seen what he was yellin' about, so I lit out like he said to."

The other police officer was on his radio. Soon the place would be alive with them. Tidwell knew he was going to miss his flight, but knew equally well there was nothing he could do about it. Melendez looked more closely at what had once been Colum Tobin, aka O'Neill. There was the edge of a boarding pass just under the lapel of his jacket, pushed a little from its snug berth of an inside pocket when he had been dropped on the seat as he fell. Melendez, careful to disturb nothing else, gingerly pulled it out and inspected it. "Joe," he said to his colleague, who was momentarily off the radio, "get this flight stopped."

"Done better'n that already," Joe told him. "Whole damned airport's being sealed off."

The sealing off of airports, although much practiced and re-hearsed at a time when terror attacks are on everybody's mind, is still not an instantaneous process. In this case, it would have made little difference if it were, since nearly half an hour had elapsed between Tobin's death and the finding of his body—more than enough time for a man to find a cab and leave the area. Surveillance tapes would be no more of a threat here than they had been at the Hilton restaurant the previous evening. Youssef was well on his way to Manhattan by the time the alarm was raised. He left the taxi at Penn Station and took another to Grand Central. There he bought a ticket to White Plains. At the station there, he took yet another cab to Scarsdale, where he borrowed an elderly Oldsmobile from the small garage whose owner owed him a favor and his life. Youssef had, quite gently, reminded the man of that day years ago in East Jerusalem and the car was instantly available.

"Report it stolen tomorrow morning. Not until then."

"I understand."

"It's insured? I don't need any trouble." He had enough already.

"Yes, the papers are in the glove box."

"You'll get it back eventually, but there will be questions."

"I know nothing."

"Good." Within an hour he was headed north, well along I-87 and, in the early afternoon, he crossed into Canada with minimal dif-ficulty. The road continued, now as AutoRoute 15, straight to Mon-treal. He parked at the Place d'Armes Hotel near the center, went into the lobby, and arranged for the concierge to rent a car for Monsieur Jacques Dutoit of Toulouse. He then returned to the Olds to remove any vestige of his presence, quite a lengthy process. That done to his satisfaction, M. Dutoit went back to the lobby and found that the rental car was ready. A decent tip to the concierge and, bag in hand, Jacques Dutoit went to the waiting Chevy, got in, and drove away. "Business in Trois-Rivieres and Quebec," he'd told the concierge be-fore taking the opposite direction to Ottawa.

LaDonna's elegantly-organized fax report arrived on Ziplich's desk at the same time that news was coming in regarding a suicide bombing in Tel Aviv and a major shutdown at Newark airport. Ziplich himself was deeply immersed in the finding that Ralph Ferguson, deceased, had been an imposter. As a matter of routine, the bodies found in the destroyed Fergoil building had been fingerprinted, as much to eliminate them from other prints which might be found amid the rubble as anything else. They were automatically compared to file information as a double check. It was at that point, Ziplich's partner Benny explained, they had found that the Ferguson of Fergoil had prints which differed from those of First Lieutenant Ralph Ferguson, U.S. Army (Ret.) Yet they were supposedly the same person. Two questions immediately arose: who was the dead man in the morgue, and what had happened to the original Ferguson? Ziplich was pondering about these points and listening with one ear to the NPR Newark report on the radio that he kept on his desk, when the British fax appeared. Please, Ziplich thought, no more complications. He was to be disappointed.

Rachel Taylor was the daughter of a Polish Zionist, had spent time in Israel, and had at one time been the girlfriend of a man who might have had radical Irish affiliations. She had managed to put herself in a position where she could enter the U.S. more or less at will, and had eventually become the mistress of a very rich man more than twice her age, a man who—it had just become clear—was masquerading as someone else.

"Damnation, Benny, it's only just nine o'clock and the whole day's a mess already."

"Just be grateful you're not trying to get home from Newark," said the philosophical Benny.

Nobody was going home, or anywhere else, from Newark for a considerable time. The entire perimeter of the airfield was ringed with police and other security vehicles, every entrance and exit was guarded, every concourse and departure gate under strict surveillance. Once the cordon was fully in place, the questioning would begin. It might have taken much longer before the investigation reached Riordan if he had managed to remain calm. Once it became clear, however, that there was an investigation at all, he began to pester the security personnel, the coffee having had only a marginal effect as yet.

"It's Colum, y'see. Went to the bog and didn't come back and what's happened at all?" The less reaction he got, the more strident he became, eventually earning himself a place in the Chief of Security's office, an armed guard holding him firmly.

"I think he may just be a drunk, sir, but I'm not sure. Keeps shouting about a pillar and a marsh."

"Colum and a bog, y'fool. D'ye understand nothing at all? He went to the bog—oh, shit, bathroom to youse—and never came back. Then y'stop us going anywhere or doing anything and ye wonder why we don't like it. I've lost me friend, can't you understand? And I don't know what the fock's going on and it's not right. This is a bloody democracy, ain't it? So democratize us." After a little more in this vein, Riordan seemed to run out of steam. But Chief Phelps noted the main point: this man's friend had gone to the toilet and not returned. The whole security alert had been triggered by the finding of a dead man in a toilet. Hardly coincidence, the Chief thought but, even if it were, it had to be looked into. So it was that, some four hours after Tobin had gone to meet his maker, Jimmy Riordan—now desperately sober, and wishing he were not—looked, for the last time, upon the face of Colum Tobin.

"That's him. That's Colum. Oh, Jaysus, he only went for a pee. We were going home, we were." Riordan was choked up: he and Colum had been friends since that first meeting. They'd been runners for the Cause when they were children, they'd worked for it since they were grown. They'd carried messages and Semtex, they'd done time in the 'Kesh, they had embraced the views of the dissenters who refused to accept what they regarded as IRA treachery in its cease-fire with the hated British; they'd been involved that long. And always together.

Jimmy's mind wandered back to the day, long ago, when a weedy little boy in the Crumlin Road area of Belfast was being tormented by a group of older children. They were prodding at him, pushing him, jeering at him. "Is yer mother Orange or Green?" came the taunts, "or yer faither if ye know who he is?" More shouts, more abuse, and finally, a blow that sent the thin boy sprawling. Jimmy was furious: all he had ever been taught was brought to bear on bullies who targeted the weak—a philosophy that dictated his later political views. Without a moment's hesitation, Jimmy had launched himself at the three largest tormenters and in seconds they, and their supporters, were bloodied and in full flight.

Jimmy gently helped the smaller boy to his feet. "I'll walk home wit' youse," he offered, and so was born a lasting relationship.

The Chief knew that he'd found at least a partial answer to his own problem. He asked quietly, "Do you have any idea who would want to hurt your friend? Or why?"

"That I don't, but if I ever catch the bastard..." He stopped. Then, bitterly, "It's the bloody Brits, isn't it; just can't bear to think they can't hold us down. Well, they never will, the scum. People think we've sold out to the 'peace process,' but that's only political talk. Just wait until Paisley's gone."

Phelps supposed he meant the ultra-hardline Irish 'loyalist' Ian Paisley, now a part of the power-sharing he had so often stridently vilified. "Have you ever seen this before?" Encased in a plastic bag Phelps dangled between them was the ceramic knife.

"Never!" Riordan said emphatically, and the Chief, a man of many years' experience, recognized the lie.

Chapter 3
June, 2011

"Riordan got back today."

Grayson was less than excited. "Should I be interested?"

Jacko Perkins suggested that perhaps he should. "He came back from somewhere. Alone. He went away a couple of weeks ago with Tobin, and he came back without him. One has to wonder why. I just had the foolish idea that, since you've been tossing messages to and fro with that Yank, the one with the funny name, about possible IRA connections, you might want to add this to the mix."

"You're the one who keeps his finger on the Republican pulse, not I. I'm simply naughty British expats. I was merely answering a few questions in your stead for our transatlantic friends while you were away reveling with that Mata Hari from Belfast in the fleshpots of Ramsgate."

"Actually she was from Newtownards, and it was Margate."

"I imagine the fleshpots are similar."

"That's true but, by golly, you should just see Whitstable."

"No doubt, no doubt."

"Anyway, Riordan went off, we presumed to the States, about a fortnight ago with Tobin, and arrived back today without him. That's unusual. Those two elegant fundraisers are almost as conjoined as Siamese twins." Perkins's educated Public School tones sounded aggrieved. "Your, what's her name, Rachel Taylor, died three or four days back, and not by accident. She may have been a sympathizer. I know America's a big place,"—did he and LaDonna have the same scriptwriter, Grayson wondered—"and it's most likely only coincidence, but it has to make you think, if only a little."

"Oh, all right," Grayson sighed. "I'll think—but probably only a little, as you suggest. Seems to me they're much more your bailiwick at the Irish Desk. I will, admit, though, that Taylor was a British expat, naughty or otherwise."

LaDonna appeared in the doorway, holding a small sheaf of papers. "Jacko," she said, "I'm sorry, I mean Mr. Perkins." It was generally believed that Perkins was in line for the currently vacant position of Deputy Director General—the previous holder of that position having suffered a massive stress-induced heart attack—and it would be as well to keep him happy.

Perkins smoothed a hand over his immaculate hair and unnecessarily adjusted his Old Etonian tie. "It's all right, LaDonna, Mr. Grayson here knows my nickname well enough to make constant fun of it, and I can't really say I blame him. Blame him for lots of other things, but not that. You were saying?"

"Messages via Century House, Scotland Yard, and all the usual stops along the way, from the Chief of Security at Newark International Airport in the US of A, concerning a dead man named O'Neill. Ulster-issued passport, knife in his chest, and a travelling companion called Malone who's been allowed to return to the U.K because there's no evidence that he had any hand in the killing. In fact, he was very clearly not involved, because a number of impeccable witnesses, including an American senator, saw him alone at the time of the death. On the other hand, the security man is certain that Riordan was lying when he was shown the murder weapon and denied all knowledge of it. Not evidence, of course, but the Chief has an excellent reputation for sniffing out things like that."

LaDonna waved the papers. "It's all in here. Pictures, too."

"Let's have a look." Perkins took the sheaf and flipped through it. His eyes narrowed sharply. "Oh, my. Just look at this, Dan. Here is Mr. Riordan, with a caption identifying him as James Malone, and here is Colum Tobin—now the late Colum Tobin, it would seem— who led America to believe his name was O'Neill."

"And now Riordan is back in Belfast?"

"Yes. Maybe one of our chaps ought to go and chat to him. Poor fellow must need a bit of sympathy."

It had taken a full twenty-four hours to get Newark Airport back to normal running. Normal, that is, except for the milling of frustrated passengers, the repositioning of cancelled, delayed, and diverted aircraft, the angry telephone calls to family or friends or employers to explain why they were having to wait. It would take days to straighten all that out. The Head of Security was profoundly grateful that was not part of his responsibility. Shut everything down, yes. Get it all started again when the perceived threat had been dealt with, that was the airport authority's problem, thank heaven. He leaned his considerable bulk back in his "Executive Swivel/Recline Leather Chair" and considered the question of the knife in O'Neill's chest. Ceramic, clearly intended to defeat the scanning machines, and successful at having done so. Forensics had found prints on it, nice clear prints. Trouble was, they didn't match anything on record. The Police and FBI were checking with foreign allies, but there was no certainty they'd find anything. Britain was probably most likely, the victim and his travelling companion both having been British citizens, but Phelps wasn't very hopeful.

There was something wrong about that Irish Malone guy. The Chief knew he'd been lying about the knife and had tried leaning on him a little, but to no avail. He'd gathered the impression that the man was not unaccustomed to interrogation techniques, which gave him, in turn, to consider the recent troubles in Ireland. Any connection? Possibly, but nothing of substance, especially now that the IRA had renounced violence. Since a senior senator had seen Riordan throughout the entire period during which the murder must have occurred—enjoying a cup of coffee himself—Malone was definitely off the hook. Besides, nobody could fake distress that well. So, in the end, he'd had to be allowed to go. He'd be back in Britain by now, while his former companion was lying in a chilled drawer. O'Neill wouldn't be going home for some time. The phone rang. "Phelps."

"Ah, Mr. Phelps. You won't know me, I'm afraid. Name's Grayson, Dan Grayson. I rather wondered if we might have a little chinwag about two of my fellow countrymen who seem to have caused you a modicum of distress over the last few days."

I think I'm going to need an interpreter, Phelps told himself.

Ziplich was still wondering who the hell the late Ralph Ferguson had really been and, at the same time, where was the original? He and Benny, together with three other detectives, were searching the Ferguson residence more fully than they had been able to do the previous couple of days. There were latex gloves, dusting powder, cameras, evidence bags, the usual paraphernalia of a murder investigation, and so far they had discovered precisely nothing to shed light on a reason for the killing. There had to be one, obviously. What was not obvious was what that motive might be. There were not many company papers in the house. They'd had a check done of the premises and, finding no safe, had contacted both the bank that Ferguson had used for his corporate and private accounts and the representatives of all known safe manufacturers and dealers in the area. It quickly became apparent that the search for a hidden safe was a waste of time: there wasn't one. Ferguson kept his business affairs confined to the office and his private affairs were taken care of by his secretary and the bank. His secretary, a thin, distraught woman by the name of Jenna Grant, had been almost prostrated by the news of her employer's death.

"He's, I mean, oh dear, I mean was, such a lovely man to work for. I've been with him more than fifteen years, and I..." There was a good deal more of this nature, but nothing to shed light on the crime. The wilting Ms. Grant was eventually allowed to go home, with the admonition that, if she thought of anything...

Benny and Ziplich were about ready to call it a day. They'd been here since the early morning and found nothing that advanced their investigation. Ziplich called the other members of the team. "Okay, guys, take off. Anything you've got in the bags, drop off at the office and we'll check 'em out in the morning. See you then." They departed through streets still showing scattered branches and other signs of storm damage. Benny and Ziplich were left in the empty and, by now, chaotic house.

"Know what, Benny?"

"H'm?"

"I could use a drink. We been at this three days now, and there's nothing, no clue. Carol's on my case because I'm never home, the lieutenant has been patient, but I know he's getting flak from up the line, and the Brits will probably start whining. Time out tonight. So, this is what I saw earlier."

He led the way downstairs from the elaborate bedrooms, one of them clearly containing the king-sized bed that Ferguson had shared with Rachel Taylor—no clues about anything there, except the obvious—and into Ferguson's library.

"There are," Ziplich announced, brushing his unruly mop of hair from his brow, "people who call rooms libraries, and people who really do have libraries. Ferguson was one of the latter." He pushed the door open, revealing a spacious room lined with filled bookshelves and furnished with leather chairs, a magnificent stereo with a selection of classical CDs, largely Wagner, and a couple of fine mahogany tables. "He also had," Ziplich continued, opening a cabinet door, "a very respectable taste in liquor. Now, as far as we know, the late Mr. Ferguson had no heirs. Should all this inheritance go to the taxman?"

It was a rhetorical question. Benny had no objection to sampling the largesse revealed by the open cabinet door. It had all been fingerprinted and recorded, a couple of measures in the cut crystal glasses wouldn't bring Ferguson or Taylor back, and it was already far into cocktail hour.

They were, in fact, on their second—Jack and Seven for Benny, Skyy and tonic for Ziplich—when Benny paused. He'd been wandering about the room looking idly at the shelves of books and delicately enjoying his drink, his bulky figure a strange contrast to the (Ziplich thought) too carefully contrived elegance of the surroundings. Ziplich himself, shirtsleeved, was sunk in the comfort of a vast leather armchair. Benny stopped abruptly, his swarthy face reflecting curiosity.

"Zee?"

"Yeah?"

"C'mere a minute."

Ziplich didn't stir. "What is it?"

"Crosswords."

"So?"

"Well, look, there's a whole bunch of crossword books here. There's," he started to count, "more'n thirty of 'em. And," he was flipping the pages, "they're all done, completed."

"Just because you can't complete the crossword on the children's page doesn't mean everybody else has the same problem, Benny ol' pal."

"Zee, they're done in ink."

Ziplich remained unimpressed. "So Ferguson was sure he was always right. Lotta executives like that."

Benny gave an exaggerated sigh. "Will you look at the books, Zee?"

"What's your point, Benny? Ferguson did crosswords. Lots of people do crosswords; maybe lots of 'em do 'em in ink. It doesn't help."

"Might," Benny told him. "See, these are all English crossword books. Look—selections from the Daily Telegraph, Times, Guardian, Independent. All British newspapers. And Ferguson had an English mistress. Now, did she do the crosswords, or did he?"

Ziplich was fully alert now. "Graphology will soon tell us. Grab a couple more of those books, Benny, and let's get going." He drained his glass and stood up. Then, belatedly, "Good work, feller." Starting towards the door, he paused for a moment. "Benny, can you hear anything, or is it just me?"

"I hear you good enough, but nothin' else. Well, a car just went by on the street. That what you mean?"

Ziplich was straining his ears. Several seconds passed before he relaxed with a rueful smile. "Must be the air conditioning. I guess I'm losing my touch. Let's get out of here."

In Belfast, Jimmy Riordan was not appreciative of the company's concern for his wellbeing and the loss of his lifelong friend. To say that the snarling reception young Peter Ngami received in Riordan's dreary flat was rude and insulting would be overstating its warmth. On the other hand, it did reveal one thing. Riordan, in his fury, let slip that the knife he'd seen at Newark was of Middle Eastern origin. He tried to cover up the error, but Ngami, although a recent recruit, was very well trained and observant. He gave no sign that he had picked up on what Riordan had said, and continued questioning for some time, sure that he already had all he was going to get. Eventually he left, went directly to Aldergrove, and flew back to London. He was in the office again by four o'clock, and went to report to Grayson and Perkins.

"You didn't get any elaboration on 'Middle Eastern,' did you?" Grayson asked, fiddling with several indecipherable pieces of paper.

"'Fraid not, sir. Actually, I was surprised to get that much. Riordan was not," he said tactfully, "particularly welcoming."

Jacko smiled at that. "No, I hardly thought he would be. All right Peter, well done. Push off home now, to that delightful lady of yours." When Ngami had gone, Perkins turned to Grayson, a thoughtful look on his face.

"D'you think we could get a photo of this knife from your friend at Newark? It could be a crucial link in the case." Grayson thought so too, which was how he had come to be speaking again to Chief Phelps.

"A picture of it? Sure. I'd offer you the genuine article but, of course, the police are gonna be hanging on to that as evidence. So those two guys were IRA, eh? I kinda felt like they were, but didn't have more than intuition. Certainly Malone didn't have any connection with the killing; his reaction alone convinced me of that. If I'd known that they were travelling on false passports, I could've had them held—well the Malone guy, anyway."

Grayson was grimacing over a rapidly-cooling cup of tasteless tea. "Yes, well, actually the passports were genuine enough. It was the names that weren't. We haven't yet found the source of the passports, but we will, and we'll cut it off. Then, naturally, it'll all start again somewhere else. It's what keeps us employed, this sort of thing. As for IRA—well, maybe. Problem is, the IRA has—for public consumption, anyway—renounced its evil ways. In other words, they've sworn off 'armed struggle'. It'll probably be some years before we can be sure they mean it. On the other hand, there are plenty of extremists on both sides who see the current reconciliation efforts as treachery, and they'll be glad to keep the fires of hatred stoked. We'd like to deal with them. Not cut a deal," he added hurriedly, lest the

American misunderstand. "Our other problem is that we can't prove that Riordan used a fake, because he was careful to lose it before we questioned him, and it's too late for Tobin."

Phelps was beginning to warm to this unseen Brit at the other end of the telephone line. "Anything else?"

"Well, yes, Chief, actually there is,"—*these guys really do say "actually" all the time*, Phelps thought—"We'd rather like to have a sample of any fingerprints you might have been able to lift from the knife. Could you manage that, do you suppose?"

"No problem. I'll get 'em sent over to you right away. I was going to check with your Scotland Yard to see if you had a match in the archive, anyway, but now I'll send 'em to you instead. Difficulty is, you see," he continued, "we have these jurisdictional concerns here. There's us, Airport Security, then there's the City, County, and State authorities—they're divided oftentimes between police and sheriff departments, too—and then there's the Feds. We try to keep *them* out of the loop as much as we can, since they usually seem pretty heavy-handed. So far, we're managing to keep this to the police and ourselves. Still, you see, it can slow things down trying to be careful of the sometimes fiercely-protected demarcation lines."

"Oh, I do understand, I do indeed. We're not free of such little jealousies here, either. Which is a good reason to leave Scotland Yard out of that same loop, by the bye. Well, thank you very much, Chief. I'll look forward to receiving your pretty pictures. Perhaps we'll have the opportunity to meet sometime. I do manage to get about quite a bit."

"Great idea. 'Bye Mr. Grayson."

"Oh, do please call me Dan. Goodbye, Chief." Grayson finished his tea.

At first, the accountants hadn't seemed to be much help. The books of Fergoil were impeccably kept, meticulously accurate, and went back in an unbroken line to 1974, when Ferguson, or whoever he was, had first manipulated the purchase of Grebe and Oliver, and changed the name to Windfall, then Fergoil. There, the trail went cold. There was absolutely no indication of where the money for that acquisition had come from, Ferguson's earlier career having yielded no information on that front. Certainly, it hadn't come from his modest family. Anyway, he wasn't really Ferguson, so that was all nonsense. Inquiries as to the Ferguson family had ground to a halt, too. There were no surviving relatives, which Ziplich regarded as being, perhaps, too convenient. So where was the real Ralph Ferguson and, the question yet again, who was the dead man? On the other hand, the graphologist, a middle-aged man with a pony tail, and not much else by way of hair, had been quite positive.

"The writing is Ferguson's. The characteristics are unmistakable. The Taylor woman had a totally different 'fist.' May I make a point?"

"Sure," Ziplich said. He needed all the help he could get, and it was getting late. Carol wouldn't be too happy if he showed up at eight or nine.

"These British puzzles' clues are more cryptic than ours, and they oftentimes require what you might call specialized knowledge; you know, about the British way of life, their 'public' schools, cricket, the armed forces and so on. Most particularly, there are spelling differences, differences of pronunciation, and awful puns. Look here." He pointed. "Clue is 'extinct elephant.' Answer: mastodon. OK, so far. Next clue: 'salad plant.' Answer; 'cress.' We'd call it 'watercress,' at least the few who're familiar with it would. Now, put those two answers together as the clue to eighteen down, and you get 'mastodon cress.' 'So what?' you ask. So this: mustard and cress is an English sort of salad plant, hotter than watercress, but looking much the same. Bad pun, and most Americans couldn't make that connection. One example doesn't prove anything, but these books are full of 'em. Look here: 'Man rises above it.' Answer, Irish Sea. The Isle of Man rises out of the Irish Sea, a bit to the west of England. Again, a bad pun, but typically English and, like I say, the books are full of them. Your Ferguson was an Englishman."

Ziplich went home, mentally exhausted, to be greeted by a radiant Carol. "I got the promotion, Paul, I got it!"

"You're gonna be a partner? Oh, honey, that is the greatest—no, you're the greatest. Oh, boy! Tonight we celebrate! Hey, girl, get your glad rags on, an' I'll brush my teeth. You didn't defrost the TV dinners yet, did you?" Carol aimed a poor right hook, which missed by a foot or so, and then sniffed.

"You had a drink." It wasn't a question.

"Yep. Tell you all about it over dinner. Go get your on-the-town clothes. I'll book a table."

Jacques Dutoit had disappeared, and the man who boarded the Air Canada flight to London in Ottawa a couple of days later—a Mr. Vincent Callio—didn't look like him at all. Gone were the sleek black hair and the conservative business suit. The auburn-haired Mr. Callio wore Reebok shoes and a remarkably ugly microfiber "TravelSuit." Clutched in his hand was a sports duffle. He had no other baggage. "Gonna buy me a whole new wardrobe in Paris, France," he confided to the desk agent, who had looked a trifle askance at his traveling so light. "Had a bit of luck with a horse."

The agent gave a wan smile. This jerk looked exactly like the sort of person who would have "a bit of luck with a horse," while she was stuck at this damn desk, feet aching, putting up with the gripes of ill-mannered passengers with whining kids and stupid questions. What she wouldn't have given for a little of Callio's luck.

Monsieur Dutoit's rental car wasn't discovered in the Ottawa airport car park for several days. Avis had been a little disgruntled at its absence but, after all, it was covered by the credit card. Except the credit card had proven to be a fake. Avis contacted the police, and eventually the car was found. Little else was, not even a fingerprint. Just one thing: a single strand of auburn hair—from a wig.

On the same day, a car reported stolen from a garage in Scarsdale, New York was recovered from the parking lot of a Montreal hotel.

A staff of police and other authorities had spent a great deal of time trying to gather the papers scattered over a huge area by the tornado. The storm had continued its rampage northeast from Tulsa, ripping buildings apart, seemingly at random but without more casualties, eventually running out of force after a final burst of fury destroyed Joplin, Missouri. The destruction and loss of life there eclipsed even what Tulsa had suffered. Papers from destroyed buildings were scattered over hundreds of square miles, and most of them were soggy and indecipherable. But there were a few which could be assembled together, and some of them, ripped and blurred, were found to refer to Fergoil. "Received of Ralph Arthur Ferguson, in return for valuable and agreed property both real and financial, together with all rights and assigned ownerships...." There was a good deal more in this style, but the end product was that Ralph Ferguson had paid, in cash, more than $500,000 for Windfall, which had itself bought out Grebe and Oliver. That was an enormous sum in 1974. Yet there was still no indication where Ferguson had acquired it, especially in cash. Had the brokers not questioned a cash sale of that size? Apparently not. Ziplich decided that, if they hadn't asked questions back then, they most certainly should answer a few now.

Herbert Langfeld—"Call me Herb," he wheezed genially—was the largest man Ziplich had ever seen. He must be six-foot-six in any direction you care to measure, he thought. No wonder he's short of breath. The aroma of expensive cigars might also have been a clue to the huffing of the good Mr. Langfeld.

"So, you want to know about the purchase of the Windfall company by Fergoil. Well, I do remember the sale. I was just a very junior broker back in those days, but I did do some of the general paperwork. Since you called me, I've had all the records pulled and, in essence, they say what you already know. Fergoil did indeed pay cash to Bill Hewitt and, sure, that surprised just about everybody. I remember ol' Joe Wagner—he was the boss back then—telling me to get the bills down to the bank and have them checked for authenticity. Cigar? No? Well, if you don't mind I will." Langfeld selected carefully one from a box of what seemed to Ziplich identical cigars, rolled it in his fingers, sniffed at it, put it close to one ear, and rolled it again. Apparently satisfied, he performed a swift amputation of one end with a gold cigar cutter, stuck the cigar in his mouth, and lit it with a match.

"Never light a cigar with a lighter," he advised Ziplich, "Totally ruins the flavor." He leaned back in his vast chair and emitted a cloud of blue smoke toward Ziplich, who had no intention of ever lighting a cigar with anything.

"See, this was a young company back then," Langfeld resumed, "and we didn't have a whole lot of clients, not like now. So Joe was ready to take on anybody that wasn't clearly a felon. Ferguson didn't seem like that. He was quite young, I'd guess about thirty five, forty or so, but he had an air of, well, honesty about him. I remember being struck by his New England accent. I thought that was real classy, back in those days. 'Course he lost it over the years. I'd run into him time to time—fundraisers, that kind of thing—and, shoot, he sounded just like the rest of us Okies. I'm sorry he's gone. I'll tell you, he was a great asset to this city. We'd probably have had to wait years longer for our storm sewer project after those last floods if he hadn't stepped in and underwritten a lot of it. Even set up his own contracting companies to do the excavatin' and lay the pipes; did it at cost, too. Yep, we have a lot to thank that guy for. 'Course, he had a talent for turning a profit, but then that's what business is about. Like I say, gonna miss him."

Ziplich leaned forward. "You said his New England accent. Are you sure it wasn't Old England?"

"Could've been, I suppose. It's awhile back now, you know."

"Have you a copy of any letters he might have sent you?"

"Sure, of course. You want to see 'em?"

"Just one or two, the very earliest ones."

"You got it." Langfeld buzzed the intercom. "Juanita, bring in the Fergoil file, will you?"

Juanita was at the door in moments. "We had 'em ready when we knew you were coming," Langfeld explained.

Ziplich took the file and opened it. There were a few pages of office preamble, and then the first of the Fergoil letters. Slipping it out of the folder, Ziplich looked at it carefully. There, at the bottom, handwritten, "Thank you for your help, Yours Faithfully, R. A. Ferguson." Yours faithfully, eh? Time for another session with the graphologist and, perhaps, some more communication with Dan Grayson.

"Could I have copies of these, please?"

Paul Ziplich was in an upbeat mood. His dinner with Carol last night, at the Chalkboard, had been outstanding, as had been the balance of the evening. Amazing, Ziplich had managed a moment to think in the turmoil of the bedroom, that she should still be so passionate. But she had been.

The graphologist, of whose name Ziplich had never been entirely certain—Groen? Petty? Orbach?—confirmed his earlier diagnosis.

"Yours faithfully? Not, as you noticed, 'yours truly' or 'sincerely.' No, 'faithfully.' Classic 50's and 60's British business procedure. It's not quite as distinctive as 'I have the honor to be, sir, your obedient servant,' but near enough. And the handwriting is classic British, too. When he was growing up, handwriting in Britain was based on what they called 'pothooks,' an angular style, while Americans were being taught the rounded 'Jack be nimble' Cursive method. I tell you again, your alleged Ferguson was British. He may have acquired a veneer of Americana over, as you say, a good many years, but whatever name he was signing, he was a Brit. Period."

❖　❖　❖

"The Feds gave it all a good going over," Chief Phelps said, " they didn't find much, not that they figured was of much interest, anyway. They passed the information on to us as a procedural matter, and then washed their hands of it. But"—Grayson's ears pricked up at the inflexion of that 'but'—"the forensic report did include the news that some grit found in one of the outer seams of this suitcase was similar to some building materials being used in airport construction. Now, Newark is not currently doing any construction, for a change, but many airports are. So, I put one of my youngsters here on finding out which ones, and he came up with a pretty long list. What may be the interesting point here, Dan, is that one of those on the list is Tulsa."

Phelps had rung Grayson with a rundown on a piece of baggage found when the chaos of the flight on which the ill-fated Colum Tobin had been booked finally began to subside. There had been no one to claim it. It wasn't "O'Neill's." The baggage tag linked it to one Henry Millen, who had never checked in at the departure lounge, so the suitcase was removed for further examination. Nothing suspicious had been found.

"Tulsa, eh?" Grayson murmured. "Chief, how about prints?"

"Don't know. There were some, of course, but none on our records. We did eliminate the baggage handlers here, naturally, but there were just too many, often partial or smeared, to check 'em all out. A piece of airline baggage goes through a lot of hands."

"Yes, of course. I was just wondering whether any of those hands had also touched a ceramic knife. I've got your copy of the pictures you sent me, for which many thanks, but nothing to compare them with." At the other end of the line Phelps was already gesticulating to one of his assistants. "It's probably too long a shot to be helpful, but then you never know, do you?"

"You're right, of course, Dan. Should've thought of it myself, but that set hasn't been entered in our archives yet. It's been pretty busy here recently." Grayson could well imagine. "Are you thinking that the guy who wasted your O'Neill, I mean Tobin, may have had a connection with the other killing in Tulsa? It looks a bit shaky to me, but coincidences do happen." A young man across the room from Phelps was tapping at a keyboard and gazing intently at a screen. "You're thinking that what we're looking at is a professional hit man who blew away the two in Tulsa, met up with the Irish guy on the way home, and took him out, too? But why, if there is, as you suspect, an IRA connection, would he attack his own man? And why only one, not the two of them?" A computer printout was thrust into his hand.

"Those are some of the things I'm wondering, too, Chief."

"Well, we can stop wondering about one thing, at least, Dan." Phelps was peering at the sheet of paper he held. "Some of the prints on the bag do match the knife. So the unclaimed bag was owned by O'Neill's—dammit, Tobin's—killer. The bag may have been in Tulsa; we'll have to get a more exhaustive analysis on building materials before we can confirm that. If it really had come from Tulsa, we have to look at a possible link to the murder of your Ferguson and his girl friend." *Why,* Grayson wondered, *had Ferguson become "his?"*

"Well, there's this other point. The gun used in the Tulsa killing was British. Old, true, but originally from this country. There are lots of old war souvenirs still floating around, most of them illegally, many in Ulster."

"Ulster?" broke in Phelps.

"Northern Ireland. Now Riordan and Tobin are both from there. Rachel Taylor once had a boyfriend who came from there, who is believed—only believed , mark you—to have had IRA sympathies. I know we're looking at coincidences again, Chief, but I can't help wondering whether Taylor might have done something to upset the leadership of some renegade Irish group. There are several of those who haven't taken kindly to what's called 'the peace process.' It could just be that Ferguson simply happened to get in the way at the wrong time."

"Didn't you tell me his legs had been kneecapped according to that guy in Tulsa, what's his name? Zip something."

"Ziplich. Yes, you're right. That was too deliberate to be simply eliminating a witness. Classic IRA tactic, too. Thing is, we still don't know who Ferguson really was, and certainly not why some Irish group might want him out of the way. Maybe this Irish business is all red herring."

"Maybe," Phelps agreed without conviction.

Ziplich looked around the room again. He'd collected Benny from the office and returned to the Ferguson house to see if there were any papers they might have missed in their three days of searching the place. He couldn't have said why, but he felt uneasy that there was a missing part to the puzzle which the building might resolve, and so had determined to check all the library shelves for something—anything—which might shed light on the Ferguson story. The two of them set about a methodical scrutiny of the contents of the bookcases, taking down each volume and examining it for any unexpected papers or entries. They were aided in this by another determined assault on the Ferguson liquor cabinet. It hadn't helped, and after several hours they were no nearer a solution. Ziplich freshened his glass and sank into the armchair he had favored previously.

"I'm sorry, Benny, I've brought you out on a wasted errand. I had a hunch, and it was wrong. Let's go home." He paused, cocking his head a little. "Is it me, or is there a kind of humming here? I thought

I heard something last time we were in this room, but put it down to air conditioning. Now I'm not sure. You hear it?"

Benny listened, then said: "There's a faint sound, yeah, but I'd've said the air, too. You got another idea?"

"Not really. Let's go round the place and see if we can find anything."

The two of them made a careful circuit of the home, both inside and out, but found nothing out of the ordinary except a cellar flap just outside the kitchen door. Opening it, Ziplich saw that it was the entrance to a storm cellar, a tornado shelter, and was struck by the irony of Ferguson and Taylor having been discovered as murder victims, and not storm casualties, due to the arrival of that tornado the night they died. About to close the flap, Ziplich realized that the hum here seemed a little more pronounced, so instead he ventured down a few steps into the gloom. It was very late in the day by now, and the sky provided little light.

"Benny, would you get that flashlight from the glovebox of the car, please? We ought to take a look here, I think."

Moments later Benny was back. "The guys checked this out, y'know," he remarked and Ziplich grunted. The pair descended into a spacious cellar, meticulously clean and dry, with a large steel door facing them. There was a light switch on the wall which Ziplich flipped on and the area was flooded with brilliance. They approached the door. It had no lock and opened on silent hinges, revealing a well-prepared shelter. There were three double beds, two of them arranged as bunks, a table with six chairs, a buffet furnished with cutlery, drinking vessels and plates, a small but fully-equipped kitchen area with a propane stove, and several closets and cupboards containing linens and clothing. In addition to the existing overhead lights there were several oil lamps; a small propane refrigerator sat in one corner, but it was empty. Not so the kitchen cabinets, which were fully stocked with enough canned and freeze-dried food to last six people several weeks. There was also a huge water tank, with a filtration system built in. An Incinolet toilet, tucked away behind a slatted door, answered the unspoken question.

"Jeez," murmured Benny, "they were ready for World War Three."

Ziplich nodded abstractedly: he was listening again.

"Can't you hear it, Benny?"

Benny could. Down here the sound was more pulsating than it had seemed up in the main house, although still very muted. One thing was certain; it was not air conditioning. There was a condenser-operated system fitted into one wall—leading, they presumed to the outside—but it was turned off.

Ziplich suddenly realized he was still holding a glass of vodka and tonic, and he set it down on the table. The liquid in the glass quivered very slightly, as if at some vibration.

"There's something here," Ziplich declared, "that we don't know about." He prowled around the space, trying to locate the source of the noise, tapping occasionally on the walls for any hollow sound, but without success. Taking out his mobile phone, he dialed headquarters, only to find that the cellar was insulated too well to connect. Swearing quietly he climbed the steps and tried again.

Sergeant Schmitz answered. "Yeah, of course, Zee, if you say so. Listening equipment? Like, y'know, spyin' an' buggin' an' such?"

"I've got walls here, Pete, and I got to know what's behind 'em. Maybe even a stethoscope. Hell, I don't know. Contact the emergency services, maybe. They find people under rubble, I guess. Use your imagination, but be quick. I think we've found something, but we can't find it." Ziplich was immediately embarrassed by this contradiction, and cut the connection.

Ten minutes or so later they heard the sirens, and climbed out of the cellar. The emergency response vehicle pulled up, lights flashing, and the sirens droned down to nothing. Captain Wright approached at a trot and, catching sight of Ziplich, said: "This better be good, Zee."

"You bring the listening stuff, Cap?"

"Yep. Show me."

Ziplich led the way into the storm room, indicating the shaking vodka, and said: "Hear anything?"

Wright strained his ears. Then; "Yeah, a kinda humming, I guess."

"We need to know what it is and where it's coming from. Can you guys find it?"

Wright smiled sympathetically. "It's what we live for."

The response team was quick and very efficient. Armed with seismic devices that caused Ziplich to gaze in awe, within seven minutes they had isolated an area underneath the toilet, and painstakingly revealed what amounted to a concrete trapdoor. It was so well concealed and so thick that no hint was seen of its presence at all. Ultrasound had been the key. Now the question was how to open it.

Benny said: "If it's under the john, how about trying to flush?"

"It's an electric incinerator. That's why it's called Incinolet. Reduces waste to ash. It doesn't flush."

"Then why's it got a flushing handle?" Benny pushed the handle down, and the floor heaved open. Suddenly the noise was much louder, and fluorescent lights flickered on below them. Ziplich peered down into the vast chamber revealed below.

"Oh, my God!" he breathed.

Chapter 4
June, 2011

Grayson had received not so much permission as a thinly-veiled order to go to Oklahoma. The authorities in Tulsa had come to the conclusion that they really needed somebody British to try to unravel the Rachel Taylor business, and problem expatriates were Grayson's responsibility. Then there was the matter of the old Webley revolver. Where had that come from? For that matter, where was it now? Not least, the crossword books. Was there something more to them than just the hobby of a man who liked words? Ziplich and his superiors had decided they needed answers to these and many other questions, and they had asked London for on-the-spot help. The Director General himself who, together with his decrepit Basset hound, had unexpectedly visited Grayson's office, awe-inspiring eyebrows lifting significantly at the first sight of the unkempt desk, had issued the invitation. The implication was not lost on Grayson, who had readily agreed that, since he was the head (and sole member) of the Expatriates Desk, he was probably exactly the man the Americans needed for the job.

It was probable that the DG was right: he usually was. That had been one of the remarkable things about him during his early years with the company, when he'd been a humble field agent in an agency devoted to thwarting the plans of disgruntled Britons against their own country. Not quite treason, perhaps, but "unfriendly activities." For some reason, never satisfactorily explained, M.G.Conroy clearly had an instinct that led him to accurate conclusions, often in direct opposition to the wisdom of his superiors. This frequently gave rise to acerbic meetings with the higher echelons, but the fact remained that he was much more often right than they were. It was a source of constant irritation to the brass that he was smarter than they, and there were several machinations designed to bring about his downfall. Each had signally failed in its objective, and Michael George Conroy had risen inexorably to the top.Only one person had ever expressed real satisfaction at his swift progress; his recruiter, a teacher at the Grammar School that Conroy had attended.

"Michael," she was occasionally heard to say, "had a *gift*."

No one had the temerity to call him "Mike," even at school, where he had a reputation of tolerating neither overfamiliarity, cheating nor bullying. He also had the skills, learned in his tough home Tyneside neighborhood, of making sure his views were respected. Grayson liked him very much, but was not fond of the dog.

A few days were taken up with arranging tickets, currency and the inevitable bureaucratic requirements of a large, if unacknowledged, government agency. Grayson needed some sort of a cover story, so Cover instructed him that he was to be a "communications specialist." It was generally assumed that nobody would question what that meant, precisely. In the event, there was not the slightest interest displayed by the American immigration authorities once it was clear that this was not a potential terrorist.

Farewells were muted. Most of Grayson's colleagues were of the stiff-upper-lip, no emotion school, so "Bye, old chap" or "Bring us back some of that Maker's Mark whisky" were about the sum of them. LaDonna's leave-taking was the exception.

"Do take good care of yourself," she pleaded, eyes brimming with unshed tears. "I'm going to miss you dreadfully. " She hugged him with quiet desperation.

Grayson himself was a little hoarse when he said: "I'll be back before you know it. Then we'll really try to straighten out my desk." He smiled fondly at her, wishing he had the nerve to tell her what he really meant, then turned and left. He could almost feel LaDonna's gaze on his back, and it took a determined effort not to look round. He'd be back soon, and then..? He shrugged the thought away, and headed for the Underground Station, dragging a wheeled suitcase and with a briefcase slung over his shoulder.

Tube to Heathrow, British Airways to New York, American Airlines to Dallas, and then on to Tulsa. At least he'd earn some air miles. Unless the department took them.

At the airport, Grayson's security search presented no problems. He was using his own name, and the only cover was the "communications" label, which seemed to interest nobody. The flight, cramped and boring for more than eight hours, provided little excitement. The in-flight entertainment was utterly dull, and Grayson ignored it. He ate the food—*do they recycle this stuff from cardboard and foam plastic?* he wondered—merely to pass the time. Later, he managed to doze a little.

Once he had landed at Dallas, however, Grayson had an uncomfortable feeling that he was being observed. He was waiting his turn in the Visitors Passports line, when he realized that a small man, one who had sat across the aisle from him on the flight, seemed to be looking speculatively at him. The moment Grayson's eye caught his, he glanced away hurriedly. Training immediately took over. Grayson started to fidget with his carry-on bag, and managed to drop some of its contents on the floor. Clearly flustered by his own clumsiness, he bent to retrieve his plastic bag of toiletries, thus dropping his passport and landing card. Shamefaced, he gestured to the two people behind him in the line to go ahead, then slowly recovered his items. The small man, one of the two who had gone past him, would now have to go through immigration before Grayson, allowing time to assess the situation.

When Grayson had cleared immigration, the little man was nowhere to be seen, until he finally spotted him collecting his baggage from the farther end of the vast reclaim area. At about that moment, a police officer with a sniffer dog approached the baggage carousel, and the animal at once displayed a keen interest in one of the small man's suitcases. Moments later, the man was ushered away, and Grayson relaxed. It had been a long time since he'd had to worry about surveillance, his days in the field being long gone. And it was all a false alarm, anyhow. Hadn't he read somewhere recently that more than fifty per cent of sniffer dog alarms turned out to be false anyway? Grayson wondered for a moment if he were becoming paranoid. Perhaps—ah, that was it—the man had resembled his recruiter all those years ago in Oxford. His fears for his mental health were allayed by his welcome to Oklahoma.

Ziplich was at the Tulsa airport to greet Grayson. He was armed with a faxed photograph of a slender, vaguely elegant man—with the exception of an obvious 'comb-over'—and a face which could only have been, to Ziplich's mind, English. *I'll bet he's carrying an umbrella*, he thought. He wasn't: security regulations had seen to that. What he did have was a slightly bewildered look on his face when Ziplich spotted him coming through the arrivals exit amid a crowd of passengers.

"Hi, Dan, it's good to meet you at last." Warm handshakes, and a murmured word or two of appreciation from Grayson, who still looked a little perplexed. "Something wrong?"

"I was looking for the cameras."

"Security, you mean? Sure, they're all over the place. You can spot 'em pretty easily if you look up a bit."

"Well, no. Actually, I meant the film, that is to say movie, cameras."

"Don't think there's any movies being made in Tulsa right now. We sure could use the extra dollars that'd generate if a movie got to be made here. Has happened, in the past."

Grayson continued to seem nonplussed. "You mean that all these cowboys aren't extras?"

He knew it was rude, but Ziplich guffawed; he just couldn't help himself. "Dan," he finally managed to gasp, "you're in the Great Southwest." He looked about him at the sea of Stetsons and Wranglers, Noconas and big buckles. "This is how folks dress here—lots of us, anyway. Even your Ferguson" *Here we go again with my ownership of this Ferguson,* Grayson thought, "had a pretty good set of western wear. And I'm wearing the boots, myself."

Looking down, Grayson saw that it was true. Ziplich's footwear showed every sign of being ostrich skin, with pointed toe, stacked heel. Yes, a cowboy boot, all right. Grayson smiled wryly at his own ignorance.

"Never been this far in the States before, you see," he told Ziplich. "Spent more time on the continent, you know. Europe, I mean," he added, suddenly aware that he was on a different continent now.

Ziplich tried to ease his discomfiture. "Let's go get your bags, and we'll head out to my car. Then you can rest up at your hotel after your trip. I guess you're pretty bushed?"

"Not too badly, really, thank you. I would rather like a shower, though. It gets a bit sticky."

"Dan, you wait till you step outside into a Tulsa afternoon in June. Then you'll find out about sticky."

As they drove into the city from Tulsa International Airport, the two, in addition to sizing each other up, did a quick review of where their respective investigations stood. Except for the Ferguson storm cellar, there had not been much in the way of new development during the last week or so. Ziplich had decided that the Lieutenant could break that news. Phelps had established for certain that the Henry Millen suitcase had, indeed, been in Tulsa recently. Careful analysis had finally made that clear. What was more, it had to have been within a week of the incident at Newark Airport, since that was when that particular batch of materials had been delivered.

There was, however, no link to the murders of Ferguson and Taylor other than shrewd suspicion. The Webley from those killings had not yet been found, and no suspect prints had been discovered at the crime scene. Attempts to match any fingerprints found there with the Millen bag or the ceramic knife had failed.

Equally unsuccessful were the efforts to find out who Ralph Ferguson really was, or what had happened to the man whose identity he had assumed. One theory floating around was that the real Ferguson had been murdered for his money, but that his associates— if he'd had any—had traced the bogus Ferguson to exact revenge. The Irish connection, maybe? What about the Taylor woman? Had she, perhaps, been sent as bait? If so, why was she killed? Too many questions, too few answers. And there was always the specter of the FBI or Homeland Security butting in. The Tulsans wanted to avoid that: this was their case and, like Chief Phelps, they'd select their own allies, which was why Grayson was here. Both Malcolm and his superiors felt that the Federal authorities had been too compromised by "extraordinary renditions," wire tapping, and Guantanamo Bay to be objective. *"Change We Can Believe In"* might not yet have filtered far enough.

Grayson had been booked into the Downtown Doubletree hotel because of its proximity to Ziplich's office. Even the short walk from the car to the front door was a trial for the Englishman, who had already been assaulted by the mid-ninety-degrees heat, the high humidity, and the blazing sun of an Oklahoma June on his way to the car from the airport terminal. Officially speaking, it was still only springtime, the summer solstice being a few days away, and Grayson had brought his spring weight clothes: English spring, that is, a time of showers and temperatures rising—occasionally—to seventy-five or so. It had swiftly become clear what Ziplich had meant when he referred to "sticky." What also became clear was that Grayson was going to have to acquire a more suitable wardrobe, and soon.

❖   ❖   ❖

Wardrobe changes were a commonplace for the man who had been Henry Millen, Jacques Dutoit, Vincent Callio, and many others during his career. Today he had changed again. He wore a gray suit—beautifully tailored, naturally—and his shoes were obviously handmade. A dark blue shirt, with blindingly white collar and cuffs, clearly another bespoke garment, set off a Brigade of Guards tie. He sat, quite at ease, in the lounge of the Dorchester Hotel, and over his glass of lemon tea contemplated the rumpled man who faced him.

"I carried out the operation as it had been put to me by my superiors and your own Malone," he said in impeccable, accent-free Oxbridge English. All his many languages were impeccable and accent-free. "The woman got in the way and, as there were no instructions to the contrary, I disposed of her. The setting of the fire"—again he remembered that distant night when his course had been set—"would have worked perfectly, had it not been for the tornado. That was unforeseeable."

"Don't you listen to weather forecasts?" sneered the other over the rim of a glass of Tullamore Dew.

"I was, as you well know, otherwise engaged with our late friends. It did not seem appropriate to stop in the middle of proceedings to listen to the weather news."

"Maybe, but what about Tobin? O'Neill, as you knew him. You did do away with him, didn't you? That was unnecessary." The Ulster accent was more pronounced now, as the other man began to lose his temper, which was always on a short fuse.

The Chameleon sipped delicately at his tea. "I think not. He had seen me, and was certainly going to make some kind of trouble. Otherwise, why would he have followed me? Your other lout, the drunk—Malone, or whatever his real name may be—would definitely have done so. He was still drunk at that hour of the morning. Now, as you may imagine, some hung-over oaf shouting at me would scarcely have gone unobserved. I could not, would not, take such a chance. The elimination of chances is why I survive."

"The fact remains that the job didn't get properly done, and one of our most valuable operatives is dead without his having drawn the funds from Fergoil that was his purpose in the operation. I hope you and your organization are not expecting you to be paid for a botched job. Remember what both you and we stand to gain."

Youssef put his now-empty glass gently on the table between himself and the other man, then looked up. "I not only expect, I intend to be paid, one way or another." In spite of the warmth of the lounge, the rumpled man felt a sudden chill.

"But, you see," he said in what he hoped was a more reasonable tone, "we need that money to cover expenses, including your own not inconsiderable fee. Your group needs it for its own purposes, whatever they may be, no less than we do."

"Dear me, but you do say some rather silly things, don't you? I am prepared to concede that there have been some unfortunate turns to this operation, but none of them is irreversible. The money is still there for the taking. True, the originally planned taker is no longer available, but don't expect me, Mr." here he hesitated almost imperceptibly, "Smith, to forego my, let's say, emoluments." Youssef leaned forward, his face close to that of the other; a deliberate invasion of personal space."Find another accountant, find another way, but do not imagine for a moment that I shall waive my fee for 'disposal as requested.' I will not. What I am prepared to do, since you have at least some justifiable grievance, is delay payment due by up to sixty days. Note, 'up to.' After that, I shall feel free to exact payment in my own way. You already know," he continued with a bland smile, "that I am quite capable of doing so."

"I think you should, in your own turn, remember just which organization it is that hired you." Smith leaned forward too, his voice low and filled with menace. "We are not without our own resources. You would also do well to remember that one of the purposes of this arrangement was to benefit your own organization, hence your involvement. Co-operation between our two groups could be immensely useful to both, but operations which do not achieve their objectives are an indulgence we can't afford. Least of all can we afford them when they fail to deliver the very finances upon which success for all of us depends. So don't bother threatening me, it won't work."

Youssef didn't deign to respond and, with a brief sneer, the other was gone. The look in Youssef's eyes would, if anybody had noticed, have indicated a man lost in his own thoughts. In his mind, triggered by the arrogance of the lout he had so summarily dismissed, Youssef was a twelve-year-old back in Ramallah. His uncle was pointing at a rough map drawn in the dusty ground with a stick.

"They have taken our land, here." He indicated with his stick. "It was always our land, and they stole it. Now," he gestured again, "they want more of it—all of it!" He spat at the image. "But it is ours! We have a sacred duty to guard it, to protect it from these savages, to return it to its rightful heirs. You are one of those heirs, boy, and so is your little brother. You must be patient, you must be stealthy, you may have to lie and cheat and even attack some who are innocent, but you must, *you must,* rid our soil of these evil people. They are people of Satan, and they must be destroyed like the vermin they are. You boys, and others like you, will take over from the old men like me. And you will win the blessing of our God. Many will die, but they will have their reward in Paradise. Here on Earth, the banner goes forward in the hands of the young—your hands, for I am sure you will defeat the forces of Satan. So now, little one, I am sending you to a school."

"But I'm already in a school, Uncle," the boy protested.

"Yes, of course. But this is a very special school, were you will learn all the skills you need to fulfil your destiny. Your brother will follow as soon as he is old enough. Remember what happened to your mother. Do not become deflected from your course. You *will* be a beacon for our people, and you will destroy the arrogant ones who seek to steal your land and your inheritance."

Arrogance, Youssef reflected, ordering another lemon tea, was the downfall of so many.

Chapter 5
June, 2011

Lieutenant Malcolm greeted Grayson a little warily. He was by no means certain that he wanted a British operative nosing around on his turf. At the same time, the Tulsa investigation seemed to have stalled, and if this Brit could offer some insight which his own team was culturally unprepared for, then he was ready for that help. He stuck out his hand.

"Glad to know you, Mr. Grayson."

"Please, it's Dan. I'm sure Detective Ziplich has already filled you in on that."

"Well, yeah, he did, but you don't like to take things for granted, y'know? Okay, then. I'm Stan—Stan and Dan, what a team—Zee you already know, and the criminal-looking Indian guy over there," he gestured, "is Benny. He may have had another name once, but everybody except the pay clerk has long ago forgotten it."

Grayson froze. "Pay clerk," he repeated in a low voice, except that he pronounced it "clahk," "pay clerk. Oh, yes, of course. That was Tobin. An accountant, and a good one, too, I understand, despite his unfortunate connections with assorted nefarious persons. He was in America either to arrange payments or accept them. Which was it, I wonder?" He paused for a moment, then: "Oh, sorry. It's only that one of those occasional chords got struck just then. May be nothing, may be useful. Something to bear in mind, anyway."

Benny was the one who picked it up. "You mean that perhaps, if the Newark thing and the Ferguson murder are connected in some way, Tobin—wasn't he the O'Neill guy?—may have been in line to cook the Fergoil books, or something?"

"I think it bears a little thought, at least."

Malcolm glanced ostentatiously at his watch. "Gentlemen," he said, greatly to the amusement of Benny and Ziplich, who were more accustomed to *Okay, guys,* "Perhaps we should put Mr. Grayson here, Dan, that is, in the picture about our latest news? Zee?"

Ziplich cleared his throat. "Well, yeah, it's sort of a surprise, and we didn't have time to get the details to you, Dan, before you were due to leave. But, well, we, er, found something in Ferguson's house." Grayson adopted an indulgent "*so tell me*" expression.

"See, Benny and me, we were giving the place another going over, just in case, y'know? And we found, well, um..." And he explained to a stunned Grayson about the basement.

Malcolm said: "Why don't we call it good for today? Dan here is probably jet-lagged out of his skull, and we'll all be better for an early night. What's waited for nearly two weeks now isn't likely to suffer from one more night. Go on, beat it. Zee, make sure Dan doesn't get lost on the way to his hotel. Benny, quit smirking and go check out the chicks someplace.. Dan, great to meet you. See you all in the morning."

Ziplich and Grayson trudged through the steamy evening to the Doubletree, where Ziplich was about to take his leave, when Grayson said; "Zee—may I call you that?—are you married?"

"You bet. How 'bout you?"

"Not any more, unfortunately. She died. Janet, her name was." Ziplich was shocked to see the sudden naked emotion on the aristocratic face of what he had assumed was the traditional stiff-upper-lipped Englishman. "Still," Grayson resumed, "the point is, maybe your good lady wife would care to join us for dinner. I assume this splendid hostelry has a restaurant?"

"Yeah, and pretty good, too. That's real nice of you, Dan, but don't you want to get some rest?"

"To tell you the truth, I'd appreciate the company. This new development has really woken me up, and I do feel just the least bit lost here. No cowboy boots, you see."

Ziplich grinned at that. "Let's find the bar, get a drink, and I'll call Carol. I know she'll be real glad to meet you."

While Ziplich went to find a phone—he had the cellular in his pocket, but had a horror of using it in public places unless unavoidable—Grayson ordered the drinks. Carol, Zee had informed him, was fond of Chardonnay. Zee himself would go for a vodka and tonic. Grayson was pleased to notice a selection of single malts on the top shelf at the back of the bar, and selected a Talisker "with a little water and no ice." He was aware that in the States, large quantities of ice were the norm, but he felt it an affront to Mother Nature to put ice in good Scotch. Sure enough, the bartender had to be gently reminded about the ice that she had automatically put in Grayson's glass. She looked at him a little curiously, but complied with good humor.

"You wanna run a tab?" she inquired of Grayson.

"I beg your pardon?"

"A tab."

"Excuse me, I don't quite understand." It was then Grayson heard the question he would hear repeated countless times during his stay.

"Say, where're you from? I love your accent."

"London," Grayson replied, "and thank you."

"You're welcome. Oh, and the tab, well that's your bill. If you decide to have more than a single round, we add 'em all up, and the total, why, that's the tab."

"I see. Well, yes, thank you, I'd like to 'run a tab.'" Grayson felt he was going to have a lot to learn. What was that expression he'd heard? Two nations united despite the barrier of a common language, something like that. Apparently there was some truth in it. Ziplich and the drinks arrived more or less simultaneously.

"Carol says thanks, she'd love to. Be here before long; we don't live all that far away. Cheers."

They clinked glasses, sampled their drinks and chatted companionably for a few minutes, avoiding their professional subjects: it's always difficult to switch off a conversation like that when another person arrives, and neither of them wanted to "talk shop" for the rest of the evening. Carol probably wouldn't appreciate it, and they were both ready for a bit of a break, anyway. Tomorrow would be full enough of it.

Mrs. Ziplich, when she arrived, took Grayson's breath away. A remarkably beautiful African-American, with a smile that could melt icebergs, she displayed a warmth and intelligence that he found utterly captivating. Her dress was the absolute model of understatement, and Grayson took a moment to think how much she resembled LaDonna. What was even more surprising, he thought, was the fact that, following the introductions, she began asking about the progress of the case.

"Or is it cases?" she asked astutely.

"We're still not really sure, Mrs. Ziplich," Grayson began, but got no further.

"The name is Carol. 'Mrs. Ziplich' is reserved for people I don't like, people I'm trying to intimidate—at which I'm quite good, by the way—and telephone solicitors. You don't come under any of those headings, so I'm Carol."

"Carol it is, then. Well, as I said, we're not certain by any means that the cases that Zee and I are pursuing are, in fact, related. But they could be, and that's reason enough to work together. After all, if one of us discovers something that the other can use, even if not directly relevant to his own inquiries, something has been accomplished to the good."

"Of course. Well, I may have a little something that might, possibly, help out there."

Grayson was surprised, but Ziplich broke in: "Carol is a partner"—he slipped the promotion in seamlessly—"in a law firm which has had dealings with Fergoil. I got news for you about Ferguson, but first, you pick up on something, Hon?"

"I do believe so, in full compliance with the requirements of client privilege, since the client is deceased by way of a felony."

"Told you she was a lawyer," Ziplich put in.

" You see," Carol continued, unabashed, "we deal with the real estate aspects of businesses. We're not concerned with the day-to-day running of companies, the profit-and-loss accounts, that sort of thing. No, we're property attorneys. Now, Fergoil has acquired a lot of property in the course of the last thirty or so years. Nothing unusual there. What is unusual is the original purchase of Grebe and Oliver, which became Fergoil, by way of Windfall. It was a cash sale. Five hundred thousand dollars. Cash! In 1974 that was a very large sum. Not enough to buy a Sinclair or a Getty by any means, but quite enough to buy Grebe and Oliver. In case you're not familiar with this, Dan, Oklahoma was once a major oil-producing state, and Tulsa was known as 'The Oil Capital of the World.' That may have been a little grandiose, but it wasn't far off the truth. Huge fortunes were made here, and in the immediately surrounding area. Most of the big oil companies had important offices, if not headquarters here. Names like Skelly and Phillips are still to be found on streets and buildings wherever you look. 'The Golden Driller,' a statue outside the Tulsa State Fairgrounds—well, Expo Square, as it now is—emphasized that point. But it wasn't only the behemoths of the industry who flourished here, there were many small companies, too, and oilfields were all over the place. As time went by, the big fish swallowed the smaller ones, as they often do. There were holdouts, though, right up into the seventies and the oil crisis of those days. There is still a handful, and they fight strongly to defend themselves against takeovers. Grebe and Oliver was one of those." Grayson's name was called, and they added another round to 'the tab' before following a willowy young woman to their table in the dining room.

Grayson, surveying the menu, had some mental difficulty in reconciling the oxymoronic concept of "fat-free fresh sour cream," but held his peace. Selections having been made, Carol continued.

"So, Grebe and Oliver, which owned a handful of gas stations and a small oilfield—sometimes a 'wildcat' well goes to a company like that—hung on, by one means or another, until 1974. By then the Middle East and OPEC thing had started, and Grebe and Oliver, like several others, began to find that they couldn't meet their expenses. Their own field was pretty much worked out, the cost of imported crude had skyrocketed, and OPEC was cutting off much of the flow, anyway."

Ziplich sipped at his iced water. "Then along came the guy in the white hat?"

"Not quite yet. The company began to sell off some of its assets; you know, a gas station here, another one there, none of them at a price that would help raise them out of the mire. Eventually, they were down to just the really pathetic field—they didn't have their own refinery, of course, had to contract that out for more expense — and two gas stations. This is where the white hat arrives."

"Worn by Ralph Ferguson," Grayson supposed.

"Exactly. In the guise of The Windfall Company, which bought Grebe and Oliver at a bargain basement price, even taking into consideration their considerable liabilities."

Salads arrived at this point, and the conversation stalled for a short time while dressings, freshly ground black pepper and the like were distributed.

"So now we have our Ralph as the owner of what amounted to a large debt," Ziplich said,." Not a very promising start to what became a pretty successful career. 'Course, we now know he had an additional source of income."

"Well, now here's the interesting part," said Carol. And both the men stopped chewing at the inflection of her voice. "Grebe and Oliver became Windfall and, eventually, Fergoil. A large amount of capital arrived from perfectly legitimate investing sources—brokers, banks, that sort of thing—and Fergoil began to buy property. That's when our company got involved. I've been looking over all this stuff for the last several days, what with Paul's investigation and all, and I found this. The very first, indeed the only, properties Windfall purchased were the same ones which had been sold off by Grebe and Oliver. What's more, they were bought at almost nominal fees. What's more than that, they were bought from the people who had originally picked 'em up from Grebe and Oliver. I checked a bit, and none of those people is in any way connected to the oil business except for that one transaction. What's even more, they're all individuals; not a company among 'em. Just one additional thing. The corporation, Windfall, that collected all these properties and then sold out to Fergoil, was established by..."

"Ralph Ferguson," breathed Ziplich.

"Right on the button. His name was no longer associated by the time Fergoil did its first transactions, but the nominal head of the company, which had only six employees, was one William Hewitt, another man with no oil industry experience. He's dead now, has been for years, but I bet you'd find that was his only dabble in oils, unless he was an amateur painter."

"So Ferguson engineered the whole thing to get himself set up at minimum cost. Quite ingenious," Grayson said. "The question of where his original money came from remains, though, as does the question of where he came from himself. In short, who is bloody Ferguson?"

"Honey," Ziplich said, "d'you know anything about the company Ferguson set up for the flood control project?"

"Well, a little, but only to the extent of the properties he bought for the project. He set up a handful of companies, that I do know. One was for the excavation; that was Flieg and DeHollander. The other was Lowe and Greene, the pipeline providers."

Ziplich slapped his thigh delightedly. "If only he'd managed to have one called Masters, Singer Inc!"

"But he did. It was the transport company."

Both Ziplich and Grayson were convulsed. Carol was bewildered until her husband explained about the Ferguson collection of Wagner. "Oh," she said. "Well jazz is more my style."

Another break in the conversation was brought about by the serving of the main dishes. Carol had selected a shrimp platter, Zee barbecued ribs, and Grayson had ordered a steak. Not knowing the niceties between a "ribeye," a "KC strip," a "NY strip," and a "T-bone," he had opted for a filet mignon. His opinion of steaks had risen several grades with his first taste. *Why,* he wondered, *can't we cook steaks like this at home? We grow the wretched cattle, Angus and so on, and then destroy them in the kitchen. No wonder so many of my fellow countrymen subsist on egg and chips.*

"I had a thought," Ziplich put in between forkfuls. "Ferguson— let's call him that for the time being—was about seventy-six when he was murdered. Agreed, that's according to the age of the real Ferguson, which we know, but he must have been around that. Now, we're convinced that he was British. If so, he would have been drafted at the age of eighteen or so, back in the early fifties. Isn't that right, Dan?"

Grayson nodded. "Yes, assuming he was medically fit and wasn't in a protected occupation. He might have been deferred to go to university or something, but other than being a conscientious objector, those are just about all that could keep him out of doing his National Service."

"That's what I thought. Now, are your servicemen fingerprinted when they enter the military?"

Grayson looked dubious. "You know, I haven't the faintest idea, though I rather doubt it. I would doubt it even more for all those years ago. Security back in my father's day wasn't what it is now. I remember being told by a friend of his, who'd been stationed at Aldershot, that the gate was protected by a soldier carrying an ancient Lee-Enfield three-oh-three with no ammunition. Not much of a deterrent, so I imagine fingerprints weren't part of that equation. Anyway, I can certainly have inquiries made. What you're wondering is if our Ferguson," *share the ownership*, he thought, "has prints that might match up with one of our servicemen, is that it?"

"That's exactly it."

"Right-o, I'll set about it in the morning." He leaned back from the table. "That is indubitably the finest steak into which I ever sank a tooth. Thank you both so much for your company, and equally much for your research and your insights. I do believe we're getting a little bit along the way. I hate to appear ill-mannered, but I rather feel the infamous jetlag has finally caught up. Would you mind awfully if I bid you good night and seek out my chamber of repose?" Assured that they would not, he took his leave, while they remained to take coffee.

"Paul, d'you suppose he always talks like that?"

"Nah. Probably seen too many episodes of 'Inspector Morse.'"

"So what about those companies that Ferguson set up for the flood control project? Seems like a decent thing to do for the community, even if the names were a bit funny. Maybe he just had an odd sense of humor."

"Maybe. Or maybe he was being just a *teensy* bit illegal." Ziplich was remembering the basement in Maple Ridge.

"How so?"

And Ziplich told her what had been found in that basement with an I still can't believe it look on his face.

Benny and Ziplich had descended the steps which led down from the trapdoor. The humming had become quite loud, and they both could feel the quivering of the concrete beneath their feet as they reached the floor. The fluorescent lights were efficient in illuminating the entire huge space.

"He must have excavated right out under the grounds," Benny said in awe. "Just look at the size of this place." The emergency rescue team had followed them down from the basement, and stared open-mouthed.

Ziplich said sharply: "You have seen none of this, you understand? Everything that has occurred here is confined to your official report of answering a false alarm. Not one word, I repeat, *not a word* of this must leak out while our investigation is ongoing. Is that clear?" The others nodded silently. "I'm including pillow talk with wives or girl friends or whatever. We're talking serious repercussions. Got it?" They nodded again and continued to stare about them.

On one wall was a vast control panel, filled with dials and switches and knobs whose functions Ziplich could merely guess at. Pipes snaked across the floor; others spread above the men's heads. What was completely unmistakable though, to anyone from Tulsa, was the fact that they were looking at a working oil well.

Up in his room, Grayson took stock for a moment. On the infrequent occasions he had been called upon to go abroad for the firm, he had always had to make do with inexpensive lodgings and small rooms. In particular, he remembered one place in Stockholm where the shower and bedroom were one and the same, with no dividing door—or even curtain—to prevent the place from being permanently damp. Here, the bathroom alone was bigger than the entire Swedish "suite," while the bedroom seemed to him enormous. Two vast beds ("King size," he later learned, putting their British namesakes to shame) and a large television with remote control and more than sixty channels of programs which held no interest. He did pause for a moment to reflect that at home, where the topic of conversation so often seemed to be the climate, The Weather Channel might be a welcome addition to the usually dreary selection most of the TV companies seemed to provide. There was a coffee maker, too, unfortunately without real milk, a clock with a radio and built-in alarm, a telephone, even a chocolate chip cookie (he thought of it as a biscuit) on the pillow of one neatly turned-down bed. *I could,* he thought, *come to enjoy this sort of thing.*

He had also enjoyed dinner with the Zipliches, and he thought what a fortunate man Zee was to have such a delightful and intelligent wife with, he'd been pleased to notice, a sense of humor. He had always thought that, no matter how physically attractive a person might be, or how clever, it all lost its point without at least a glimmer of humor. That was one of the nice things about LaDonna, she had much more than a glimmer. Carol Ziplich reminded him greatly of LaDonna, and Grayson suddenly realized how much he missed his secretary, and how much she meant to him. *Watch it, lad,* he thought, *you'll be getting maudlin in a minute.*

His thoughts turned to the matter of the amusingly-named Ferguson companies and the remarkable oil well. Plenty to work on tomorrow, he yawned.

Unpacking his well-worn bag, Grayson put away the few clothes he had brought. He hung the suits and shirts in the spacious closet— in which, he noted, there was even an ironing board—and placed socks, underwear and so on in one of several drawers provided in the bureau which housed the television set. He stripped off his clothes and, uncharacteristically, tossed them carelessly into a corner. He'd deal with them in the morning. Anyway, he was going to have to purchase a wardrobe more suited to the Oklahoma temperatures. Into the bathroom for a quick shower and toweling, then after making use of the thoughtfully-supplied hair dryer, he cleaned his teeth, got into bed and checked the time. Almost eleven. That made it five tomorrow morning at home. No wonder he was tired—been going more than twenty-four hours. Pausing for a moment to set the clock-radio for 7 a.m., he sought a radio station that did not merely offer raucous rock, "contemporary gospel" whatever that meant, or nasal country, finally—blessedly—finding the sound of a Mozart symphony. He was sinking into oblivion when the music ceased and the announcer bade his listeners a deeply sincere farewell. A few moments of station identification, and then: "Four hours, GMT. BBC World Service.."

Drowsily, Grayson was amused at the position. Five thousand miles away from home, and the only radio station he could bear turned out to carry the Beeb news. "....the death of Michael Nolan, believed to have had connections with a splinter group of the Provisional IRA." Suddenly, Dan Grayson was wide awake. Must get hold of LaDonna in the morning and have her check that out. And Ferguson had a hidden oil well under his house, he thought before sleep finally came.

An hour or so later, LaDonna Chauduri was waking up to essentially the same news on BBC Radio Four in her small flat in Bounds Green. She'd moved there nearly ten years ago, after her parents had died in a senseless bank robbery shooting in Brixton, where they had then lived. Rajiv and Swapna Chauduri had come to England in search of what they hoped would be a life better than that of their impoverished Indian province. At first, it had seemed as if they had made a bad mistake, for they could find only poorly-paid, menial jobs. This was discouraging for a well-educated and personable couple, but gradually attitudes had changed and, by the time LaDonna was born, her father had a teaching position at the London School of Economics and her mother was a senior nurse at Guy's. They remained in the Brixton house they had moved into when they first arrived. "Don't want the neighbors thinking we're getting uppity," Rajiv had told his wife, who had agreed. They had been on the best of terms with those who lived in the area, a racial melting-pot which became more diversified with the passage of time.

LaDonna had done well at school and gained an exhibition to the University of Kent at Canterbury, whence she had graduated with a First. She had enjoyed living in Canterbury during term time, but had always returned home during the holidays and remained there after graduation. She answered an advertisement in The Guardian for a secretarial post, and found herself in an office for which security clearance was required of all and granted to few. She had been one of the few, and before long was the personal assistant to two young men named Bloom and Perkins. It wasn't until after her parents had died, and she had moved away from a home which no longer seemed welcoming, that the name Grayson had been added to her list.

LaDonna listened to most of "Today" while making tea and toast, which she ate in her tiny kitchen. Michael Nolan? There was no certainty, but when she got to the office she'd make it her business to find out if this were the same Michael Nolan who'd had a romance with Rachel Taylor. If it turned out to be so, then the long arm of coincidence was being stretched too far for credulity. If it were he, then she'd need to get in touch with Dan Grayson. Jacko Perkins was away on leave, and John Bloom had been shifted to a different department—"a sideways promotion," he had described it to her as he moved things from his desk— so this would give her something useful to do. She carefully washed her plate, knife, cup, and saucer, dried them, and put them away. No dishwasher here, not worth it for one person. She had no boy friend—there had been one, once, Harry, but he had a proclivity for illicit substances, and she would have no part of that —and few close acquaintances, but she never thought of herself as lonely. Her hopeless attraction to Grayson ruled out romance. She read a great deal, articles connected with her work, books of all sorts, and two newspapers, The Times and The Sun. "Get both ends of the spectrum," her father had advised her, and she still heeded his words. Occasionally she tried the Times crossword, but she usually became irritated by the more arcane clues.

Time to go. She picked up her handbag, checking to be sure it contained her travel card, her security pass, and a few pounds. She had a credit card if needed, but seldom used it. And so to Bounds Green Underground station.

❖　❖　❖

"It was you who killed Nolan? That was very unwise of you." The leader's eyes were hard.

"And you know that he could have led the British to us, by way of the Irish, and that would be bad news for us all."

"The British, who caused the trouble here in the first place, are now so feeble in the world arena that they have little importance to us." The leader loathed the British with the intensity reserved to those who have been defeated by an inferior. "They are," a strong emphasis here, "a spent force. There is no Churchill," now the voice held a suppressed fury, "no Margaret Thatcher, not even a John Major. Oh, yes, they've had a minor presence in Iraq and Afghanistan as lapdogs of the Americans, but Britain is a spent force. You have, it seems, forgotten the reason for your mission."

Youssef was very angry; but wise enough to control his own voice. "I have spent nearly twenty five years in the service of my country. Do not, ever, suggest otherwise." He remembered the night attacks, the killings, the misery of the survivors, all the things that had triggered his original attraction to the movement. *That terrorism,* he thought, *will never be either forgotten or forgiven.* That he had become, over the years, a killing machine himself did not for a moment reduce his evident and dangerous fury.

"Calm yourself, man. There is no suggestion that you are disloyal, merely that there may have been an error of judgment. Like that in killing that Taylor woman"

"The error of judgment is assuming that the British are a spent force."

The leader glowered. "And another is allowing your personal enmity to influence your actions."

"Nolan was a fool, and I'm sure the British are aware of his affiliation, even if they haven't yet been able to prove it. What's more, he was trying to cheat us. He's gone, and there's the end of that, but as one door closes, another may open. This one in the shape of Jimmy Malone."

"You maintain he's a hopeless drunk." As if that were a cue, the leader sipped at his bottled water.

"I said he was drunk at the airport, obviously from the previous night. I met him once, at the beginning of this operation and I also said, as a result of that meeting, that I think he drinks too much in general. But he gave me the final briefing about Ferguson, and was even interested in the possible use of the ceramic knives. What I have never said is that he is to be dismissed as of no danger. He may be a lout, but he wouldn't have held the confidence of his superiors to run the Fergoil operation if he were an idiot. It's clear that he has abilities of which we may be unaware. One other thing is obvious; they'll find a replacement for O'Neill. Remember, they still rely on us to provide them with the arms they want—the arms I now understand their money will also help us to acquire. So they'll send their replacement to Tulsa to finish the job that O'Neill didn't, and you may be sure that Malone will go there too. If nothing else, he'll be looking for revenge for O'Neill's death. In other words, he'll be looking for me. Naturally, he won't find me, I'll take good care of that, but I'll find him and his new accomplice. Then, when the money has been pulled out of Fergoil, I'll take care of two things: first, that Malone ceases to be an embarrassment, and second that the new accountant—whoever he is—sees fit to ensure that we are paid in full. I can guarantee that, after he's seen what happens to Malone, he will comply. The money, of course, will come to the organization, less my legitimate expenses."

There were some minutes of discussion among the delegates, then: "Very well. Our situation is becoming more pressing by the day. The question of the new settlements has created stresses which will be increasingly difficult to control. There are questions, too, as to survivability on the political front. Arafat's gone, Abbas is virtually a cipher and there's no telling how long or how far this Hamas versus Fatah business will continue unless we take action. Worse than all that, however, is the fact that our friends in Russia are becoming restless. They even hint that if we fail to fulfil the promised financial requirements by the specified date, they will entertain rival offers. So we haven't got a lot of time available. What we do have is virtually complete infiltration of all the necessary official bodies. It's taken since the 1967 war, largely due to insufficient funds and the stealth needed for the operation, but we are now in a position to take over as soon as we have the essential weaponry. Suicide bombers can only do us so much good, but we now control most of the fighters, although they don't know it, and a major part of the political arena—although the opposition doesn't know that either. Our source in Britain assures us that the Fergoil money is still accessible." He paused, and noted the nods of the others around the table.

He turned to Youssef. "You have one chance to put matters right. We give you a maximum of three months to do so. After that..." The sentence was left hanging. And Youssef was left wondering whether he knew who the source was in Britain who had access to information about an American oil company.

Ziplich picked up Grayson from the hotel at nine o'clock By that time, Grayson had eaten his "complimentary breakfast"—not bad, as it turned out—and spoken to LaDonna in London about the death of Michael Nolan. LaDonna had left an early message which established beyond any doubt that he was the former lover of Rachel Taylor. "It's too much to believe all this is by accident, although the difference between Nolan and Ferguson is notable as an extraordinary change in her taste" she'd said. "There's something going on that we have to, let's say, decode."

Grayson read the fax, agreed, then went with Ziplich to the nearest WalMart to buy some warm weather clothing.

WalMart was just as surprising as the hotel had been. Grayson had been well aware that the American giant had bought out the appalling ASDA chain in Britain, but he hadn't seen much improvement there. Here, the WalMart store seemed to stretch for acres and, while the selection of items—everything from fruit to tires to saucepans to computers—was enormous, the general feeling wasn't much better than ASDA. Grayson yet again regretted the loss of most of the local shops of his youth. Still, under the expert tutelage of Ziplich, he managed to acquire an adequate selection of warm weather clothing.

"'Taint fancy," Ziplich said, "but you won't"—he hesitated for a moment— "bloody well fry."

Grayson enjoyed the touch. "'Preciate it, pardner," he replied.

Newly arrayed in chinos, a chambray shirt and loafers—"It's not a reflection on your work," Zee assured him, "just the generic name for the shoes," Grayson, with Ziplich, returned to the police center.

"Oh my goodness me," said Lieutenant Stan Malcolm, "whatever happened to that Limey you brought me yesterday?"

The Ferguson home in Maple Ridge was surrounded by official vehicles and yellow tape. The discovery that there had been a hidden oil rig under the house had astounded the few authorities who had been informed about it. Grayson had asked about oil derricks and gushers, and had been quietly told of changes in the way petroleum was now extracted—small equipment, no tall derricks, no spraying "black gold." All the sub-basement had contained was a pair of large "nodding donkeys," which pumped up the oil, the control panel and a tangle of pipes to siphon the oil away.

"It's been known for decades that there's oil under Tulsa," Malcolm had said, "but ordinances have always prevented drilling within city limits. Smartass Ferguson got the franchise to install the storm sewer system, and used that as cover to drill a well and pipe it to his refinery across the river. No wonder he had the profit margins he did. Shit, the man was a devious crook—just think of how much money we found he'd taken from the real Ferguson's accounts—but you gotta give it to him for ingenuity."

Chapter 6
June, 2011

Michael Nolan had died in a second floor bed-sit in Kilburn, an unimposing room he had inhabited for several years. He was known to his landlady, Mrs. Flavell, his fellow tenants, and the regulars at The Black Lion as a pleasant, quiet man. His rent was always paid on time, he always bought his round, he was seen at the local launderette on Saturdays and at Sacred Heart on Sundays. General opinion was that he was a building worker, "on the lump," probably, but no one much minded the Inland Revenue missing a few tax pounds. "Not many visitors", Mrs. Flavell had mentioned across the fence to Mrs. Next Door, "but 'e don't seem lonely ever."

Unfortunately, he had evidently had at least one recent visitor, since his death was brought about by a knife to the throat. The blood had dried to a hard crust by the time his body was discovered, so Mrs. Flavell did not have to wash her hands before she called the police. Yes, of course she had checked to see if he was alive, and he wasn't. He was cold and stiff, and who was going to take that room now, after a murder had been committed there? Mrs. Flavell was quietly looking forward to the brief notoriety she'd get from all this, but it didn't pay to gloat, did it? After all, nobody really knew the man, and if he had been murdered, he must have had something to hide. And, of course, he was Irish, and we all knew what that could mean. When the police had gone, except for a constable at the front door, Mrs. Flavell went down to the Black Lion and had, of all things, a Guinness.

It was not the normal routine by any means: suddenly, LaDonna Chauduri was thrust into the forefront of an investigation. She was used to doing the background checks, the peering into the hidden corners of people's lives, but now, with both Perkins and Grayson away, she was abruptly—and unhappily—in the front line. What she wanted above all, at this point, was to have Grayson to fall back on, but he was out somewhere in Tulsa, and her most recent phone call had so far elicited no response from him. LaDonna assumed he was tied up with some promising lead. At least, she hoped so. Things weren't going so well at her end. Maybe she should contact John Bloom. Even though he'd been moved to the SNP/Plaid Cymru desk (now, how much threat did *they* represent?) he was slightly familiar with the Ferguson affair and might be able to offer some suggestions regarding this new Nolan complication. Better look further into that Taylor woman, too. Was there something she'd missed? She had decided that Bloom was probably her best choice—certainly better than admitting her lack of experience to the Section head—when the phone rang. It was Grayson.

"Promising lead? About the killing? Well, no, actually. I've been buying some clothes."

LaDonna was staggered. "Buying clothes? While I've been going frantic trying to cope with this Nolan business? Have you decided to take a holiday, or something?"

An outburst of this nature was most unlike his calm, efficient secretary, and Grayson was taken aback. He managed to produce a soothing reply, explaining the heat problem, the hidden oil pumps, and the fact that it was still only just after ten in the morning, while it was four o'clock—tea time—in London, and gradually LaDonna reverted to her usual quiet manner. "Oh, I'm sorry, Dan. It's just that I feel so lost without you. You know, unable to cope. No, I don't suppose you do know, because you always seem able to cope."

"If you did but know, my sweet," said Grayson. A momentary thrill coursed through LaDonna. My Sweet. Did that mean what she had always hoped for, ever since she'd known him? *Don't read too much into it, girl. He's your boss, and he's not even here. Still....* "Coping, you see, is more of a show than a fact. Learning the show's rules, that's what keeps one going, no matter the occasional cock-up. That's my system and, by and large, it works. Now, to business. What have you found out about this Nolan thing?"

LaDonna had recovered her composure and was once again the complete professional. "Found early last evening, about six o'clock, by his landlady, a Mrs. Flavell. She went into his room to put clean sheets on the bed. 'Do it regular, once a week,' the police report quotes her. She was rather surprised—her own words—to find Michael Nolan sitting in his chair by the window, a favorite place for him as he read the paper, she said, with a knife wound in his throat. She'd thought he was out at work, had no idea when he'd returned, or whether he came in alone or with his assailant. She'd not opened the door to anyone, but then she had been out to the Safeway, so there were two or three hours when she wasn't home. My guess is that some of that time was, in fact, spent in a pub. That's the impression that comes across in the official rundown, although it's not explicit. Anyway, by the time she found Nolan's body, the blood was dried, she said, and he was very obviously dead. Mrs. Flavell says she touched nothing and immediately dialed 999."

"You said blood. There's been no report that I've heard here on the World Service about the cause of death."

"That knife in the throat."

"In the throat? Still there when he was found?"

"Initial report doesn't say. You want me to find out?" LaDonna's fingers were already flickering over her computer keyboard as she cradled the telephone receiver to her left ear with a hunched shoulder.

"It could be significant. What I really wonder is if this knife was of local or foreign manufacture, specifically Iranian. That would tie in with what happened to Tobin, but I suppose it would be asking too much."

LaDonna was gazing at her screen. She was using the department's secure link to Scotland Yard, and was checking the Nolan file. "No knife," she told a disappointed Grayson. "Wait a moment, though. There was a flake of something that looked like a bit of china up against the Atlas bone; seems it was a very deep stab, according to Forensics."

Grayson grunted. "Get them to analyze that flake. It's a long shot, but if there's any sort of match to the weapon that took out

Tobin, we can definitely rule out coincidence in this and the Tobin death. And since Tobin's killer was known to have been here in Tulsa, probably to dispose of Ferguson, we can almost assume that these really are all parts of the same puzzle. And, while I think of it, I've got another little job for you." LaDonna rolled her eyes. Here she'd been dying to talk to Grayson just a few minutes ago, and now she was being swamped. Oh, well..."I'm sending you some fingerprints, Ferguson's. This is likely to be a waste of time, frankly, but we need to see if there are any matches in military records of the fifties: nineteen fifty to fifty eight, say."

"Have you got a service branch in mind? Army? Navy?"

"No idea. As I say, it's only a very long shot at best, but we've got to try it, at least. So that means the lot: Army, Navy, Air Force, Marines, everybody."

"Going to take time." LaDonna automatically glanced at her watch

."And probably for nothing, but it's got to be done. Keep you off the street corners for while."

"Thanks for that!"

"I'll get back with you tomorrow. Going to look a little further into Ferguson at this end. My colleagues here have come up with some quite interesting aspects of his business dealings, and I have a feeling we may be on to something. Off now. We'll chat in the morning. 'Bye."

"I can't tell you how much good it's done me to hear your voice. Come home safely—and soon. 'Bye."

Chapter 7
June 2011

"Mr. Smith's" sixty days hadn't been anything like up, but he had thoroughly annoyed Youssef by his insistence that payment was not due in full since the job had been, as he had put it, botched. So Youssef had followed "Mr. Smith"—a matter of great simplicity with London's crowded buses and trains—and watched for a few days. Once he had established to his satisfaction the "Smith" routine, it was quite easy to take the bus to Kilburn, wait for Mrs. Flavell to leave for her midday trip to the pub—by now he knew her habits very well—and open the front door with a piece of stiff plastic. Then he went silently up the stairs, and listened. There was the sound of music coming from what he had determined was Nolan's room. Youssef paused only to draw his new ceramic knife from its sheath on his calf, then quietly opened the conveniently unlocked door.

Nolan was sitting by the window reading The Sun newspaper. The music was emanating from a laptop which sat on what was clearly the dining table-cum-desk. Youssef crossed to the table and switched off the computer. Nolan turned and was greeted by the point of a knife an inch from his right eye.

"Good afternoon, Mr. Smith," Youssef said silkily. "It's time to settle your account." As was his habit, he made the man suffer first. This time he used only psychological means, striking terror into Nolan with the threat of what he called "prolonged discomfort." Youssef then described in minute detail what that discomfort would consist of. Then, without warning, he plunged the knife into the cowering Nolan's throat. This time he had removed the knife, wiped it carefully on the Irishman's somewhat crumpled shirt, collected Nolan's laptop from the table, shut the door, and left. No one had noticed him arrive or leave, and if anyone had, all they would have seen was a nondescript man with jeans and trainers, a British Home Stores shirt and a tool bag, all common enough sights around here. He had, of course, been wearing thin surgical gloves, but one has to look carefully to see those.

The question now was, how was he going to get his money, since O'Neill and Nolan were no longer in the equation? It had to be Riordan, or Malone as Youssef still thought of him. That meant a trip into dreary Belfast, but somebody was going to pay; he needed the money for the organization. He had another mental snapshot; five men breaking into the modest house, tearing away from his mother the baby she was nursing—his little brother—raping her and coolly shooting her in the head. He remembered their faces to this day, and the sneering threats they had made to him. Three of them were dead. The others would be, eventually. And the younger brother to whom he had become both father and mother had grown to be a source of great pride to Youssef, though contact was out of the question. Their father had died of tuberculosis while Youssef was not quite six.

Or, perhaps, there was an alternative to Belfast.

At just about that time. James Riordan, stone-cold sober as he had been ever since returning home, was talking to the committee of the PFRI. "I'm telling ye, I didn't know why he left me, except that he said he was going for a pee. That's reasonable enough, isn't it?'

"Of course it is, Jimmy," the Chairman soothed, "but y'have to understand our concerns. We've a hit that turned out to be a miss, at least in part. We've two of our best men, one of them your closest friend, dead. We have, at this moment, no way to access the Fergoil account, since the company has been pretty well on hold following the sad demise of its CEO. Agreed, nobody can control the weather, but it's unfortunate that it was so clearly not an accident, and Ferguson's girl friend is dead because nobody told that Mediterranean madman to leave her alone. A communication failure, at the very least. Look here, now. We've our whole network ready to complete the job that the IRA and the Provos sold out when Adams, McGuinness, and the rest went all respectable. We *will* free Ulster from the Brits—not to mention that snake Paisley—but we need that money. It's how we'll be able to buy the weaponry from those Wogs. Their own agenda, whatever it is—a big hit at the Jews, I suspect—may well take some attention that might otherwise be focussed on us. Why the hell else d'ye suppose we let them provide our hitman instead of doing the job ourselves?"

"I'd like to get me hands on that..."

"It doesn't matter, Jimmy. You can't undo what's already done. What you can do, and what we shall do, is adapt to the changed circumstances ."

Changed circumstances were pretty much the state of everything at that time. America and Britain had invaded Iraq years before on the flimsiest of evidence—later proven to be false—destroyed an already faltering economy, killing tens of thousands in the process, and installed a "democratic" regime in which the Iraqi public had virtually no confidence, although "free and fair" elections had been promised and, it is true, held. Fergoil's Iraqi connection, under siege since the Gulf War of the early '90s, was essentially defunct.

"At least under Saddam Hussein," Ralph Ferguson had declared in an interview following a trade conference some weeks before his death, "the locals were pushed around by their own people, and not a bunch of foreigners. Fact is," he had continued, "Bush One should have taken out Saddam during 'Desert Storm.' Oh, I know the U.N. was against it, but it would have given closure. The U.N. were also against the British and American invasion this time, and were totally ignored by Bush Two and Blair—in fact, those two misled their countrymen about the Iraqi situation."

"Don't you mean they may have been mistaken?" a journalist had asked.

"No, I mean they lied." Ferguson's patrician face was hard with anger. "For example, when Bush was talking to the media immediately after the onset of the Iraq campaign, he said that the UN had been trying to get inspections of the so-called Iraqi Weapons of Mass Destruction program. Those inspections had, in fact, been going on for six months under Hans Blix without finding any 'smoking gun,' but Bush said of Saddam Hussein, regarding the inspectors, 'He wouldn't let 'em in,' claiming that as justification for the coalition invasion. It was a blatant falsehood, and Blix refuted it. Whether or not a speech-writer laid out the actual words, the President should be held responsible for what he says, particularly when it concerns going to war. The ability or otherwise of a President like Clinton to keep his fly zipped doesn't affect the nation's or the world's security. Declaring an unjust war does. What's more, notwithstanding the absurd 'Mission Accomplished' claim on an aircraft carrier, the situation in Iraq got progressively worse. Civil war seemed almost inevitable. Nothing could be more calculated to inflame Arabic and Muslim sentiment against the west. They're convinced that it's all part of a conspiracy to support Israel against the Islamic world: maybe to lay hands on Iraqi oil, too. Perhaps there's some truth to that, I can't say. What I can say is that, as an oilman myself, I want no part of any such plot."

The interviewer had then turned more fully to the Israeli-Palestinian conflict. Ferguson said: "Of course we should all be against terror, and we've had plenty of occasion to know why. One has to ask oneself, though, what causes people—mostly young—to feel so oppressed that they will deliberately kill themselves in an attempt to inflict damage on a perceived enemy."

"You're talking of the Palestinians, or Al-Qaida?"

"Not Al-Qaida. They, for the most part, appear to be religious fanatics of the most twisted kind. It's the same mentality, seems to me, that encouraged the Spanish Inquisition, Jonestown, and the Nazi atrocities, and today the Taliban, with followers who have so little identity of their own that they get sucked into an organization, headed by psychopaths, that seems to offer them some, well, family."

"Well, not Fatah, surely?"

"I agree that Fatah is largely a toothless tiger, though still wily. It's anybody's guess what'll follow the Hamas election, even so late in the game. Some people have not forgotten that Arafat was himself an instigator of terrorist acts. What does get overlooked is that so were Ariel Sharon, Menachem Begin, and even Anwar Sadat, among so many canonized others. No. I mean that terrorism begets terrorism, and until the Israeli tanks and bulldozers stop destroying homes and even towns, until helicopter gunships and missile-firing F-16s leave the sky, and as long as poverty-stricken people are prevented from earning a living by a 'security fence'—which looks like a wall to me and is built inside their territory—and a whole population is denied the right to its own nation, we can expect the violence to continue. If George Bush wanted to make the impression he constantly sought in the world, he'd have done well to emulate a man he had always greatly admired, Reagan, by imitating his famous words into 'Israel, tear down this wall,' instead of blindly backing Israel at every turn."

"What about Hamas, then?" somebody asked.

"They're crazy," Ferguson replied bluntly. "They keep firing their pathetic little rockets into Israel with essentially no effect, other than to incense the hawks in the country. Israel is bound to react, although the actual danger at an American July Fourth firework show is greater. Still, with the ferocity of response Israel shows each time this occurs, it's clear that someone in the country actually likes killing civilians. What amazes me is that the western powers, after touting 'free and fair elections,' refused to accept the outcome of the one in Gaza because that outcome didn't please them. Instead of talking to a legally-elected government—obviously the sensible thing to do—they cut off Hamas from the outside world. It's madness. Of course the Palestinians decided to strike at an easily-identified enemy. But they haven't got the tanks, the Mirages, the personnel carriers, the standing army that Israel has. They've some essentially useless rockets, a few RPGs and Kalashnikovs, brought in through hand-dug tunnels, and rocks to throw. And Israel shreds the ghetto it created itself. Does that sound familiar?

"Well, maybe the Obama administration can do something to redress these terrible imbalances."

Ferguson shrugged dismissively. "Then they'd better do something about the illegal building of settlements on Palestinian land. Netanyahu talks about accepting the idea of two states co-existing, while demanding conditions that Hamas can't possibly accept. If he's going to demand full disarmament of Palestine, is he also going to disarm Israel? I think not. And just look at Egypt, Tunisia, Libya, and the rest. Israel must be quaking at the possible outcomes all over the area."

Then they went on to discuss the Iranian nuclear threat and the peace process in Ireland, Ferguson's opinion being that the IRA was no longer a significant factor. One member of the group that was listening remembered all that had been said, and early in the morning reported to a contact in London.

And just a few hours later, the word from Tulsa had been forwarded by Greyhound to the JUA Council.

Ziplich, Grayson, Benny, and two other officers had been pawing through the mass of mangled documents relating to Fergoil that had been collected so far, but had not really found anything new, when LaDonna's phone call came. "Every now and then," she told Grayson, "we do get something right. This time, it's fingerprints."

"You don't mean you've found Ferguson?" Grayson was, to say the least, surprised." I wasn't sure the Services had stuff like that or, if they did, they would have kept them for so long."

"Well, turns out it was really a bit of a mistake. Our boy was originally to have been sent to a nuclear weapons training school, which did require a good bit of security classification. As it happens, he wasn't posted there, but his fingerprints had been taken, as were those of anyone seconded to that particular unit. It would have involved his going to Aldermaston or some similar site, but he actually ended up in Air Traffic Control at West Malling, and then he applied for an overseas posting. Clerks in the Gloucester records office had a reputation for sending personnel to exactly the opposite of what they had asked for, so our boy found himself stuck at Malling. Later he was sent to North Weald, so his contribution to the Korean War was mostly to go home every weekend. He lived in North London, Hornsey to be precise, and both those air bases are—that is to say were, since they're both long since closed—within easy reach of his home. He was National Service, 1952 to 1954."

"So he was RAF. You call him 'our boy.' Did 'our boy' have a name, perchance?"

"Verily. Bernard Gerald Phipps."

Grayson was scribbling notes—he had already established a reputation with his hosts as a manufacturer of desk chaos. "I don't like coincidence, 'Donna, and I notice that Ralph Arthur Ferguson also has the initials 'RAF.' Accident?"

"Who knows? That's all I've got so far. I'm sending a copy of Phipps's very good but not quite exceptional service record to you, and I'm working on what happened to him after his 'demob,' but that'll probably take a bit of time."

"'Donna, you are a wondrous lady. Thank you so much. I'll be back to you before long."

"There's something else."

Grayson, about to hang up, paused. "Yes?"

"That flake in Nolan's neck. It *was* ceramic, and it does match knives known to have been made by a rather unsavory individual in Abadan. Does that tie in with the unfortunate Colum Tobin's departure from this world?"

"It could well. Any more on Rachel Taylor?"

"You didn't ask for more, but I was intending to have a go at her again."

"I repeat, you are the woman of any man's dreams. Thank you, 'Donna, thank you very much."

Grayson rang off and turned to his colleagues. "We have some progress," he reported.

❖　❖　❖

Finally, the Committee began to see things Riordan's way—the murder of Nolan, their London paymaster, had changed their views of the man they had accepted as executioner. There were still questions as to how they should deal with his organization, which was even more elusive than their own and upon which they depended for their armaments, but clearly he couldn't be allowed to pick off their operatives at will and without retribution..

"He'll be after me next," Riordan declared. "I know who it must have been—that Youssef creep—and I know what he looks like. That makes me dangerous to him, so he's bound to come looking for me. This time I'll be ready for the bastard and, by Jaysus, he'll wish he'd stayed home before I'm done with him." Riordan, however, was not familiar with the frequent changes of appearance made by the man he hated so bitterly. Just now his whole attention had been diverted from the detested British to this one person. With him out of the way, they could all concentrate again on acquiring the Fergoil money, use it to further their ambitions for a federated Ireland, and screw the people who had presented them with a homicidal maniac instead of a simple executioner. After the arms deliveries, they'd not see another penny. 'Twould be an epitaph for Colum, so it would.

"Who's our best accountant, now that Colum's gone?"

"We've already given that some thought,' replied the committee Chairman, a man who looked like Mr. Pickwick. His name was Luke Parsons, and he was a greengrocer. "'Tis our belief that that we'd better get Bernadette Riley back in."

"That girl!" snorted Riordan, horrified. "Are youse all out of your minds? We need a hard case: a harder case than Colum, God rest his soul, was. Not a woman."

"Jimmy," the Chairman snapped, "remember who's controlling this operation, remember your own place in it, and remember how far it went astray while you were running the American side. You'll do as you're instructed, and you're instructed that the person who drains the Fergoil bank account will be Bernadette, since she's the one who worked so closely with Colum. Now, if you want to argue, you're aware of what that could mean."

Riordan was, and he subsided.

"Right, then," Parsons said brightly. "That's settled. Bernadette will re-lay the groundwork for getting access to the Fergoil books, which will, it's true, take a little extra time, now that Colum's no longer able to. Still, before too long we'll no more be dependent on nail bombs and ancient AK47s, the UDA, Paisley and their like will get what's been coming to 'em. Maybe Adams, McGuinness, and their band of crawlers, too. So we'd better have another round to celebrate." Business was usually brisk at Mason's Bar when the committee met there. Riordan had a tonic water.

Assembling all the papers she'd printed out from her hours of research, LaDonna placed them carefully in the safe and was about to close and lock it, when it occurred to her that it was nearly nine o'clock. That would be three p.m. in Tulsa, and she realized that if

[]

she delayed sending them until the next day, Grayson wouldn't get them until the following morning, his time. She was tired, and her eyes ached from the nearly twelve hours she'd spent peering at the computer screen, but she felt she had better transmit the material now to avoid lost time. With a slight sigh, she took the folder out of the safe again, sat down at the secure fax machine, looked unhappily at her paper cup of cold office coffee, sipped at it resignedly, and started to transmit. Supper tonight, if any, would mean ripping open a tin of baked beans.

At his secondary base in Geneva, his preparations were, as always, meticulous. Youssef assembled eight sets of identity papers from five different countries—three European plus Canada and the United States, but none from his own—and a selection of Italian (mostly Armani) and British (mostly Anderson and Sheppard) clothing, together with a number of more proletarian items. His toiletries were French, his shoes handmade, his luggage Hermes (with some modifications not provided by the maker) and he had a new ceramic knife to tape to his calf, since the old one was missing a chip from its point. He collected currency of each of the countries from his usual source in Zurich, including several thousand US dollars. Then, using different public telephones, he booked his flights. Again as usual, he would be taking a convoluted route to his destination. On this occasion he would fly on from Zurich to Frankfurt, then to Paris, Copenhagen, Toronto, Chicago, St. Louis, Dallas, and, finally, Tulsa. Each segment was under a name separate from that used on the previous leg. The reservations were made direct with the airlines, and no two legs would be with the same carrier. That did mean, it was true, that there would be lengthy layovers on some stops. No matter: he had both time and patience. The system was very simple: he would fly from Zurich to Frankfurt. There, he would leave the arrival terminal, go to a men's room in one of the adjacent buildings, remove all baggage tags, and dispose of his ticket, change clothes, add a pair of glasses, comb his hair differently, and then check in at the next airline for a flight under a different name. This would be repeated, with variations, until arriving at Tulsa. The one exception was Copenhagen, where he would spend the night, and a hotel reservation was made accordingly. He had made a hotel booking in Tulsa, as well.

Since he had stayed at the Ambassador on his last visit, he made sure to select a hotel at some distance from it, and settled on the Renaissance. He also rented a vehicle from Avis, and in this case his habitual expensive taste was muted: he ordered an economy car. When all the arrangements had been completed, he went to bed, satisfied that his travels would not be traceable. He was certain that Malone would go to Tulsa, for the two reasons he had given the council, and he was equally sure that the accountant, whoever that turned out to be, would, after being forced to see Malone's ordeal, become highly cooperative. He'd get the money he had promised to deliver to the JUA Council, extract his own not inconsiderable expenses—all his new bookings were again first class, naturally—and the Irish could have whatever was left over. Didn't make much difference, really, whether they did or didn't; they were so pathetically incompetent he almost felt sorry for them, but he had made a promise. He always kept a promise—as long as it wasn't to his own or the JUA Council's disadvantage. At least now he wouldn't have to go to Belfast.

The Phipps post-National Service career had been traced through his National Insurance number, which his Royal Air Force records had provided. True, there had been gaps, but they were few and of short duration. Once he had been honorably discharged from the service in 1954, former Corporal Bernard Phipps had joined an office machinery company as a salesman—not a particularly successful one, it seemed. He then had a succession of other sales jobs, none of them notable for his conspicuous abilities, until, in 1965, he had been taken on as a tour guide by a Swiss-based company. Here, he seemed to find his milieu, for the company gave glowing reports of his success with his mainly American clientele. Phipps traveled almost the whole of Europe, including many of the then Iron Curtain countries, for the next several years, and apparently picked up at least a working knowledge of a number of languages. Then, quite suddenly, in 1972, he failed to report for his next assignment after heading a lengthy tour which took in most of Western Europe. And here was the interesting point: one of the passengers on that last trip had been a man named Ferguson, traveling alone, the record showed. But that was not all LaDonna had found.

Rachel Taylor, following her brief affair with Michael Nolan, had joined AllGlobeProductCo as a clerical assistant. Up to that point, she, too, had held a number of nondescript jobs. However, she clearly had a talent in this sphere, and was rapidly promoted until she reached the level of product manager and found herself sent to New York. At this point in her search, LaDonna had a bit of luck. AllGlobe's records (which the resourceful LaDonna entered clandestinely) showed that, in the mid-nineties, Rachel Taylor had reported that she had been introduced to Ralph Ferguson, and that Fergoil might prove a useful source of further diversification for the company.

All this LaDonna transmitted in detail to Grayson. Then, exhausted, she locked the papers away and went home. She fell into bed without opening the tin of beans.

For Riordan and Riley, the trip to Tulsa was a great deal simpler than that of their adversary. They drove from Belfast to Dublin, flew Aer Lingus to London and American Airlines to Tulsa, with a change of planes at Dallas. They arrived in Tulsa in the early evening. James Riordan, obviously not able to re-use his earlier persona, any more than his own name, was now Brian Hearn, and Bernadette Riley had become a very carefully selected Candace Simpson. Although on the same flights, they did not travel together, nor acknowledge each other at any point.

Bernadette had proven a great surprise to Riordan. She was petite, young—Riordan judged not more than twenty eight or so—and sounded American, with no trace of Irish accent.

"Did my business degrees at Harvard," she told him when they were first brought together. "Got a pretty good grasp of American practice, probably better than Mr. Tobin had." One of her traits was that she usually included "Mr.," "Mrs.," "Doctor," and other honorifics in her speech. "I know it seems a bit old-fashioned," she had said when Riordan remarked upon it, "but the American media's habit of simply using surnames has always irritated me, so I make it a point not to do that. Did you know that there is a booklet known as the 'AP Style Book,' or something like that, whose sole purpose seems to be to encourage journalists to write badly? I can, of course," she had continued, "turn my prejudice off if the occasion demands it but, overall, I prefer the small courtesy."

"What about the man we're going to have to kill?" Riordan asked brutally.

"He'll be the late Mr. Youssef," she responded without hesitation.

Riordan changed the subject. "And will you be able to get the money out of Fergoil, now that the principal's dead and the whole company's ground to a halt?"

"Oh, I think so. All I have to do is identify all creditors—the accountants' records will do that pretty much for me—and pay them. At least, it'll look at first like they're being paid, but a little creativity will send the money in a different direction. Few companies of any size are without considerable debts to banks and the like. By the time realization sets in, the money will have disappeared. That's what offshore banks and shell companies can do for you," she smiled cheerfully, "and we'll be long gone."

"Why should the company, no matter how moribund, show you its books? And won't a Receiver, or whatever the American name is, have been appointed?"

"Fergoil isn't bankrupt, far from it. I've been studying that for months now, remember, and the company is really quite sound, so there's no question of it being put under court control. As for why they'll show me the books," she smiled even more broadly, "that's because I'm from the IRS. Sorry, the American tax authority, that is. I'll do an audit— not particularly unusual for a large company to undergo that, and we—Colum, God rest his soul, and I—had been preparing them for this for some time, with a little professional help." Riordan wondered who might have provided that help, but kept quiet. "And then I ensure that the appropriate checks are written and transfers made. They'll just go to the wrong people—us. It's really ours anyway—and the amounts may be just slightly higher than might have been expected." She grinned disarmingly. "And then we'll leave."

Riordan shifted in his seat. "You make it sound very simple."

"Really, it is. You'll see. We won't get it all, of course, since a lot of paperwork, including bills due and accounts receivable, was scattered all over the place by that storm, never mind the smashed computers, and the accountants won't have gotten them: there'll have to be new ones issued or programmed. But we'll get most of it." Bernadette glanced at the wall clock. "Now, would you like to take me out to dinner?"

The sun blazed down, partially obscured by a haze that covered Tulsa. An ozone alert had been issued; residents were discouraged from using lawn mowers, driving when not absolutely necessary, and "topping off" their fuel tanks if they did have to drive. They were, on the other hand, encouraged to car pool in order to reduce the number of vehicles on the road or, better yet, use public transport, which was free on such days. Grayson could not see any discernible difference in the general level of traffic.

"The bus service is so pathetic," Ziplich told him, "that only those who can't afford a car use it. Half the time buses don't show up on schedule, most of the services aren't timed to coincide, so that changing from one line to another may mean a wait of an hour or more, and the whole thing shuts down in the early evening, anyway. Besides, the transit system leaves huge areas of the city unserved. Ozone alerts," he went on, "are a means of showing federal authorities that the city takes its responsibilities seriously. It has to: no one else takes them seriously."

"There's no underground, I mean subway?"

Ziplich snorted. "There's only one passenger train service of any kind in the state, and that's from Oklahoma City."

"And I thought our system was bad."

"It is," Ziplich retorted. "I've been to England, and I've endured late trains, overcrowded trains, trains unheated in winter, and overheated in summer. I've waited interminably at London bus stops, and once I missed a flight from Heathrow because the Piccadilly Line had a signal failure. The British transportation system is awful—but it's a whole lot better than ours."

The two men were walking through the steamy morning from Grayson's hotel, where Ziplich had joined him for breakfast, to the office. Grayson, bristling slightly at Ziplich's assessment of British public transport, said: "What about all these huge van things, or whatever they're called?" He gestured at the crowded street.

"SUVs," Ziplich told him. "Sport Utility Vehicles. Intended originally for people who live in the boonies—back country areas—where the roads can be marginal, at best. Now they're simply a means of trying to impress the neighbors. Eight miles to the gallon, with the price of gasoline what it is. Not as high as it was for a time, but still crazy."

"The price of your gasoline would make a European green with envy."

"Yeah, I know, yet it's where Ferguson made his fortune. Phipps, I guess I should say. And the company's still booming, even without that basement well."

They entered the blessed cool of the air-conditioned building, took the elevator to the fifth floor, and went into what had become known as "the situation room," where the stocky figure of Benny was already ensconced in a comfortable chair in front of the computer. LaDonna's fax awaited them. After that had been carefully scanned, it became clear that next on the agenda would be finding out what happened to the real Ferguson on that European tour, and whether he ever returned from it.

"Benny," Ziplich said, "I got a little project for ya."

"Also," Grayson added, "we'd better look more closely into this early contact between Taylor and Ferg...and Phipps."

Bernadette, Riordan, and Youssef had all arrived in Tulsa before those tasks were completed.

"Tell me, Zee," Grayson said that evening over a glass of refreshment in McNellie's, a pleasant version of an Irish pub (Ziplich's sense of humor at work) in the downtown area, "do American policemen really burst into places with guns stuck out two-handed in front of them, no matter what the investigation?" He'd found single malt here, too. Ziplich, not finding his favored brand, had opted for Grey Goose and tonic, with lots of ice.

Ziplich controlled his dislike of Grayson's constant needling. "Been watching too much television, pal, like I told Carol, only I suggested 'Inspector Morse.' Must have been 'Law and Order' or sump'n instead. Anyway, no. The gun is our last resort, but we're not scared to use it if necessary. Why?"

"I was thinking; it does happen occasionally, you know. We're unlikely, aren't we, to have seen the last of this Irish connection. I mean, the Taylor woman, the Nolan man in London, and Tobin at Newark. They're all, one way or another, tied up with the Ferguson murder. Then there's Riordan: we know he's implicated, but we can't prove anything. Somehow, Ferguson annoyed an Irish faction and paid the price. What's unclear is, was it the real Ferguson or the copy they were after? My guess is the copy, since the original dropped out of view nearly forty years ago. On the other hand, maybe he got lost because he'd offended them. Such people do have long memories, you know."

Ziplich signaled the bartender. "Then why would Phipps have assumed his identity? That would have been asking for trouble. No, I'm sure you're right, they were after Phipps for some reason. It seems clear that they were expecting to get into his money somehow, hence O'Neill, I mean Tobin. And since they failed there, we're probably going to have a long haul tying up all the loose ends. And the lieutenant has been told to try to keep the Feds from nosing this out—they can be pretty heavy-handed, and we're not real happy with the way they seem to trample on people's rights these days. Homeland Security and the Patriot Act have been used as cover for a great deal of dumb stuff, so we try to steer away. The new people may prove better, but we're being careful, anyway."

Grayson drank the last of his scotch and graciously accepted its replacement. "Well, you see, that's why I asked about the guns. Ferguson and Taylor were shot—and with a British weapon. The money remains secure, at least so far. But if this rogue Irish gang didn't get it the first time as we think they tried to, why should we suppose they've given up? Fergoil represents a very great deal of money. It's my belief that they'll be back with a Plan B. And, possibly, with guns."

"Or knives?" Ziplich suggested.

"Or knives," conceded Grayson, "or even both." He sipped at his drink. "You know, this stuff is frightfully good. Sure you won't try some? My round next."

"Not on your life. Scotch tastes like medicine."

"Of course it does, because it is. The very name whisky derives from the Gaelic 'Uisce Beatha' meaning 'Water of Life,' and the inventors of it ought to know. Have you ever noticed, in passing, that Americans and Irish spell it whiskey, with an 'e,' while the British and Canadians usually spell it without? No matter." Ziplich wondered, with increasing irritation, whether all Englishmen were so damn pedantic.

"Back to the point. These people are likely to return, looking for the money they didn't get last time and, most probably, revenge on whoever it was knifed Tobin. Admittedly, that was in New Jersey, but he'd intended at some point to come here, that's pretty well certain, since he was the accountant. They'll have another one available, and he'll be here sooner or later. I can almost smell it. And with him will be Riordan, looking for the one who killed his life-long friend, and with murder in his heart. We have just one advantage; we know what Riordan looks like, but he doesn't know us. Is it too much to ask that his picture be circulated to your law-enforcement officers and security guards, especially those at the airport? I wouldn't want him, or his accomplice stopped, but it would be nice to know where they go."

Ziplich, still annoyed by Grayson's didactic manner, said curtly, "Of course not. I'll get on it first thing in the morning."

Unfortunately, Riordan and Bernadette were at that very moment collecting their bags from the carousel at Tulsa International Airport.

Neither had been to Tulsa before, Riordan's intended arrival previously having been cancelled by the Fergoil building fiasco, and Bernadette having been limited to the east coast as she completed her years of study in Boston, so neither was fully prepared for the fierce heat and oppressive humidity. Stepping outside separately, for they still had not acknowledged each other, into the furnace, they were dismayed to discover there was no bus service into the town center. Riordan immediately re-entered the terminal, into the welcome cool of the air conditioning, and sought out the car rental agencies. Bernadette followed at a discreet distance. At the Budget desk, Riordan found he could rent a Chevy Cruze at a cost that would hardly have got him a push bike at home, so his misgivings about the expense were somewhat allayed. "I'll need air conditioning," he said.

The desk clerk looked at him pityingly. "All our vehicles have air, sir" he told Riordan in an Oklahoma twang that dripped with the implication "idiot," and Riordan was soon armed with paperwork which would allow him to pick up the car from the adjoining parking lot. Signaling Bernadette to wait, he went off to find his vehicle. He was pleased to discover that the Chevy had an automatic transmission, since he would be driving in an unfamiliar city on the wrong side of the road.

"All our vehicles are automatic, sir," said the attendant, with only slightly less sarcasm than the rental agent. By the time he'd tossed his bag into the boot, "trunk" they called it here, he remembered, Riordan was dripping. For a moment, after starting up the engine, he thought he'd switched on the heater instead of the air conditioning, for a blast of hot air hit him. He fumbled with the controls, but in a few moments cool, then cold, air began to blow. Something new learned; let the thing run for a few seconds before panicking. He set the seat and the mirrors to his satisfaction, put the transmission in "Drive," released the brake, and set off to collect Bernadette from the terminal.

Road signposting was adequate, and they were shortly on I-244 heading west into Tulsa proper. Bernadette noticed a sign for a La Quinta Inn on Sheridan Road. "They're not bad," she told Riordan, "and not too badly priced, either, so let's try that." Riordan was bewildered that he had to cross several streams of traffic to reach the exit ramp, which was off the fast lane, of all things.

"Must have been designed by an apprentice," he muttered as he negotiated the hair-raising maneuver, but he managed it safely, and they swung into the hotel parking lot without further drama.

As it turned out, the desk clerk assumed they were a couple and offered a good rate for a double-queen room for the three-week period they had allowed themselves. Bernadette looked dubiously at Riordan, but he had already accepted and was signing the agreement. "Look," he said as they entered the room, "I have no designs on you. We're here to do a job, and that's it. We haven't got unlimited funds, and this is the cheapest way for us to spend our stay." He looked around.

"Coffee machine, fridge, microwave. See, we can even save on meals if we buy stuff at a supermarket some of the time, and breakfast is included. Once you've done your financial magic, then we can think about bluing a little. Until then, we need to be just a bit frugal." He'd also come to the same conclusion that Grayson had some days earlier. "And we'll have to pick up some clothes we can live in without melting." Bernadette had reluctantly admitted that he was right.

"Another good thing," Riordan observed, "is they've got a pool and a fitness room. Now, I really appreciate that."

Bernadette was surprised. Riordan had a deserved reputation as a drinker, and it had never occurred to her that he might indulge in exercise. What she did not know, and neither did many others, was that having a background in the mean streets had encouraged him to take steps to ensure his safety, and he held a black belt in martial arts. Still, looking at him closely for a moment, she realized for the first time that his considerable bulk was due to muscle, not fat. Reassuring, that, to some extent, because they had no weapons, and she knew that this Youssef had. Nor had he hesitated to use them. Could she rely on Riordan to cope? She could only hope so.

She selected the bed nearer the window, so Riordan deferred to her choice. They unpacked their bags, with the exception of the document case Bernadette had brought, and took turns cleaning up in the quite adequate bathroom. Then: "Let's get something to eat," Riordan said. They went back to the front desk, Bernadette clutching her briefcase, and asked for suggestions.

"Depends what you're looking for," the clerk told them. "There's plenty of choice: burgers, Mexican, barbecue, steaks, pizza, Chinese, you name it."

"Well, I'd like something typically American," Riordan declared.

"Then Frank's Country Inn is what I'd recommend. It's not far," and he gave them directions.

Youssef was, at that same time, sleeping peacefully at the Copenhagen Radisson. He would arrive in Tulsa the following evening.

❖   ❖   ❖

LaDonna took the Tube from Bounds Green to King's Cross, and then to The Angel. She'd decided to spend this glorious spring Saturday working her way through the antique stalls and shops of Islington, although she didn't expect to buy anything. Still, you never knew: most of the items were far beyond her limited means—the vendors were much too canny to be caught out underpricing—but she had picked up the occasional print or a small piece that attracted her eye. Her little flat was a tribute both to her taste and her budgetary awareness. It was true that she had inherited quite a handsome amount from her parents, and the sale of the Brixton house had realized far more than she had anticipated, but carefulness was part of her nature and most of the money had been prudently invested. She sometimes amused herself by imagining some Scottish ancestry to account for this; *the Black Watch, perhaps?* she would think.

Today, as usual, she attracted many an appreciative look and the occasional suggestive remark, but she mentally shrugged them all off. Her light summer dress—too warm today for jeans—was of a pale yellow, which accented her dark skin and green eyes, and the small feet of her long, elegant legs were thrust into heeled sandals. A small purse hung from her shoulder on a slender strap. Her nails were impeccable. It never crossed her mind that the headquarters of All-GlobeProductCo was only a few hundred yards away on Essex Road.

Camden Passage was as crowded as she'd anticipated, but the people were mostly good-natured as they shouldered past one another. LaDonna stopped here and there without making a purchase; she felt the selection wasn't as good as usual, and the prices seemed to be getting sillier. The traffic roared a few yards away but the faint breeze seemed to be blowing the pungent smell of exhaust fumes in the opposite direction, more toward Pentonville Road. She had pretty well decided, after a couple of hours, that there was nothing she couldn't live without here. Maybe she'd pop into one of the pubs surrounding the Green for a glass of lager.

And then, there it was. As she turned to leave the shops and stalls with their sometimes elegant, sometimes tawdry contents, a locket caught her attention. It wasn't very large, but it was clear to her experienced eye that it was gold, as was the delicate chain on which it hung in an illuminated jewelry case. She pointed to it and the shop owner said: "Pretty, isn't it, love? Used to be the property of a titled lady, I understand." He took the piece out and opened it. "That's her, on this side. And the man on the other side, well, that's said to have been her lover . Look," he turned the piece over, "there's her monogram, RNT. I'll make you a good price on it, miss, since I've had it for a while now."

LaDonna's haggling was desultory: she had to buy this thing. In a matter of minutes a deal was struck, LaDonna's credit card had been charged, and the locket changed hands. "Want to wear it, miss? Look lovely on you."

"No, I'll put it in my bag for safekeeping." LaDonna went straight home before checking her purchase again. Drawing it carefully from her purse, she examined it minutely. There was no doubt. There, looking out at her with a faint smile, was a young Jimmy Riordan. On the other half of the locket was the owner of the monogram. RNT. The "titled lady" was Rachel Naomi Taylor.

LaDonna studied the two pictures. She could almost see Rachel breaking off with Riordan and selling the locket in a fit of petulance. She realized now how close Camden Passage was to the AllGlobe building. *Probably got rid of it during her lunch hour,* she thought. *Better get word to Dan.* Her eyes misted over a little as she repeated the name to herself. *I'd like us to have a locket like this. I'd never sell it. Never!*

Chapter 8
June 2011

Lieutenant Malcolm listened intently to Grayson's news. "So," he said, "there's no longer any doubt that all our suspicions are confirmed. No question, the Ferguson and Taylor murders and the deaths of Tobin and Nolan are all part of the same Irish connection. How come there's been no tie-up between Taylor and Riordan before? Even the Feds didn't make one in Newark. But you guys..."

"Our resources are no more limitless than are yours," Grayson pointed out. "We can watch some of the people all of the time, and we can watch all of the people some of the time, but we can't watch all of the people all of the time. After all," he added," we're not police states, either of our countries, despite the recent attempts of our respective governments." Malcolm, a staunch Democrat, bridled somewhat, but said nothing. " Better the occasional slip than that."

LaDonna, once she was certain of what the locket displayed, had returned to the company headquarters. Since it was a weekend, there was only a skeleton staff on duty and she had the office almost to herself. Still, she did manage to find an operative in the photography section who could produce enlarged images of both front and back of the locket, which she then sent off to Grayson, alerting him by phone that they were on the way. Grayson himself had been spending the day with Benny, who had promised to show him what a real baseball game was like. In the middle of the ninth inning at the ball park, Benny's mobile phone had sounded.

"Better finish that hot dog," he'd told Grayson. "We've got news. Pity. Looked like our guys had a chance here." They had left at once. Next morning, Benny read in The Sunday Tulsa World that the Drillers had eased to a 5-4 victory over the Springfield Cardinals in the bottom of the tenth. By then, Grayson had read LaDonna's news and looked at the pictures.

"It's a bugger," he had said to Benny. "Here we have two suspects, and we never had any idea they even knew each other. I wonder just how well they did. Pictures in a locket smack of romance, wouldn't you say?"

"Unless it's a plant."

"I somehow doubt that. Who was to know that 'Donna would go shopping in Islington? No, I think it's real enough, but I think it also shows that whatever these two had going was over. My guess is that Taylor sold the locket simply to help get Riordan out of her system. It had to have been some time ago; just look how young they both appear. Youthful indiscretion, perhaps. However, she then hooked up with another possible IRA fellow, Nolan. Once again, I have to say I don't like coincidences. Well, that's not entirely true: I do like the coincidence that led LaDonna to find this."

LaDonna had also forwarded a report from Peter Ngami, who'd been assigned to keep the occasional eye on Riordan. Jimmy Riordan had been seen to take a London flight from Dublin, but his trail ended there, as there had been no one available to intercept him at the airport.

"He's on his way here, I just know it," Grayson asserted. "Zee, did you get your chaps to circulate that photograph?"

"They're on it right now. Y'know, Dan, I got to thinking..."

"Congratulations," Benny chipped in.

"...that the security folks at the airport check people boarding—photo IDs and all the rest—but arrivals just walk through. So if this Riordan guy has come to Tulsa, he probably wouldn't have been noticed unless he was wearing a big sign saying 'suspect.'"

"Which would be open to some doubt. So what do you suggest?"

"If he has arrived here, there's no bus service so he has only three ways to get out of the airport—aside from walking, which would really make him look suspicious. He could be picked up by someone, which would mean an accomplice in Tulsa, he could take a cab or a limo, or he could rent a car. Let's get them checked out." Benny was already dialing his cellphone.

The call came in from Officer Tony Billings about an hour later. "Got your guy, I think," he told Benny, who handed the instrument to Ziplich. "Rented a car last evening from Budget. Man at the desk, who's pulling back-to-back shifts, so he was here then, says a guy who resembles the photograph rented a Cruze, red one. He remembers him for two reasons. One, he had an accent—he thought maybe South African or Australian, although he had an EU license—and the other because he said he wanted air conditioning. Whoever heard of renting a car in Oklahoma, or America, for that matter, that doesn't have air?"

"Does this memorable individual have a name?" *God, I'm starting to sound like this Limey, myself,* Ziplich thought.

"Hearn, Brian Hearn. You OK?"

"Yeah. How about a contact address and a tag number?"

"No address, no phone number. Touring vacation, the guy said. But a tag number, yes." Ziplich wrote it down

"Anybody with him?" There was a moment while Billings talked to the rental agent.

"Says as far as he knows, Hearn was alone."

"Good work, Tony. Keep your eyes open, and thanks."

"You bet."

"So. He's here, then, and he seems to be alone, so the money man must be coming separately," Ziplich told the others. "He's driving a rental red Cruze, and he's using the name Brian Hearn, but we don't know yet where he is. Still we've go the car tag number and we'll circulate it to all units. He's got to show up somewhere."

"Motels, hotels?" suggested Lieutenant Malcolm.

"You're right, lieutenant," exclaimed Ziplich. "Benny, got a little job for ya."

"Why am I not surprised?"

It was more than three hours before there was a break. Benny, together with several other officers, had been calling all hotels, suites, motels, and bed and breakfasts in the area. It was Grayson's opinion that Riordan would try to stay out of easy view, and he suggested that they start with outlying areas. He was a little put out when Benny said: "The guy at La Quinta on North Sheridan won't tell me if he's got a Brian Hearn staying there." Up to this point, all the establishments had simply said "there is no one of that name registered here," or a slight variation. But the clerk at La Quinta had said, "We're not allowed to reveal the names of guests without their permission."

"This is the police, and we need to know."

"I'm sorry, sir, but I can't tell over the phone that you're the police, and I can't tell you the names of our guests. Perhaps if one of your officers came…"

"That's where he is," Benny declared, "otherwise the desk clerk would have denied all knowledge of him. Whaddaya say we go welcome him to Tulsa?"

"Okay," Malcolm said, "Take four cars—unmarked and stealth approach—and see if we can pick this guy up. Let me know what goes down."

"You got it, lieutenant."

Ziplich and Grayson entered the La Quinta lobby. Unmarked police cars were covering the entrance and exit.

"May I help you?"

Ziplich displayed his badge. "TPD. You got a Brian Hearn checked in here? Guy who looks like this?"

The clerk looked at the picture of Riordan that Ziplich was holding. "Haven't seen him, but he might have come in while someone else was on shift. What's the name again?"

"Hearn. H-E-A-R-N. First name, Brian."

The clerk was checking his computer. "We had a Mr. and Mrs. Hearn check in last evening 'bout 8.15 That be who you want?"

"Mr. and Mrs. Hearn?" asked Ziplich incredulously.

"Yes, sir."

"You got a car tag number for them?"

He had, and it matched.

"I don't believe this," Ziplich growled, "Mr. and Mrs."

"The money man," said Grayson, "is actually a money woman. Who'd have thought it?"

Mr. and Mrs. Hearn had, unwittingly, emulated Grayson in that they, too, had gone to WalMart to buy some clothing more suited to the Oklahoma summer. They had to wade through a great deal of Stars-and-Stripes merchandise (made in China) for the Fourth of

July was approaching, when patriotism would reach its annual frenzied peak. Each picked out a selection that seemed more appropriate to near hundred-degree weather and, when they met near the checkout desks a little later, Bernadette said: "You know, we ought to buy some red-white-and-blue things. They'll be a good cover. Who's going to be suspicious of a car that's displaying an American flag?"

Riordan was about to protest, when she added quietly; "Just remember where you are."

They bought the flags and ribbons.

Frank's Country Inn had proven to be exactly the sort of Americana that Riordan had hoped for. There were strange things like "chicken-fried steak" and "fried okra," "country gravy"—a peculiar, gelatinous substance—and "catfish," not to mention a "bodacious salad bar."

"What the hell is 'bodacious?'" he asked Bernadette.

"Comes from an old newspaper cartoon featuring hillbillies," she informed him. "also included 'corn squeezins,' meaning moonshine whisky, and such phrases as 'Land o' Goshen.' Bodacious is the main one to survive."

"L'il Abner!" exclaimed Riordan, anxious not to seem totally ignorant.

"Snuffy Smith," said Bernadette, and concentrated on a peach cobbler with ice cream.

"We'd like to look in the room of Mr. and Mrs. Hearn," Ziplich told the clerk.

"I can't let you do that, sir," he was told. "That's private."

Ziplich gave a little sigh. "Listen, son. I can get a warrant to turn over this whole place. You'll be out of business for days, you'll have guests who can't reach their things, who'll miss flights, who'll be unable to see clients because their sample cases are locked away, who'll be raising hell with your company, all because you refused a police request. And who will get the blame? Now?"

The room hadn't been made up yet, and the first thing they noticed was that both beds had been slept in. So, Mr. and Mrs. Hearn were a business arrangement, not a romantic one. More careful searching revealed nothing more even remotely incriminating than a cigarette end in what was, nominally, a non-smoking room.

"Does Riordan smoke?" Ziplich asked Grayson.

"The question has never, to my knowledge, come up. May I borrow your phone for a few minutes? I can soon find out."

"Sure."

Ten minutes later Grayson, having rousted out the weekend operative, who in turn checked with the weekend Irish desk, said to Ziplich, "Riordan doesn't smoke."

"Then it's Mrs. Hearn who does."

"So it would appear."

"Your next move, then, would be to find out who, among known women associates of the nefarious" *here I go again; this Brit is infecting me* "the nefarious Mr. Riordan, is a smoker."

After picking up their new wardrobes at WalMart ('You'll be much more comfortable in those," Bernadette had told Riordan, who was aghast at the thought of wearing shorts until he looked around and saw that men who weren't in jeans were in shorts) they went back to the car and headed for the motel, which was only a mile or so away. There they'd change into their new warm weather gear.

Turning on to Sheridan from Admiral, Riordan noticed that there were cars, each with two men sitting in the front seat, parked curiously close to the entrances of La Quinta. For momentary flash, he was back in Belfast's Falls Road, so instead of turning in, he drove straight on.

"You missed your turning," Bernadette said testily, "The motel is back there."

"So are the police, I think,' he snapped. "Now shut your face and give me time to think."

"I have an idea, if you think they're on to us."

"And that is?" Riordan was driving through an area of tumbledown homes and decrepit commercial buildings.

"Change the tags."

"What the hell are you talking about, woman?"

"The tags. Oh, dammit, the number plates. If they know we're at that motel, they know we've got a car, and they'll know its registration. So we need to change the number. Once they know the one we've got, the whole damn police force will be on the lookout for it. We need another.'

"Brilliant. We'll go and buy them."

"No, we'll go and take them off a car in a secondhand dealer's. They're not likely to be open on a Sunday. That'll give us a bit of time."

She was right. There were many used car dealers in the area they had come to by dodging in and out of streets in the hope of throwing off any pursuit. Riordan looked at a street sign. E.3rd St. And there, the answer to their prayer. Four, five, maybe more, used car lots. Riordan, who had seen some junk vehicles in his time, was struck dumb at the sheer awfulness of many of these knock-kneed horrors. But, as Bernadette had pointed out, they would have license plates. Riordan pulled up.

"Have you got a nail file?"

"What for?"

"The plates will be screwed in place, and we haven't got a screwdriver. The blunt end of a nail file should do, though."

Bernadette scrabbled through her purse and came up with the desired file. "Now, don't spoil it," she exhorted Riordan, and despite their situation he had to laugh..

Riordan got out of the car and looked up and down the street. No traffic, no pedestrians. He went to the back of the Cruze and unscrewed the number plate, then went to the front. There was no number plate, or "tag," there. "*Shit*," he thought, "*that's all we needed, a car that was illegal to start with.*" Then he noticed that none of the appalling wrecks in the dealer's yard had a front number plate either. He walked to the back of them and, sure enough, there were the tags. *They only have 'em on the back*, he realized, and thought how handy for a bank robber who could back away quickly from the scene of his crime. Ah, well. He took a plate at random from one rusting wreck, replaced it with the one from the Cruze, then put his new acquisition on the rear of his Chevy. There had still been no passing traffic. Sunday morning. Everybody's at church. Had to be. Riordan had never seen a town with so many churches, or so many denominations, and he wondered briefly how they all managed to make enough income to keep going. Then he remembered his strict Catholic boyhood: guilt, that was the key. Make people feel guilty enough, and they'll try to buy their way out of damnation. Maybe he should have gone into that line of business, instead.

Just now, however, his focus had to be on three things: how to avoid being caught by the Yanks, how to get the Fergoil money, and how to kill Youssef. Bedding Bernadette wouldn't be a bad bonus, either.

"I'm sorry," said the manager, "it has happened before, but it won't happen again, I can promise you."

"We do not," Ziplich informed him with great delicacy, "give a flying fuck whether it happens again or not. It's just wasted a lot of our time." It had turned out that one of the room cleaners was inclined to have a quick smoke when no one was looking. Clearly she had done so yesterday, and a faint trace of her lipstick on the cigarette end found in the Hearn room waste basket had proven the butt to be the reddest of herrings.

Youssef (now Mr. Alfred Combs, from Peoria, Illinois) arrived late on Sunday afternoon. He collected his rental Focus, and took I-244, then highway 169, to the Renaissance Hotel, where he was expected. He was conducted to an excellent room, and later enjoyed an equally excellent dinner.

Bernadette and Riordan, the Stars and Stripes proudly floating from its perch on a rear window of the Cruze, found a seedy motel on 11th Street. They still had their travel papers with them, and Bernadette never moved without her document case. The WalMart clothing selection would do for the time being. They phoned an order for pizza to be delivered from Papa John's.

After some hours, it looked to Ziplich and Grayson as if Riordan and his companion had either decided to take the day off, had gone to check out the Fergoil office, now temporarily housed in a "business park" near 101ˢᵗ and Yale, or become suspicious and gone into hiding. One of the police cars was dispatched to keep an eye on the office, an APB had been issued for the Cruze, and the clerk who booked the Hearns into the motel had been summoned. In addition, Ziplich had initiated a search into the credit card Mr. Hearn had used when he registered. The room had been systematically taken apart, as had the luggage, but all that came to light was the fact that most of the couple's personal effects were of British origin.

"Of course!" said Grayson as it dawned on him. "They did what I did—went to get some clothes they wouldn't stifle in."

"Then why haven't they come back here to change?"

"Couldn't they have done that in the shop? Surely there are fitting rooms?"

"It'd be unusual, but not impossible, I guess."

"Then we'd better check the stores, get an idea of what they may be wearing."

"That's a hell of a tall order, Dan," Ziplich said with some irritation. "Do you have any idea how many stores there are?"

"Can't be that many open on a Sunday, surely."

"Most of 'em. Maybe it's different in England, but here pretty well everything's open. There's dozens of 'em—Kmart, Sears, Kohl's, and a whole bunch more, and the majority with a number of branches. We just haven't got the manpower to check them all out."

Grayson was disappointed. It had seemed like a promising idea.

Last night's desk clerk was ushered in and shown Riordan's picture.

"Yeah, sure. Came in eight, eight-thirty last night."

"Man have an accent?" Ziplich asked him.

"Yeah, kinda funny one. Sort of Scotch-sounding, I thought."

"What about the woman?"

"Don't remember her saying anything. If she did, it didn't strike me."

"Okay, thanks. Give a statement to the officer in the lobby, and then you're free to go. Oh, one more thing. Did they give any indication of where they were going?'

"Well, the guy asked me about someplace to eat, and I suggested Frank's Country Inn."

"Did they go there?"

"Can't say, but I gave 'em directions how to get there."

"Thanks again. If you think of anything else, let me know." Ziplich gave him one of his cards, and the man left.

"Benny."

"Don't tell me, let me guess. Will I go down to Frank's, show the picture, and ask the questions."

"You got it."

"See you guys later," and Benny departed, too.

"Now," Ziplich said to Grayson, "we wait awhile."

❖　❖　❖

On Monday morning, after a leisurely breakfast, Mr. Alfred Combs, immaculately attired in a Zegna lightweight suit and carrying a briefcase, strolled out to his Ford Focus and went to look at Fergoil's new premises. He had no intention of trying to enter, but he wanted the inspect the lie of the land.. There were liable to be police guarding the place, given the recent circumstances, but what interested Youssef more was what sort of approach might tempt Malone, should he accompany his financial expert. It was a pity he didn't know what the new man looked like, and he rather hoped that he might catch a glimpse of someone with Malone at some stage. He didn't rely on it, but it would be useful to be able to identify his other target. Youssef had an almost photographic memory, as many who had tried to outwit him had discovered to their cost, and he would not forget the face of any associate of Malone's.

He selected what seemed to him the simplest route. 169 to I-44, I-44 to Yale, then turn south. He had already made it his business to find out the address of Fergoil's new headquarters, and the map of Tulsa was well established in his mind from his previous visit here.

Sure enough, there were police cars. They weren't marked, but too many radio antennae gave them away. The building itself wasn't remarkable, a concrete block with dark-tinted windows. *Was there a rear entrance?* He started slowly to circle the place, but the parking lot didn't go all the way round, so he had to turn; still, he had already noticed a side door. *Good.* He drove round to the other side and, a bit of luck, another exit. He turned again, and noticed a man in one of the police vehicles eyeing him. Attack being the best defense, he drove over to the car, rolled down his window, and adopted an inquiring expression. The police car window rolled down, too. "Say, can you tell me where the Spirit Bank is?" he asked in his well-honed Midwest accent.

The plain clothes officer regarded him for a moment, then replied: "I guess the nearest is on Harvard, just north of 51st. Don't know the exact address, but it's easy enough to see. Big white building with a curved front. Got a feeling there may be a newer one a bit closer, but I'm not certain about that."

"Okay. The one you told me's good, 'cause I gotta go up that way, anyhow. Thanks a lot.'

"Sure."

Mr. Combs, senior sales representative for a noted insurance company, drove away.

❖ ❖ ❖

Malcolm, Ziplich, Benny and Grayson sat around a table, reviewing yesterday's results. The credit card Riordan had used at both car agency and motel was false, or to be more accurate, was an instance of "identity theft." Somehow, and this was the subject of yet another investigation, the credit card information of one Francisco Muniz, of Redding, California, had been purloined and transferred to a card bearing the name of Brian Hearn. Mr. Muniz, a retired social worker, had no idea how his information had been obtained, but he was (to put it mildly) outraged. The card company had already agreed that his account and credit rating would not be adversely affected.

Benny had found that the cashier at Frank's recognized the picture of Riordan, but could remember nothing of his accent. The Country Inn was a buffet, where customers made their selection from a vast array down the middle of the restaurant and really said nothing much to the staff except to order beverages such as coffee or iced tea. They paid at the cash desk as they left, and "thanks" or "have a nice day" were about the limit of the conversation. The cashier had recognized Riordan's picture, and remembered the woman with him.

"Pretty big guy, he was," she informed Benny, "y'know, not fat, but big."

"What about the lady?"

"Well, that's kinda funny."

"How, funny?"

"She was, like, small. I remember thinkin' to myself," she giggled, 'I wonder how they 'do it?' Y'know? Ain't that naughty?"

"Deeply sinful," Benny had agreed, with a broad wink, and she giggled again.

"Okay," Benny persisted, "she was small. What else did she look like, can you recall? Hair color, eyes, anything?"

"Well, let's see. Dark hair, kinda short. Not like Liza Minelli's, but, like, what'd they use to call it? Gamine. That's it." She was pleased with her grasp of phraseology. "Don't remember her eyes, though. Sorry."

"You done good, Honey," Benny had assured her, and left after leaving the usual card and "if you can think of anything else…"

Mr. and Mrs. Hearn had not reappeared at La Quinta, certainly a tacit admission that they had something to hide, even if the spurious credit card hadn't been enough on that score.

There was no news about the missing rented Cruze.

What there was, however, was a report from one of the units keeping an eye on the current Fergoil office. A car had come into the parking lot there, driven round to both sides of the building, and then started to leave. Before departing, it had stopped by one of the unmarked squad cars of the watchers, and the driver had asked directions to Spirit Bank. The description of the driver bore no resemblance to that of either Mr. or Mrs. Hearn, but Officer Kohler had noted the car tag number, just in case. Malcolm had it traced.

"Avis," he told Ziplich. "Some guy named Combs. Said he's staying at the Renaissance. Better get someone there. And find out if anyone has gone to Spirit Bank on Harvard that can't be accounted for."

Benny was on his feet.

"You can never say I don't know my duty," he gave as his parting shot.

There had been one more development. The two other members of the team that had been trying to put the scattered Fergoil documents into some sort of order, Officers Ryan and Kachel, had found a reference to a hitherto unknown property in Missouri. Together with the papers which were gradually being collected from over literally hundreds of square miles—and they were still coming in, even after all this time—the pair were collating material from the various Fergoil fuel station properties in the hope that they might build up a coherent picture of the company's situation prior to the night of the tornado. A telephone call by Ryan to Ferguson's former secretary, Jenna Grant, who was overseeing the establishment of the temporary Fergoil offices, garnered confirmation.

"Yes, he had what he called a cabin on Lake of the Ozarks. I went there quite a few times for company weekends and, if that's a cabin, I live in a dog kennel. It's all a question of what you're used to, I suppose."

"Company weekends?" Ryan asked.

"His way—one of his ways—of thanking staff for a job well done. He did all kinds of things like that. A weekend at Six Flags for staff members with children, a Caribbean cruise for the top producers, Christmas parties, Fourth of July picnics, that sort of thing. He was very generous."

"With company funds, I suppose."

"Yes, of course. But using funds like that meant that he would get less. If he'd been a greedy man, like a Madoff, he'd never have spent the money he could have kept for himself."

"What about the stockholders? Wouldn't they have been annoyed to see some of their dividends used up that way?"

"Stockholders? There are no stockholders. Haven't you realized that yet? Even all the early investors have been bought out. Mr. Ferguson owned the company outright."

The benefits of a covert oil well, Ryan said to himself. He paused a moment at this news, then: "Can you tell me, Ms. Grant, where the Lake of the Ozarks property is? Have you got an address?"

"Yes. Give me a moment while I look it up." There was the sound of tapping computer keys over the telephone line, then she said: "Camdenton, Missouri. It's a lake road address. I believe the roads all have names now, to help with emergency services finding their way to some of the more remote properties, but I haven't got that, just the old lake road number."

"That will do very well, thank you, Ms. Grant, " Ryan assured her.

❖　❖　❖

The Renaissance Hotel had no difficulty in finding Mr. Combs's reservation. "Sure, officer. Booked direct about a week ago, with the usual credit card confirmation."

"You got the card details?" Benny wanted to know.

"Be in here," said the desk clerk, tapping at her computer. She was quite pretty, and Benny wondered if she was a free agent. He looked at her left hand. No ring. H'm.

"Here you go,' she said, and handed him a printout . Benny took it and ran an eye over the information, noticing the fact that a Visa had been used. He took out his cellphone and dialed the office.

"Leona, I need you to check out this Visa card number for me," and he gave her the details. "Gimme a call back ASAP, okay?"

"Benny, you know that for you I'd go to the ends of the earth, mortgage my soul, ride through the desert on a horse with no name..."

"Yeah, I know all that, babe. Just find the stuff, will ya?" Leona, a very well-upholstered lady, had set her sights on Benny a couple of years ago, seemingly never to be deflected, and Benny lived in constant fear that one day he would simply capitulate. Not today, though; there was too much still to be done.

He turned back to the desk clerk. "You do understand, don't you, that this is entirely confidential? Your guest is probably just who he says he is, but we have to check every lead in an important investigation." She was wide-eyed. "One of these days I'll probably be able to explain to you what it's all about."

"Oh, I do hope so."

Hope, thought Benny, springs eternal, and he had some hopes of his own where she was concerned.

There was no news of the Hearns, the Cruze, anything, until the call from Ryan.

"Ferguson had this place in Missouri, on the Lake of the Ozarks," he told Lieutenant Malcolm. "Jenna Grant—that's his secretary—says it's a big lakeside house in the resort area just outside Camdenton. Called it a cabin apparently, but Grant says it's the size of a castle, with several acres of land. A few small log cottages, too. He used to give deserving employees vacations there. Seems to me it wouldn't be a bad idea to take a look at it."

"Thanks, Jerry," Malcolm said. "We'll do that, if the Missouri authorities don't put up obstacles." Privately, he thought *the hell with States' rights.* Benny had called in to say that Alfred Combs appeared to be, as he put it, legit. Leona had traced the Visa, finding it had been issued to Alfred Combs.

" Works for Mutual of Omaha, and they confirm that, so we can cross him off our list." *Pity,* Malcolm thought.

The actual Alfred Combs, who had, unfortunately for him, run into Youssef while on vacation in Switzerland about two weeks earlier, was no longer taking an interest in matters. However, he had been kind enough, during that meeting, to ring his company and tell them that he had met a hot prospect from Tulsa, to which city he would immediately travel after his break. He'd get back to them after that. Mr. Combs had then gone for a prolonged, and unexpected, swim in Lake Geneva.

Both Riordan and Bernadette had, to their own surprise, slept well. The pizza from Papa John's—which had been ordered at random from the phone book—had turned out to be really rather good, and it had included a big bottle of cola. Bernadette had done the actual ordering, since she had no foreign accent, and they had paid for it in cash. Riordan had cut up the credit card he'd used to rent the car and the room at La Quinta, and flushed the pieces down the toilet. That didn't matter too much: he had two more.

The problem had been that this, shall we say "inexpensive", motel room had only one bed, albeit a queen-size, and no sofa. It was a question, then, of whether Riordan slept on the not-very-sanitary floor, Bernadette slept on the floor, or they tried to make the best of it together in the bed. Riordan was relieved when Bernadette actually suggested that they share the bed. Apparently she had decided that the tension of the last several hours had made Riordan no threat. If that's what she thought, she was right. Under more relaxed circumstances, she might have had to fear for her virtue.

They went for breakfast at Tally's, another inexpensive establishment down the road, to which the somnolent desk clerk directed them. Again, they were surprised by the quality of the admittedly simple food they were served. Riordan dug into a vast array of eggs and bacon, sausage, hash browns, grits ("What's them?" he'd had to ask Bernadette) and Texas toast, which latter elicited a similar inquiry. Bernadette's choice was rather more modest. Then they returned to the motel room to plan out their strategy.

"I've got to get into the Fergoil office," she impressed on Riordan.

"Sure, and I know that full well, girl."

"Don't call me 'girl,'" she snapped. "I'm a woman doing a job you're too thick to do, so watch your mouth.'

Riordan recoiled. This was something he wasn't used to, a woman not deferring to him, and he didn't much care for it. He remembered his dismay when the committee had told him the accountant would be this woman. Then he also remembered the reaction his complaint had aroused, and he decided to swallow his pride. After all, he told himself, the main thing is to get the job done. And so he assuaged his manly honor.

"Look," he said, "we don't need to fight. We both have the same objective and, what's more, we're both in the same jeopardy. Let's just find a way to get you into that office."

"A frontal assault."

"What?"

"We—I—just walk in. I've got all my IRS credentials," she flourished her document case. "I just walk in and demand to see their books. They haven't got that many, because they've mostly been scattered to the four winds, but enough, and anyway they've been conditioned to expect someone. And they'll have some check books and certainly a number of computers. Those're what I want."

"Easy, then. I'll drive you over there, and you walk in."

"Wrong. *I'll* drive me over there, and *I* walk in." Riordan was about to protest, when she went on: "Don't you understand yet? They've got you nailed. They know what you look like, you've got a record that stretches from here to Rangoon and back. If you go anywhere near that place, which will have cops hanging from every rafter, we're finished. The only thing they've got, so far as we know, on me is a description from the guy at the motel, and descriptions are notoriously inaccurate. So you stay here and watch television, grow a beard, trim your toenails; whatever. But you don't come with me to Fergoil. Give me the keys." Chastened, Riordan did so. "See you later." She picked up her document case and was gone, leaving Riordan to watch the soaps.

Finding the Fergoil office should have been easy enough, given the grid system that Tulsa, like so many American communities, had adopted and Bernadette set off confidently. She was driving south on Yale, nearing her target, when she noticed flashing lights in her rear-view mirror. Red-and-blue flashing lights, immediately behind her. Her pulse rose and her heart sank. She'd been busted. Had they acquired a picture of her from the airport surveillance cameras? She hadn't thought about those until this moment. She had to stop. You don't start a high-speed chase with armed American police unless you're suicidal, which Bernadette emphatically was not. She pulled to the side of the road, stopped, rolled down the window, and waited.

The day had been almost entirely spent trying to find the connection between Rachel Taylor and Jimmy Riordan, and LaDonna had come up with precisely nothing. She had found liaisons between Riordan and at least three women, none of whom gave any cause for concern. Just "a bit of the other" from time to time was her assessment. Very much the same held for Taylor. Her romance with Nolan was known, although there had been no evidence that she had any involvement with the Provo splinter group he had espoused. It hadn't even been completely certain that he really was part of the group until he had been murdered. An odd thing, that. Nolan had been stabbed, probably by the same man who had stabbed Tobin in Newark Airport.Killing a man in a public lavatory is rather different from doing it in the victim's home. In the former case, you get out as quickly as possible. In the second, you might stop to search the place. There was no evidence that had happened in Nolan's flat, and LaDonna wondered why. The authorities had taken the place apart and found all manner of incriminating evidence against Nolan—too late to use that now—and several other operatives, who were duly rounded up. There were indications of a widespread plot to renew the terrorist attacks in Northern Ireland, unfortunately lacking several crucial details as to who and how. And money. A very great deal of money, more than fifty thousand pounds, in several currencies. Mrs. Flavell had been distressed that most of it had been hidden under the floor of the bathroom that the two top floor residents shared.

"It wasn't even in 'is own room," she complained over the fence to Mrs. Next Door. "I mean, I could of gorn in there and just pulled up the floorboards any time. 'E wasn't to know, was 'e?"

"'Ow much floorboard pullin' you done recent, Madge?" Mrs. Next Door asked, but was not favored with a reply.

The simplest answer was that the killer was probably uninterested in anything but disposing of Michael Nolan, and the two obvious motives here were a) to shut him up or b) revenge. Now, which was it, LaDonna mused. Her hunch was on b),otherwise she would have expected at least a cursory search to remove any form of incriminatory evidence, and that apparently had not happened. Revenge then, but for what? An internecine dispute between two rival groups? Prods v. Papists? A wrong, real or imaginary, from some unconnected source? No, of course not. The piece of ceramic knife blade, which pretty well matched that in the chest of the late lamented Colum Tobin, had to be the key. It didn't get her any closer to the Riordan/ Taylor business. Unless—it flashed upon her—Riordan had used the Tobin death as a cover for his own vendetta against Nolan who had, apparently, taken his girl friend away. If the locket had any credibility, that was. Certainly Riordan hadn't killed Nolan himself, for he was known to have been in Belfast at the time.

The trip from Tulsa, quickly approved by the Missouri authorities, was accomplished without drama. Overall, the Interstate road system seemed to Grayson to be rather well designed, despite the frequent road works. "But I do believe," he remarked to his companions, "that Britain scores higher on the cones per linear mile than America seems to." *And,* he thought, *we have those uncounted cameras spying on us all the time in the name of safety. Big Brother is alive and well in the UK.* On the other hand, the density of American truck traffic—and the often illegal speeds at which it traveled—struck him forcibly.

"Lack of railroads," Benny informed him. "The arrival of the Interstates, combined with the huge increase in available air travel decimated the railroads. There's still some passenger trains in a few areas of the country, but not many, and commercial traffic has dropped right off. A lot of railroads have been torn up, so there's not much chance things'll get better. 'S a pity. A place this size could sure use TGVs to real benefit. Not likely, though."

"For the Land of Opportunity, that seems like a bad opportunity to have missed," Grayson said. Ziplich seethed inwardly: this damn Limey was too smug by far.

The rolling hills of northeastern Oklahoma gradually gave way to the foothills of the Ozarks. Grayson noticed a sign which read "Leaving the Cherokee Nation," and remarked upon it. Benny, who was driving, murmured something about his home territory and kept the "Police-package" Charger's speed set on the cruise control at eight miles per hour over the limit. "Most folks can usually get away with that," he confided." Any more and the troopers begin to take an interest. What sometimes catches a driver out is that the limits often change from state to state," he went on. "F'rinstance, it's seventy-five in Oklahoma, but seventy here in Missouri." He pronounced it Mizzourah. "Okay, you'll most likely get away with your eighty-two or so in Oklahoma, that's only seven over the limit, but in Missouri it's twelve over—too big a margin for comfort. Radar's pretty accurate these days and there's lidar, too. Even have spotter planes sometimes. Fines can add quite a lot to the state coffers. Some small towns have even been known to earn thirty percent or thereabouts of their income from speeding fines. A few courts have cracked down on that practice, but don't imagine it doesn't still happen."

They had barely passed Joplin, shattered by the recent tornado but not visible from the highway, when Ziplich's cell phone chirped. "Yeah?" He listened intently for a few moments, then: "Okay, have her fax it to the Ferguson place in Missouri. You got the number, don't you? Fixed it, too? Good. We'll be there in about a couple hours, I guess, and the local guys should already be there. Later." He switched off and turned to Grayson.

"Your secretary, what's her name, LaDonna, has come up with something she believes is big. Gonna fax it to the Ferguson number at his lake place."

"But that's not a secure line, surely?"

"It is since we found out we were gonna be there."

"You really are rather forward-thinking, Zee."

"Easy on the compliments," Benny put in, "he may not be able to get his head out of the car door."

They turned off I-44 at Springfield and drove the remaining distance on Highway 65 to Buffalo and then over mostly winding country roads to Camdenton. Agent Ryan had obtained detailed directions to the Ferguson property from Jenna Grant. "It's not on any GPS," she had told him, and he had passed the information on to Ziplich who, in turn, now navigated Benny along a couple of smaller roads. They were called "lake roads" here, and numbered as well as named. Grayson was fascinated by the variety of homes he saw, everything from decrepit trailers surrounded by rubbish to large and elaborate mansions set in groomed gardens. They turned onto a dirt road, which started to descend. Grayson had been told that Lake of the Ozarks had been formed by damming a handful of rivers, both large and small, and flooding their valleys. The land here was poor for agriculture, but there was some cattle-grazing locally. The big industry was tourism—though the recession had hit that hard—brought about by the formation of the lake whose origin was clear when you looked at a map. In plan, Lake of the Ozarks resembled an elongated centipede with stomach cramps. There were also the occasional meth labs. Grayson, wondering if the white lightning stills of legend were around these days, got his first glimpse of the water as the car negotiated a sharp turn and the ripples glittered in the sunlight through the trees which covered the hillside.

"How deep's the water here?" he asked Ziplich.

It was Benny who answered. "Better'n a hundred feet at its deepest point," he said, "and more'n six hundred above sea level." Grayson began to understand why the Ozarks were called mountains rather than hills. Six hundred feet added to the distance they had descended on this track added up to some pretty impressive height.

"Used to be Indian country," Benny observed, with some pride. "Still find bunches of axe and arrowheads if you take the time to look."

"Snow caps on the hills in winter?"

"Snow everywhere." Benny replied. "Even ice on the water. If you want to get out of this place in mid winter, you sure better have serious four wheel drive." He swung the wheel upon seeing a sign which read "Peacehaven," and started down an asphalt driveway. Ferguson had evidently not wanted his property coated with the dust which plumed from the tires of vehicles on the dirt road that had brought them to the edge of his land. The drive wound down the hillside, then began to level off. One more turn and there was "Peacehaven" at the edge of the water, a vast, rambling wood-and-stone building with a green roof and manicured lawns.

"It ain't much," Benny remarked as he took it in, "but I guess you could learn to live with it."

A cooling breeze from the lake mitigated the sultry heat as they got out of the car. The Camdenton Police and a County Sheriff were there to greet them, and introduced themselves as Sergeant Balfour and Deputy Krauss—"Bill an' Tony"—and the three from Tulsa returned the compliment.

"We bin lookin' around a bit," Balfour announced, as they went inside, "an' we found sump'n we kinda feel y'all might find interestin'." And in the lobby—you couldn't call anything this size an entrance hall—he gestured toward a pile of notebooks on a table.

Krauss said: "Ferguson's diaries, looks like."

"Where'd you find 'em?"

"Bill was checkin' the library and the living room real careful, an' he noticed they didn't match up size-wise with the dimensions of the house floor plan. So he guessed a hidey-hole, an' he was right. In a wall behind a bookcase."

Chapter 9
June, 2011

Before they could examine the diary—or diaries, for there were several volumes of various shapes and sizes—there was LaDonna's fax to be read.

"I think I have the basis of what has happened re the Ferguson affair, and the reason for it. What I am uncertain about is the identity of the person or persons who carried out the operation. Ferguson was murdered for his money.

"He was killed by someone who failed to ensure that the money could be accessed.

"His killer also killed Colum Tobin and Michael Nolan. Tobin was killed to shut his mouth. Nolan was killed for revenge. Nolan had large amounts of money hidden in and around his bed-sitter in London. He was a paymaster for his organization.

"Since the money remained, it is clear from documents recovered that the assassin had not been paid for his work in eliminating Ferguson, probably because the arson failed to function properly. Non-payment can be sufficient motive for a killing in these circles.

"Fergoil's assets remain inaccessible to those who intended to obtain them. Only the renegade Irish group has been implicated in that. But why did they target Ferguson particularly? Because it was their money originally.

"The real Ferguson disappeared at almost the same time as the, now wealthy, bogus one appeared. That his new riches were illegally obtained seems obvious. It also seems clear that it was obtained from an organization which was itself illegal, and which, having finally traced him in his new identity, was determined to seek both redress and vengeance. Rachel Taylor, who had liaisons with both Nolan and Riordan was dispatched to discover the inner workings of Fergoil, pass that information on, and Colum Tobin would arrange the transfer of funds. Her murder was probably a case of being in the wrong place at the wrong time.

"There has been no physical connection established between the Irish group and the death of Ferguson. The knives used on Tobin and Nolan were Iranian. There have, in the past, been known contacts between extremist Irish and Middle Eastern groups. Thus, an assassin was hired to do the job, his payment to go to his own cell, probably together with a proportion of the Fergoil money. Fergoil's financial assets remaining intact, another attempt to siphon them off is certain to be made. What form this attempt will take can only be surmised, but any unexpected caller at Fergoil should be regarded with suspicion.

"Riordan has left Belfast, and we have to assume that he is in Tulsa with the new financial expert. Where these Irish extremists are, death also seems nearby. I strongly suggest a close watch for any untoward activity in the vicinity of the Fergoil premises. I think the assassin will be there to complete his work."

Grayson put the fax down. "So, the bloody Irish splinter group hires its assassin from somewhere among the many factions of the troubled Middle East—I'm sure LaDonna has that right. Someone else does the dirty work, they collect the cash. I smell double-cross here on both sides. Taylor, sent here to sniff out the best way to get at the Fergoil money, sets herself up as Ferguson's doxy in order to do so and then gets murdered with him. Another double-cross, this time on her part?"

"She probably just got in the way, as the fax suggests" Ziplich replied. "Remember, Ferguson was tortured, had his legs shot up. Maybe that upset her. Weak stomach, perhaps, or she may actually have come to like Ferguson. Or," he added slowly, "Nolan or Riordan wanted her taught a lesson for dumping them."

"Have we still got the watch on the Fergoil offices, Zee?"

"Yeah, but it's kinda low-key. We don't have personnel available for a major, long-term surveillance."

"We need to get someone into the Fergoil offices. Inside, not out. As LaDonna says, any visitor must be regarded as suspicious. Can we ring the office now? I mean, we're sure that Riordan will show up with his financial expert somewhere, even though they've gone to ground. It's obvious that they know we're on to them, but they've still got to get into Fergoil's bank information, now that their original source is dead. It's just a pity that we don't know what the woman with Riordan looks like. You did the best you could at Frank's, Benny, but it's pretty vague, and the airport security cameras were no help at all."

Ziplich said: "I'll call the lieutenant and ask if he can get someone over there ASAP. You're right, Dan, we do need somebody inside. Should've thought of it before." He took out his cellphone just as it trilled. "Ziplich. Yeah, lieutenant, I was just gonna call you. You have? Hey, that's great. Sure, I'll pass it on. Now, I wonder if we can get a bit more help, here," and he went on to describe what was needed at Fergoil. "Great," he said again, "thanks, lieutenant, I'll be back to you when we've had a chance to really look around here. 'Bye."

Dropping the phone back in his pocket, Ziplich told the others: "There's been one development. Seems a used car dealer on Third Street had a customer for one of his vehicles and he noticed, when he was filling out the paperwork, that the license tag was wrong; it should've been taken off, anyway. He immediately called our guys— no used car dealer needs trouble with the cops—and it was found that this tag belonged on a Cruze rented from Budget. Our friends Mr. and Mrs. Hearn had made a switch. So now we know the number on the car they're driving, and we also know that it's expired, so we're requesting all units to keep alert for it." The phone rang again.

"Ziplich. Yeah, lieutenant." There was silence for a few moments, then: "And he let her go? No, I guess he couldn't have known. Did he get a good description? Uh-huh, uh-huh, yeah. Okay, then, let's hope for a break. Sure, we'll be in touch."

"Let me guess, Zee," Benny said. "Some traffic duty guy stopped this Hearn woman because of an out of date tag, then let her go with a warning."

"Right in one, Benny. Two things going for us, though. One, he's got the number of the stolen tag, which we already knew from the dealer and two, he gave a good description of the girl. Only thing he couldn't judge was her height, because she never got out of the car.

Still, we know from the woman at Frank's that she's petite. But best of all, he got her driving permit number."

"What about her name? Didn't he get that?"

"Can't read his own writing on the copy of the warning he wrote her up. We'll trace the name through the Massachusetts records." Benny's face registered an unspoken question. "That's the driving permit she was carrying, Massachusetts. Shouldn't take long. I see a noose closing here, and when we find her she'll lead us to Riordan."

"All we need after that," Grayson said dryly, "is to find a multiple killer."

"Dan, you damn Limeys sure can be a real pain in the ass sometimes," Ziplich shot at him, and Benny nodded agreement. "Just let us get on with our work, will ya?"

"Oh, dear, I must have touched a nerve. Frightfully sorry, old bean," Grayson said with exaggerated British courtesy. "I'll try to remember my place as a foreigner. Make that *alien*."

Balfour and Krauss regarded this display of acrimony with considerable discomfiture.

It was almost pathetically easy, Bernadette thought, and that eased her nerves a little, since they had been stretched almost to snapping point by the incident with the traffic cop. He had let her go with a warning, since she was driving a rental car, but advised her to have the outdated tag taken care of immediately. At the Fergoil temporary headquarters, she flashed her identification, demanded to see the records for the past seven years and was ushered into a conference room. There a computer was provided, together with all the information needed to access any financial file.

"We've been expecting you. The only things that you won't be able to able to read," said the wan woman who was taking care of the unwelcome visitor, "are confidential personnel files and items of a personal nature. All business and financial records are as complete and available as possible following the disasters of the tornado night. Anything that isn't there is because we haven't got it. I'll have some coffee brought in. Is there anything else?"

"Does this computer have Internet access? In case I need to check with our Austin office?"

"Of course."

"Then I'm fine. I just want to get the formalities out of the way with as little disruption to you as possible, and then be out of your hair. I know how difficult it must be after...after what happened."

"Yes, thank you. Well, I'll send the coffee in to you, and let you get to it." She slipped out quietly, and Bernadette set immediately to work. All she really needed were the names and numbers of the various Fergoil bank accounts, and their respective balances. The rest would be simplicity itself. She would transfer the great bulk of those accounts, via the Internet, to a selection of offshore accounts in such places as the Bahamas or Caymans, whose numbers and passwords she had memorized. The main problem would be hacking the passwords of the Fergoil accounts in order to make the actual withdrawals, and that might—almost certainly would—take time. Time, indeed, was her arch enemy here, even though the provision of a computer was infinitely preferable to reams of paper to sift through. Sooner or later, probably sooner, the police would get a line on her, and she needed to complete her work and get out of Tulsa, with or without Riordan. No, wait: if she dropped him in the shit, he was stupid enough to blow the whole business, just to get at her. He'd have to go with her. Bernadette turned on the computer and was preparing to look at access information when the coffee was brought in. She had already made an adjustment to the telephone line, in case an attempt were made to confirm her with the IRS. That had all been prepared before she'd left Belfast.

❖   ❖   ❖

They had barely opened the first page of the Ferguson diaries, when Ziplich's phone rang yet again. It was Agent Ryan.

"Lieutenant Malcolm told me I better let you know this, Zee," he said. "I had a call from Jenna Grant, you know, Ferguson's secretary. She tells me there's an IRS agent in the office, checking up on all the Fergoil finances using a computer and some paper records. She knows there's something wrong about her. The IRS ran a check immediately after the company offices were destroyed, to confirm the insurance information, and she can't see why there'd be another so soon, although a check was expected eventually."

"Did she call the IRS for confirmation?"

"She sure did—this is no stupid woman, Zee—and she said she was told that an agent named Candace Simpson had been assigned to the case right after the Ferguson death. There've been quite a lot of comings and goings with the IRS about an audit, too. And this is Candace Simpson in the Fergoil office, right now."

"So what's Ms. Grant's problem, then?"

"She happens to be an acquaintance of Candace Simpson, they belong to the same health club, and the one in the office is a total stranger. You want us to pick her up?"

"No. This may be our break. We need her to lead us to her accomplice, this Riordan guy. He's holed up someplace, and we need to talk with him, to put it mildly."

"So whaddya want us to do?"

"Ask the lieutenant to get that computer whiz—what's his name? Norton, something like that."

"Nordstrom."

"Right. Get him to block any activity out of that computer that the Simpson woman is using—anything on the Internet, that is. She mustn't know about it though. Nordstrom'll know how to do that. And watch her till we get back. You got anyone in the Fergoil place yet?"

"Kohler's on his way there now."

"Good. If that woman makes a move, except to the restroom, follow her. We'll be on our way back in just a few minutes. Call me if there's any new development."

"Gotcha."

Ziplich briefed the others on what he'd just heard.

"Ah, well," Grayson said, "we can pick up the diaries, ensconce ourselves in your splendid vehicle, and peruse them as Benny whisks us toward Tulsa."

"At the rate of whisking that Benny is liable to use, you probably won't be perusing anything, except maybe a prayer book, until we arrive."

So it proved. With lights flashing and siren wailing, Benny had them in Tulsa in nearly half the time it had taken to reach the Ferguson 'cabin.' The diaries remained unopened.

Lieutenant Malcolm's phone rang and, much to his irritation, it was not news on the Fergoil front, or so he thought at first. "Some guy named Phillips from Nebraska. Says it's real urgent."

"Okay," said Malcolm with resignation, "put him on. Lieutenant Malcolm."

"Lieutenant, my name is Carl Phillips, and I'm with Mutual of Omaha." Malcolm was suddenly alert. "It's about our Alfred Combs. You called a few days ago to ask about him, and we confirmed that he was coming to Tulsa after his vacation. Thing is, he hasn't contacted us in over a week, and that's totally out of character. He's our most meticulous and reliable of sales agents, and it's his habit to be in touch almost daily. We're wondering if anything could've happened to him since he arrived in Tulsa. Is there anything you can do to help us connect with him? Do you have a hotel where he's staying, something like that? He hasn't answered his e-mail or his voicemail, and we can't raise his cellphone. We haven't heard anything and we're concerned about him."

"I'll certainly look into it, Mr. Phillips. Tell me, do you have a photograph of Mr. Combs?"

"Sure, our personnel files will have one."

"Then please fax it to me right away," he gave the number, "and let me have a phone number I can call you on when I've checked this out, okay?"

"Yes. Thank you, lieutenant, thank you very much."

"I'll be in touch."

A few minutes after the conversation with Carl Phillips, the fax machine printed a clear black and white image of Alfred Combs. The lieutenant used his considerable influence to discover, very rapidly, where a Mr. Alfred Combs might be sought. Malcolm summoned one of his most recent recruits, Officer Judy Black, who belied her name by being a natural blonde.

"I need you to take this picture over to the Renaissance Hotel and have the desk clerks, waiters, cleaning staff, anybody, tell you whether this is the man they know as Alfred Combs. Get his room number. If they'll let you, and if he's not there, try to get into his room and have a look around. I can't tell you what to look for, since I don't know myself, but there's a definite smell of fish here, so maybe you'll spot something. Anyway, don't press them about the room if they're hesitant, but do be absolutely certain whether or not the guy in this picture is their Alfred Combs. Got it?"

"Got it, lieutenant," and she was on her way.

Malcolm was musing at his desk, the routine paperwork pushed to one side. If, and it was a big if, this Alfred Combs was a phony, the question arose as to who he really was, and why he had shown an interest in the building which housed Fergoil. Coincidence? He doubted it. Like most people in his profession, he was profoundly skeptical of coincidence, while admitting that it did occasionally occur. His gut feeling told him that the man calling himself Combs was the third corner of the triangle that Ziplich, Benny and that Limey were trying to piece together—the killers of Ferguson and Taylor, Tobin and Nolan. Malcolm did not like murderers. If this guy was the one they'd been looking for, he was going to pay the price, and the price Malcolm wanted was available in Oklahoma—the death penalty. Then there was the question of "Candace Simpson" over at Fergoil right now. It all tied together pretty well, and that worried Malcolm, too, because things which tied together on the face of it were so often not connected at all. So, wait and see what Kohler had to say when he called in.

The call wasn't long in coming. "I asked Ms. Grant if she could give me a description of the woman calling herself Candace Simpson, an' it matches with what we have from the motel, the restaurant and the traffic cop. In short, boss, I think we have found 'Mrs. Hearn'."

"Have you had a look at her yet?"

"No, she's in an office—well, conference room—an' there's no window from the main offices. Maybe she'll come out to go to the john or something. I've been in touch with Nordstrom, an' he says this broad can't get anything worth jack on her internet connection, now that he's jinxed it, but it'll just seem like a normal glitch to her. He's monitoring her line, an' he says she hasn't tried to use the net so far. His guess is that she's checkin' files to see where she can hack most efficiently."

"Did you ask Ms. Grant if this woman has a British, or maybe Irish, accent?"

"No, but she's right here, so hang on a moment an' I'll ask her." There was the muffled sound of a conversation as Kohler talked to Jenna Grant, then: "No foreign accent, boss, but Ms. Grant thought she detected New England, Boston, maybe."

"You're sure she doesn't mean Old England?" Malcolm asked, echoing Ziplich's question to the Fergoil accountant weeks previously.

"She's quite sure. New England, probably Massachusetts, likely Boston."

A bell rang in Malcolm's mind. "Hold on a minute, Joe, while I check this out." He fumbled through the papers on his desk, coming up with a copy of the traffic warning, issued to an illegible name, for driving a car with an out of date tag. What was legible was the driver's license number and state—Massachusetts. "Joe?"

"Yeah, lieutenant?"

"Stay there at least until you can get a glimpse of this woman. If you do see her, call me."

"Sure."

"And if she leaves, follow her. You got an unmarked car?"

"Yep, got that little Toyota, the one with no antenna. If I follow her, I'll be invisible."

"Good. Let me know any developments."

"You got it."

Malcolm now rang the communications room. "Darlene, honey, I need a favor."

"Tell me, lieutenant."

"I want you to get on to Massachusetts DoT and ask them about this driver's permit number," he read it to her, "and find out everything you can about the owner. It's probably phony, but might just possibly be genuine, and we need to know."

"Leave it with me. I'll call you back real quick."

"Thanks, sweetheart." Malcolm sat back for a moment, then, with a faint sigh, set about clearing up the matter of official paperwork.

Officer Black showed the photograph of Alfred Combs to the desk clerk at the Renaissance Hotel.

"No, nothing like him. Our Mr. Combs is much thinner, and has dark hair. He's older, too, I'd guess—unless this isn't a recent picture."

"Is Mr. Combs in at the moment."

"I'm not sure, officer. Give me a moment to check, please." He performed some esoteric rites at his computer, then said, "No, he left a few hours ago. His car isn't in the lot, and his room is empty."

"You can tell all that from your computer?" Black asked in disbelief.

The clerk looked a little shamefaced. "Well, to tell the truth, I saw him go out and I haven't seen him come back . It just impresses people to do a little magic now and then."

Black, usually a mild-mannered young woman was stung. "Do not," she said slowly and distinctly, "attempt to impress police officers by wasting their time with your stupid ego trips. I want to look inside Combs' room. Now. And don't give me more cause for irritation."

"I can't just let you into a guest room without his permission."

"You are beginning to look like someone trying to obstruct an officer in the course of duty." Black was now unwittingly emulating Ziplich at La Quinta. "I can get a warrant which will shut this whole place down while we search it from top to bottom. All your guests will be disrupted and the company will lose untold amounts of business, for which you, *you*, "she emphasized, "will be responsible. Just think how that's going to look on your resume when you're looking for your next job. You want to re-evaluate your attitude?" He did.

Darlene rang Malcolm within a matter of minutes. "Got your Massachusetts stuff, lieutenant."

"And?"

"The license was issued to a Bernadette Riley, in the States on a student visa. British citizen, attended Harvard and got her Bachelor's and then a Master's in Economics. She went back to Britain after graduation last spring. No record of her since then."

"Darlene, you're a wonder. You don't happen to have her British passport number, do you?"

"Matter of fact I do."

Malcolm jotted it down. "Remind me to buy you a real good dinner sometime."

"All in a day's work, lieutenant."

Grayson, Ziplich and Benny returned a short time later, having made the journey from Missouri in a time which would have had a NASCAR driver grinning broad approval. Grayson, himself a fast driver on occasion but a nervous passenger, was decidedly shaken after the trip, although Ziplich appeared unconcerned and Benny was his usual insouciant self. Malcolm told them of the latest developments. "There's no certainty that our Candace Simpson hasn't just stolen the license and had it doctored, but it bears more investigation, don't you agree, Dan?" Malcolm inquired.

"Most definitely. I'll get hold of LaDonna and have her make the check." He glanced at his watch. "She'll have left for home by now, the time difference being what it is, but I'll ring her at home and tell her what we need. She'll have it to us by early morning. In the meantime, I assume there's a watch on this Miss Simpson?"

"Joe Kohler's on it."

"Then we wait to see what he comes up with," Ziplich suggested.

"Right."

"What about this Alfred Combs guy, then?"

"Judy Black hasn't reported back yet."

"More waiting," Ziplich complained. "Oh, well, maybe we can finally have a look at those diaries." But the phone rang. It was Officer Black. Malcolm turned on the speakerphone for the benefit of the others.

"Nothing in Combs' room that looks suspicious," Black began.

"Hell," Malcolm muttered.

"But what may interest you, lieutenant, is that the staff here at the Renaissance state that the man calling himself Combs bears no resemblance to the picture you gave me to show around. Looks like we got us an imposter."

"My God," Malcolm groaned, "another one. That makes—how many?—four, at least."

"May I venture to suggest, Stan," Grayson said, "that this may well be the assassin we've wondered about. After all, he was spotted driving around outside the Fergoil premises. He wants to dispose of Riordan, and that's the obvious place to start looking for him."

"But Riordan isn't there."

"No, but Simpson, Riley, whatever her name may be, is. Perhaps Combs knows what she looks like. If so, he'll follow her in an attempt to find Riordan. That's what we're going to do, after all."

"And if he doesn't?"

"*We* follow her anyway. We'll have lost nothing, even if we don't gain this Combs fellow straight away."

"Okay. Officer Black?"

"Yo, lieutenant."

"Stay there, unobtrusively. Impress on the hotel staff that they are to tell you the moment he reappears—and that they are by no means to raise his suspicions. Remember that he may be entirely innocent, although I doubt that. I want you to give me a detailed description of this guy."

"Lieutenant, I'm in uniform. How unobtrusive is that?"

"Use your imagination, officer. You're off-duty police acting as a security guard. Dammit, the whole country's full of 'em. Just act like you belong there."

"Okay, lieutenant, I'll try."

"No, officer, you won't try, you'll succeed. Now go to it."

"Yessir."

After leaving the Fergoil office building, Youssef had gone shopping, in the belief that there was nothing to be gained by lingering—he might attract unwelcome interest. There were all manner of goods available in America which were sometimes difficult, if not impossible, to obtain at home and at prices which never failed to amaze him. It seemed almost incredible that a nation so corrupt, so inimical to his own beliefs, could serve its people so well. Clearly, it was the government's way of blinding its citizens to the evils of the regime. *The opiate of the people isn't religion,* he thought, *our own religion proves that. No, it's opulence.* The irony of his own addiction to the trappings of wealth, no doubt a result of the deprived and dangerous youth he had endured in his homeland, never occurred to him.

He lunched well at The Wild Fork before returning to the Fergoil building. No police cars visible. Had they been called off for lack of results? He scanned the parking lot carefully. No one sitting idly in a driver's seat anywhere. Had Malone appeared and been caught, perhaps? He had reluctantly to believe that Malone was smarter than that. Precautions, then, were still in order, and he remained ignorant of the identity of the financial expert he knew had to be here somewhere. It was very frustrating, but Youssef was a patient man, and his patience had proven one of his most important assets over the years, second only to a cold-blooded determination to destroy his enemies without mercy or compassion. As a precaution, this time he took up position a couple of hundred yards down the street, in a Burger King parking area from which he could observe the Fergoil building, and settled down to wait.

By six o'clock Youssef was convinced that he had nothing to gain by remaining longer. The Fergoil parking lot was almost empty, so most of the office building must be empty, too. Also, he'd noticed a few questioning looks at his car, which had been in the Burger King car park for a considerable period. It was definitely time to move: there was always tomorrow. Youssef decided to take the fruits of his shopping expedition back to the Renaissance. Perhaps he'd change his name and appearance again, move to a different hotel, rent a new vehicle. It didn't pay to be the same person in the same place for too long, and there was always the chance that Alfred Combs would soon be missed. Yes, he'd check out in the morning, turn in the car at the airport and hire another one in one of his other names. Then, with his physical appearance totally altered, he would continue his surveillance.

❖   ❖   ❖

"Candace Simpson" felt that she was making significant progress. She had not yet gone on the Internet, but she had searched a large number of the Fergoil financial files and found assets in excess of twenty three billion dollars. "That's billion," she told herself. "For convenience sake just halve that; you get twelve and a half billion. We'll not get it all, but let's just project a third, which seems conservative," she smiled to herself at the use of the word, "say four billion. Four billion dollars! Let's see what the Brits can do to counter that, when they're already overstretched and cutting back on every damn thing. We've got the bastards by the balls."

There was a knock on the door, and Jenna Grant put her head in the room. "Ms. Simpson, we're shutting up the office for the day, is that all right?"

"Oh, I'm sorry, I didn't notice the time. Yes, of course. I'll come back in the morning and I'll probably be able to clear this whole business up by the end of the day. I'm really sorry to have disturbed you. Just let me save my stuff to disk, and I'll be out of your way."

Joe Kohler followed Bernadette to the motel on Eleventh Street, and reported to Stan Malcolm.

Jimmy Riordan was watching drag racing on The Speed Channel.

Judy Black called in to say that Alfred Combs had returned to his hotel, and that he bore not the slightest resemblance to the picture furnished by Mutual of Omaha.

And Dan Grayson, Paul Ziplich and Benny—who may have had another name—were reading the Ferguson diaries. These were meticulously kept, and spanned the time from his days as a schoolboy in Hornsey during the Second World War right through until a week or so before his death. This looked like being a long haul. Nothing much looked particularly helpful until they eventually reached Phipps's eighteenth birthday. There had been reflections on the air raids (including the scramble by young boys in the streets to collect pieces of shrapnel while they were still hot), rationing (mostly annoying because of the restrictions on buying "Crunchie," for which Bernie clearly had an addiction), VE Day and the ensuing austerity of the late '40s. Phipps had made a brief trip to Brittany in 1950, and had been incensed to find that the French, who had been occupied, were far better fed than the still-rationed British. Still, there was no light shed on his acquisition of money until...

Chapter 10
The Diaries

October 18, 1952

I'm at RAF Padgate with considerable misgiving. A series of mostly black-painted wooden buildings, which I have learnt are known as Nissen huts, seem to stretch away into an indefinite future. They are anchored to the world by a series of whitewashed stones. Groups of new National Servicemen—I've already determined to claim to be a "conscript"—stood around uncertainly, waiting for some coherent information. Most of them, like me, are barely of school-leaving age. They mill about unhappily, dreading more shouting, we having already learned that recruits are shouted at without much re-lief. My first day, and already we're being treated like cattle. Most of the time we just sat around in a big, bare hut, waiting for something to happen. Finally, late in the afternoon, a corporal came in and made us line up outside. It felt freezing, but we were soon taken to another hut, more of a hangar, where we were "kitted out." This consisted of being asked our sizes for chest, collar, inside leg, shoes and so on, and having things thrust at us to push into a kitbag we had each been given when we arrived. Then, outside again and off to more Nissen huts. There are to be forty new arrivals in each hut, with beds lined up on each side and a small locker per bed. All the blankets and so on were folded into neat squares when we arrived. I am ready to bet we shall have to fold them that way again in the morning. There was a small cubicle at one end of the hut which, we were told, will contain a corporal at some point, and there is a coal stove too, that is supposed to warm the place but seems mostly to smell of hot metal. It is black and polished. Everything is polished. I am ready to believe that we will all learn a lot about polishing, too. And whitewashing. When we finally arrived at our hut, we had to change into our uniforms, which were scratchy, stiff and uncomfortable, and then were marched (with much shouting from the staff) to the mess hall for supper. One look at the food and I knew why they called it "mess," but I was hungry and ate it. Quite a lot of the others scarcely touched theirs. Along with our other equipment, we had been issued with what were called "mug and irons," meaning *eatin' irons* like something out of the Wild West, I suppose, and the recruits had to rinse them in a trough of hot water outside the mess. I wonder if the RAF has ever heard of hygiene.

I heard someone saying "If it moves, salute it: if it doesn't, whitewash it." But that elusive hygiene doesn't seem high on the list, and my first trip to the "shower block," which is to say outside latrines, pretty well confirmed that. There is a dreadful noise coming from a loudspeaker in the hut, and now here is that corporal, shouting of course. Apparently the noise meant "lights out." Welcome to Padgate.

Grayson skipped through several pages of complaints concerning Phipps's experiences at "'square-bashing" camp. Not having been a victim of National Service himself, he had no means of judging the accuracy of the diaries, but he remembered some of his father's reminiscences and imagined they weren't far off the mark. Benny and Ziplich had selected the next two volumes, one each, and were engaged in the same pursuit as his own, trying to find a clue as to how Phipps became Ferguson. The saga continued:

November 1
They try very hard all the time to talk you into applying for aircrew. I had not really meant to, but I did get a bit carried away after the propaganda film they showed us, and tomorrow a few of us are off to Hornchurch to find out if we are POMs, *'Potential Officer Material'*, Grayson dredged out of his memory's *'Miscellaneous' file*. Flying could really quite be fun, I imagine. Well, we shall see.

November 2
Lots of aptitude tests and more films about the joy of flying. It covered all sorts of areas, like Coastal Command and Transport Command and a good many more, but if I am selected, I want to

be in Fighter Command. They have got these new aircraft like the Swift and the Hunter on the way, and I would be finished training just about the time they come into service. Not that a Meteor would be too bad. After supper (the food is better here than at Padgate) they showed us "The Sound Barrier," guaranteed to set every heart a-flutter. Much less Bull here than at Padgate, too. Perhaps that is how it is at operational stations, which Hornchurch is. Old Battle of Britain airfield, it seems.

November 4

Those of us selected for aircrew training were told today. I was not one. My maths are too poor, they said, which was hardly news. Pity, though. I think I would have enjoyed it. Back to Padgate tomorrow. What fun.

So Phipps was bad at maths. I wonder how he managed his financial expertise.

November 5

Back at Padgate. Guy Fawkes Day, but no fireworks here, unless you count being fingerprinted for some reason, and the yelling of the DIs. *DIs? Oh, yes, Drill Instructors.* They have put me in a different billet, but it is not full of strangers, because there are two blokes from school here, Gibbins and Moore. Funny, I did not see them when we all arrived here the same first day. Rumor is we will get our first leave at Christmas, but I have already learnt to distrust rumors here. It is cold in this damn hut.

December 17

It is official, now, no Christmas leave for me. Now I have finished square-bashing, I will be one of the skeleton crew that keeps this wonderland going over the holiday. Getting New Year, though. Nina will be disappointed, at least I hope she will be, but we will be able to see the New Year in together.

Nina? Make a note to find out about her.

December 25

Funny, but we had quite a good time today. There was no real duty, and everybody dined in the same mess, including the NCOs. The real entertainment was that the officers served the food to us, brought it to the tables instead of us lining up at that long hotplate thing. Food was really rather good, too. Of course, there were not that many of us, so it was probably easier to keep it decent. Turkey, stuffing, all the veg, Xmas Pud, even beer! Quite festive. Not as good as being at home, but at least bearable. Sang Carols before turning in.

January 7 1953

Back at Padgate seems almost like home. New Year leave was lovely; lots of time with Nina. I suppose I have got used to this place. I did not like having to leave Nina and Mum, but it was not as bad as I had expected.. Change tomorrow. When I got here I was notified that I am posted as of tomorrow to West Malling. It is in Kent, so it will be nearer home, which is nice. It is a Fighter station, too, and I am posted to Air Traffic Control. I suppose that is the next best thing to flying. Wait and see.

January 9

RAF West Malling.

Had a lousy journey getting here. Left Padgate early with three other blokes who are all posted to Lossiemouth. At least we had transport to Warrington Station from the MT section. My train was late, of course, so I missed my connection, and finally arrived in London at rush hour, lugging a bloody kitbag. The tube was jammed and then I had to wait another hour at Victoria. Nearly went to Chatham by mistake (wouldn't the Navy have laughed) since the train divided at Swanley, and I was on the wrong bit. Luckily I heard the announcement, and managed to get on the right one. There is a bus from West Malling village to the front gate here, but I had to wait for that, too, When I finally got here it was after nine, and no one knew I was coming. Chap at the gate found a fairly pleasant sergeant who showed me an empty room in one of the barrack blocks (real brick! No Nissen huts! Hooray!) and the NAAFI, since the mess is closed for the night.

He also told me to enjoy myself because tomorrow is Saturday and Admin will not be open until Monday. He said there are some decent pubs in the village, and it is quite possible to walk there if the weather is ok. There's a pub just outside the airfield called "The Startled Saint," he told me. Who dreams up these names? Some chaps here have cars, and it is often possible to get a lift. He showed me how to get to the Control Tower, too. I can hear aircraft now, so evidently there is night flying here. Tired, so the tower can do without me for one more weekend.

Grayson leafed rapidly through the increasingly brief entries in the diary, noting that Phipps had been one of those who spent many wet, cold, miserable hours fighting the disastrous floods of late January/early February and that his love affair with Nina seemed increasingly shaky. Phipps had an eye for the pleasant countryside of the Weald of Kent, and was increasingly at home with his duties in ATC. He was promoted from AC2 to AC1 and then to LAC, so he must have been pretty competent. Then came a Friday in June.

I was in the tower alone, first one in the place, about half an hour before flying was scheduled to start, when there was an RT call on Local for permission to taxi. I told the pilot to hold his position, then rang the Officers' Mess to see if the SATCO was there. He was, and I asked him what I should do. "You're experienced enough, Phipps," he said, "so let him go. I'll be up there shortly. Just make sure you know who it is and where he's going." So, for the first time, I was a controller. Quite a feeling. Have to go back again after lunch, because Wilson is sick and I am doing his watch, too.

The next entry was made three days later.

It seems like a month, but it has only been a few days. After I went back to do Wilson's watch, I was due for a weekend pass. PO McDonough was doing circuits and bumps after just having flown back from Aldergrove, where he'd been home for a bit of leave. How he managed to wangle having the aircraft for a week is a mystery. He called to say he was going to do a couple of asymmetrics before landing, and was given permission. *Asymmetrics? Grayson didn't know and nor did his companions, so he took a few minutes to do a search on the Internet. It seemed that the term, in this context, meant flying a twin-engined aircraft with one engine disabled.* He was just turning onto Finals when we heard him yell 'Flameout' and he ploughed in. *Flameout, Grayson recalled from somewhere, meant an aircraft's engine had completely lost power.* Poor bastard had no chance at that height, and we saw the smoke and flames as he hit. Crash crew rushed out, but there was nothing they could do but douse the flames. They cobbled together a crash guard, six of us plus Flt. Sgt. Blackman, and we went out in a gharri to where the wheat field site was. It was strange; there was an awful smell of burning aircraft, and the ground was blackened, but a lot of the grain had been ripened by the heat, and birds were pecking at it. It was like a great golden eye with a huge black iris. We were ordered to points around the field to keep gawpers out, but nobody ever came to look. We stayed overnight, standing two-hour watches, and the boffins came next day, when we left. Blackman told us not to touch anything, but to keep an eye open for anything we saw scattered on the ground. I found a helmet with half of McDonough's head in it, and threw up. Blackman gave me a bollocking for that. Then we went back to Malling, and I changed into best blues and went off on my pass. Nina has found some fellow in the RAAF. They get paid a lot more than we do, so that's that. Got drunk. Came back on Monday and found a wallet in the BD that I had worn on crash guard. It is McDonough's. I must have picked it up, but I do not remember doing so. Should I turn it in? There is not much in it except his 1250 and a ticket for a suitcase at the Victoria Station left luggage office. His family must be very sad just now. I think I will pick up the bag and see if it is anything they should have. If not, I will throw it all away. They do not need me making matters worse for them.

Never mind about checking on Nina, then, Grayson was thinking, when Benny, who was looking through a big ring-folder said: "I may have something here." The number of an account in an unnamed Swiss bank.

July 4
Independence Day in America. Independence Day for Bernie Phipps, too. Went to Victoria, took the ticket to the left luggage office and collected a suitcase. Took it home before opening it. Mum was out. The case was locked, but it was not difficult to open. It was full of money, all those lovely black and white notes that mean five

and ten and twenty and fifty pounds. I counted them. Fifty thousand pounds. Impossible, so I have counted again. Fifty thousand pounds. There is an unsigned typewritten note that I am looking at now. It says "Delivery to be made on August the 12th at the arranged time and location." Something illegal has been going on, that is obvious. Now that McDonough is dead, I inherit his money and there is no reason that anybody will know, as long as I am careful. Maybe I will send an anonymous amount to his family. They do not need to know that he was involved in anything shady. Nina would be cross to think what she missed! I have hidden the case under my bed. I will leave this part of the diary with it, for safety's sake. Must find a proper hiding place soon. I will decide how to proceed while I am at Malling during the rest of the week. Maybe I should take one of those classes the Education Officer is always on about. Perhaps there is a course about the stock market.

So that's where his money came from, although it's a long way from fifty thousand pounds to five hundred thousand dollars. If he really got the hang of the stock market, though...Got to check that Swiss bank account that Benny found. Grayson kept searching.

August 12

Delivery day. I wonder who is waiting where for what. Have started on an investment course. Applied for an overseas posting a couple of weeks ago and was refused. Well, they cannot say I did not volunteer. On the other hand, I am not too disappointed. It could have been Korea and they are shooting real bullets there. I am no Speakman. I cannot help but think that he must have gone a bit crazy. Still, he got a VC and he is still alive. I get a Coronation medal because my name was drawn out of a hat. Do not think I shall wear it.

September 12

Have made my first stock purchase, in ICI. It is not likely to make a killing, as they call it, but it looks like a steady earner. Maybe later, when I feel more confident, I shall try to "speculate" a little. Have taken my SAC exam. It did not seem too difficult.

October 23

Have been posted again, this time to North Weald. Seems they need a SAC in the Ops Room. I am not quite sure what an Ops room is, but I suppose I can cope.

November 30

It is so cushy, except that I am back in a Nissen hut, I can hardly believe it! Five day week, just like a union man. Home every weekend, and all I have to do is take the Tube. Gives me plenty of time to examine the papers for good prospects for investment. So far, I am doing quite well. Met a nice girl named Rebecca last week at a dance in Epping. Mum sometimes wonders how I am able to pay her so much for my part of the housekeeping expenses. I tell her that I win it playing brag with my oppos. *'Playing a kind of simplified poker with my pals,' Grayson translated.* I am not sure that she believes it. I would like to give her a lot more, but it might look suspicious. Perhaps I could tell her I have had a win on the Pools. I will think about that.

December 18

Mum's funeral was very quiet. We do not have many relatives, as most of them went during the War. She just died. I was not even home at the time, I was out with Rebecca. When I came home, she was sitting in her chair by the fire, and I thought she was asleep and I crept around so as not to waken her. I went to bed, and when I came down in the morning, there she was. She had not moved and I realized something was wrong. I looked more closely and saw she was sort of waxy. Then I knew. I called the doctor and he came and examined her and said that she had had a heart attack. Poor Mum, she never quite got over losing Dad on D-Day. I wish I had done more for her.

December 20

It has happened again. I have drawn Christmas duty. Two years on the trot, and Mum just gone. I suppose it will be better than sitting in an empty house.

(No date)

I have finally decided what I am going to do. It has been worrying me having all that money sitting in a suitcase under the bed in what is now my house. I haven't used much of it, and my few investments actually mean that I now have more than when I started. There has been no outcry about the missing money and I am convinced that I am right in believing that something highly illegal was going on when McDonough got the chop. I have tried to guess what he was to have delivered that would be worth so much, but have not had any useful ideas. I have some leave due soon. I shall go to Switzerland and put the money in a bank there. They have numbered accounts and do not require a lot of personal information. All they want is the money and their fee for looking after it. Then I can arrange any stock market dealings to be paid from there and for dividends to be added direct to that account. That should reduce the chances of being caught out by paying huge amounts of income tax if I do well. Demob in just over nine months! I had better decide what I am going to do when I get out.

The next couple of months shed no new light on Phipps's activities, and Grayson flicked quickly through the entries. Benny had been on the phone, trying to twist arms in an effort to crack information on the Swiss numbered account. So far, Ziplich had uncovered nothing of significance.

June 19 (1954, presumably)

It was ridiculously easy. I collected my travel warrants, leave pay, ration cards etc. I had already packed a few civvies. Instead of taking a train, however, I got a ride to Gutersloh with my Ops. Officer, Flt. Lt. Parkinson. It was a "liaison" flight in the Station Flight Oxford, which usually means picking up some cheap cigarettes and brandy to bring home. Parkinson is a man who nobody except me seems to like. He agreed to take me over and we arranged for me to be picked up again on his next trip ten days later. I was lucky enough to get a lift to the French Zone, which borders on Switzerland. The French pilot spoke only a little English, but my schoolboy French got me through. Then I got a bus to the Swiss border and just walked through. No one paid me the slightest attention, and me with a suitcase full of cash! This was at Basel. Some nice chap gave me a lift in his car and took me to the station, where I got a train and went to Lucerne. I had decided not to do my banking too close to the frontiers, and on the map Lucerne looked pretty well placed. It was pretty, as well as pretty well placed. In fact all the country I saw was pretty, with mountains, of course, many of them snow-capped. It was the towns and villages that surprised me. They were all so neat and clean and tidy, not like at home. I thought to myself, "they must wash the streets." Then one morning I saw a woman actually washing the pavement outside her shop. Another lesson: do not make fun of the tidiness of the Swiss. I stayed at a hotel called the Wilden Mann in a simple but comfortable room. The day after I arrived I went out to look for banks, and finally settled on one in the middle of the town. It was called (*this entry had been blacked out. Grayson asked Ziplich if there were an expert who could, perhaps clear it up. Ziplich promised to find out. "Probably turn out to be the same as the numbered account Benny's working on," he suggested, and Grayson agreed that was likely*) It was only about half an hour later when I walked out with an account number and my money safely deposited. No questions about how I got it or anything. You would think this kind of thing happens every day. Maybe it does. Spent a few days just being a tourist, having changed some money into Swiss francs at the station in Basel. Went up a funicular and a couple of cable cars, quite interesting. The food was very good, no rationing here, but their beer is not up to much. Some of it is called 'hell' and that seems about right. Then I went back to Basel, crossed into Germany, where the French officials did look at my passport and RAF identification, but gave me no trouble. Once again I struck lucky and got a lift to Gutersloh. These "liaison" flights certainly use up a lot of taxpayers' money. A couple of days later, after I had been amazed by the scale of destruction the war had caused, and I only saw a tiny fraction of the country, Parkinson came and picked me up, this time in a Meteor 7. Bonus! He gave me a flying lesson on the way home. I go back on duty tomorrow.

June 29

They have promoted me to corporal, which is unusual for a National Serviceman. Now I get the corporal's room, which has been empty, in the billet and there has been a lot of pushing for me to sign on as a Regular. Good prospects for promotion, they tell me, and a pension at the end of it all. If only they knew. I have made several investments now, which should certainly produce better than an Air Force pension can. I am thinking of finding a stockbroker who can help me with this buying and selling business, but I have to be careful because of taxes. Everything has to be done through Lucerne by post, and that is a slow process. I shall have to go there after I get out and make arrangements about doing business by telephone or telegram. Probably need some sort of password to be sure the instructions are legitimate. Less than four months to demob.

July 4

One year exactly since I came into money, and still no indication of what its original purpose was. I suppose that one day something will happen to solve that. I just hope that whoever was the person who paid out so much and got nothing in return is not with Cosa Nostra or the IRA or something. It is probably foolish of me to write this stuff down, in case it gets found, but I want to remind myself from time to time that I come from a poor family, and that I must use some of what I make to help out those who have not had my luck. 106 days to demob.

July 22

With the help of the bank, have found a broker in Zurich who will handle my financial matters. He will get a fee of 10% of each transaction, buying or selling. I think it is well worth it. The bank speaks highly of him, and I have come to trust their advice. 88 days to demob.

August 15

Very hot today. Had a message from Zurich suggesting the purchase of De Haviland stock. The company is in trouble following the crashes of Comets because of metal fatigue, and the price is quite low, but Konrad thinks they will rise as another company, Supermarine or Hawker perhaps, offers to buy them out. That will be the time to sell as the price rises. I think I will do that. 64 days to demob.

August 30
For some reason my share prices spiked, so I sold at a handsome profit through the standing arrangement I have with Konrad to take care of such matters. Now he is looking for new ventures. He is doing quite well out of me already, but he is proving a valuable asset. 49 days to demob.

Benny said; "I've got the name of the bank. Can't pronounce it, but I got it written down," he brandished a piece of paper, "an' all we got to do now is persuade them to let us have Phipps' account info."

"Which may not prove so easy," Ziplich remarked, his own attempts to get the blacked-out bank name deciphered not yet having borne fruit. " No wonder you were having trouble, Benny," he added.

"Dan, how the hell do you say this?" He pointed and Grayson read "Vierwaldstatterbank AG.

"Ah, yes," he said, "known and loved by all."

September 21
Konrad is buying some oil company shares. He says that in the long term that will be a good investment because oil reserves are not limitless. Some experts have said that they will run out by the turn of the century. He doubts that, but says that increasing demand as the world gets back to normal and nations are rebuilding so fast after the war will ensure oil price increases, and so share prices and dividends. I hope he is right. Less than a month to demob, now.

Oil shares. So that's how he got started in it.

October 4
A landmark day. Just a fortnight until demob. They're still trying to get me to sign on as a Regular, even promised me promotion to sergeant if I do. Parkinson says he'll never find an assistant like me

and will be very sorry to see me go. It seems silly. This job is a doddle, and anyone who isn't mentally deficient could do it in his sleep. I do quite enjoy my work, but certainly not enough to stay. If it were flying, or if I was not a man of means, I might consider it, but as things are...

October 11

The question of McDonough's crash has suddenly resurfaced. A couple of SIB men appeared out of the blue asking for me. Apparently, anybody who was involved in the crash guard is being interrogated, no matter how far away from West Malling they may now be. They asked me if I had found anything, and I told them about the helmet with the piece of head in it. It still turns my stomach to think of it, and I suppose that showed, because they left me alone after that. No one mentioned a wallet, but I shall have to stop direct contact with Konrad for a time, just in case. One week to demob.

October 17

DEMOB TOMORROW. Showed Filkins, who is taking over the Ops. Room from me, the last few things he needs to know; what time the NAAFI van comes, for instance. I have completed all the handoff paperwork except travel warrant and final pay and packed everything except what I am going to wear. I shall be on the Central Line by 10 o'clock and in the Maynard Arms in the evening. The next day, I will start looking for a job.

There were no entries for the next several days, and then for a few weeks only sporadic notes on attempts at finding a job. He found employment in an office equipment manufacturer, and was later moved to the company's West End showroom as a salesman. Evidently he gained little satisfaction from his work. There were no references to Zurich or Lucerne.

Ziplich got a phone call and, after a number of grunted "uh-huhs" and "yeahs," hung up and turned to Grayson. "They've been able to clean up that bank name and, like I expected, it's the same as the one with the number Benny found. We'd better get the wheels moving on getting details of that account."

"I've given that a little thought, you know," Grayson said to Ziplich, who hadn't known. "That could be an area where my firm might have a

certain influence, if I may put it thus. May I suggest that I give LaDonna a ring in the morning?"

Ziplich glanced at his watch. "Jeez, it's after six already. Okay, guys enough for today. Get a good night's sleep. For some reason, I have this feeling that tomorrow is going to be very busy.

Grayson was in the office very early next morning, in order that La-Donna's day should not be too advanced when he spoke to her.

"No," she said in answer to his question, "Jacko isn't back from leave, yet." I wish you were back, she thought. "So I'm all on my little ownsome for the moment. In what fashion may I be of assistance to Sir?"

"We would rather like to obtain details of a certain numbered Swiss bank account"—he gave her the bank and account information—"belonging, probably, to one Bernard Phipps or, possibly but less likely, Ralph Ferguson. Unless, of course, he used yet another name. What think you?"

"It can be done, yes, but it will not be very quick. How much time have I got?"

"We don't really know, 'Donna. There are people here in Tulsa who are being watched, one of whom is quite possibly our assassin, and another who may be the financial genius who's trying to milk the Ferguson company. I really need to know how much is tied up in this account and whether it's vulnerable to attack. So, ASAP is about the only answer I can give you at this point in time, as they say over here."

"I'll start on it right away."

"Bless you, my child."

And bless you, you lovely man, she thought.

"This looks interesting," Benny said. He had been looking through the volume comprising the years 1970-1974, Phipps's years as a tour guide, when a name had caught his eye.

July 12

Collected a new tour group from Gatwick and took them into town. Staying at the Buckingham, which is all right, because it's handy for the changing of the guard and West End theatres and the concierge is very adept at getting good tickets. They're the usual motley collection: a couple of families, a couple of pairs of women travelling together, a group of business pals from Boston who decided to have a holiday without their wives, and two loners—one male, one female. Got most of them sent off to decent restaurants and/or shows. A few of the older ones opted to stay in and get some rest, what with full-day sightseeing tomorrow and the Windsor/Blenheim/Stratford run the next day. The single man, a Mr. Ferguson—*Benny pointed this name out to the others*—wanted to know where the best nightclubs are. That's never come up before, and I have no interest in "nightlife," but I dragged a few names from my memory and off he went. We'll know in the morning how it went.

July 13

Most of them were pretty exhausted by the end of the day. It's a fairly busy trip, and the majority of them are really feeling the jet lag at this stage. All except Ferguson, who extolled the delights of the previous evening, and set off again towards Soho. I'm vaguely interested to know what he's up to. I'll keep an eye open for city nightclubs during the course of this tour, and then I'll not look too stupid if he asks again. Anyway, the hotel concierges are bound to be able to help. I've finished up the paperwork for the last trip, and now I'm going to bed.

July 14

As good a way to spend a birthday as any, I suppose. Did all the usual stuff at Windsor, decent lunch at Woodstock and an evening performance at the RSC. This damned hotel looks like a gasworks, but it's comfortable enough and it has a fair bar. Several gathered there, some chose the White Swan, the Dirty Duck to the initiated, over by the theatre, but that's too crowded for me. Ferguson will be disappointed in the night entertainments, I fear, but he went out anyway.

July 15

Broadway, Oxford and back to the Smoke. It drizzled a bit, but not enough to be really annoying and the people seem to be getting along pretty well together. It remains to be seen who will cause the inevitable problem later on. My money's on the two middle-aged Lesbians, the Misses Gluck and Braden, with one of the rather boisterous stag group a close second, but you never can tell. They have their Day at Leisure tomorrow, so I'll be free until the evening. Then off to Amsterdam next day. We'll be at the Krasnapolski, which is convenient.

July 17

Easy enough trip over, but the airports are getting steadily more crowded, and it can only be a matter of time before they become unbearable. Michel turned out to be the driver waiting for us at Schiphol, and he and I have always got along very well, so that should minimize difficulties. Did the usual brief rundown on the way in, and we were pretty soon booked in with the passport requirements efficiently done by the hotel staff. It's weeping a few showers, so most have decided to stay in and dine at the hotel's quite good restaurant. Not the rowdies, though; they've decided to sample the Dutch gin. Regret it in the morning, probably. Tomorrow we'll do the sightseeing and canal cruise in the morning, afternoon at leisure, next day on to Koblenz. Ferguson has gone seeking who knows what. He didn't ask for advice this evening, so Amsterdam's red light reputation has no doubt reached his notice. Michel and I went out for a couple of beers, and a chat about what's happened since our last trip together. His English is really improving.

July 18

As usual, the first true Continental breakfast came as a surprise to the group, but they accepted it without demur. I'd given them my "the customs are not better or worse than ours, just different," pep talk, with the customary "don't forget we are guests in someone else's home, and if they have ways which are different from ours, that is their right." It's never fully effective, but it cuts down on the worst offences. The Misses Braden and Gluck do not seem to be talking to each other today. Bought a nice leather jacket cheaply in the Kalverstraat. Michel picked up a couple of bits of really good Delft for his mother.

July 19

Border crossings are becoming simpler almost by the day. The drive from Amsterdam to Cologne was quick and easy, with minimum delay, and we were actually a bit early for lunch at the restaurant, but they were most accommodating. Quick sightseeing before coming to Koblenz. The concierge here gave me an address to pass on to Ferguson. This is the first of the older German towns the people have seen, and they are enchanted. Can't tell about Gluck and Braden, since they seem to have been struck mute. Also much subdued today, the Genever topers of last night, most of whom look haggard.

July 20

Rhine cruise went well. The women seem to be on speaking terms again, and the Boston Brotherhood stayed sober last night, and actually took an interest. The children, all of whom have behaved very well so far, enjoyed the boat as much as anything else they have experienced. I must say that the parents have done a good job with their kids, which is all too often not the case. There have been some real little terrors on occasion. As for the rest, they have proven friendly and thoughtful of one another. I know this is pessimistic, but I can't help feeling there'll be an explosion at some point. Good lunch at the Klosterbrauerei near Ulm. Had venison. Staying at the Astoria in Lucerne. Stadtkeller tonight, Pilatus tomorrow, clouds permitting. Will have to find time to get to the bank and contact Konrad

"Who or what is a statt killer?" Benny wanted to know.

"A tourist trap. Yodelling, dancing in lederhosen, fondue eating— all very, very Alpine," Grayson told him.

"And Pilatus?" put in Ziplich. He pronounced it Pie Laid Us.

"A mountain near the town. Cog railway, cable cars, restaurant near the top."

"You been to this place?"

"Just once, on my honeymoon."

July 21

Pilatus was clear and nobody screamed when the cable car lurched on the way down. Miss Humphries has begun to pay attention to Michel, and he is highly embarrassed. You'd think he would be used to it after so many trips, good-looking as he is. Konrad says things are going very well, and he's made another big deposit. He sent a detailed account, which I collected while I was at the bank. Made a largish withdrawal, because I want to pick up a few things on this trip. Oil is being rather good to Konrad and me, and so is the American car industry, as well as Farber in Germany. What they call a diversified portfolio, I believe. I'm thinking about newspapers, too. This Murdoch fellow seems like one to watch.

July 22

Uneventful drive to Innsbruck, with the usual stop at Vaduz for the passport stamps that tourists always seem to want so desperately. Lunch at Neufeld, overnight at the Europa. There's another folklore show if they want it, but most opted to go walkabout as the weather is fine. Michel is carefully avoiding The Humphries.

July 23

Quite a lot of snow on the Brenner, but no delays, except with the Italian passport control people, who seemed to be in one of their more officious moods. Run down to Venice easy enough. Many commented on the much warmer weather here. Hot in Venice in July? I should bloody well think so. The canals are a bit smelly. We're at the Bauer Grunwald. Nice to be able to eat on the terrace. The Humphries tried to get Michel to sit with her at dinner, but he cited company policy forbidding fraternization. Several other tours are here, including one with Pauline as leader. The three of us, and her driver, Kees, ate together. We hatched a plot to save Michel's virtue. He and Pauline swapped rooms, just in case.

July 24

O Joy, O Rapture! It actually happened. Pauline heard a tap at her door just after midnight. When she opened it, there was The

Humphries with a bottle of spumante, a couple of glasses and a bewildered expression. "Excuse me," Pauline told us she said, "I thought this was, er, someone else's room." "Yes, that's right," Pauline replied, standing there in her nightgown, and The Humphries retired in embarrassed confusion. I would love to have seen it. The Humphries has been subdued all day. She did the walking tour, but missed the gondola ride "'con musica" in the evening. Ferguson missed it, too. Something more interesting to do, I suppose.

July 25

Day off today, while the travelers made their own arrangements to amuse themselves. Did a bit of shopping, got some really nice Murano and had it shipped home, then spent most of the rest of the day at the Lido. Got a bit sunburnt.

Several more entries revealed nothing new about either version of Ferguson, and the trio skipped through the pages at some speed, until

August 1

They are beginning to flag a little, all except Ferguson, whose stamina is quite remarkable. We had the full day sightseeing, after that long drive yesterday, and most of them chose to wait until tomorrow to do one of the options like Versailles or the nightclub tour. Not Ferguson. He's gone off to research Pigalle. It beats me how he keeps up the pace. Once I've got them set for any trips they want to make on their day at leisure, I have a day to myself, as soon as I've confirmed all their flights home. Most are going TWA. A handful, including Ferguson, The Humphries and two of the Boston Brotherhood are staying here for some extra days, and they'll make their own arrangements. It is amazing, a whole tour without a really major upset. This must be a first. I'm off home a day after I see them to their airlines. Got 4 days off before the next one starts. Mostly Scandinavia this time. Good. Should get some cool weather.

"*I wonder how he coped with Tulsa's temperatures,*" *Grayson commented.* "*Must have taken a long time to get acclimatized.*"

"*He had enough money to import cooler weather from Siberia, if he wanted,*" *was Benny's opinion.*

August 3

The hotel tells me that Ferguson has not checked out, and they need the room, so I went and packed up his stuff and brought it to my own room, with instructions left at the desk to tell him what has happened when he does turn up. Home tomorrow.

August 4.

Still no Ferguson. I took his suitcases down to the desk and told them to hang on to them until he gets back. I shudder to think what he's been up to. Hotel says it will put his passport, which he had unwisely left in his room, in the safe until he claims it, or up to ten days. After that, they'll have to inform the police of a possible missing person. Told them I would be back in 9 days and check with them. It is nice to be home for even a short break. Have to find a girl friend for the off season to share the flat. The Murano stuff hasn't arrived yet.

Apart from small domestic matters, Phipps had little to tell his diary until the next tour group arrived, when he performed very much the same duties as previously. This, time, however, the first port of call, rather than the last, was Paris. Phipps was back, as promised, at the desk of the Meurice in nine days. Together with the usual outline of the progress of the tour, the diary continued:

August 13

I debated what to do about Ferguson's luggage and passport, since he still hasn't shown up. What *is* that man doing? I finally decided to take charge of them. I'll take them to the company office here tomorrow, and they can take whatever steps they deem necessary.

August 14.

The damned office is closed for a week. I know that Paris atrophies in August, but a tourist office? And we leave for Copenhagen in three days. By train. I'll just have to take bloody Ferguson's bags with me. What the hell has happened to that bloke?

August 15

The picture in Paris Presse is Ferguson, I know it. Body found dumped under a bridge, reported to the police by an early-morning runner. Evidence of extreme sexually aberrant behavior leading to, probably accidental, death. Some money, but no identification on the body. Has he family? He never mentioned any. I shall examine his possessions to see what I can find out.

I have now gone through Ferguson's things and his papers. Among them was a traveler's accident insurance policy, listing under "next of kin," none and naming a cat's home as beneficiary in the event of death. What is more, he was due to start at a new job after his holiday, with a month between arriving home and relocating. I am sorry for Ferguson. He seemed harmless enough, and even if he was a pervert of some sort, as he obviously was, he did not deserve that. On the other hand, there may be an opportunity here.

August 16

Head office contacted me to ask if I will accept another 3 tours this season, as well as a Christmas/New Year 3 cities whoopee. I told them I would do 2, not 3, and the Xmas thing. It will give me some time to work out my plan of action regarding Ferguson. I am going to wait and see if the office gets any inquiries about him. If so, they will certainly get hold of me, and the matter will then be resolved. If nobody asks, then I believe I have found a way to make use of my resources. At the same time, I should finally be in a position to offer help to some of those who really need it. That would feel good, as well as being some kind of memorial to poor Ferguson. I cancelled his air ticket, which was for Friday, and left the new return date to New York open. There will be an additional cost for the change.

August 17

I got rid of Ferguson's dirty laundry, which was what his luggage mostly contained, by the simple expedient of giving it to an Algerian clochard down by the river. He invoked God's love on me. The bags themselves, and the clean clothes which remained, from which I removed the labels, I gave to a homeless shelter. Small stuff, like toothbrushes and so on, I simply stuffed in a street rubbish bin. We are on the way to Denmark, and most of my group are napping after lunch. They'll enjoy the ferry over from Germany and, most likely, endless Hans Christian Andersen thereafter.

Phipps had added little more for the next several weeks, during which he completed his last tours of the season, except to say that there had been no inquiries regarding Ferguson.

November 22

The arrangements are all set. I have sent a quarter's rent in advance, which should put people off the scent, cancelled the paper and milk, asked for the phone line to be cancelled as from January, and filled in the Post Office change of address card with some totally illegible information. By the time they've realized they can't deliver anything, I shall be only a memory. Sorry to let the company down, but they'll have no trouble finding a replacement who wants to spend New Year in Paris. Tomorrow I go to Dover, take the ferry to Calais, then the train to Paris. By the time I arrive, I shall be Ralph Arthur Ferguson. Using his name and passport—funny how a little change in my appearance can make me look so close to his passport picture—I fly out of Orly to New York. I'll stay there a few days, then start looking for my opportunity. 'Ferguson' wrote to his future employers to regret his inability to accept a position with them, after all, as he had elected to spend a year in Europe, 'to broaden his horizons.' I was quite pleased with that touch. Easy to contact Konrad from the States by phone or wire, the bank, too. I have a bank draft for a tidy sum in my wallet, and the information of the Ferguson account to which it will be deposited. I still marvel at the risk that man took, leaving all that personal information in a hotel room. Evidently, though, nothing to the risks he took when he went out at nights, poor bugger.

Ziplich, Grayson and Benny looked at one another. "It was all so simple," Grayson said, "The fellow merely took over a dead man's identity, a man with no other ties. It's as easy as that, provided you have the luck, and Phipps certainly had that."

"Didn't you Limeys ever wonder where Phipps went?" Benny inquired.

"At the time, probably not. As far as we know, nobody ever asked. Now, yes, of course. LaDonna looked all that up, checked his history, looked at his service record—well, you've seen all that. He sold up the house he inherited from his mother, I expect he invested the money, and moved into the flat he mentioned in the diary. We know what jobs he had until he disappeared some time before Christmas, when he failed to report for his tour assignment. The company just wrote him off as unreliable when their communications were ignored, but never thought of reporting it to any authority. Tour leaders are notoriously temperamental. Eventually a missing person notice was issued, but nothing ever came of it."

"No record of that ferry trip to Calais? Surely there was some sort of passport check?" This from Ziplich.

"No. As a rule the officer would check the passport but, as it was British, he might not even have opened it."

"Well, what about the ferry company? They'd've had a manifest of passengers, wouldn't they?"

"Certainly, but remember there was no reason to suppose he'd gone abroad. Phipps took quite a lot of care to avoid that impression. We'll check, naturally, now that we have this somewhat sparse information, but I doubt that any ferry company keeps passenger lists for thirty years or so."

"And that was before any mass computerization, of course. No, you're probably right, Dan. Phipps just disappeared, and Ferguson never did. That's ingenious. But I do wonder how the real Ferguson came to his sticky end. No suspect ever caught for that, was there?"

"If," Benny observed, "his playmates were so kinky, chances are they continued indulging in similar games, possibly with similar results. We might could get the Feds to try the French and see if they have any info on that front, huh?"

"Good idea, Benny, but let's keep the national authorities out of things. They'll want to take over the entire business, and I doubt if any of us would like that. I'll get LaDonna to contact our friends across the Channel."

Ziplich sipped at a cup of cold coffee. "How about the French Customs? Would they have a record of ferry arrivals?"

"Most doubtful. Even in today's security-conscious world such inspection is none too rigorous. Back then, it meant a glance at a passport and an *'anything to declare?' Phipps would have been far too careful to take any risks on either of those fronts. I'll have the queries made, but.." He shrugged, rang LaDonna and told her what was needed, and they went back to their reading.*

November 23

The crossing went well enough, although it was rough and we were late arriving. Amazingly enough, the boat train from Victoria was smack on time. At Calais, nobody showed the least interest in Mr. Ferguson. Bernie Phipps had been burned in an ashtray in the men's loo aboard ship, then his ashes scattered to the winds of the English Channel. That way, anyone looking for a connection between the missing money and Bernie Phipps will run up against a dead end. And I should not have any trouble entering America, since I am now a "US Citizen". Must remember not 'loo,' now, but 'bathroom.' Tried out my American persona on a family from Texas. Accent slipped from time to time, but they didn't seem to notice. Train to Paris had been delayed for us and was fast, so we got to Paris at very nearly the advertised time. It was foggy when we arrived, so I rang the airline to ask if the flight had been delayed. It has, and we are being put up at an unlovely hotel for the night, at airline expense. I could have paid for better, but that might raise unnecessary questions. We will be off, weather permitting, at 11 in the morning.

November 24

I am here without a hitch, sailing through passport control and customs without the least difficulty, and with even a couple of "welcome homes." Took a taxi here from the airport. I chose the Empire Hotel on Broadway because some people on my last tour told me about it. Mr. and Mrs. Weiss, a very nice older couple from Albany, said it's where they stay when they're in New York. I made sure that they had no plans to be here at the same time as me, then booked ahead. They were right, it is ideal, well-placed for just about everything I want to see. Funny that there should have been another Ferguson on that tour, too. Made me feel a bit conspicuous, I can't think why! I intend to take a Gray Line tour tomorrow, to help me learn how to navigate this unfamiliar place. I have to listen to the accents, too, because I know mine is shaky, and I have to be truly American.

"We can stop the search we started on this other Ferguson, then," Ziplich observed. "When we found one on this last trip, we never thought to look farther back, because the connection was so obvious. Too obvious."

November 25

It's cold and gray and miserable weather, and the Gray Line was a good choice. You could see all the sights from the warm and dry bus, getting out only if you felt like it. I really felt quite at home, although it was funny not being the guide. Saw Times Square, the Statue of Liberty, the Empire State Building, the World Trade Center (remember to spell American-style) Wall Street, China Town, Central Park and all the rest. Really quite impressive, but a lot of it seems very dirty. Tomorrow I will do a little exploring on my own. I need to get my money into Ferguson's account. I have been practicing his signature from his passport, insurance policy and other papers he had, and I think I am getting pretty good. It will mean a trip to Rochester, and I think I shall hire—I mean rent—a car. I shall have to get used to American traffic sooner or later, and while I have spent plenty of time on the wrong side of the road in Europe, I am sure the feeling here will be much different. I hope Ferguson was not a very well-known customer.

November 26

Spent the day crisscrossing the city by bus and subway. They use tokens here, although you can put cash in a device next to the bus driver. It won't give you change if you overpay, which I did. You can get transfers from one bus line to another instead of having to pay twice. The subway trains and stations are filthy, encrusted with grime and daubed with graffiti. You can see huge rats in the tunnels and even on the platforms. New Yorkers do not, so far, impress me as outstandingly friendly. I asked a policeman the best way to find my way to the Empire State Building, as I wanted to see the view from the top, and yesterday it had been in cloud. He told me to buy a map. Went to the Times Square area by bus (which is much nicer than subway) and realized it would be possible to walk from the hotel. Times Square is really quite small, more triangular than square and there were lots of people. Turned out that, in addition to all the theatres around here, since Broadway is one of the cross streets which make up the square, there is also a thriving pornography, prostitution and drugs industry. The original Ferguson would probably have loved it. Maybe he did. I think I shall set up a rehabilitation centre—center—when I am able, in his (unacknowledged) memory.

November 27

I am in Rochester. I had not realized the distance, and did not really allow enough time. Got my Avis Ford here barely in time to make the deposit into "my"' bank account without anybody commenting about the appearance of Mr. Ferguson. Thank goodness banks here stay open later than at home. By then it was nearly dark and I didn't fancy the long drive back, so am spending the night here. Shall drive back in the morning. I'll be in need of a shave.

November 28

Returned the Ford, had a meal. Tomorrow I shall start looking for a permanent place to operate from. And something to operate on, since I really have no idea what I am going to do. I certainly have a big financial cushion, but I need an occupation.

November 30

Have found what I think could be an opening by reading the Wall Street Journal. There is an oil company in Oklahoma, Grebe and Oliver, which is selling off some of its assets. The article implies that the company is in financial difficulty, without saying so openly. I think I shall go to Tulsa and take a look. Can't do any harm, might do some good. Will see if I can keep my room here for a couple of months. It's quite a busy place, and they may have some policy about long-term stays, but I'm used to it now, and I like its location. Am running low on cash, will have to start on the American Express card. It works OK, I've used it once, for the car. When I have a permanent base, I'll see about moving the bank account to somewhere more convenient.

December 1

Hotel says I can keep the room at the same rate until the Christmas season starts in earnest, so I have taken it until the 17th of January and will pay the difference for the season. That will give me two weeks to look things over, and a couple of extra days before I hit the much higher rate over the holidays, not that I can't afford it. It still seems funny, even after so long, to think that I really don't need to pinch pennies. On the other hand, it makes no sense just throwing money away. Have booked a flight to Tulsa for tomorrow morning.

December 3

Arrived in Tulsa yesterday, hired (this was crossed out and 'rented' written in its place) a car because there is virtually no public transport I heard someone say, and so it turned out. The agent at the rental desk recommended the Hilton as a good place to stay, so I took his advice, and it seems all right. Drove round the town a little bit. It really is a sprawling place, with some utterly hideous shopping areas and some very pleasant residential neighborhoods. The Downtown district is not very large, but clearly has a few of the better stores as well as offices. Oil companies seem to be everywhere. The local motto appears to be Oil Capital of the World. I thought that was Texas or the Arabian Gulf or somewhere, but there's certainly plenty of oil business here. Nice to see where some of my money may be coming from. Drove past the offices of Grebe and Oliver. Not notably impressive. Today I have put an ad in both of the local papers: "Investor seeks managerial and office staff for oil-related concern. Must be experienced." Got a box number for each paper, which they took care of. Will be running the ad for 4 days, and will see what it reaps. Will go to Bartlesville, about 70 miles from here, tomorrow. It has the headquarters of the Phillips company, and a Frank Lloyd Wright building I would rather like to see.

December 8th

A busy few days. Found several potential employees. One, a William Hewitt, strikes me as a capable man trapped in a dead-end job. He is not in the oil business, but he is certainly intelligent, and

I think he'll serve my ideas very well. He seems like one who is too old (about sixty, I would guess) to take a risk with his retirement. I shall offer him a very good salary and pension plan and see if he bites. I have opened an account at National Bank of Tulsa, with money transferred from Rochester. They gave me a toaster! Tomorrow I am to look over a small house in the Brookside area. It would make a good starting point, I think. I shall also set up a company to make my first transactions as soon as money from Lucerne arrives at the bank. It seems to be quite a simple procedure, and there are lawyers who can take care of it. Thinking of calling it The Windfall Company, in view of its financial origin.

December 15

It seems incredible, but I have done it. Windfall is established, Hewitt is hired as manager, and there are three to assist him in organizing the whole business. What I have learned are called "straw buyers" have been arranged and have already purchased two of the properties Grebe and Oliver had offered for sale. Windfall will, in turn, buy from them. Windfall will take a loss on this, but it will put me in a strong position to get the whole company when it eventually goes down the drain, which it undoubtedly will. Then I can start to build it up again. It's quite clear that the senior management at G&O is hopelessly outdated. They'll have to go, while the few remaining staff will have to be carefully evaluated. I am determined that G&O will become a viable company again, albeit with a different name.

Ziplich, Grayson and Benny skimmed through the details of the various legal and financial transactions—they were the areas the legal experts were already analyzing—and moved on to:

December 30

Back in New York to see in the New Year with the big crowds that gather in Times Square. Christmas alone in Tulsa was very lonely, and I concentrated mainly on being sure that Windfall is going to work. I really believe it is. My little house on 36th Street is modest, just what I want. It's funny, but as an Englishman I couldn't have bought it, since Oklahoma has a law preventing foreigners from legally owning what they call Real Property. Liberty and Justice for All applies selectively, it seems.

January 1 1975

Hung over. Celebrated New Year in a bitterly cold Times Square, with several thousand other fools, and with a good many trips to a Blarney Stone bar. Lots of expatriate Paddies there, and a lot more Americans of Irish extraction. They are far more madly Irish than the real thing. No wonder the IRA manages to raise funds here so easily. Saw two men I had a beer with on the Channel ferry, but turned away before they saw me, as I was behind them. I wonder what they are doing here. Could they be trying to get American money to fund terrorism? Or are they utterly harmless? Difficult to say, but I wonder how they are able to afford a trip to America if they are, as they told me on the boat, clerks in a surveyor's office. I dare not interfere yet, but when I am properly established in business, I shall try to find some way to help prevent the mindless violence on both sides of the Irish dispute. Returning to Tulsa at the end of the week. I shall pay the hotel the agreed costs up to January the 17th, so as to leave a good impression for the future. I daresay I'll come to NYC fairly often in the course of business, and it will be nice to have a decent welcome.

"It is," Grayson said, "time to speak again to LaDonna. My colleague, Jacko Perkins, described Riordan and Tobin as 'fundraisers.' We should find out if they were away on one of their fishing expeditions at this period. If so, then the Irish connection to Ferguson's death becomes almost inescapable. It would be entirely possible that these two could have noticed Ferguson, despite his belief that they hadn't, followed him back to his hotel, and found out who he was."

"Why would they do that? What was to gain?" wondered Benny.

"They'd probably seen him on the boat. Ferguson said he'd seen them. They might well find it difficult to believe that a man who had been on the ferry with them would find them by accident in New York. They'd smell a rat."

"Then why not waste him right away?" Ziplich asked.

"*They would have had to be sure. Irish terrorists didn't kill individuals at random. They may have blown up innocent civilians en masse, but they didn't target just one person without a good reason. Good to them, that is,*" Grayson added. "*To do so in a foreign country, especially this one, would not have been at all in their interests.*"

"*It sure took 'em a long time to be certain,*" Benny remarked.

"*Think about it, Benny. The two follow Ferguson back to his hotel. They find out his name from the desk clerk, if they can get that information. Even if they do, they won't know where he's based, because he certainly won't have given his old address, and his new Tulsa one didn't exist when he checked in. So that's a dead end for them. What do they do? They could watch him, but he was leaving, and they wouldn't know his destination when he departed for Tulsa. You can be sure that the airline won't give out passenger information without an official reason, so they're stuck there, too. How much time could they spend on this if they were supposed to be fundraising? When were they due to return to Belfast? A lot of questions, all fruitless until we determine whether or not these two really were Tobin and Riordan. If they were away from home during that period, I'd say we have strong grounds for suspicion, rather than our present mere speculation. As I said, I'll get on to LaDonna. She'll be able to find out from Jacko, or through her own channels. We can rely on her, as you well know. We have no way yet of knowing how they finally managed to find the right Ferguson, the one who had taken their money, or whether they ever connected him to the man in New York at a New Year celebration three decades ago. In a country the size of this one, someone who wants to disappear can easily do so, as long as the law isn't looking for him. In Ferguson's case, the law had no reason to take an interest. Anyway, I'll get with 'Donna first thing. Maybe she'll have gathered something from the French about the real Ferguson's unpleasant playmates, too.*"

After consulting his watch, Ziplich suggested it was time to call it a day. "*We still got a long way to go, and a lot to read,*" he said, "*and we'll do it better fresh in the morning.*"

As it turned out, the morning was to prove quite busy.

Chapter 11
June 2011

Grayson had set his alarm for three thirty, reasoning that La-Donna would have had plenty of time to get settled in her office if he called her at four, which would be 10 o'clock London time. That would enable him to make a cup of coffee; he had learned to bring enough coffee and some real milk from the nearest QuikTrip to satisfy his morning wake-up needs. LaDonna was a little surprised to hear his voice at what she knew to be a very early hour in Tulsa, but she listened to his request about Riordan and Tobin's whereabouts at the end of December, 1974, and promised to find out. Then she gave Grayson the news that the French investigators had, indeed, uncovered a ring given to extreme practices of a sexual nature, and there had been two more deaths in the five years following that of the real Ferguson. His body, incidentally, had never been officially identified and, after the statutory period with no claim made for it, was interred. The file remained dormant, but not closed.

"Fourteen of these odd people, there were," LaDonna informed Grayson, "and it seems that they liked to pick their victims up in the sleazier places of Paris. They worked on the assumption that frequenters of such establishments were likely to be responsive to their suggestions, and apparently they were only too right. Three have themselves died, and the others are locked away and won't see daylight for many years yet. There's no telling how many other people became involved with them over a period of several years, but speculation is that it runs at least into the hundreds. They, of course, are not likely ever to offer information. My opposite number at the Surete, Lisette Blondel, tells me that the authorities over there are of the opinion that a good many may have changed their ideas of what the definition of 'fun' is."

"I can well imagine," Grayson told her. "Well, I hope life isn't too depressing without my sparkling company, but I rather feel we're getting somewhere with this case and I expect to be home before much longer. Can't really tell you what 'much longer' means, since oddities keep popping up, but a week, ten days should probably put this business to bed. The people here are quite splendid, but the heat is appalling, and I shall be delighted to return to gray skies and drizzle."

"Actually, it's twenty-three degrees and sunny," he was informed. "I'll get back to you with the information on the Irish gentlemen."

"Thank you, 'Donna, you're a treasure." LaDonna experienced a little frisson of pleasure at his words, and set about her latest task. Grayson made some more coffee.

Kohler had followed Bernadette to the motel, and reported back. Lieutenant Malcolm arranged a relief system for round-the-clock surveillance there, and a similar set-up for Officer Black to be replaced at the Renaissance Hotel. The man calling himself Alfred Combs had dined at the hotel, then retired to his room. The police watchers took up station in the room across the corridor from his and took it in turn to peer through a spyhole in the door. Mr. Combs remained in his room until the morning. At eight o'clock precisely, he went down to breakfast, after which he returned to his room, leaving it again at nine-fifteen and carrying a suitcase. He checked out, with profuse apologies for having to leave at such short notice, went to his car, and drove off. Officer Thornton followed at a discreet distance, reporting in on his cellphone that Combs seemed to be heading for the airport and receiving instructions from Malcolm to stick to him "like shit to a blanket." Combs returned his car to Avis, then entered the terminal and went into a men's restroom on the upper level. Thornton went to the Dollar Rent-a-Car desk, from which he could watch the entrance of the restroom, and browsed through a couple of brochures. A man came out of the men's room, but it wasn't the elegant Combs. This guy was wearing jeans and a plaid shirt, a baseball cap and rimless glasses. He had almost passed out of sight when Thornton realized the man was carrying Combs's suitcase.

Thornton was in a quandary. Did he go into the toilet to look for Combs, or did he follow the suitcase? He opted for the latter, and strode after the loping figure, which was by now leaving the terminal and heading toward the taxis lined up outside. Thornton's car was parked on the lower Departures level. He dashed down the nearest stairs to his vehicle, pulling away with a squeal of tyres which made the duty airport security officer, who knew him, look up in surprise. It was close, but Thornton glimpsed a plaid shirt and a ball cap in a cab about a hundred yards ahead of him, and he settled down for a leisurely pursuit, reporting in on his cellphone to Lieutenant Malcolm.

Malcolm, in his turn, contacted the airport security office to request a search of the men's toilet, and was assured a few minutes later that there was no unexplained person there. Thornton, then, had been right to follow the suitcase, which was by now heading into the downtown area, arriving at the Doubletree Hotel. Thornton watched his quarry enter the lobby, then pulled his car into the forecourt and followed. A flash of his badge forestalled the protest of the doorman at such flouting of the parking regulations.

Youssef, no longer Mr. Alfred Combs, was at the desk arranging for a room and a rental car, this time from Hertz. Details having been settled to his satisfaction, he turned and walked toward the elevator, passing Thornton on his way. He gave no sign, but Youssef recognised Thornton immediately as the man at the Dollar desk in the airport, and realized that he was being followed. His life, given his profession, had often depended on his finely-tuned powers of observation and this development meant that he was, at the very least, under suspicion.

Youssef wasted no time speculating how it was he had come to be watched, but concentrated his mind on the best means of leaving the building unobserved. Was it surrounded? Probably not, otherwise there would have been an attempt to stop him. Very well, he would find a way out that avoided the lobby. Luck was with him. A notice proclaimed that there was an air bridge to the parking garage. Youssef took the elevator to the sixth floor, where his assigned room was, waited a few minutes, then took the elevator down again, sharing it with a thin, balding man and getting out where the air bridge would allow him to cross to the garage. The other man continued to the lobby, where Thornton, who was on his phone to Lieutenant Malcolm, recognized him as that Limey who was working with Zee and Benny.

Walking across the bridge, Youssef found himself in a typical multi-story car park with ramps to go up or down and marked parking spaces. There were plenty of cars to choose from, and he selected an older Pontiac, which, he judged accurately, would not have an alarm. It was the work of moments for his expert hands to open the door, hotwire the ignition and start down the ramp. There was no attendant at the exit, and the gate was up. Youssef turned onto Seventh Street just as a police car drove up to the hotel entrance.

Kohler was back on watch when Bernadette set off to the Fergoil building. Jenna Grant greeted her unwelcome guest in her usual pale way, and conducted her to the conference room, promising that coffee would be forthcoming shortly. Bernadette lit up the computer and set about completing her preparations for cleaning out the Fergoil bank balances. The actual transfers would be electronic to a variety of mostly offshore accounts, untraceable through the Internet. It did occur to her that they hadn't considered acquiring Ferguson's personal money, which was doubtless considerable, but that might be tempting Fate a bit too much. Miss Grant phoned Lieutenant Malcolm's office to report Bernadette's arrival, which Kohler had already done anyway, and was told that the lieutenant was on a case but was expected back shortly; the information would be passed to him.

Grayson had walked down the road to the office. Ziplich and Benny were already there, leafing through the diaries when he arrived, since Grayson had dozed off again after talking to LaDonna, and he apologised for being late.

"No problem, Dan," Ziplich said. "Seems we got ourselves a bit of movement." And he told Grayson what had happened on the "Mr. Combs" front.

"So he's in my hotel?" Grayson was surprised. "Any idea who he really is? Damnation, there are just too many people who are somebody else in this affair, what with the Irish, Ferguson and now this character."

"No, we don't know who he is, but he's a real chameleon. If Thornton hadn't been sharp, the guy would've gotten away clean." The phone rang. "Ziplich. Yeah, lieutenant? You're kidding. Got a description? Of course, from Thornton. Okay, I'll get it circulated. You coming back here? Right, I'll get on it right away." He hung up and turned to the others. "The bastard's disappeared, changed his appearance again. Got to get his new description out ASAP." He picked up the phone again and dialled. "Yeah, Lena, this is Zee. Listen, I need an all points on this right away. Looking for a guy, white, medium height, dressed in plaid shirt, jeans, baseball cap, rimless glasses, carrying an expensive leather suitcase. Probably armed, believed extremely dangerous. Stop and arrest if possible, otherwise observe. Don't put anyone in harm's way. Hang on a minute." He turned to Grayson, who was gesticulating at him. "You got something, Dan?"

"I rather think so. Chap fitting that description came down with me in the lift. I saw him heading for the air bridge to the parking area when he got off, and just a moment before I got here, he passed me driving a grey car."

"You get the make?"

"Unfortunately, I'm not yet familiar with American cars, so no."

"Lena? He may be driving a grey car, make unknown. I'll get back with you if I can get a tag number. Thanks, hon." Next, Ziplich called Malcolm. "Lieutenant, it's likely our suspect stole a car out of the hotel parking garage. Can you get the guests alerted, and see if anyone is missing their vehicle? If someone is, let's get the tag number. At the very least we'd have a theft felony here. You'll get back to me? Great, thanks." Once again he turned to the others. "Now we wait a bit."

They didn't have to wait long. A Mr. Trent Lowther, salesman from La Cygne, Kansas, burst into the hotel lobby, shouting that his car had been stolen. Malcolm and Thornton managed to get him calmed down, explaining that they were police, and copying down the licence number of a 1995 Pontiac Grand Am, which they then passed on to Ziplich. He rang Lena with the information, and the waiting started again.

❖ ❖ ❖

Carol Ziplich, as the most junior of junior partners, had been selected to do the liaison work with Jenna Grant, of Fergoil, regarding properties held both by Fergoil as a company and Ralph Ferguson as an individual. Some properties, notably the private houses owned by the late Ferguson, would have to be sold, while others would be merged to produce a new, more streamlined, company. Fergoil would survive, that was the general consensus, but it would take careful management. Careful, not over-cautious. So Carol arrived at the Fergoil office confident that she was going to have a hand in shaping the future of what could become, she thought, a major factor in petrochemical development. This despite the capping-off of the clandestine well in Ferguson's basement. She was greeted by Jenna Grant, who displayed more than customary animation.

"We have something of a situation, here," she told Carol. "There's a phoney IRS woman in the conference room, and she's trying to cook the books. We don't know who she is, but I guess the police have got their eye on her."

Carol, who had noticed Agent Kohler at the concession stand, nodded her understanding. "It's the view of the police that she's connected in some way with the death of Mr. Ferguson, but there's not, as far as I know, any real hard evidence, so they're just watching her."

"At the very least, she's impersonating an official, and that makes her a criminal," Jenna Grant continued. Carol, who had rather more knowledge of police strategy, held her tongue. Although her husband, in accordance with his orders, had not given her details of the operation being mounted to find the killer or killers of Ferguson and Taylor, she was well aware that there would indeed be a careful eye kept on Fergoil, and she had been by no means surprised to see Kohler downstairs.

"Well, I don't doubt they know what they're doing," she assured Jenna. "Maybe we could take a look at this person, just out of curiosity. In the meantime, there are a few points I'd like to go over with you." Jenna led her to only the third office she had occupied ever since first joining Fergoil almost twenty years previously. The first move had been from clerical work in the general office to becoming Ferguson's secretary when the company had transferred from its original premises to a newer, larger building, the one which had been destroyed by the tornado. The second had been, of course, when that office had ceased to exist. The room into which she now ushered Carol was unremarkable, containing all the essentials of her profession, but few light touches. There was, Carol noted, a framed photograph of Ferguson on the desk. There was a coffee maker on a credenza, and Carol accepted Jenna's offer of a cup, no cream or sugar, then settled herself in a chair across the desk from Jenna.

After a few minutes of conversation concerning the everyday running of the company, Carol explained the main purpose of her visit. "It's the real estate, you see, that concerns us a bit. Fergoil holds a large number of properties, some more profitable than others, some not profitable at all, and there are three cases where Fergoil holds adjacent pieces of real estate. While Mr. Ferguson was alive, he insisted to us that he had good reasons for these, sometimes unusual, arrangements. Would you have any idea what those reasons might be?"

Jenna shook her head. "No, he seldom explained his reasons for what sometimes seemed slightly strange decisions. The thing is, though, he was almost always right, and very seldom did any of his purchases or sales go wrong. Oh, there were one or two, naturally, but overall he had an amazing success record. That was his biggest strength, I suppose, his ability to judge the value, or more frequently the potential value, of a transaction, and the company did very well because of it."

Consulting some notes from her briefcase, Carol asked, "How about personal property? As you know, our firm handled all the company real estate deals, but we don't really know much about other buildings or land. We do know, of course, about the house in Maple Ridge, that's common knowledge. Everybody knows, too, that he shared it with Miss Taylor. She, I believe, once lived in the Brookside area, and I wondered if that were one of Mr. Ferguson's houses, too. Perhaps there are, or were, others?" Carol avoided any mention of the basement oil rig.

"Well, there's the lake house, of course," Jenna began, and Carol remembered the little Ziplich had told her about that, "and he owns a few small rental houses in the TU area, although fewer now since the college has built so many dorms. He rents them out to students at very low rates, thinking that it's a way to help out needier students without making it look like charity. I believe he takes—took, I mean," she said sadly, "a considerable loss on those. If you'd like more details about all these things, I can give you the name of the attorney who handled all the transactions. There's another example of the kind of man Ralph Ferguson was. He could have hired anybody, but he selected a young woman, who'd shared a rental in one of his houses while she attended the University, almost as soon as she graduated. It was a great start for her, and I know she didn't disappoint him."

Jenna tapped for a couple of moments at her computer keyboard, and in another few seconds, the printer presented the name of Althea Gurney, attorney at law, together with both her home and office addresses and telephone numbers, as well as numbers for fax and cellphone, and an email address. Jenna passed the sheet of paper to Carol.

"She'll be able to answer all your questions, I'm sure."

"I'm very interested about this lake house you mentioned," Carol said. "Is that the one up in the Missouri Ozarks?"

"Yes. I've been there a few times—well, a lot of times, really. He used it as a place to get away from business pressures, as well as giving top employees a break from time to time. The actual house is huge, bigger than his Tulsa home, and there are cabins in the grounds for extra guests. That's where Fergoil employees went when they'd done especially well. There's a caretaker couple who look after the place, and I guess they have it pretty easy most of the time."

"Why not somewhere nearer, Grand Lake, say?"

"He said there were two reasons for that. One, the land was for sale cheaply— not all the big developments they have going there nowadays. Two, it was far enough away that he wouldn't be bothered in the same way as if he were real nearby. There's the phone, fax and all that stuff, naturally, but not the physical presence. He valued that distance, sometimes."

"But it's, what? Two, three hundred miles? That's a lot of commuting time."

"Not for Mr. Ferguson. He keeps a Cessna at Jones airport, and a Range Rover at Camdenton airport. He just flew up there in an hour or so, had what he called his 'down time,' and flew back again. To go by road takes somewhere between four and five hours, depending on traffic."

"Sounds like a place I'd like to see."

"By the time all the legal points have been cleared up, you'll probably have seen more of it than you care to remember. After all, you won't be flying."

Which goes to prove that it is unwise to make predictions.

Youssef, never a man to waste time on wondering what had gone wrong, made a rapid decision. If he were under surveillance—and he quite obviously was—then that meant that the Irish money man must be here. Why would anybody but the Irish be interested in him? There was not, to his knowledge, any official concern with him so, yes, it must be the Irish. That, in turn, indicated that they were preparing to extract money from Fergoil, the money he wanted himself. It also meant that the oaf, Malone, was here. Malone had to be disposed of, representing, as he did, a possible danger. Besides, it would be a pleasure to deal with him, just as it had been with Nolan in London. Youssef regarded the Irish as a bunch of clumsy fools, and was irritated with his own organization for doing business with them, even though he understood the potential benefits to be enormous. If the money were being removed from Fergoil, somebody was at the Fergoil office to do the job. That was where he should seek his quarry. No time like the present.

Parking the Pontiac well away from the street, where the casual eye would not immediately notice it, Youssef took the side entrance into the office building, and was at once confronted by the sight of the policeman he had spoken to on his first reconnaissance. Officer Kohler displayed no interest in the man who bore not the slightest resemblance to Alfred Combs, but to Youssef he offered both a danger and an opportunity.

"'Scuse me," he said, "I sure hate to disturb you, but is there any chance you could give me a jump start? Looks like my battery's dead."

"Sure," said the obliging Kohler, figuring a couple of minutes would be safe enough, and the pair went out to the Pontiac. Kohler brought the Toyota over, pulled some jumper cables from the trunk, then opened the hood to connect the cables to his battery terminals. From behind, Youssef used both hands to jerk back and twist violently Kohler's head. The sound of a neck breaking was unmistakable. Youssef, with a quick glance about to ensure there had been no observers, pulled the inert body to the back of the Toyota, dropped it in the trunk, and relieved it of the standard-issue hand gun that Kohler had carried. He shut the lid, closed the engine hood, and drove the car to an empty parking space. There he locked it, then returned to the office building and took the elevator up to the main Fergoil floor.

At the reception desk Youssef said; "You the lady who called about the computer problem?"

The receptionist, a pretty but inexperienced young woman, looked puzzled. "Computer problem?"

"Yeah, with the person who's doing the audit, I guess," said Youssef, who really was guessing. He had made a note of the names of two of the other companies in the building to provide him with an "I'm sorry, I must be in the wrong office. This isn't the Batby Company?" exit strategy. It wasn't necessary.

"Oh, yes," the receptionist exclaimed, "she's in the conference room. Down that corridor, first on the right."

"Thanks," said Youssef, heading in the direction indicated, at the same time thinking; *She?*

He knocked on the door and entered upon a called out "Come in." A petite, dark-haired young woman was seated at a computer, whose screen displayed rows of figures, apparently in various categories.

"Yes? Can I help you?" Her accent was pure American, not Irish, and just for a moment Youssef wondered if he'd made a mistake and this really was a legitimate auditor, but her immediate move to insert her body between him and the screen, then to close the program, told him otherwise.

"I do believe you can," he told her with a smile, and then the door opened again, admitting two more women. This was not what Youssef had hoped for at all, and he slipped behind the new arrivals and shut the door, leaning against it.

"Who are you?" demanded the older of the two newcomers, a wispy woman with a slightly defeated air. The other woman, the black one, just looked at him.

"I doubt that my name would mean anything to you," Youssef said, "although I strongly suspect that the names Malone and O'Neill might." He noted with satisfaction the reaction of the "auditor". "Ah, I see I was correct. You, madam," he was addressing Bernadette, "will continue with your work. Do not try to deceive me by meaningless inputs: I am quite familiar with financial practices, and will be able to pick up on any false move on your part." This was totally untrue, but he was banking on it that nervousness would work in his favor. To reinforce his words, he partially drew Kohler's handgun from his pocket, allowing the women to recognise it as a weapon before he dropped it back.

"When you have fully identified the total assets of Fergoil, which you are attempting to steal, you will, instead, transfer them to an account number which I shall give you. Again, do not attempt to encrypt or to add worms or Trojans," he was throwing out any computing term he could remember, "as they will be instantly recognised, and you will regret any such attempt. Is that clear?"

Bernadette nodded mutely, mentally cursing herself for forcing Riordan to remain at the motel, and returned to her program. She was quite sure that this man was coldly vicious, and that he would not hesitate to use any form of violence to attain his ends. While she was devoted to her cause, she was not suicidal, so she continued from where she had halted. She had been, indeed, on the brink of finishing her task. It had merely remained to open the Internet and make the electronic transfer. Now, with everything set to pull up the 'net, she tapped 'enter.' Nothing happened for a few moments, then large red letters filled the screen "ACCESS DENIED." Frustrated, Bernadette made a few adjustments, then tried again. "ACCESS DENIED."

She muttered a few muffled curses, and was about to make a third attempt, when Jenna Grant said mildly, "You won't get access, you know. It's been blocked all the time. We just needed to give you enough rope..." She left the rest to the imaginations of both Bernadette and Youssef. Carol Ziplich, who had been brought in here to get a look at the "IRS auditor," had so far said nothing, merely standing close to the older woman with a faint smile on her lips.

Youssef could feel his control of the situation slipping away, an unwelcome sensation to which he was not accustomed, and one to which he now responded with a growled "Who are you?" directed at Carol.

"Me? Oh, I'm nobody important. Just passing by, so to speak, and getting caught up in a surprising piece of excitement. Tell me, sir, are you a terrorist or something? I've never met a terrorist."

Stung, Youssef snarled, "I am not a terrorist! I work for my country and the majority of its people who do not even realise how they could be made free for ever, just as your own people do not fully understand what the whites subject you to. Terrorist? There is your terrorist"—this pointing at Bernadette—"her and her fool of an accomplice. He's somewhere here, I know it, and he will show himself, the precious Malone." Bernadette's head jerked up again at the name. "Ah, yes, you do know him. Then know, also, that I shall destroy him, and you shall help me do it."

He drew the gun from his pocket and, gaining more control of himself, smiled without humor. "Now, ladies, we shall leave, because I still have work to do. Since it seems that can't be done here—a clumsy attempt on your part, Irishwoman—we'll have to make different arrangements."

"May I make a suggestion?" Carol asked.

"Don't think you can trap me: I am very experienced in..."

"But you're right, don't you understand?" Carol broke in. "I'm sick of being treated as a servant. It's a double insult: one to me as Black—I refuse to say 'African-American'—and one as a woman. You say my people don't understand. Well, that may be true for some of them, but not for me. I want freedom, the freedom I've been denied since I was a child." Her voice was rising, a note of hysteria faintly discernible as her words now came rushing out. "The freedom my parents never knew, or my grandparents. Why do we always have to be second class, despite the new President?

"Why does this woman here," she gestured at an aghast Jenna Grant, "get to hold a decent position while I'm only allowed to bring in coffee and clean offices? They show me a woman working at a computer, but she's white, too. She may be a terrorist, I don't know and I don't care. She's obviously got some kind of trust, the kind I never get. The hell with all of them! They call this the Land of the Free. Only if your face isn't black!" She stopped suddenly, as if she had lost all energy, and started to weep. "I'm sorry, I'm sorry, it's just that...." Carol broke down completely, slumping into one of the chairs placed around the conference table at which Bernadette had been working.

"That man," the words were almost inaudible, "that man. He deserved to die. He treated us like dirt, paid us starvation wages, and all the time he had his big cars, his country estates, his private airplane. Did he ever think of the people who made it all possible? No! We were used, exploited..." The rest of what she said was lost in great heaving sobs.

For a moment, the sobs were all that could be heard. Then Youssef said, very softly, "Airplane?"

LaDonna's latest news for Grayson was threefold. First, the French had no record of the entry of either a Phipps or a Ferguson—or anybody else, for that matter— that long ago. Second, the Swiss bank account had no name attached to it, merely a password known only to the account holder. However, the bank, mindful of complaints levelled at some of its rivals concerning illegal deposits made as a result of World War II crimes, agreed to reveal certain transactional information, while preserving the anonymity of the account holder. The Phipps/Ferguson account, as LaDonna knew it to be, currently held more than two billion dollars. Sums totalling in excess of one billion had been defrayed over the past four years, but dividends and other deposits had far outweighed that figure, enhanced during the petroleum crisis. Certain charities, notably the Windfall McDonough Trust and the Windfall Paris Victims' Fund, had received substantial figures on a regular basis. In addition, large sums had been intermittently transmitted to a bank in the Cayman Islands. Third, Tobin and Riordan were known to have been in the United States at the time Ferguson was enjoying the 1975 New Year celebrations.

"We now have a virtual certainty on our hands," Grayson informed Ziplich, Benny and Malcolm. Lieutenant Malcolm was having some problems in keeping his superiors from becoming over anxious about the Ferguson murder, but contended that a solution was not far off. He hoped he was right. The Ferguson case was taking a lot of his department's time, and the backlog of other important—if less pressing—cases continued to grow. So far, at least, there had been no interference from the FBI, Homeland Security or other law-enforcement agencies. "Riordan and Tobin must have seen Phipps at the New Year thing in Times Square. They probably followed him to his hotel and found out that he was a Mr. Ferguson from...well, we don't know where he claimed to be from, but it was certainly an American address, probably Ferguson's old one in Rochester. So, the Englishman they had talked to on the cross channel ferry was now an American. If you were a member of a covert society, wouldn't that make your whiskers quiver? Someone, evidently of a certain substance, with something to hide. A prime target for blackmail. What a nice fundraising device!"

"I still don't see how they traced him to here," objected Benny.

"Neither do I," Grayson agreed. "We really need to talk to these people, this Bernadette Whats'ername and the ubiquitous Jimmy Riordan. Shall we collect 'em, Stan, and see whether they're ready to chat a little? Bernadette, at least, is committing a felony, probably as we speak, while both she and Riordan are here on false papers. Since your Mr. Kohlcr followed the lady to an insalubrious hostelry, we may assume her nefarious partner has taken up temporary residence there. Let's pick him up. Mr. Kohler is at the Fergoil building, so let's ask him to go inside and invite the Irish lady to come here for a few quiet words, as well. What say you?"

"I say 'Aye,'" Malcolm returned, and thought, *Ouch, he's got me at it now, too.* He used the office intercom to send word to Officer Black to collect a couple of colleagues, "Wilson and Steinmetz will be fine," and go and offer hospitality to Jimmy Riordan. After all, his present accommodation was less than luxurious. Then Malcolm tried to raise Kohler on his cellphone, but there was no answer. Three attempts later and Malcolm was becoming concerned. "Benny?"

"On my way, lieutenant."

Jimmy Riordan, watching "Ellen," heard a discreet tap on the door. "Have ye lost the bloody key, woman?" he called out, and a female voice responded,

"I must have. Let me in, Jimmy." Riordan opened the door, and was confronted with two police officers, with handguns drawn, and a young woman in plain clothes. He decided not to decline their invitation to accompany them.

Benny called Malcolm to report that Kohler was nowhere to be seen, although his car was here. Benny had not yet approached the Fergoil office, but was prepared to do so, if those were his instructions.

"No, Benny, not yet. Have you checked out Kohler's car? Did he leave anything in it that might help?"

"I tried the door, that's all. It's locked."

"Can you open it anyway?"

"That a serious question, lieutenant?"

"No. Open it."

"Okay." A pause. "Nothin' useful here that I can see."

"How about the trunk?"

"Hang on just a minute." Another pause, then: "I got Kohler here, lieutenant. He's in the trunk and he's dead. What's more, his piece is missing."

"Stay right where you are, Benny. I'll get backup. Do not approach the Fergoil office on any account. Someone is very dangerous, and I believe it's the guy who wasted Ferguson. He's back to finish whatever his original job was meant to be, and that's somehow connected with the Irish. It's got to be the money. Anyway, stay put till our guys get there."

"Okay, lieutenant."

Ziplich was already setting the wheels in motion, and in minutes a contingent of five cars was on its way from the Riverside police station, with four more heading from Downtown. Another three were pulled off routine patrol and instructed to join their colleagues at Fergoil.

"Silent approach," Malcolm ordered, "and no lights. Surround the building, and wait for the negotiating team to arrive. I want to avoid further bloodshed if possible, and at least one of our suspects is an armed killer. We're on our way."

Malcolm, Ziplich and Grayson dashed to the parking area, pausing only for a moment to pick up a gun each.

"Can you use this?" Malcolm asked Grayson, indicating a Smith and Wesson.

"I think so," replied Grayson, who had an awesome reputation with the weapons instructor at the range in the basement of his own office building.

Within moments their car was hurtling through the streets, lights flashing and siren wailing. Traffic before them parted like the Red Sea at the command of Moses. "Is this 'silent approach?'" Grayson asked nervously, as the speedometer topped eighty-five on Riverside Drive.

"It will be, when we get a bit closer to the target," Malcolm replied, swinging past an elderly lady so small she was scarcely able to see over the steering wheel of her Cadillac, and narrowly missing a car heading in the opposite direction: neither vehicle made any attempt to pull over and allow the police car through. In less urgent cases, Malcolm might have paused to have well-chosen words with the drivers. Grayson, remembering the trip back from Missouri, was glad that it was not Benny driving. Leaving the lights flashing, Malcolm cut the siren several blocks from the Fergoil offices. "Here's your 'silent approach,' Dan," he said, as they neared the building. He switched off the flashing lights, and turned into the parking lot.

Ten of the twelve other assigned vehicles were already there, and the remaining two arrived almost simultaneously. Malcolm sought out the senior officer present, Sergeant Schenk. "Got your men deployed, Matt?"

"Yeah, lieutenant, got the place surrounded, like you said, with the exits all covered, but no one's gone inside yet. No one's come out, either," he added with a grim smile. "I guess the sight of nearly twenty armed cops helps 'em to stay where they are."

"Where's Benny?"

"Benny, lieutenant? I haven't seen him. He supposed to be here?"

With the thought of Kohler's death still fresh in his mind, Malcolm was distinctly worried. "Yeah, Matt, he should be. Seen his car?"

"Don't know what he's driving, lieutenant. Do you?"

Malcolm didn't, but Ziplich said: "Blue '09 Honda Accord."

They all glanced around the parking lot. Four Accords, none of them blue.

"Where the hell's he at?" Malcolm demanded of nobody in particular. "I told him to stay put. He hasn't called in. It's not like Benny to just vanish. Must be a reason."

"Following the suspect?" Ziplich suggested. "After all, his car's not here."

"Then why didn't he tell anybody? Zee, I'm worried about him after what happened to Kohler. Get on to the office and tell them to relay any communication they get from him. The rest of us, let's go see what's going on at Fergoil."

Several people were in the lobby as the officers entered cautiously, and the questions were all the obvious ones. "What's happening?" "Who're you after?" "Can we get out, now?" "Is it safe in here?" and the like. The police response was equally predictable: "Just keep calm, let us handle things, it's going to be alright." Malcolm directed the operation, herding the onlookers to one side, sending a contingent of officers to the Fergoil office via the stairs and then taking the elevator, along with Ziplich, Grayson and two more policemen, up to the reception floor. The elevator door slid open, and they slipped carefully into the office. The pretty receptionist looked up with her professional welcoming smile.

"Good morning, gentlemen, how may I help you?" Then she noticed the five drawn guns. "Oh!" And she fainted.

Leaving one of the officers to revive her, Malcolm and the others entered the main offices. Everything appeared normal, with computers much in use and the usual office hum in the air, the smell of coffee from an industrial-size dispenser in one corner. Nobody took the slightest notice of the intruders. Indeed, it's doubtful whether they even noticed anyone was there, so deeply did they seem immersed in their work. The four moved on to what turned out to be a conference room. It was empty, except for the long table, the chairs, a credenza, a projection screen at one end of the room, and a computer on the table. The computer screen read "ACCESS DENIED." The next office, smaller, was evidently that of Jenna Grant. Ziplich suddenly remembered that Carol had been coming to see Jenna today to deal with some legal property issues. He was appalled to realise that he hadn't even connected her professional interest in Fergoil with his own investigation. What was he thinking? How could he have allowed her to be sent here when he knew that the Ferguson murder inquiry was centred in this very office? And where was she now? Where, for that matter, was the Bernadette woman? Or Jenna Grant? Ziplich felt a deep sinking in the pit of his stomach. The unknown man, the one who had called himself Combs, had been here. He just knew it. And suddenly he had a mental picture of Malcolm passing a little old lady in a Cadillac, and almost hitting another car. A grey Pontiac Grand Am! Ziplich strove to recall the face of the driver; man in a plaid shirt and baseball cap.

"Shit!" Ziplich snarled bitterly, and the others stared at him. "They were in the car we nearly bumped on Riverside. It was heading north as we were heading south. Grey Grand Am, the one stolen from the Doubletree."

"Zee, how do you know?" Malcolm asked him.

"I can see him now. It didn't strike me then, but now that the Irish woman has disappeared, Jenna Grant isn't here either and neither is Carol, who had an appointment here this morning, I just know that's it. They've been taken hostage, and I'll bet Benny is on their tail."

"Then why didn't he report in? Judging from poor Kohler, we have reason to fear for Benny's safety, too."

"Don't know why he hasn't communicated—lack of time, maybe—but his car's gone, and this Combs guy, or whoever he really is, can't drive two of 'em. No, Benny's behind him."

"Could Combs have an accomplice?" This from Grayson.

"Been no indication of one up to now. No, Benny is on this, and sooner or later he'll be able to let us know what's happened. Let's get out of here." They returned to the reception desk, where a very shaken young woman was being soothed by a policeman clearly out of his depth in such a position.

Malcolm asked her gently: "Do you know where Miss Grant is, please?"

"She...she went out with the lady from the auditors, and the man who was fixing her computer. There was something wrong with it... the computer, I mean, and he couldn't fix it here and they...they had to go to his workshop, or something. I...I guess I'm a bit confused. I don't like guns," she ended lamely.

"Of course not. Tell me, was there anyone else with Miss Grant when she went out?"

"Yes, there was another lady, an African-American. She's an attorney, I think, and she came to see Miss Grant at about, oh, nine-fifteen."

"And what time did they all leave?"

"Around twenty, thirty minutes ago, I guess." She glanced at her watch. "That'd be just before ten."

"Thanks, Honey, you've been very helpful. You better get some coffee, maybe take the rest of the day off. I'll see to it that it's okay."

"Oh, I'm alright now. But I would like to know what's going on."

"It won't be long before you do. Right now, though, it has to remain confidential." They went back to the parking lot, where Malcolm sent most of the officers back to their regular duties, at the same time sending out a renewed APB for the grey Pontiac and another for Benny's blue Honda. While that was being done, Ziplich's cellphone rang. It was Benny.

"I'm at Riverside airport," he said. "Followed almost every damn suspect you can imagine: the guy in the plaid shirt, the Irish woman, Jenna Grant and," he paused fractionally, "your wife, Zee."

"We figured he's taking hostages, Benny, in Carol and Jenna. Don't know about this Irish woman, whether she's working with him or against him but, for the moment, we'll assume with. He's armed, as you know, since he took Kohler's weapon. You got yours?"

"Course."

"Good. Listen, don't approach them, but see if you can find out what these characters are up to. Why didn't you contact us sooner?"

"Cellphone died; don't ask me why, battery, maybe. I'm on an airport payphone right now."

"Okay, we're on our way over. See ya."

Within moments, Malcolm, Ziplich and Grayson were speeding towards the river, crossing by the 71st Street bridge, and turning south, a road sign reading "Jones Airport."

"I thought you said Riverside," Grayson said to Ziplich.

"Same place," Ziplich told him. "It's just that a lot of us use the old names of things we're used to, even if the name changes at some time."

"Ah, yes," acknowledged Grayson, "I'm the same with pubs."

There were small aircraft taking off and landing with considerable frequency.

"Flying schools," said Ziplich in answer to Grayson's unspoken question as a small twin-engine plane passed overhead. "Sky gets pretty crowded, sometimes." They pulled up next to a blue Honda. A short distance away, a grey Pontiac was parked. Benny appeared from a doorway.

"They've gone. Turns out Ferguson kept a plane here, used it for business and pleasure. Guys here know Jenna Grant, allowed her to check out the aircraft by phone, and had it all ready and warmed up by the time they arrived. Guy with her has a valid pilot's license in the name of, can you guess, Alfred Combs. They filed a flight plan for Dodge City."

"Alert the authorities there," Malcolm snapped. "Then let's see them try to 'get out of Dodge fast!'"

"One moment, lieutenant," said Benny. "I'd like to show you this. I found it outside the hangar." "This" was a small handkerchief, the initials CZ delicately embroidered on it. There was a lipstick smear.

"So?" demanded Malcolm.

"It's Carol's, lieutenant," Ziplich said, his throat dry with apprehension.

"Look carefully," Benny said. "See how she dabbed at her lips while putting on her makeup or something. She's one smart cookie, that lady of yours, Zee."

Ziplich peered at his wife's damp handkerchief. There, blurred but legible, was one word. "Ozark."

Youssef had realized that he might have an ally in this disaffected black woman. He had known, of course, that black Americans were oppressed by the system; women, too. Here, he had both. He wasn't at all concerned with women's rights, except in any way their lack might be used to his advantage and that of his brethren, but it seemed that he had come across a doubly useful circumstance—a black woman who hated the society that repressed her. Maybe he could use her to slip through the net that was so clearly closing around him.

"Airplane?" he repeated.

"Yes, yes, of course. He was rich, the bastard. He had an airplane, country houses all over the place, a mansion not far from here, all the money you can imagine. But us, us, hell no. We got the leavings. He had a lover, a whore, who got all she wanted out of him, just for opening her legs. Other things, too, maybe. I'd of done that, too, for the kind of stuff he gave her. But no, I'm black. 'I's not able to please de Massa de way he wanna be please. I jes' fit to slice de melons an' sweep de flo'.'"

"You think I'm stupid, do you? You're beautiful and well-dressed. You haven't been ill-treated at all, you're just trying to waste time. It won't work."

Carol lunged at him, beating her fists pitifully on his chest. "Get me out of this stinking place," she screamed, "Get me out!'

Mindful that he could lose control of the situation, Youssef took rapid mental stock. It would do him no good to eliminate his hostages, since that would leave him no point of negotiation if he were backed into a corner. This black woman might, just might, prove his salvation. "Tell me about the plane," he demanded.

"It's at Riverside—Jones, that is—airport. He uses it to fly around on business. He's got houses and businesses all over the country, and he's always going away. She"—an accusatory finger pointed at Jenna Grant—"goes with him a lot. Probably she's another one of his whores, I don't know. I don't care. I just want out of here. I got a bit of money, Ferguson's dead and got no hold on me now, I just want out."

"What hold on you?"

"He...he caught me one day when I was cleaning the finance office. There was some money in an open drawer, an' I thought nobody would miss it, but then he came in." She looked up at Youssef, tears streaming down her face, dabbing uselessly with a handkerchief. "Take me with you. Anywhere, I don't care, just so long as it isn't Tulsa. He's got places everywhere; San Antonio, Taos, La Jolla, Pensacola— everywhere. Cars at all of 'em, too. We could go anywhere: they'd never find us. I'm not," she said apprehensively, "trying to tag on to you. I just want to get away.' She was obviously struck by a sudden thought. "You don't know how to fly, do you? Oh, Jesus." She started sobbing again, the handkerchief now on overtime.

Youssef, a graduate of Saint Paul School of Aviation, had said, "Tell me where Riverside is."

Chapter 12
June 2011

"My name is Brian Hearn," Riordan insisted. "I am a British citizen here on holiday—that's vacation, here, I'm told—and I have no idea what you want with me. What's this all about?"

Lieutenant Malcolm, who had returned to his office after being notified that Riordan had been picked up, said: "We want to have a little talk with you. You see, we don't think you're Brian Hearn at all. No, your name is James Riordan, and we want to know what you can tell us about the death of Ralph Ferguson."

"Never heard of him."

Malcolm sighed dramatically. "Next you'll be telling me that you've never heard of the late Colum Tobin," he noticed the flicker in Riordan's eyes, "or Bernadette Riley, who's changed her name, too, to Candace Simpson. But, you see, we know who the real Candace Simpson is, and she is not the woman who went to the Fergoil offices and attempted to steal a very large sum of money by computer fraud. The phony Candace Simpson is the same one who was sharing a motel room with you, incidentally. Now, would you like to rethink your answer?"

Riordan knew when he was beaten. "I want to make a deal, a plea bargain," he muttered.

"Oh dear, you must have been watching too much television. The police, Mr. Riordan, do not make deals. That's up to the district attorney. In your case it may well involve the federal prosecutor's office too, since there are questions about how Tobin came to be murdered. That's not within my area, since it occurred in another state, but you must surely know something about it. But there is now the death of one of my officers to consider, too, and that of Ralph Ferguson."

"I know nothing about them."

Malcolm ignored the interruption. "Right now, you're looking at a life sentence at the least and, I should tell you if you don't know already, Oklahoma still has the death penalty. You're in trouble big time, Riordan, and the only way you can help yourself is by telling us what you know. After that, I'll make my recommendations to the DA, and we'll see what she has to say. If you choose to remain silent, which is your right, the inference will be obvious. Now?"

"Is this being recorded?"

"Naturally."

"Good, because I don't want any mistakes."

"The mistakes have already been made, Riordan, and you're one of those who made them."

"The Ferguson money wasn't his, it was ours."

"Ours? Then who are 'we?'"

"The Cause. We want freedom for the whole of Ireland, not the stupid partition we've had to live with for ninety years. Yes, we had our armed struggle against the Brits, but we were always outgunned. We lacked firepower, and we could only fight back in a modest way because the whole British system is geared against us. We have the manpower, but not the armaments, and that's what we need."

"The peace process in Northern Ireland is going ahead, now. You mean you intended to destroy that?"

"Peace process?" spat Riordan. "A sellout by Gerry Adams and his cronies! They gave in to the Brits, collapsed like a pack of cards. Never saw any action themselves, did they? No, they're like Arafat and bin Laden, Blair and Bush; send out some other poor sods, fools who've been fired with the patriotic urge for freedom, while they sit comfortably in the rear and issue orders."

"And you are one of the 'fools' who go out and do the dirty work?"

"My job is to raise funds. Noraid was quite helpful at one time, but that's changed, particularly since the Twin Towers attack has taught Americans what it means to be at the receiving end of the results of their own arrogance."

"You approve of the 9/11 attack?"

"Good God, no, man! I understand how it could happen, but the massacre of innocents is not part of our strategy. We aim at the head, not the tail, of the beast that suppresses us."

"The IRA made many attacks on innocents, as you put it," Malcolm sneered. "You approve of it when it's your organization, but not when it's someone else?"

Riordan seemed somehow anxious to reason with the lieutenant. His craggy face was earnest, his voice persuasive. "Ye've got it all wrong. When we made an attack on a target, it was with one of three objectives—either to disrupt the foreign economy which holds us down, to destroy a carefully identified target, like the attempt on Margaret Thatcher, or to make the general populace so nervous that they'd pressure the British government to order a withdrawal from Ireland. When there was a chance that ordinary people were in danger, we gave a warning ahead of time."

"There were many occasions when no such warning was given."

"I know," said Riordan, with what seemed to be genuine regret, "but mistakes are sometimes made. You know about 'collateral damage.' Just look at Iraq and Afghanistan, even Pakistan."

Malcolm nodded without speaking.

Riordan continued, apparently feeling a need to justify his actions. "We had to get the tools to rid ourselves of the British occupation. We tried to acquire arms from various sources..."

"Such as Libya," put in Malcolm. "Strange Marxist bedfellows for a Catholic movement."

"Ach, 'tis not religion that our fight is about, and anyway that Libyan shipload was years ago. Sure, the Republican sympathizers in Ireland tend to be Catholic for historical reasons, and the Unionists mainly Protestant, but religion has become the scapegoat, not the reason. Not like your radical Islamists. Sure, now, they're real religious fanatics, most of 'em. See, 'twas like Churchill when he said of Stalin that he'd make a pact with the Devil if 'twould help defeat Hitler. We got our equipment where and how we could. Unfortunately for us, there's always a tout..."

"A tout?" Malcolm wanted to know.

"A grass. Oh, what the hell d'ye call 'em here? A paid informer."
The word he'd sought suddenly occurred to him. "A snitch. So the
Brits often intercepted our shipments, and a great loss to us it was,
too."

"I don't understand," Malcolm said, "what all this has to do with
the death of Ralph Ferguson." He took a sip at the appalling coffee in
his Styrofoam cup.

"I told you, he took our money. Money that would've bought us
enough weaponry for us to win the war. That's how he got himself set
up in business."

"Where did the money come from?"

"I told you that, too. We have fundraisers. A lot of them were in
this country. Ah, Colum was an artist at soaking sympathetic Americans who had no real idea what goes on in Ireland."

"And how did Ferguson get your money?"

"A flying accident."

❖ ❖ ❖

"Ozark," Ziplich had said. "The bastard has gone to that Ferguson place that Jenna Grant pointed us at, the big house. But what the
hell for?"

"Doesn't matter," Benny told him. "We've got a destination.
Let's get onto the guys in Camdenton, what're their names? Balfour
and Krauss. Have 'em set up a watch at Camdenton airport, and
another at the house. When they land, follow 'em and pick 'em up.
They'll need a sharpshooting team, in case this Combs guy threatens
his hostages. It can't be at the airport, though, because there's too
much chance that a bystander could get hurt. And they can't clear the
airfield, because that'd look suspicious and he might not land. Gotta
be at the house."

"You're right, Benny. Let's get to it."

Malcolm's phone buzzed. He listened for a few moments, then
said: "Right, I'm coming in." He turned to the others. "We've got
Riordan. I'm going back to question him. Keep me informed." And
he was gone.

❖ ❖ ❖

In his hotel room, Greyhound watched the news on television, as usual. There was always the chance he'd pick up something useful, even this far from home. But there was nothing that told him what he didn't already know, and there was always the problem of his difficulty with a language which was so different from his own. Most of the news was so skewed anyway that, despite his own personal convictions, he became so irritated that he eventually switched it off with a muttered imprecation. The BBC represented a regime which he regarded as corrupt and effete, but at least it had the virtue of considerable accuracy and he wished he were able to receive it here. Cable and satellite providers were always, he reflected, bound by their own prejudices, as were the broadcast networks. Perhaps he should have elected to become a media mogul; then he could bend the news to his own purposes. Well, too late now. He sipped at a glass of cool white wine and anticipated the next few days.

His intuition had proved right, Youssef thought. The black woman had said: "I've got to repair my face. If I show up with tear stains, someone's gonna notice. These two," she indicated Jenna and Bernadette, "better keep their mouths shut. We can dump them someplace where it'll be hours before they're found, and by then we'll be long gone." She dabbed her newly made-up face with her sodden handkerchief and looked again at Bernadette. "That one, anyway, is gonna want to get out without more trouble with the law. She"—this meant Jenna—"will try to finger us, for sure. She's got to be put out of circulation for several hours."

"Or permanently," Youssef suggested.

"You crazy, man? We already got theft, hijacking and kidnapping on us, but murder—that's something else. Ain't much hiding from a rap like that. No, let her sweat 'til we're gone."

Youssef decided not to mention the passing of Detective Kohler. Once they were clear, he'd decide what to do with her, but just for the time being she was proving a useful asset.

At Jones airport, the twin-engine Cessna was already on the concrete and warming up. The flight plan Youssef filed to Dodge City was dealt with in minutes, the three women within his sight throughout the process, and his hand significantly in his pocket most of the time. Carol dabbed at her face one final time. "Let's go, Honey," she simpered at Youssef, and within another five minutes they were airborne, the aircraft passing over the arriving vehicle of Stan Malcolm and his colleagues, and swinging away toward the northwest in the direction of Dodge City until out of range of the airport. Altering course, Youssef then set a heading to the northeast and Camdenton.

"A flying accident? What do you mean, Riordan?"

"We had a source who knew where there was a huge cache—well, several caches, really—of arms. See, when the allies pulled out of Austria after the end of World War Two, they left a whole series of hidden weapon depots. Most of 'em were buried, some were hidden in mountain caves—the sort of place Hitler had concealed one of his secret hideouts—because the Americans, especially, didn't trust the Soviets to keep to their word about withdrawal. The arms were there for partisans and infiltrated Allied forces to combat the Russians if they tried anything funny. In the event, that didn't happen, so the arms just stayed there, waiting. Well, a greedy ex-GI, who'd been one of those involved in the operation, decided to make capital of it. It didn't hurt us that his family had been Fenian sympathizers. So by devious routes—and I don't know what they may have been—he contacted our High Command, and promised to deliver the goods in return for a large payment. Seems he was by now running his family business, which was international transport, and he reckoned he could get the stuff away under guise of industrial machinery, or some such."

"How much money?" Malcolm asked.

"Fifty thousand pounds or so, I understand."

"Doesn't sound like much."

"Not now, no, but this was over fifty years ago. It was a huge amount then, worth at least a million in today's terms, if not more. And, remember, that's pounds, not dollars. At that time the pound was four dollars or so. So, we're talking two million dollars or thereabouts in today's terms. That's not small change, even now."

Malcolm had to concede that it was not. "So where did the money come from?"

"I told you, for Christ's sake. We have fundraisers."

"Okay, okay. So you had the money. Then what?"

"It had to be delivered to the contractor. Now, that's not the kind of transaction you could just do by wire or Internet back in them days. But we had a bit of luck, finally, or so it seemed at the time. The RAF—the British Air Force—had quite a lot of Irishmen, from both north and south, and one of them turned out to be a patriot. He was a pilot, and at the time there were lots of military flights between Britain and the British Occupation forces in Germany. All our man had to do was collect the money, arrange a flight to a British base in occupied Germany, and pass it on to the contractor. It was a 'cash only' arrangement, to avoid the chance of being traced, and the contractor knew the consequences of failing to keep his end of the bargain."

"I can well imagine," Malcolm murmured.

"Obviously, no civilian could expect to walk through the security of the occupying forces. So, the money was left in a suitcase at a railway station in London, at the left luggage office, and the redemption ticket was sent to the pilot."

"Name?"

"McDonough. So all he had to do was collect the money and fly to Germany on one of the so-called liaison flights. Then the stupid son of a bitch went and killed himself in a crash. When our people tried to get the suitcase back from Victoria station, they found it had already been picked up."

"How could they have gotten it without the ticket?"

"Sure, we're not eejuts. A copy was made of all the details, just in case."

"Didn't help, did it?"

"No. But what it proved was that someone had the real ticket—and the money. The question then became, who? This was urgent, because delivery of the goods was due in only a month or so, and without payment we could kiss it goodbye." Riordan helped himself, unasked, to a cigarette from a pack on Malcolm's desk, lit it, and went on. "Then we'd be left without the either the money or the goods.

An intensive investigation was launched, but we found nothing. Oh, there were suspicions, especially of the flight sergeant who had headed the guard at McDonough's crash site—thought maybe he'd found the ticket amid the wreckage—but there was no real proof. We examined all the information we could get about the other members of the crash guard, but nobody suddenly seemed to have money to burn. Same with the experts who examined the site. We were stumped. Delivery day came and went and we were left with nothing."

"So, what happened to the arms?"

"Nothing, until the US acknowledged their existence a few years ago. Then they were dug up and destroyed."

"I still don't see what all this has to do with the death of Ferguson."

"Ah. Well, that was Colum's doing, y'see."

❖ ❖ ❖

The Camdenton police and sheriff's departments had a quick consultation following the communication from Ziplich in Tulsa, and it was decided that the police would monitor the airport, while the sheriffs would take over surveillance of the Ferguson house. No general alert was to be issued to avoid any chance that the incoming aircraft's pilot might be inadvertently warned off. Official vehicles would be concealed within hangars at the airfield and parked lower down the dirt road from which the Ferguson driveway branched off. Armed officers would be deployed at both locations, with strict instructions not to use their weapons unless ordered or there was an immediate threat to life.

These arrangements were relayed to Ziplich, who approved them, adding his thanks to his Missouri colleagues. By now, a police helicopter, which would transport Ziplich, Benny and Grayson to Camdenton, had been called in. It arrived within a few minutes, and settled on the concrete, rotors whirling. The three scrambled aboard, buffeted by the downdraft, and the helo lifted off, bowing to the ground as it set course.

❖ ❖ ❖

Under different circumstances, Youssef would have enjoyed the flight. It was some time since he had piloted an aircraft, but the

Cessna was a familiar plane to him, and the cockpit check, taxiing and takeoff had come to him as naturally as if it had been yesterday. Had it really been over ten years since he'd been instructed to familiarize himself with small aircraft? It seemed odd, particularly when one considered what had happened on 9/11. Youssef had been appalled by that event. The slaughter of innocents was the reason he had chosen the path he trod, and indiscriminate murder seemed to him quite loathsome. Death for a reason, yes. Death of hundreds for its own sake, no. He never for a moment considered his own career as an assassin as anything but justifiable.

He had placed Bernadette in the seat next to him, while Jenna and Carol were in the seats behind.

"Just remember," Youssef had told them, "that I am the pilot, and if any of you has an intention to interfere, a crash will kill all of us. I doubt if you want that any more than I do."

Jenna cowered, Bernadette fumed, and Carol smiled happily.

It was a simple course, at first following more or less the same route as the tornado which had sparked this entire episode. Along I-44 northeast to Joplin, then Springfield. Youssef then banked slightly toward the north, passing over the rolling hills of the Ozarks. Away to the south gleamed Table Rock Lake, to the north, Truman Reservoir. Farther away, his immediate destination, Lake of the Ozarks. In the far distance, through the crystal clear air, he could just discern the tiny shape of an aircraft landing at Fort Leonard Wood. Overhead, arrow-straight contrails of airliners on their way to Chicago, Los Angeles, Dallas and Washington left their ephemeral marks in the sky. Not much wind up there today, Youssef thought idly, and began his descent.

Camdenton Memorial Airport was not large, being mainly given over to small aircraft owned either locally by wealthier residents of the Lake of the Ozarks resort area or those, like Ferguson, who had vacation homes there. A newish concrete runway blessed what was otherwise an open field, while there was a small group of hangars, a basic control building, and several parking lots holding a few cars. Good. No sign of what Youssef had now begun to think of as The Enemy. The next move was to find Ferguson's Range Rover.

The landing was feather-light, and Youssef was pleased that he had not lost his touch. He taxied round to one of the hangars and cut the engine switches. The propellers turned gently a few moments, then were still. Youssef opened the door and, before climbing out, said warningly: "I have the gun. Don't forget that. Now, come out and leave the talking to me. We'll soon be gone from here, and you'll remain unharmed as long—and only as long—as you do exactly as I say. You can agree with anything I tell people here, and that's all. I repeat, that's all." He dropped to the ground and the women followed him. A man was approaching.

"Who the hell are you?" he demanded, "landing here without authorization."

"My apologies," smiled Youssef. "I filed a flight plan from Tulsa. It must have got misrouted."

"Got a radio, don't you?"

"It's died on me. I need a technician to fix it. In the meantime, Miss Grant, here, is Ralph Ferguson's secretary,"—this much he had gleaned from the terrified woman—"and she needs to use his Range Rover to get to his house. Important papers," he clarified.

"Oh, sure. Hi, Ms. Grant," the man said to a Jenna who had never seen him before in her life, but who understood immediately that they had been expected—a comforting thought. " I didn't see you. Bit upset about the unauthorized arrival. Yeah, well, the car's over there," he gestured. "You got the keys?"

"Of course," Youssef replied. "You'll have to excuse us, but this is urgent. Would you mind taking care of the plane?" He produced a roll of bills and peeled off a few. "I'd be real grateful."

The man accepted the money without demur. "Sure, I'll see to it. Nice to see you again, Ms. Grant. Have a good day." Youssef ushered the women toward the parking area.

From the gloom of a hangar, Sergeant Bill Balfour watched. "They've arrived," he said quietly into a hand-held radio. "Going to the car now." There was an equally quiet acknowledgement from Deputy Tony Krauss.

"I know who Colum was," Malcolm interrupted. "He's still in a chilled drawer in New Jersey," he added callously.

Riordan was clearly distressed. "He was me lifelong friend. Don't be so bloody cruel about a man who's lost his life."

"My God!" Malcolm burst out. "You've been instrumental in maybe hundreds of deaths and you have the nerve to complain about the loss of your precious Tobin. I'm beginning to lose patience with you, asshole, and I'm also beginning to reconsider talking with the DA about you. Now tell me, or expect to see a lethal needle."

Once again, Riordan saw how precarious his position was. He stubbed out his cigarette. "'Twas the McDonough thing," he said ingratiatingly.

"What McDonough thing?"

"Ferguson—well, Fergoil, really—set up a fund called the McDonough Trust, and it paid the family of the pilot who was killed. All anonymous, of course, but Colum traced it to Ferguson through the Windfall trusts. 'Twas the name of McDonough that gave it away, he said. Ah, he was a financial genius, was Colum. And then we got to thinking about this Ferguson feller."

"Was he the same Ferguson that you saw in Times Square one New Year's eve?"

"Y'know about that? How could you know that, at all?"

"I know, that's all. So?"

"So we came looking for him here in Tulsa, and found him. He was the same man we'd seen in New York. More than that, we knew he wasn't really an American."

"Because, on a cross channel ferry, he'd been English."

"If you know everything," Riordan almost shouted, "why the hell are youse asking me?"

"Because," Malcolm smiled benignly, " I want to know who actually killed Ferguson, you or Tobin?"

"We were in New York," Riordan snapped. "You can check that out. Maybe you have, I don't know, but we were not in Tulsa, neither of us."

"But you know who was." It was not a question.

"I might, but I need some assurances."

"You'll have to talk to the DA."

"So bring the DA. I'll say nothing more until I have some kind of a deal. I'll claim your precious Fifth Amendment, to use your own word."

"You've said too much for that already."

"Ah, but I haven't. I've just remembered what you said about watching too much television. Well, I learned something from TV anyway, and it's this. Without my Miranda rights being read to me, nothing is admissible. And nobody read me those rights, so you're just beating your jaws."

Malcolm realized with a sinking feeling that it might be true.

It was only the work of moments for Youssef's skilled hands to open the locked door of the black Range Rover, and the police watchers gave him grudging credit for his abilities. A few seconds more and the engine burst into life. The three women were already inside, and Youssef put the transmission into drive, pulling smoothly away.

"They're on their way," Balfour told Krauss. "Should be with you in ten, fifteen minutes. We're following."

"Copy that," Krauss responded.

"Where's this house of Ferguson's?" Youssef demanded.

"I don't know," said Carol, "but I'll bet she does," indicating Jenna.

"I don't trust her to direct us," Youssef said. "She's as likely as not to head for a police station,"— which was exactly what Jenna had in mind. "So what's the nearest town?"

"Of any size? That's got to be Osage Beach. It's a resort area."

They were coming into the main part of Camdenton, and a traffic light was just ahead.

"I remember," Carol announced suddenly. "You turn right at the light and just keep going. There are lots of little side roads where we can dump these two, and they'll have miles to walk. We can be long gone by the time they can alert anybody. She," this scornfully directed at Bernadette, "won't want to be found too quickly, anyway, and the other one hasn't got the chutzpah to do anything alone. We've got it made. From here you can go to Saint Louis or Kansas

City and be on a plane before the law has even realized you've been here." A helicopter clattered overhead. "Me, I'll just disappear into the big city."

"They've turned off of 5 onto 54," Balfour told Krauss in some dismay. "We're still behind them, but they're not coming your way. Hold your position, just in case, but I got a feeling we've misread their intention."

"Copy," Krauss said again. "Have you told the Okies in the chopper?"

"Christ! I forgot them. You're right, I'll get 'em." Balfour changed channels and called up the helicopter pilot.

"They're in a black Range Rover, headed east on Highway 54. We're behind them a few hundred yards, in an unmarked car and with a half-dozen vehicles between us, so we shouldn't have been spotted. We've got the number advantage, now, so waddya say we stop 'em?"

A few moments hiatus, then the pilot's voice crackled through. "Guys here say yeah, so let's do it. You pull up right behind 'em an' I'll set down in front. They'll have fun coping with that."

Balfour performed a number of highly illegal passing maneuvers, until his car was directly behind the Range Rover. "Ready, now, guys," he said to the two officers with him, and made as if to pass the target. At that moment, the helicopter suddenly burst over a knoll ahead and to the right, heading directly at the Range Rover. Youssef, startled, swung the wheel and the car began a wild slide. Regaining his composure, Youssef straightened up, only to find the chopper settling onto the road a hundred yards or so ahead. Cars were swerving all over the road, both behind and in front of him, and he had no choice but to jam on the brakes. The Rover screeched to a halt in a cloud of tire dust, slewing sideways. Balfour's car had not even stopped before his officers were out, guns covering the Range Rover. A door of the Rover opened, and a terrified-looking woman stepped out, Youssef holding her shoulder and with his gun pressed into her neck. He edged toward the helicopter, and Grayson understood his intention. So, clearly, did the police, since they aimed their weapons at the two figures.

"Don't shoot, don't shoot," the woman screamed, and Ziplich, who had leapt from the helicopter ahead of Grayson and Benny, recognized Jenna Grant. He also recognized a standoff when he saw one, since the sharpshooters weren't here.

"Here's where the negotiations start," he thought, but he was wrong.

With a speed and agility Ziplich and the others would not have thought possible, Jenna swiveled on her heel, breaking Youssef's grip on her, at the same time lashing out with her left hand at the gun, with the right at Youssef's throat and one foot at his right kneecap. The weapon skittered across the road, and Youssef collapsed choking and clutching at his damaged windpipe. Jenna stepped back, smiling.

"Health club," she explained. "Same place I met Candace Simpson. They have a martial arts class. Seems like it has its uses."

Balfour used his car radio to call for an ambulance to take the injured Youssef to hospital.

"One thing we don't need," Benny remarked, "is for this joker to die on us: not yet, anyway, not before he's had the opportunity to unburden himself. Trouble is, he's in Missouri, and we had first dibs on him in Oklahoma."

"I wouldn't concern myself too much about that if I were you," Balfour told him. "We Missourians really don't like the look of him, so you'd be doing us a favor if you took him away when we weren't looking."

"What about her?" Ziplich indicated Bernadette, who was standing disconsolately in the road, watched over by two policemen.

"We don't know she's done anything wrong, pal, so she's all yours, too."

"We owe you one, Bill," Ziplich said. "In fact, we owe you plenty."

"Nuthin' you ain't seen yet, Zee. I haven't had the chance to tell you before, but me and Tony found some interestin' stuff in that Ferguson place after you guys went tearin' off the other day. Since you're here, why don't we go take a look-see, once we got this guy tucked away. Who is he, by the way?"

"One of the things we got to find out, Bill, and that may take a little time. So far, he's proved less than approachable. We'll get him back to Tulsa, once he's fit to be moved, and then we can really put the squeeze on him. We can take him in the Range Rover, since the chopper won't hold seven of us as well as the pilot, and Ferguson sure won't be needing it." They heard the wail of the ambulance siren drawing rapidly closer. "Can I get one of your men to go along with Benny and keep an eye on this guy?"

"You got it," and Balfour gave the necessary instructions. When the ambulance arrived, a groaning Youssef was bundled onto a gurney and placed in the vehicle. Benny and Officer Hong went next, and last of all a medic. The door shut, and the ambulance departed, siren on full song.

Ziplich went over to Carol and Jenna, who were standing together near the helicopter. "Honey, you were wonderful," he said as he took his wife in his arms.

"Oh, Paul, I was so scared."

"But you came through. That handkerchief thing was brilliant. Did you talk that guy into coming here"

"Well, I may have planted the idea," she admitted. "So many of those 9/11 guys knew about flying...."

"She was great," Jenna said firmly. "She even almost had me fooled that she was joining up with him, but I eventually realized she was hoping to set a trap. "

"Remind me," Ziplich said to her, "never to get into an argument with you. Health club, huh? Not so healthy for the bad guy."

"Now," Balfour began, "about that house..."

"Sorry, Bill," Ziplich interrupted, "but we've got three women to take care of."

"They can come back with me." It was the helicopter pilot, who had been silently taking all this in.

"Jack, you're a treasure. And a helluva pilot, too. That was great stuff on your part."

Jack smiled modestly, saying nothing.

"Okay, Ziplich agreed, "you can take 'em. The two nice ones better get a check up before going home. The baddie," he nodded toward Bernadette, "better rest in a comfortable air-conditioned cell. I'll be back later."

Ziplich kissed his wife. "'Bye, Honey. I'll be back soon. I love you." The three women climbed into the chopper, which lifted off immediately, curtsied again to the watchers on the ground, and set off on a southwesterly course.

"The house," Balfour said again.

"Lead on, MacDuff," Ziplich proclaimed.

"Actually, that's 'Lay on, MacDuff,' you know," Grayson corrected gently.

Once again, Ziplich felt a twinge of annoyance. He liked Grayson well enough, but found that know-it-all attitude tiresome. This was not, however, the moment to mention it, so he contained himself.

Chapter 13
June 2011

At Lake Regional Hospital, Youssef was placed in a single room. With Benny and Hong watching carefully, he was thoroughly examined by a doctor, who announced that, apart from severe bruising and a cracked patella, Youssef appeared to have sustained no serious injuries, certainly nothing life-threatening.

"He'll be very sore for quite a while," she declared, "and his throat will hurt like the dickens: he'll sure not be doing any sprinting. Aside from that, he's in particularly good physical shape. Is he an athlete?"

"Sorry, doc," Benny replied, "but we're not at liberty to discuss the prisoner at this time. Tell me, when can he be moved?"

"I'd like to keep him overnight, just for observation. After trauma like the one to his throat there can occasionally be minor complications: a blood clot could form, for instance, although that's highly unlikely. For now, I'll prescribe a couple of sleeping pills."

"Okay, doc, thanks, This room has to be off-limits to anybody not approved by us, you understand."

"Of course." The doctor departed.

"You got a radio or a cellphone?" Benny asked Hong.

"No. Sorry."

"Pity. My cell's down, and I gotta report in on the situation. Listen, you watch this guy while I go find a phone." He suddenly realized he hadn't eaten. "You hungry?"

"Yeah."

"You like pizza?"

"Sure."

"Well, I'll order us some in, then."

"I'm hungry, too," Youssef, still clad in plaid shirt and, by now tattered, jeans, croaked unexpectedly from the bed.

Benny looked down at him. "Nah. Pizza might hurt your throat. Watch him closely, buddy." Benny left in search of a telephone.

He found one at a nurses' station, and a flash of his badge brought him immediate use of it, on which he entered Ziplich's cell number.

"Ziplich."

"Zee, we got the guy in a private room, and Hong's guarding him. Doc says he'll be okay to move tomorrow."

"Good. I'll get Bill to arrange reliefs for you. He's talked to the Osage Beach police already, and they've agreed that, in the circumstances, Hong's presence—and yours, too, for that matter—is acceptable, even though you technically have no jurisdiction there. Just behave yourself, that's all. For instance, leave the nurses alone, y'know?" Benny glanced at the nurse who had let him use the phone.

"That won't be a problem," he assured Ziplich, who immediately understood.

"I'm pleased to hear that. Listen, when the Osage guys arrive, I'll be sure that you get transportation. Right now, I'm going to take a look at the Ferguson house. Bill tells me that he and Tom Krauss have found interesting stuff there, and I want to see it. You better call me first, but I expect we'll still be there when you're free to leave."

"Gotcha." He closed the connection, and asked the nurse for a phone book. Under "Restaurants" in the Yellow Pages he found Domino's, called them, and ordered two large pizzas with everything. He hadn't asked Hong his preferences, so he reckoned the officer could just remove anything he didn't like. Then he went back to Youssef's room.

It was called, euphemistically, an "interview room," but to Riordan it was, unequivocally, a cell. He had been languishing there alone except for two visits from an officer—whom Riordan thought of as a jailer—to offer some barely palatable food and coffee. The latter was particularly rank, evidently the result of stewing for several hours. Fortunately, there was the ubiquitous, in this country, "ice water." Riordan wondered idly if it came from melted glaciers.

On the most recent visit from his unloved young guard he had asked: "How long am I to be here? Sure, it must be eight or nine hours now, and I've seen nobody but you. Am I being charged, and if so, what with?"

"You'll have to ask the lieutenant."

"How the hell can I ask the lootenant if he doesn't come here?"

"I can't tell you. I just work here."

"Then make some of your work to find the man and send him here."

The officer snorted. "Me? Send the lieutenant? No way, buddy, I don't tell the lieutenant to do anything. Still," he considered for a moment, "you been here a long time, so I'll pass on your request. Best I can do. Enjoy your meal."

Riordan eyed the unwholesome mess on his tray. It looked even worse than the stuff he'd been given in the 'Kesh at home. Like Youssef nearly three hundred miles away, he was hungry. But "enjoy?" Hardly.

Malcolm was in conference with his captain and the chief of police. "We know who he is, and we got a pretty good idea of why he's here. He was riding herd on the accountant woman, Bernadette Riley. But he's somehow connected with the Ferguson murder, even though he couldn't have been directly involved. The actual job was done by this guy calling himself Combs, we're sure of that, but we still have no hard tie between the two of them, and it looks like his confession is inadmissible because of the oversight on the Miranda thing."

"Have you questioned the officers who brought him in? They're experienced, except Black, and that seems like an odd thing for them to have missed," the chief said.

"I checked with both Wilson and Steinmetz, and each of 'em said he thought the other had done that."

"What about Black, then?"

"I think she deferred to the two more experienced officers."

"You think? Don't you know?" This came from the captain.

"Well, I, er, didn't think it necessary..."

"Get her in here, now," the chief rapped. "Holy shit, Stan, what's happened to your professionalism?"

"Been a long few days, Chief," Malcolm countered, picking up the internal phone. "Get Officer Black to the captain's office, now." He listened for a few moments, then: "Well, get her back here. On the double. Make that triple."

There was a knock on the door. The captain called out "Come in," but instead of Officer Black, a very junior member of the staff stood there.

"Well?'

"It's, um, the prisoner—I mean suspect—you know, sir, the Irish one. He, um, wants to know when he can talk to Lieutenant Malcolm, sir."

"Oh, does he? Well, he's SOL until we get a couple questions answered, so you just go tell him, son, to display that legendary Irish patience. We'll see him when we're ready. That could be any time before his statutory twenty-four hours are up, which still gives us plenty of time."

"Yessir." The junior officer scuttled out.

"I swear these kids are getting younger every day," Malcolm said.

"Signs of age, Stan," observed the captain, "include finding stairs steeper, TV programs sillier and policemen younger."

Grayson surprised Ziplich quite a bit when he demonstrated how to deal with hotwiring a car, which was how Youssef had started up the Range Rover at Camdenton airport. The vehicle had stalled during its confrontation with the helicopter, and was still partially blocking the road. Traffic was backed up in both directions, and with several police cars adding to the general confusion, motorists' tempers were growing short. Once the chopper had lifted off and the ambulance departed to Osage Beach, Grayson pulled the Rover to the side of the road, and the police and sheriffs' vehicles followed suit. Traffic began to flow again, drivers and passengers alike peering out, trying to determine what had been going on. Arriving too late to make any "live on the spot" reportage, a couple of TV and radio station news teams strove to provide interesting—and largely inaccurate—recreations of what had transpired. For the most part, they had to make do with inspired guesses based on what they had heard on their police band scanners, and an interview with Bill Balfour, who told them sagely that a suspect had been taken into custody. One alert reporter had spotted the helicopter as it climbed away, made a note of its registration letters, and had the station trace it to the Tulsa police. What it had been doing in the middle of Missouri remained a subject for speculation, of which there was a good deal.

"How'd you do that?" Ziplich asked Grayson as the Range Rover engine burst into life.

"Well, you see," was the reply, "starting cars without their keys is an art gained, like being able to play pool, as the result of a misspent youth," but he would not elaborate further. To admit that it was part of the training in several arcane skills used in the course of his sometimes dangerous career was not a matter he cared—or was permitted—to discuss.

Once the road had been cleared, Grayson and Ziplich in the Range Rover followed Balfour's Ford back to Camdenton, turning right onto Old Route 5 for about three miles, then onto the minor road down toward the lakefront. Another turn put them on the dirt road that led to Ferguson's asphalt driveway. The house spread out before them, the small cabins dotted the wooded hillside, and the men were again amazed at the sheer scope of Ferguson's country "cabin."

"Must be tough to live like this," Ziplich commented.

"Let's not forget that Ferguson didn't live," Grayson suggested wryly.

The two cars parked next to another Ford with "Sheriff" emblazoned on every available surface, and the men got out, to be greeted by Tom Krauss and a junior deputy.

"Hi, guys," Krauss welcomed them, "good t'see you again. Been expectin' you for awhile. I guess you had a bit of fun up the road, eh?"

"Indeed," Grayson confirmed. "I take it you've been making good use of your radio."

"Indeed," Krauss mimicked, and Grayson smiled in appreciation. "Sorry to've missed it all, but them's the breaks. Well, come on
in," and he led the way through the huge front door.

It was blessedly cool inside, and Grayson suddenly realized that
his WalMart shirt was sodden with perspiration. The outside tem-
perature was over ninety, there had been a prolonged period of stress,
and he'd forgotten to turn on the air conditioning in the Range Rover. For a moment he yearned for the damp, gray streets of Willesden,
wondering how anyone could survive in this climate for years on end.
Still, not as bad as Riyadh, he supposed.

Krauss must have read his mind, for he now ushered everyone
into the vast kitchen and opened a refrigerator door. Oh, joyful sight!
Rack upon rack of chilled beer; such a selection Grayson had hardly
imagined in his wildest dreams (some of which, despite his quiet de-
meanor, really were wild.)

"Hep y'sevs, fellers," Krauss invited. "Ferguson won't mind."

He and Balfour selected Miller Lite, Ziplich a Rolling Rock and
Grayson an Amstel. The junior deputy found a lonely Mountain Dew
and appropriated it.

"Gonna be drivin'," he explained.

The others were more sanguine. After all, today they'd captured
a vicious killer, a grand larcenist and a probable accomplice to both
those crimes, so it would not be amiss to indulge in a modest celebration. Besides, they were hot and the beer was cold.

The party now retired to the library. Once again, as in Tulsa,
it was impressive: bookshelves lined the greater part of three walls,
while the fourth was practically all window, giving a fine panoramic
view of the lake and its farther bank, where a few houses could be
glimpsed nestled amid the trees; a couple of boats sliced through the
calm waters. Grayson could well imagine how much Ferguson—as he
still thought of Phipps—valued his "down time" here: he would have
felt the same way himself. It was not the view, however, that Krauss
had brought them in here to see: it was a series of neatly stacked papers reposing on the long, highly polished, library table.

"Found 'em in Rachel Taylor's closet." Krauss paused: "Under
the floorboards. Y'see, there are two big, walk-in closets in the master

bedroom; a kind of his'n'hers arrangement, an' it's perfectly obvious which was whose from the contents. Lots of nice clothes, of course, Ralph Lauren an' such; a vanity unit in each; a big bureau with plenty of drawers; a computer work station, all of it built-in; an' in Taylor's, a carefully hidden cavity in the floor. After we found those diaries earlier, we been takin' special care to double an' triple check everythin'. It's all carpeted, of course, real thick stuff, so there was really nothin' to give it away to the casual glance; doesn't even sound hollow when you walk over it. Wasn't until we pulled up the carpet that we found it: very professional carpentry work. We contacted the builders, an' they tell us that there was no such hidin' place in their plans. It seems like Taylor had it done later, but we don' know who constructed it, or when; could've been anybody from anywhere, anytime. So she kept her little secrets under her closet floor, just like Ferguson kept his behind that bookcase." He gestured toward the end of the room. " Still, that's not the point. The point is what these papers tell us about Rachel Taylor's personal life, the one she kept from Ferguson."

"May we look?" asked Grayson.

"'Course, that's why you're here."

They all moved to the table, and Grayson selected one of the stacks at random. It appeared mainly to comprise letters, together with a few photographs. The men studied everything with considerable care, but eventually came to a unanimous conclusion. Taylor had been hiding her personal peccadilloes—of which there were quite a few—from Ferguson rather than from more official eyes. Grayson was disappointed.

"Anything else?" he inquired.

"A few photo albums,' Krauss told him, "but they were just on the bureau in the bedroom. Not hidden or anythin'."

"Let's have a look anyway." They thumbed through a series of fairly typical vacation snaps without enthusiasm until they came to a couple of pages of seaside pictures. It was there that one caught Grayson's eye and caused him to murmur, "Oh, my word." There, smiling out at him from a beach in who-knew-where, were very young versions of three people whose faces he knew; Rachel Taylor, Michael Nolan and Jimmy Riordan. Who was Taylor with on this occasion, he wondered. Or was it a "menage a trois?" But what had really captured his attention was the reflection of the photographer, caught in the lenses of Taylor's sunglasses. Even in so small an image, he recognized the figure, and he recalled the locket that LaDonna had bought. *So, the plot thickens.*

Grayson turned to Krauss. "Can we get this enlarged?"

Entering the room, Benny could see that Youssef was asleep, his back to the door. Evidently the doctor's sleeping pills had been effective. Of Hong there was no sign. Probably gone to the john, now this guy's out of it, Benny thought, and then remembered there was a small bathroom through another door, which was closed. Benny tapped. No response. With a mounting feeling of unease, Benny opened the door and looked inside. Empty. Where the hell was Hong, then? He turned back into the room and went to the bed, shaking the figure on it. Again, no response. He tugged at a shoulder, and Youssef rolled over. Except that it wasn't Youssef. Staring up at him was Officer Hong, a surprised expression on his face and a jagged hole in his throat. Benny checked for a pulse, found none, rang the emergency bell, and took off for the nurses' station at a furious run.

Officer Judy Black reported to the captain within fifteen minutes. "You wanted to see me, sir?"

"Yes, officer. I need to ask you one question: did you read the Miranda rights to the Irishman you, together with Wilson and Steinmetz, arrested this morning?"

"Not exactly, sir."

"Not exactly? Now, what's that supposed to mean?"

"Well, Captain, I'm trying to be precise: you said 'read' the rights. I didn't read them, but I did recite them from memory"

"It's the same thing, provided you did so accurately. Did you?"

"I think so, sir."

"You 'think' so. Perhaps, officer, you would be good enough to repeat your performance for us now."

"Yes, sir. 'You have the right to remain silent, but anything you do say can, and will, be used against you'..." and she reeled off the whole thing flawlessly. The captain leaned back in satisfaction.

"Thank you, officer, that was correct. You're free to go now."

"Yes, sir, thank you sir," said a relieved Judy Black, and she left the room.

"Well, gentlemen, it seems we have our answer. Lieutenant Malcolm, why don't you go back and talk a little more with our guest. Maybe he'll have a change of heart." Malcolm departed on his errand.

"We got 'im, Chief, we got 'im cold."

"I do believe you're right, Rich."

The moment Benny had left the room to find a telephone, Youssef had started gasping and uttering muffled groans. At first, this elicited no response from Hong, but as the prisoner's distress became increasingly obvious, he said: "What's the matter?"

Youssef, clutching at his throat, groaned, "I—can't—breathe—I can't—breathe—I..." His voice was cut off by a deep rasping. Concerned, Hong rose from his chair and went to the bed.

"You need a nurse or a doctor or something?"

An unintelligible noise issued from Youssef's mouth, and Hong leaned forward a little to try to make it out. Youssef curled his legs up almost to his chest in agony, and Hong, sure now that there was something seriously wrong, stretched for the emergency button at the head of the bed. Like a flash, Youssef whipped the knife that he had earlier taped to his calf up and into Hong's throat. Hong collapsed with a gurgle and, leaping from the bed, Youssef caught the body, placing it on the bed so that the spurting blood was stanched by a pillow.

Within moments Youssef, wincing at the pain of his damaged kneecap, had stripped the officer to his underwear. No blood on the uniform. Good. Removing his own clothes, he bundled the now lifeless Hong into them, and placed the body in a sleeping pose, facing away from the door. Then he donned the uniform. It was slightly tight, but not too noticeably so. Hong's shoes were much too small for him, so he put on his own, hoping they wouldn't attract attention, buckled on the police belt, with its heavy pistol, picked up his own effects from the bedside table, wiped his knife on the, by now, blood-soaked pillow and slipped it back into the sheath on his leg. Amazing that he had been able to transfer the knife from his leg to inside his underpants while still in the ambulance. It had only been a brief moment that Benny and Hong had been distracted, but that had been enough. He had then only to wait for the moment he knew had to come—as, indeed, it had.

Turning the pillow over, Youssef arranged Hong's head on it carefully. Then he opened the door cautiously. No one in the corridor. He slipped out, and walked purposefully away from the nurses' station, hoping there would be an emergency exit somewhere. What he found was another corridor, one which eventually gave on to the main lobby. He saw no sign of Benny, so walked quite openly out of the entrance and into the parking lot.

A Corvette was just being locked by a man who then made for the building. This was convenient, since it meant that Youssef would have at least a few minutes before the driver reappeared and found his car missing. Time enough to be well away. Hong would be found soon, of course, but at least he had a head start. As soon as the Corvette driver had disappeared into the hospital, Youssef was at the car door and, with his usual speed and skill, he was inside and driving away within fifty seconds. The entire episode had lasted just under four minutes.

When Malcolm returned to the interview room, Riordan was pacing. He stopped when the door opened, and turned to face Malcolm.

"So, you've come at last, have ye? Well, when do I get out of here?"

"There are a few formalities first."

"What d'ye mean, formalities?"

By now, Malcolm had turned the tape recorder on again. "We feel, Mr.Riordan,'—*Mister* Riordan: now that was reassuring—"that you may have been under some misapprehension regarding the circumstances of your detention."

"I don't think so, and I've told you why. Now, let me out of here, or I call a lawyer—with the statutory call I know I'm allowed—and you'll be busted to corporal for wrongful arrest."

"Except, you see," Malcolm continued, unperturbed, "that you did, in fact, have your Miranda rights read."

"You talking about that woman? She wasn't even police."

"I take it that you've heard of plain clothes officers?"

It was the end of the line, and Riordan knew it. He blustered a bit more at the impassive Malcolm, but in the end subsided.

"Now, let's begin again where we left off."

There was a welcoming committee waiting for the helicopter when it returned to Tulsa. Jenna and Carol were greeted like heroines, Jack having radioed ahead about the circumstances of the interception, and Bernadette was ushered to a waiting van amid a group of dour officers. Carol was as popular as her husband with the Tulsa Police Department, and Bernadette's role in putting her in jeopardy was unappreciated. Once Carol and Jenna had been declared by the duty medic as totally fit, they were free to leave, transportation courtesy of TPD. Carol chose to go home, while Jenna opted to return to the office. "Never know what they might get up to when I'm not looking," she explained.

What they got up to was, in fact, a mighty roar of approval when she arrived. Employees to whom she had never even spoken hugged her and told her how proud they were. Fergoil was united against any further attack. Kohler's car had disappeared.

To Carol, the sight of her little apartment was a quiet delight. If only Paul could be there soon. She called her firm, and was assured that they had been kept informed of developments. She was to take a couple of days rest, then they could all see things in perspective. For the time being, the main thing was that she was unharmed.

"This Firm," the Senior Partner had intoned portentously over the phone in capital letters, "is Singularly Fortunate in having such an Ingenious and Competent, not to mention Courageous, Member. It's a Brilliant Episode that we won't Soon Forget." For the umpteenth time, Carol wondered why things would be "not soon forgotten" instead of long remembered, but she managed to hold her tongue, contenting herself with thanking the Senior Partner for his kind words. When she had hung up, she said aloud: "Pompous jerk. I bet he says things cost an Arm and a Leg," and poured herself a glass of Chardonnay. Silently, she toasted her absent husband.

At that moment, the aforesaid husband was asking Krauss and Balfour whether the computers of Ferguson and Taylor had been examined.

"They're under scrutiny right now," he was informed. "Takes a bit of time to get everything off of the memory and hard drive. It's not very likely, though, that they'd've put anything incriminating on 'em, is it?"

Ziplich wasn't so sure. "If they're naïve enough to hide things behind bookcases and under floorboards, it's possible that they're not very sophisticated where electronics are concerned. Let's wait and see. Let's not wait too long, though." He'd just recalled Ferguson's financial dealings.

His cellphone chirped. "Ziplich." A long pause, then a weary sigh. "Okay, Benny, just stay where you are. I'll set the wheels in motion." He turned a sad face to his companions. "Combs has escaped. He's killed Hong, and we have no idea where he's gone. Never mind taking him back to Oklahoma now. Let's nail the bastard."

The Corvette was not new but fast, a 2010 Z06 model with the six-speed transmission, and Youssef made the most of it. He was pleased to see a Valentine One radar detector, which he switched on. It would be ignominious to be caught for speeding. Not that he'd stop: they'd have to catch him, and few police vehicles could match the performance of the car he now had. He glanced at the fuel gauge: perfect, almost full. Then he remembered the helicopter, and at that moment passed a sign which read "Speed checked by radar and aircraft." Youssef had no idea how many traffic control aircraft Missouri might have, but he guessed it wasn't a lot, so he kept his foot pressed down. His knee was very painful now, but he ignored it: the self-preservation urge is a powerful one. He was following Highway

54 towards Jefferson City, which he knew to be the state's capital. There had to be an airport there.

By the time the group from Ferguson's house arrived at the hospital, every law enforcement agency in Missouri and the surrounding states had been alerted, and the hospital had been sealed off. Benny, who met the others at the main entrance, was disconsolate.

"I shouldn't've left. I should've sent Hong. I thought he could handle it. Oh, Jesus, what a fool."

"Easy, Benny, easy. Hong was a police officer, and you had every right to put your trust in him. It's the fault of all of us: we've underestimated this Combs guy at every turn. What he needs is a bullet in the gut. Not the head, that's too quick. We want to see him suffer for what he's done and, by Christ, we will." Ziplich was, like any policeman, relentless in his hatred of a "cop-killer."

Bernadette had been put in a cell. To all interrogation she replied merely, "My name is Candace Simpson." It was like a prisoner of war insisting on giving only name, rank and number.

Jenna Grant, in the Fergoil offices, began to deal, in her usual low-key way, with her backlog of paperwork. It was not quite 6 p.m.

Chapter 14
June 2011

LaDonna Chauduri's contact with Grayson had been somewhat sporadic over the last few days. The Director General's personal secretary had been in touch a number of times to inquire as to the state of the investigation, and she had given him most of the information she had available. Mr. Grayson had, she said, determined that Ralph Ferguson had actually been a Briton by the name of Bernard Phipps, who had apparently been murdered by Irish extremists for having appropriated funds which they claimed for themselves. There was, however, a mysterious third party—as yet not identified—who was involved in the case and was still at large. While two Irish activists had been apprehended and were in American custody, this third person, known to be a multiple assassin, had so far eluded capture. LaDonna did not think it necessary to divulge details of Youssef's escape, since the secretary was not noted for his admiration of his American counterparts, and she had no desire to feed his prejudices. Neither did she claim any credit for her own part in discovering many of the facts. Least of all did she reveal Grayson's most recent request to her.

He'd rung her early in the morning. It must, she thought, be the middle of the night over there. Does the poor man never sleep?

"'Donna?" Just hearing his voice, over the secure line which had been installed in Ferguson's lake house, warmed her heart.

"That's me, boss."

"Tut, tut, how many times? You mean 'It is I.'"

LaDonna was delighted: her man's sense of humor remained undimmed, despite the sad reversals of this dismal affair.

"Of course I do. Just testing you."

"I should have realized. Things are not going awfully well here," and he told her the full details of Youssef's escape. " Well, anyway, I have a couple of questions. First, is Jacko Perkins back from leave yet? I need to talk to him."

"No, he's due in on Monday morning, all sun bronzed from Ibiza, no doubt. And the second?"

"That's a bit trickier. Who's running the Irish section while he's away? That's a confidential question, 'Donna, just between you and me."

"Ted Garvey."

"All right. Now, I misled you, because there's a third question."

"I'm agog."

"No, you're not: you're a beautiful, talented woman, and I wish you were here now."

LaDonna was flabbergasted. The words she never thought she'd hear, coming over an encrypted line from nearly five thousand miles away. For a moment she was speechless, then: "Er, I mean, well, um, the third question? Sir?"

"Can you get any information about movement in the Israel/ Palestine business? Apart from the obvious, I mean. What I'm getting at is, are any Palestinian groups known to be trying to acquire funds in any way, legal or otherwise, in the US? You might try Colin Trent on the Middle East desk."

"I'll do that at once."

"Thanks. One more thing."

"And that would be?"

"When I get home, will you marry me?"

Grayson rang off before an astonished LaDonna could gather her wits, and he looked again at the enlarged photograph Tom Krauss had provided.

It was three a.m., and Malcolm was still questioning Riordan.

"His name is Youssef," Riordan said. "'Tis the only name I know him by. The Committee hired him to take out Ferguson and destroy the evidence by setting fire to the building. He's part of some mid east radical group. They were to help deliver our weapons somehow, but I don't know more about them, either. That bloody storm," he added bitterly, "prevented the fire from happening, or I wouldn't be here now."

"And what was to happen next?"

"Colum was to siphon the money—our money, after all—from the Fergoil account. Then we'd have the funds we've always needed, and to spare. We'd have paid the others their share for disposing of Ferguson and providing the armaments we've always lacked. The bloody Brits would have been kicked out of our land when we had all the weapons we needed, just the way they backed out of Palestine years ago when they couldn't defeat the Irgun and the Stern Gang, let alone the Arabs."

"And look at the happy result of that," Malcolm said. "Are you suggesting that the UDA and the IRA would then live in peaceful harmony? Not to mention all the various splinter groups. But back to this Youssef. That's not a typically Irish name, now, is it?"

"No, 'tis not, but I don't know that it's his real name, anyway. It sounds Arabic, but he looks like a European, so 'tis probably a cover name. All I know is he killed three of me closest friends, and I'll do anything to bring him down."

"Including 'touting' on your organization?"

"Without the money, that's only a wishful thinking dream, anyway. And Youssef's group is just as lost now, for they were to take a large slice of the proceeds."

"You're saying this Youssef was part of a rival group?"

"No, no. 'Tis totally different. I don't know exactly who they are, but they're nothing to do with Ireland. Got their own agenda, their own plans, but I don't know what they are, who they are. I only know the Committee agreed to share the proceeds of stripping the Fergoil accounts, Colum's job, for getting rid of Ferguson. I think they have, or can get, the arms we need. That's why we needed them, and that's why their man Youssef was chosen to take out Ferguson."

"So this Youssef was to kill Ferguson. In the ensuing chaos of the office being destroyed by fire, Tobin would strip Fergoil of its assets, and Youssef's group would get a share of the proceeds?"

"Yes."

"Then why was your former girl friend, Rachel Taylor, murdered by Youssef?"

I don't know," Riordan said through clenched teeth, "but he's that to answer for, as well as Colum and Michael. She was the other one I said he'd killed." There was a pause: Malcolm waited for what he knew had to come.

"How did you know about me and Rachel?" Riordan croaked finally.

"It's unwise," Malcolm advised him, "to allow old lockets to find their way to antique markets."

"She was a darlin' girl, Rachel was," Riordan went on after another pause, "and we had some wonderful times together. Ah, we were very young back then, and I was only engaged on the edges of the movement. She wasn't in it, didn't know I was involved at all. Her father was Jewish, y'see, so she wasn't concerned about the Irish troubles—more worried about Israel and its problems—but she wasn't an activist by any means. Not a Zionist or anything, although her father had been, I believe, and she wasn't religious, any more than I am. It's the injustices we hate, the attempt to control people's minds as well as their actions. The English have tried to change the Irish—even to destroy our language—for more than four centuries, and they've failed. Hitler couldn't eliminate the Jews, who'd suffered constant persecutions from nearly every nation in Europe almost since the Crucifixion, and now they have a state of their own that the Arabs want to obliterate. The Israelis try constantly to control the Palestinians. We can identify with the underdog, because that's what we are. You may say that we have our own state, too, in Eire, but it's incomplete without the Six Counties in the north."

"But Rachel moved on to another relationship—with Michael Nolan."

"That she did. I was heartbroken at the time, especially since he was one of me friends, and I felt betrayed. Still, you get over these things."

Coffee was brought in at this point and, to Riordan's surprise, it was very good. After changing the tape and taking a sip of coffee,

Malcolm asked gently, "Was it Nolan who persuaded Rachel to spy on Ferguson?"

For a long minute, Riordan didn't reply. Then he said: "So you understand about that. Yes, it was Michael. Rachel was reluctant at first. Sure, she'd done a few small jobs for him—he'd a tongue that could charm the birds—but this was like prostitution to her, and she fought against it. By this time she had a good job with a big company. Michael was in London as our paymaster, and they saw a lot of each other, so he finally talked her over. She was being sent to New York for her firm, and 'twas arranged that she'd come here to Tulsa and get to know Ferguson. She did that, and in the course of a few more trips she got to know him well, well enough for him to grow fond of her. Late nineties, that would be, I suppose. Eventually she moved over here permanently and made it her business to win Ferguson over completely. Finally, she moved in with him. I think, in the end, she actually grew fond of the man, too."

"But that didn't stop her from continuing to spy on him?"

"Not on him, really, but on his company. Her job was to identify all the financial arrangements, what with her sharp business brain, and all, and then pass that information on."

" To whom?" Malcolm sipped at his coffee.

"Michael, who then transmitted it to the Committee. "Twould've been too dangerous to let her communicate directly with them. Letters from America to Ireland were suspect in the heyday of the Troubles, since so much financing came from this country. Sure," he editorialized for a moment, "the so-called Irish Americans have a wonderfully romantic misconception about Ireland, which most of them have never even seen, and they thought they were helping knights on white horses. The truth is much more basic. We were in a war, and war is a nasty business, not a romantic one."

"And?"

"Well, then the Committee called in Colum and me. Colum to interpret the information Rachel sent, me to set up the disposal of Ferguson. Rachel knew nothing of that part," he added, "or I doubt she'd have gone ahead. She'd no time for violence. She thought, I imagine, that she was helping by raising money for strictly political purposes. She certainly never knew the hand Michael had in the bombing years ago in the City, for instance. That's London's financial district. She was horrified by that."

"Were you?"

"It's like I said, war is a nasty business, and people get hurt. Just look at Iraq or Afghanistan."

"So, how did you meet this Youssef?"

"The Committee contacted someone in the Middle East, that thing called the Council. I suppose they had connections with the supply of arms, but I don't really know. After all, what you don't know you can't reveal, so the organization has a lot of cut-outs. All I do know is that a meeting was arranged between me, Michael and this Youssef at a hotel in London. That's where we hammered out the details. Michael was to pay Youssef when the job was done, and then, when Colum had pulled the money out of the demoralized Fergoil, our Committee would send a large payment to the Council for supplying the operative. Probably to buy arms, too. I do know there were negotiations with a group in Russia that has access to apparently unlimited amounts of weaponry, for a price. That was the price that Fergoil would provide."

"Youssef killed Ferguson, then. But why did he also kill Rachel?"

Riordan's eyes moistened. "I don't know. I suppose it was unusual for her to be with Ferguson in his office in the evening, so she may just have been unlucky. I told you, she hated violence. See, Ferguson was to suffer a little before he died—our way of showing him the error of his ways. You've heard of kneecapping?" Malcolm flinched. "I see you have. Well, it's just one of our means of making a point. Youssef, it seems, takes a positive delight in such things. I suspect he's a psychopath. Anyway, Rachel would certainly have tried to stop him. Even if she didn't, Youssef is not the sort of person to leave a witness, the scum."

"And yet you did business with this psychopathic scum?"

"In our world, you get your help where you can find it. But if I ever get my hands on Youssef..."

"That's not likely," Malcolm said.

Youssef had made good time on the road from Osage Beach, but when he reached it he realized that the Columbia/Jefferson City regional airport was much too small for him to disappear safely, so he continued to Interstate 70. His initial inclination was to head for St. Louis, but a moment's reflection told him that an airport that size might well be under surveillance, so instead he turned west for Kansas City. In less than an hour he was at Kansas City International airport, which turned out to be much bigger than he had anticipated, and drove the car into the economy parking area, some distance from the terminals. He reasoned that this would be the long-term parking where travelers might leave their vehicles for several days, thus extending his chances of escape. He sought out a quiet section, checking to be sure no surveillance camera could identify him, and parked. Time to change cars. Then he began to search for a vehicle whose owner had left his parking ticket inside the vehicle; Youssef had done the same, occasionally, to avoid misplacing it.

On this occasion he found a dusty Isuzu Rodeo, which looked as if it had been there some time, and altered its identity by the simple expedient Riordan had used some days before: he exchanged the Kansas license plates for those of the Corvette. That way, he reasoned, police looking for the Corvette would ignore an Isuzu, while anyone on the lookout for either the stolen Isuzu or the Corvette would check the tags first. There was little likelihood that a connection would be made before he had vanished, and vanishing was one of Youssef's major talents. He had still to do something about the police uniform he was wearing, so he checked the pockets. He was in luck: in addition to his own money, which had been among the items he had snatched from the hospital bedside, he found Hong had been carrying nearly ninety dollars. Pausing only long enough to turn the shirt inside out, thus concealing the badges, Youssef groped under the front fender of the Rodeo, just in case. Sure enough, there was a spare key in a magnetic holder.

Youssef took a fraction of a second to thank the vehicle's owner. This was so much easier than hotwiring, and it allowed for locking the car up later. He drove away, and soon spotted a K-mart store where he stopped and bought shirt and trousers, then drove on. A little farther along he noticed a Phillips filling station with toilets entered from the outside, and he changed into his new clothes there, putting Hong's uniform into the Kmart bag, which he then stuffed into a trash can. The gun he retained.

Now his priority was to make a clean escape from the country, and this presented a difficulty. The only identification he had on him was the same he had used in his ill-fated attempt to book into the Doubletree in Tulsa, the remainder being in his Hermes bag, which he had abandoned in the Range Rover. Nothing in the suitcase could be traced to him, but he needed a passport. An airport was the obvious answer. Not St. Louis or Kansas City, naturally. Where, then? He tried to visualize the map of the United States, and decided upon Chicago. There he would seek out somebody of roughly his own build and appearance and relieve him of his identification and ticket, no matter what the ticket's destination. Youssef put the Rodeo in drive and pulled away. It was growing dark. He would arrive in Chicago at just about the time Riordan was making his threat.

Grayson, Benny and Ziplich had spent the night at "Peace-haven," after soothing their seething anger at Youssef by means of a sumptuous, and by no means overly-expensive, dinner at The Trail House. The restaurant had been suggested by Deputy Tony Krauss, who could clearly see the frustration the three men were experiencing. Grayson slept soundly after his conversation with LaDonna, while Krauss and Balfour had returned to their respective Camdenton headquarters, with a promise to be back in the morning.

In the morning, Benny had produced a good breakfast from the well-stocked kitchen—he was, Grayson thought, a man of unexpected talents—and then they had examined Youssef's suitcase, which they had found behind the back seat of the Range Rover. At first, it seemed, there was little of interest, other than that Youssef had expensive tastes in clothing. It was Benny who eventually found the carefully-screened hidden compartment, invisible to most standard security scanners, which had revealed a good deal more. Several sets of identification papers and credit cards in a variety of names, including that of

Alfred Combs, quantities of money in euros, dollars and pounds, and a compact yet comprehensive kit of theatrical makeup.

"This Youssef guy," Ziplich said, "gets around a lot, it seems, and in various guises."

"Well, it's no surprise," Grayson observed. "The man is an international assassin; a professional killer who probably has commissions in many countries. It's just that he happens, at the moment, to be engaged in his business here. If and when—no, when; no ifs about it—when he's caught, I'll bet we can tie him to all manner of unsolved incidents in Europe and maybe elsewhere, too. Anyway, we'll see if we can get any prints or DNA matches."

Balfour and Krauss arrived, and the group spent more time poring over the cache of papers removed from under Rachel Taylor's closet floor. There were several letters from "Michael," couched in cautious terms but, given the circumstances, of a suspicious nature and, of all things, a receipt from him for payment of carpentry work done.

"The man came here to put in her secret hiding place!" Grayson exclaimed. "How, in Heaven's name, did we miss that? I know of no indication that he ever left London except to go home occasionally. We've slipped up badly on that." And then he remembered the photograph.

Malcolm rang to put them in the picture regarding the information he'd gleaned from Riordan, and Ziplich turned on the speakerphone. "This Youssef guy was hired from some Mid East organization called the Council to deal with Ferguson. Ferguson had taken money which Riordan's group regarded as their own, but they wanted to be dissociated from his death, and it may be that these other people were able to supply arms as well."

"So we're looking at an extreme Islamist outfit, then?" Ziplich asked.

"Possibly. It would tie in with the name Youssef, but that's probably an alias, anyway, so nothing's written in stone. Still, it certainly can't be ruled out."

"What about Bernadette, Lieutenant? Has she said anything that might help?"

"Keeps saying her name is Candace Simpson: that's all we get out of her, but we already have enough evidence to put her away until she's old and gray, at the very least. You guys found anything new?" and they told him about Michael Nolan's carpentry.

"Hot damn, these people are unpredictable. Oh, did you find anything on the computers?" Ziplich had reported on the attempt to crack the contents of those of both Taylor and Ferguson.

"No news yet," was the reply, "but we may get something today." Balfour nodded confirmation. "That's all we got for now. Would you call Carol and let her know everything's okay here, Lieutenant?"

"Sure. Keep at it, fellers. Any updates about Youssef?"

"No, he's disappeared. Still, we got all his IDs, so he's going to show up someplace without 'em, and then we'll get him. Got a major alert out for him at just about everywhere you can imagine. There's no red Corvette in the lower forty-eight, plus Canada, that won't be checked out, so his time is limited."

"You made sure it's clear that he's known to be armed and dangerous?"

"Wasn't it you who trained me, Stan?"

"Okay, dumb question. We'll talk later. Anything comes up, call me."

"You got it."

❖   ❖   ❖

Elated though she was by Grayson's totally unexpected proposal, LaDonna lost none of her professional composure, and she immediately contacted Colin Trent in the Middle East section to pass on Grayson's query about movement among extremist groups in the Palestinian field.

"Nothing out of the ordinary," he told her. "There are plenty of attempts to obtain weapons, of course, although the tunnels from Egypt have, for the most part, been eliminated. There'll be more, naturally, but such things take time, and we have to go gently, given the touchy situation there right now. No one really knows what the army there will really do regarding elections, and there are plenty of disgruntled Mubarak supporters ready to create trouble. The Israelis are continuing their typically heavy-handed tactics, as one might expect, and terror groups keep launching their usual ineffectual attacks but, overall, it's pretty much the same old thing."

"No indication of special attempts to acquire money or weapons? That's what Dan wanted me to ask you."

"Not in Palestine. Iraq, Afghanistan, Pakistan, now they're another question. Then, of course, there's Tunisia, Egypt, Algeria and the rest, especially Syria. The Americans—and us too, for the time being—are having a hard time of it. Difficult to say where the arms some of them have acquired came from, although, God knows, the area was awash with them even before the invasions. What happens when the Americans pull completely out of Iraq pretty soon is anybody's guess."

"Thanks, Colin, I'll pass on what you said."

"Always a pleasure doing business with you, dear heart."

Hardly had she put the phone down when it rang again.

"LaDonna Chauduri."

It was Ted Garvey. "LaDonna, what the dickens is going on with Dan Grayson? We've had virtually no report since he drifted off to the Colonies, and the DG is beginning to ask questions. I know Jacko Perkins is due back on Monday, but he's been out of the loop, so I really need some hard information to keep the Big Man quiet. What's the latest?"

LaDonna, mindful that Grayson had said his question as to who was running the Irish Desk while Perkins was on leave was confidential, phrased her response with care.

"He's working with the American authorities, but he has, of course, no official status there, so he's pretty much in their hands. I understand there have been some developments, notably that the suspected murderer of Ferguson and Taylor is not far from being apprehended, but I've no more news on that yet."

"What about this fellow Riordan? Is he there, and if so, is anybody keeping track of him?"

Warning bells sounded in LaDonna's mind. Garvey should have known the situation already. "I really can't tell you more than I have, Ted. Dan has been involved in some kind of a chase with the Americans, but exactly what transpired isn't clear yet." *It's a prevarication, but it's not an outright lie*, she thought. "I expect to be hearing from him later today."

"Well, tell him we need to know what the hell he's up to, will you?"

"I'll do that."

"Thanks, LaDonna. Try to get it done by Friday, will you? I'm going to be away this weekend.'

"Well, I'll try, but I can't be sure when I'll have anything new."

LaDonna hung up. "Now, I wonder what has Ted Garvey so interested, especially since I've already reported to the DG," she said quietly to herself. "And I wonder why Dan didn't want it known that he'd asked who was on the Irish desk. I think I scent skullduggery in the department." She decided to pass her concerns on to Grayson

❖   ❖   ❖

His knee was sore and swollen, and his throat hurt badly. Youssef was exhausted, as well, but he dared not stop to rest. He had filled the Rodeo's tank at an all-night service station, where he also bought some cans of cola and a road atlas; then he continued toward Chicago along Interstate 55, having avoided St. Louis, choosing instead to go by way of Hannibal and Jacksonville. The few police vehicles he saw displayed no interest in him, so he supposed the vehicle's owner had not yet returned to Kansas City. Probably the Corvette had not been discovered, either. He still had a little time, then. Hong's pistol was on the passenger seat, under the atlas, but he hoped not to have to use it: the knife made no noise, and he'd have to jettison the gun anyway before he could board an aircraft. There was a faint lightening of the eastern sky.

❖   ❖   ❖

The computer lab report had found nothing of significance in Ferguson's Presario, the contents consisting mainly of routine business matters and a few items regarding the maintenance of the house. Taylor's Toshiba, however, proved more productive. Investigators recovered a large number of emails, both sent and received, which close inspection— in the light of current knowledge—showed to be rather more interesting than the apparently innocent contents at first indicated. Veiled references to financial matters, which were now understood to have a bearing on the acquisition of Fergoil's money, had been sent to an address which had been traced to Michael Nolan.

"Was a computer found at Nolan's place?" Benny asked Grayson.

"No. I suppose it's likely that this Youssef person took it, in case it had anything which might implicate him or lead to him in some way. Still, we already knew about Taylor's involvement with Nolan, so that's not really news. No, what caught my eye was," Grayson riffled through the pages of the lab report, "this bit here." He pointed to a sheet with an email, addressed to "Greyhound," printed out on it. "It looks innocuous enough, but I wonder about this 'Greyhound.' After all, we know that Youssef—I wish we could find him, by the way—was sent to do the dirty work by the shadowy Council. Could there be a connection here? What makes it the more interesting is this note at the bottom from your computer boys to the effect that the addressee can't be traced. And it's not the only one, by any means. When that much care is taken to remain concealed, there must be a reason, and Taylor may have been playing a double game. What puzzles me about that is, if she were in touch with the Council, why did they have her killed?"

"A mistake, perhaps," Ziplich suggested. "Maybe Youssef didn't know she was working for the Council. I don't suppose they give out unnecessary information to their operatives for security reasons, in case one of them gets nabbed. We don't even know who or what the Council may be, what exactly they want, or even where the hell they are. Oh, yeah, the Middle East somewhere, it seems, but that's a lot of ground. Bin Laden hasn't been caught yet, and we do know who he is. We know about Hamas, Hezbollah, Islamic Jihad and the PLO. Then there's the JUA, of course, but they're just a bunch of pie-in-the-Israeli-sky nuts. Then there's all this mess in Iraq, Palestine, Iran, Yemen, Egypt and Tunisia, not to mention the radical elements in Pakistan and Afghanistan."

"But," Benny objected, "we know quite well what their aims are, because they've said so often enough. Not the Council, though."

"Money and arms, according to Riordan," Grayson said thoughtfully. "You know, maybe we should let him escape." Ziplich raised his eyebrows, but offered no comment. "If he were to get away, he'd head back to Belfast: he'd have to report to the gang he calls the Committee on the shambles that's gone on here. There's no chance now that the Ferguson money is ever going to them, so they'll need to look elsewhere. All we'd have to do is keep an eye on him until he boards a plane, pick him up again when he lands, and repeat the exercise until he gets home. Once he's there, he'll go into hiding, of course, but we can deal with that: for a business as serious as this, we'll find the manpower, and he won't be able to take a leak without our knowing it. Eventually, he'll lead us to his Committee, and we'll be in a position to wrap up their operation. I daresay," he added mildly, "the members of this wretched Committee could be persuaded to point us in the general direction of Youssef's Council."

"I don't see my chief being very happy at the thought of letting the man go," Ziplich told him. "That's probably a felony in itself."

"It's just a version of a sting," replied Grayson, "and it'd be to everyone's advantage to crush the head of the snake, instead of merely trimming its tail. We can pick up Riordan again at any time we want once we've achieved our objective."

"Well, I'm willing to float the idea," Ziplich said, "but I doubt it'll fly. What about the girl, by the way, Bernadette Riley?"

Ignoring the mixed metaphor, Grayson answered: "Keep her. One escape would be feasible; two would be far too much of a coincidence for the other side to swallow."

"Youssef escaped."

"I'm painfully aware of it, but he's not from Riordan's group, he's a seasoned professional, and Riordan doesn't know he was even caught, let alone got away again, so he can't report on that. What Youssef will do is leave the country—if he's not found first, that is, and now I don't really think he will be—and make his own report to the Council. They're unlikely to be very pleased with him, so I expect he'll be at the sharp end of some disciplinary action, but I also imagine that they'll use him in some minor role because of his experience. He's too much of an asset to do away with totally."

Ziplich rubbed his chin, then came to a decision. "All right, I'll call Stan Malcolm and tell him what you suggest. Then it'll be up to him whether to take it higher or not."

There was a roaring from the distance, and two military A10 "Warthog" jets whistled low-level across the lake, abruptly climbing up to pass over the house and the echoing hills.

"They do that a lot around here," Balfour remarked to the startled Grayson. "If your plan works, maybe they'll have another target."

❖　❖　❖

Youssef had, indeed, left the country. It had been much easier than he had even dared hope, and his luck seemed to be holding beyond all reasonable expectations. He had arrived at Chicago's O'Hare airport in the early hours, and found a space in one of the vast parking lots. Police were much in evidence, and he supposed correctly that they were on the lookout for a red Corvette, but he was not challenged. His intention was to go to the International Departures terminal and seek out a suitable candidate for identity exchange. Then he would leave his victim, who would by then have no identification, "sleeping" on a chair or bench and take his place on whatever flight his ticket indicated.

Putting Hong's unused firearm under the passenger seat, he got out and locked the Rodeo, then started in the direction of the terminal through the acres of parked vehicles. A movement in one of the cars caught his eye. The man in the driving seat appeared to be choking, one hand clutching at his chest the other fumbling at a pocket, his eyes bulging, his face contorted and with a bluish tinge. Youssef knew a heart attack when he saw one, and he opened the car door. The man was gasping,

"Pills, pills, in my pock..." He broke off with a moan of anguish. "No, no, briefcase, I mean...in my briefca..." Another spasm shook him.

Quite deliberately, Youssef picked up the briefcase from the passenger seat and set it on the ground. Then he said: "They won't help you. Let me loosen your collar," and he leaned forward.

Three hours later, Mr. Todd Prentiss, from Cedar Bluff, boarded a flight to Amsterdam. He was somewhat slimmer than his passport photograph indicated, but possibly the Atkins Diet book he was carrying might have provided a clue as to why.

Dr. Atkins would not have approved of the unattractive mess on Riordan's plate, which remained almost untouched, not because of the prisoner's lack of appetite—he was hungry enough to have eaten "Lamb Fries" under different circumstances—but because his cell door had not been properly secured. When the officer had deposited the tray and shut the door, the key had grated, but Riordan noticed that it had not completely shot the bolt. After a careful look to see that the corridor was deserted, a few moments' work with the handle of the plastic knife from his tray retracted the bolt fully. Riordan arranged the scanty blanket and pillow on the cot, which made up the cell's sole furnishings, to resemble a recumbent figure, opened the door, stepped out, and pulled the door shut. He knew that the ruse had only a limited life, but it might be just enough to get him away from the building. Reasoning that walking boldly out, instead of trying to be stealthy, would be the most likely way to get free before he was missed, he adopted an air of determination and strode ahead. Despite the anticipated proliferation of checks and automatic doors, he was clear within minutes, with no indication of an alarm being raised. *Is this too easy?* he wondered, but decided to take the risk. After all, if he were caught, he'd be no worse off than he had been before.

There were security gates at the entrance, but nothing to stop visitors from leaving. A pair of indolent officers watched him go out, making no move to intercept him. It wasn't until Riordan had stepped into the blazing heat outside that one of them spoke cryptically into his radio.

By the time Riordan had walked the short distance to the city's main library, he was drenched with sweat, and he briefly wondered about stepping out of the frying pan into the fire. He'd taken advantage of the unexpected opportunity to escape, but he had neither a plan for his next move nor money with which to accomplish one. Get away, that was his sole motivation thus far. The library building, close to the courts and law enforcement offices was, it seemed, the gathering place for numbers of homeless people who occupied benches and scrubby bushes outside. Empty bottles and beer cans littered the area, and several of the indigents were asleep: drunk or doped, Riordan assumed. Maybe he could blend in with them for the balance of the day. One disheveled individual lurched towards him, what appeared at first glance to be a school satchel slung over his shoulder.

"Hey, Mister," the apparition whined at him, "you got any spare change? My car's broke down." About to rebuff him, Riordan realized the man was actually carrying a woman's large, bulging purse: stolen, no doubt. An opportunity here, perhaps.

"Trade you for that bag you have," he said, and the man nodded eagerly, unslinging the purse and holding it forward. Riordan took the outstretched bag, turned and walked swiftly away, waiting for the howl of protest. It didn't come. A glance over his shoulder, and Riordan saw the man simply standing, swaying unsteadily, arm still outstretched and a bewildered expression on his face but making no effort at pursuit.

Peering into the bag, Riordan found makeup, a magazine, a few papers—and a wallet, which he removed. He then dropped the handbag into a nearby trash can and continued, opening the wallet. Three credit cards, some sort of electronic door card, a condom, a packet of Cystex, a driving license, a pair of keys in a small marked compartment, and a wad of banknotes. Blessing his good fortune, Riordan walked quickly on. From a bus parked in the terminus across the road, Lieutenant Malcolm watched approvingly as Riordan flagged down a passing taxicab.

"Shouldn't really do this, y'know, buddy," the cab driver declared. "You're s'posed t'call in, y'know. Still, you sure look real hot, so I'll risk it. Just hope the law ain't watchin'," a sentiment that Riordan fervently shared. "So, where to?"

"Five twenty-nine East Eighteenth:" the address on the driving license, plus a few numbers added for safety's sake.

"Gotcha."

The cab moved off, and Malcolm watched it go.

"Seems like our man has taken the main bait," he said into his cellphone, and a blue Nissan Sentra eased into the road behind the departing taxi. When the two vehicles had gone out of sight, Malcolm called in the backup officers who had been stationed in various locations around the immediate vicinity. He now knew where Riordan was, and had a good idea of where he would be going. With keys and money, he would first try the address on the driving license, and even if he didn't, he was being followed. He certainly wouldn't head for the airport, which he would assume to be under surveillance, so he'd probably try to drive out of Tulsa, since he now had conveniently been furnished with a car key.

Malcolm had taken pains to have the house on 18th Street set up for his purpose. There would be a note on the kitchen counter advising the fictitious housekeeper that Mr. and Mrs. Smilley would be away for a couple of days, and please take care of the laundry. In an upstairs bedroom, a man's passport would be partially visible under some papers on top of a bureau. The picture in the passport did not resemble Riordan much, but some "Just for Men" hair dye in the bathroom and a pair of horn-rimmed glasses would pretty much take care of that, while Mr. Smilley's clothes would prove an adequate fit. *Oh, yes*, Malcolm thought, *he'll soon be on his way.*

Time to tell Ziplich, Grayson and Benny how things were progressing. Funny how easy it had been persuading the brass: still feeling mortified after the Terry Nichols fiasco, probably. At least they had agreed that there was no need to alert the Federal authorities. One more thing to do. He had ordered that radio silence would be observed until Riordan was safely in their sights. Now it was time to broadcast that a suspect had escaped and was being sought by the police. He was not known to be armed, but he might be dangerous, so should be approached with caution. Once that went out over the police radio band, the media would pick it up on their scanners, and it would very soon be on radio and television. Malcolm wanted Riordan to know that he had been missed: failing to let that be known would have been tantamount to admitting the whole thing was a setup, and Malcolm was determined to avoid that. If Riordan had any inkling that he had been allowed to get away, he would assuredly not lead the pursuit to his Committee. Now, they were the ones to find. Malcolm was betting that Grayson was right, and that a network—maybe two—could be destroyed. He pulled his cellphone out, and dialed the "Peacehaven" number.

❖ ❖ ❖

There was elation at "Peacehaven" when Malcolm broke the news. "This is progress," Ziplich declared. "Lieutenant, you're a genius to have gotten this approved." There were modest noises over the speakerphone. "No, really. I mean, I'd never have believed you could've done it so quickly. Boy, you must have some kinda silver tongue."

"Credit Dan, it was his idea." It was Grayson's turn to appear modest.

"So Riordan will be outta Tulsa real quick?"

"I guess so. We've smoothed his path as much as we dare without giving ourselves away—I hope. Seems to me he'll head to OKC or Dallas and try to get out from there. He'll be using the name Smilley, and he'll have dyed his hair and put on glasses. We'll follow him, of course, and be sure what flight he takes. My bet is London, because American flies direct from Dallas, so Dan's people can pick him up there and do the rest, but if there's any variation, we'll know about it."

Grayson said: "I'd better get home, then. Need to be on top of things on my own turf, don't you know."

"I figured you'd do that, Dan, and I agree. Better get going ASAP."

"I beg your pardon?"

"As Soon As Possible."

"Ah, yes. Well, I have to get back to Tulsa to collect my passport and things. Left in a bit of a rush, you see."

"We can take care of that at this end, so long as you can have your guys ready to see you through in England. We can send your stuff on later. Zee?"

"Yo."

"Get Dan to a major airport—St. Louis is probably best—and put him on a plane to the Old Country. ASAP. I'll take care of the details."

"Got it."

"I don't know how to thank you for everything," Grayson began, but Malcolm cut him off.

"You'll think of something. Maybe when I come to England some time, you can show me a real pub."

"That will provide but little challenge."

"Goddammit, Dan, when will you learn to talk normal?"

"Sorry. Old habits, and all that. Goodbye, Stan, and thanks again."

"We better get going," Ziplich suggested. "I think there's an evening flight to London you can catch. Be there in the morning."

"Right, but I've got to ring 'Donna first, so she can arrange for me to avoid deportation as an undocumented immigrant." He glanced at his watch. "Might just catch her."

Without realizing it, Riordan followed Malcolm's script almost to the letter. He found the passport, dyed his hair, arrayed himself in Mr. Smilley's garments, and drove Mrs. Smilley's Oldsmobile, on whose radio he heard about his escape, to Dallas/Fort Worth, where he purchased a ticket to Heathrow. He hoped that airline food would be an improvement on the appalling sludge that the jail had provided, and bought himself a large Jameson's, his first drink in over a month, in one of the airport bars. And all the time he was being watched and photographed.

Rather to Grayson's dismay, it was Benny who drove him to the St. Louis Lambert Airport in the Range Rover. At least the trip had the virtue of brevity. Ziplich had decided to return to Tulsa in a rented car, now that matters had been concluded in Camdenton, nominally to check in with Malcolm but, Grayson suspected, mainly because he was anxious to be with his wife after her ordeal. Balfour and Krauss bade them all farewell and returned to their everyday duties. Malcolm faxed a picture of Riordan, taken close-up in Dallas with a digital cellphone, in his new persona, and Grayson took it with him. A quick call to LaDonna to let her know what was happening and to have her arrange speedy clearance through Heathrow also gleaned the information that Ted Garvey had been asking what the latest developments were.

"He seemed, well, nervous about something. That could be my imagination, of course, but I feel that something's not quite right."

"And I think you're absolutely right to have misgivings. I'll explain why when I get back. Got to go now. See you tomorrow."

"It's Saturday tomorrow."

"So it is. I'd still like to see you, though."

"I'll meet you at the airport," replied a delighted LaDonna.

"Thank you. The other thing is, Riordan is on his way back—that's a long story, too, and he's changed his appearance, but I'll fax you a picture immediately—but the point is, he has absolutely got to be watched from the moment he steps off the plane." He gave her the flight number and arrival time. "I'm due in only about half an hour later, so maybe I'll be able to take a hand in this, since I'll be whisked through the formalities and he won't, but it's by no means certain. Can you be sure that we have enough personnel to keep him under tight surveillance without raising his suspicions? No need to mention this to Ted Garvey just yet, I think."

"I'll see to it. See you in the morning."

Once the photo of Riordan in the guise of Robert Smilley had been dispatched, Benny and Grayson had set off. True to his word, Malcolm had all Grayson's travel arrangements in place by the time they arrived and, after a warm parting from Benny, Grayson was ushered into the VIP lounge. There, provided with a very welcome Glenfiddich, he examined his ticket. First class: that was an unexpected and pleasant surprise, since his own department always sent him what he liked to call "steerage." Maybe he'd get one of those seats that convert to a bed, and perhaps even some decent food. Grayson's opinion of airline food was decidedly jaundiced. Both his hopes were fulfilled, and Grayson was pleased, after he'd settled into his seat, to find that he had not been blessed with a chatty travel companion. After takeoff, he took the proffered drink, ate the perfectly decent—if not gourmet, though it did include a quite palatable French cabernet—meal, fiddled for some time with the complicated seat controls until he finally had it into something resembling a bed, put on the supplied eyeshade, and went immediately to sleep.

Bernadette Riley ate the bad food, made no complaint about anything, did not demand to see a lawyer, and answered all questions with "My name is Candace Simpson."

Chapter 15
June 2011

From Amsterdam, Youssef had flown to Rome, then on to Cairo and Amman, where he decided to rest for two days before contacting the JUA Council. He had many friends in the city with whom he could stay, and he had yet to determine exactly how he could shed the best light on what had proved to be a disastrous misadventure. He needed, too, to find a doctor. His knee was a swollen, agonizing lump, exacerbated by the many hours in flight, and his throat continued to be extremely painful. How had that thin, terrified woman done this to him, he constantly asked himself. A woman! He had already determined to avoid the ignominy of admitting that, and to invent some heroic exploit in which he had overcome superior odds and made good his escape. The fact remained, however, that he had failed in his mission: the Ferguson money remained untouched and Riordan—Malone, as he still thought of him—his nemesis, was, so far as he knew, still at liberty. The Council, he was sure, would regard such a failure as unpardonable, and he prepared himself for the worst. That he should try to disappear before facing their retribution never occurred to him, for the Council had long arms, and would eventually find him. In those circumstances his life would be worth nothing and Youssef, who so carelessly ended the lives of others, did not want to die, least of all at the hands of people as cold blooded as himself.

The doctor, a Yemeni, examined Youssef's leg and throat. "The patella is fractured. It's not totally broken, but there's a crack, much more than a hairline, and the knee needs to be immobilized for some time in order to knit."

"How much time?"

"Difficult to say without an x-ray, and that's out of the question for you, but I'd say probably three, four weeks."

"I can't afford that long."

"Very well, I'll give you pain-killers, but you have to be aware that you could sustain serious and permanent damage if you use that leg much more. In short, you'll be crippled."

With no hesitation, Youssef said: "Give me the pain-killers. What about my throat?"

"Your own body will take care of that without interference from me. The analgesics will help you to cope with the discomfort."

❖ ❖ ❖

In a blessedly gray and damp Surrey day, and under the envious gaze of other passengers, Grayson was hustled through immigration formalities in a matter of moments. When he exited through the green Customs channel, there was LaDonna, holding a huge "Welcome Home" banner. She flung himself onto the embarrassed Grayson, and kissed him passionately on the mouth. Despite the surroundings, Grayson felt his loins stir, and he heard a faint round of applause from bystanders.

"My word," he said when he had managed to disentangle himself from her embrace, "that's more of a welcome than I anticipated."

"Oh, you're so bloody English!" LaDonna exclaimed. "If I didn't know you better, I'd say you were frigid."

Grayson leered. "Say that again tonight."

There was a discreet cough behind them. "I think you may want to check out the chap who's just come through," murmured a nondescript man in a grubby raincoat. "If I'm not mistaken, he's Mr. Robert Smilley."

It was Riordan, all right, walking carefully as he peered through the lenses of his stolen spectacles. He was carrying an American Tourister suitcase and had a small bag over his shoulder. He paused for a moment to scan the departure boards then, apparently satisfied, set off toward the Aer Lingus desk.

"On his way to Dublin or Shannon," Grayson said. "Then he'll find some means to sneak back home. Looks younger with black hair, doesn't he? Henry?" The raincoat was beside him. "Don't let him slip you, old boy."

Henry was unperturbed. "We've got more people watching in more places than we've got at all, if you take my meaning. Dear

Mr. Smilley is under the microscope, Dan, and there he'll stay until you want to haul him in."

"Right, Henry, thank you. Let me know what's happening, will you?"

"Of course. Shall I ring you at Miss Chauduri's number?" And he dodged a mock left uppercut.

The body of a man, clearly the victim of a heart attack, was found on the floor of a Cadillac in one of O'Hare's huge car parks. He had no identification, but the license tag on the car was that of a Missouri-registered Corvette. A nearby Isuzu carried the number plates of the Illinois Cadillac and a police pistol under the passenger seat. Before long, a red Corvette was discovered in the Kansas City airport, bearing the tags of an Isuzu Rodeo. Youssef's escape route had been revealed, but too late.

Carol curled contentedly against Ziplich. His unannounced arrival had filled her with joy: it was always her secret fear that his job would one day bring him harm, and to see him home and safe was an inexpressible relief, even though she knew that, on this occasion at least, he had been in no danger once Youssef had made his break for freedom. Her own experience she brushed off as nothing, although Ziplich knew better. Tonight they were not in their chairs by the window, but snuggled together on the sofa; they both needed the comfort of loving touch.

"Paul?"

"Mmm?"

"What will happen now? About Youssef, I mean. How will you ever find him?"

"That's outside my area now, Honey. Wherever he is, it's not in this country, and I doubt if he'll ever show his face—any of his faces—here again. He'll be in big trouble because of the bungled Ferguson business, and I guess he'll be kept on a tight leash by his masters for a long time. No, I think we can forget about him and concentrate on our homegrown thugs and assorted villains. Dan, on the other hand, has much wider-ranging responsibilities than a Tulsa cop does, and

I bet he'll be setting his sights on Youssef 'til the guy is nailed. Dan doesn't strike me as the type to let go of a problem easily."

"I like him very much. He's so gentle and...and, well, civilized. I'm so sorry about his wife."

"Me too, but, unless I'm very much mistaken, his secretary is soon going to fill that gap in his life."

"Oh, I do hope so. You know anything about her?"

"Not really, except that he told me you reminded him of her a great deal. That's a real compliment to her. And when he spoke to her on the phone, his voice took on a kind of, I don't know, an extra warmth, I guess. Yeah, Dan has it going for LaDonna alright."

"She's black, too? Is that okay in England? I mean interracial romance, marriage, all that kind of stuff? Folks are a bit less judgmental here these days, but what about there?"

"You know, he never said anything about that but, yeah, I suppose it's OK there. I think he said her parents were from India. Seems to me like the Brits were ahead of us on that front, anyway. I mean like Johnny Dankworth and Cleo Laine even all those years ago, right?"

Carol, the jazz lover, nodded. "I do so hope it works out for them."

"Me, too. If there's a wedding, I sure expect us to get an invite." Ziplich stroked the back of his wife's neck, and she shivered a little. "Are you cold?" he asked with feigned concern. "Maybe I should put you to bed."

"Yes, please."

.The Council met at a secluded farmhouse in Lebanon's Beka'a Valley. This was, more or less, neutral territory. True, Syria nearby, Israel and Hezbollah each had a substantial presence, but it was fairly low key—Israel's virtually invisible yet well understood—and the members expected no interference from any of them. In any case, they were pleased to acknowledge, Syria had its own hands full at home, while the Lebanese authorities could simply be ignored. There were several items on the agenda. First the Israeli attacks in Gaza and new settlements in the Occupied Territories; the current American and Israeli governments; the developments in Iraq, where the Americans were in the final stages of a phased withdrawal. Also discussed were the troubles in Pakistan and Afghanistan, the question of attacks in Saudi Arabia, the increasing unrest the Council had fomented in several mid-East countries, notably oil-rich Libya and the vast expanse of Egypt and, currently, Syria. The leader pointed out, to the surprise of no-one, that the sights were now firmly trained on Iran. "We will use its oil more wisely than they can," he said with a humorless smile. Finally, the topic was Youssef. Only the Leader was aware that this building had once been the school where Youssef and his younger brother, together with thirty or so other young colleagues, had undergone their very extensive training.

Up to this point, the delegates had been largely unanimous as to how to proceed, but there had been a few questions about what the West had begun to call the "Arab Spring."

The Leader smiled. "It is *our* spring," he declared.

When the matter of Youssef was raised, all eyes turned to the one they knew only as "Greyhound."

"Gentlemen," he began—there were no women present—"as you well know, the real success of our campaign, to 'smite with the edge of the sword,' depends to a great extent, if not entirely, upon the ability of Youssef to complete his mission in America. It is difficult to assess exactly how that is proceeding, since he has made no recent contact with us and, unfortunately, our direct source there is no longer available. I have, however, the greatest confidence in Youssef, for reasons which security prevents me from revealing"

There was a slight stirring around the table: they all knew why the source had dried up and a few were disinclined merely to accept the word of a man whose exploits they knew only by whispered repute.

"The fact that we have not heard from him is not, in itself, unusual," Greyhound continued. "Communications under such circumstances are rarely secure, and Youssef has a well-deserved reputation for taking no chances. I have little doubt that he will prove successful. Within a few weeks, we shall have acquired the means to purchase all the armaments we require. With the developments you have already discussed so fully, particularly regarding the hideous Israeli atrocities in Gaza," here he smirked briefly, "the moment is most opportune for us to move. The arms will be distributed covertly—the system for that has been established, tested in Libya and is entirely secure—to our supporters throughout the region. Many of those supporters, as you are all well aware, are now in positions of the highest importance and influence. In addition we are very strong among what I might call 'the foot soldiers.'

"In direct contrast to Hamas, Hezbollah, Islamic Jihad and the like, or even the IRA," there was a snicker among his audience, "we have never publicized our *intentions*, although our beliefs are well-known, and our attacks will come as a complete surprise. What is more, they will not be futile suicide bombers or those miserable and virtually useless rockets, both of which we have instigated to firm up support among our general population. Our weaponry will be both modern and effective. You know already of the trusted source in Russia from which they will come, and delivery plans are complete."

He paused a moment for emphasis. "We have a comprehensive network in place in even the highest echelons which will assure us of success. All we need is the money that Youssef is charged with obtaining. I should be in a position to tell you within," he glanced at his watch, "seventy-two hours from now, whether that funding has become available. There is no doubt in my mind that it will be. My confidence is based on the fact that I, together with our leader, know Youssef intimately. He is utterly dependable and supremely able. I am proud to acknowledge him as a brother. I shall contact the Chairman"—this with a nod to the distinguished figure at the head of the table— "the moment I can confirm that, and matters thereafter will proceed with great rapidity. We are on the threshold of an historic victory."

"Insh'Allah," murmured one delegate, to the amusement of the others.

The Chairman again smiled briefly. In his mind he saw the destruction of the enemy as clearly as he beheld the room in which he sat. There would be double satisfaction for him. The immediate target and the more distant object of his hatred, the people who had ravaged his adopted homeland. They would be disgraced, humiliated. And he, he, Beniamin Meier, would be the architect of their defeat.

To Henry's surprise, Riordan did not book a flight, having evidently had a change of mind. Instead, he took the Piccadilly Line to King's Cross, walked the short distance to Euston, and took a train to Liverpool. He then boarded the overnight ferry to Ireland, imbibing several glasses of Bushmills during the crossing. None of this made much difference: Henry and the others had him in sight the entire time. Watchers who had been alerted in Dublin and Shannon airports were stood down, with the caution that they might be recalled at any time, and others were activated to greet the ferry. When Riordan disembarked, he was again followed, and again he surprised the surveillance team by merely booking a train ticket to Belfast. It seemed that he had total confidence in his persona of an American tourist, although a trained ear would have found his accent highly suspect. Once in Belfast, he went straight home, once more amazing the team following him.

"The feller's just asking for it, so he is," Sean Smethwick muttered incredulously to Henry, as they watched from a battered Ford Sierra near the street corner. Henry was on his phone, arranging for immediate wiretaps on Riordan's line and a replacement for himself and Sean.

"He probably believes we still think he's in America. Well, can't sit here too long, Riordan or someone would be bound to notice us," and he set in motion a series of "changing of the guard" to provide constant coverage.

The wiretap soon bore fruit. "He rang Parsons's greengrocery," the listening post advised Henry, "and asked for a delivery to be made. 'My usual address,' he said. Since there's a shop not two hundred yards from his door, that sounds to me more like setting up a meeting than giving a vegetable order. I've got a hookup with Parsons's now, so we can find out if anyone else is liable to turn up."

"Well done, young man." The communications operative was old enough to be Henry's father. "It would be as well to know what sort of numbers we're looking at so we can arrange a suitable welcoming party. Have you got any idea where the 'usual address' might be?"

"No, but I'll keep listening. Maybe someone will let something slip."

"Good. Thanks, and let me know when you've got anything."

"Will do."

Henry turned to his companion. "Sean, can I use your phone? Got to keep mine free in case there's anything new."

"Sure."

Henry dialed Grayson. It was Saturday afternoon.When Grayson's phone trilled, he was sitting in the Hammersmith flat of one of his colleagues, appalled, if no longer surprised. When he and LaDonna had left the airport in the car she had been allocated from the Company's pool, they went neither to his house nor her apartment.

"There are several questions that have to be answered first, my love," he said, and the endearment filled her with delight.

"Such as?" she asked, threading through the traffic of the M4.

"Such as, what does this photograph signify?" He pulled out the enlargement that Balfour had provided of the figure reflected in Rachel Taylor's sunglasses.

LaDonna momentarily took her eyes off the road to glance at the picture. "Oh, my God," she exclaimed. "So that's why you wanted me to be cagey with Ted Garvey."

"Exactly. You mentioned a few minutes ago about smelling something fishy, and this is it, right enough. Who'd have thought it? At first I simply couldn't believe it, but this can't be denied. So now, we have a flat to search before we get a bit of time to ourselves. But then..." He trailed off, but LaDonna understood.

Now, in the flat, the hurriedly assembled search team, backed by a pair of armed agents in case the target was not, as expected, away until the evening, had found the incontrovertible proof in several forms, not least some emails addressed to and from "Greyhound." There were others, too, referring to the "Committee." Grayson's phone trilled.

"Grayson."

"Dan, it's Henry. We've got Riordan in our sights—at his home, would you believe?—and we think he's setting up a meeting. I'll get back to you when I have more, but I thought you'd want to know."

"Quite right, Henry. That's the sort of stuff you don't expect to hear so quickly, but it's very welcome news indeed. I have a feeling that we're beginning to wrap this damned Committee up, and that will be a huge relief. Let me know what develops."

"'Course. Back with you soon as I have more."

Ringing off, Grayson said to LaDonna: "Now it's our painful duty to talk to the DG."

The Director General, reached at his country weekend retreat, listened without comment until Grayson had finished. Then he said: "Dan, this is the most Godawful security breach we've had since Burgess and Maclean. There can't be the slightest shadow of doubt, I take it?"

"No, sir, the evidence is in front of me now and, with this, the whole thing holds together tighter than a duck's arse."

The DG gave a grim chuckle. "More like a crocodile, I'd say. Well, we'd better have a few well-chosen words, hadn't we? What do you suggest?"

Grayson told him, and received approval. Then he turned to the head of the search party. "Let's wrap it up here, son. Everything back exactly as it was. These"—he indicated the assorted documents he'd printed off a laptop recovered from a concealed under-eaves compartment—"we'll take with us. We'll have a dispatch rider pick the computer up on Monday, the moment our suspect has left. And now maybe we can all go home for a few hours."

The painkillers were quite effective, and Youssef found that his leg, if exercised with caution, was fairly flexible, while the throat was scarcely noticeable. He purchased a disposable cellular phone and, from the bustling Amman street outside the Kempinski Hotel where his conversation would be masked by the ambient noise, he rang the assistant to the Chairman of the Council. His words were selected with great care, but the listener at the other end understood the implications clearly. Youssef was back on his home ground, and requested an urgent meeting. The assistant accepted that Youssef could not be more explicit, since the CIA and other unfriendly entities were known to intercept calls of this nature, so he immediately contacted the Chairman, who at once agreed to the meeting. The venue was identified by the standard coded reference, as was the time. It would take place at a restaurant on Tuesday, four o'clock, local time. By then, Meier reasoned, Greyhound should have reported and he hoped that Youssef would confirm what he expected to hear and add the relevant details. Youssef, cold with apprehension at his failure, acknowledged the rendezvous, broke the connection, and threw the phone into a rubbish bin. Then he began preparations for departure.

He was about to use a public telephone to make his next reservation when a face caught his eye. A familiar face, older and more lined, maybe a little fatter, and no longer crowned with a head of dark hair. What hair there was had turned a dingy gray, lost its tight curls and receded far from its original forehead line. But Youssef was in no doubt; the large black eyebrows, the cruel, almost lipless mouth, the expressionless eyes were unmistakable. The final, irrefutable evidence was the sniggering, odious laugh as the man made a remark to a young woman at his side while the two were crossing the road in front of him.

Youssef had found another of his mother's killers.

"I was quite serious when I asked you to marry me, you know," Grayson told LaDonna. "I'm aware that it wasn't the standard down-on-one-knee proposal of bodice-ripper novels, but I suddenly realized just how much I missed you, how much I rely on you—God! How much I love you. Does that sound foolish?"

"It sounds like the words I've been longing to hear from you for years. Didn't you realize that I absolutely adore you? You men can be really thick, sometimes."

"Thank you for your own kind words," Grayson retorted dryly.

"Oh, you know what I mean, Dan. I've loved you for so long it's almost been pain, but I thought you merely regarded me as part of the office furniture, and that's been hard. I was afraid that because of my color..."

"Never, never, mention such a thing again," Grayson interrupted. "It's what's inside that counts with any rational being, and I hope I'm that, at least. It's you, not your skin, that I care about, lovely though it is." He chortled. "Just think what they'll make of this back at the firm."

LaDonna pulled up in front of the Willesden house. "Well, here we are. You're home. What now?"

"Do you really have to ask?"

"Sir! What will the neighbors think?"

"The neighbors can go and take a funny run at themselves, for all I care, although the fact is I'm very lucky in that respect."

"Talking of respect, will you still respect me in the morning?"

"That, I take it, is a rhetorical question."

Grayson's phone interrupted. "Damnation! Have they no sense of decency or timing?" Irritably, he pulled the instrument from his pocket and barked: "Grayson."

"Sorry to break in on you Dan, " said a slightly miffed Henry, "but I thought you'd want to know. Riordan's arranged a gathering of what must be the entire Committee, judging by the number of people who've been contacted by Parsons, so we may be able to make quite a catch."

"And I'm sorry to have been short with you, Henry. Tired, I suppose." There was a sympathetic grunt from Henry. "Any idea where or when?"

"No, but we'll have both Parsons and Riordan trailed, and they'll lead us to the place. Once we've established the spot and the rest have arrived, we'll call up the reserves and surround it. Then," he paused dramatically, "We Swoop!"

"Henry, my lad, you're beginning to talk like a B Movie. Have you had any rest?"

"No more than you, but then I haven't flown the Atlantic, either."

"Okay, keep me up to date, will you? I promise not to snarl at you again. Not often, anyway," he added.

"It shall be done."

"Now," Grayson said to LaDonna, "would you like to come up and see my etchings?"

"Only if you promise not to offer me Madeira, m'dear."

"Cup of tea's more like it."

Henry's men waited and watched outside Riordan's house and Parsons's shop: eventually, as dusk was falling, they were rewarded for their patience. First, Riordan emerged, minus the horn-rimmed spectacles, but still with black hair. He was dressed in jeans and a denim shirt. With a glance up and down the street, probably for any sign of surveillance, of which there was none—the team was far too well-trained for that—he set off on foot.

Parsons, looking more Pickwickian than ever, took his delivery van, a decrepit Morris Minor of '60s vintage, and headed towards the Falls Road. Within twenty minutes, both men had entered Mason's Bar. Henry was surprised. The bar had been, like almost all similar establishments, under scrutiny on many occasions, but there had never been a whisper of impropriety. Clearly, they'd missed the connection here. Henry spoke quietly into his radio, and the net began to close. Over the course of the next ninety minutes, nineteen men and five women were seen to go into Mason's. It was possible that they were not all part of the operation, but Henry was certain that he now had sufficient cause to make his move, and he whispered again into his radio.

It was done very quietly: the expected lookout was located and placed in one of the unit's vans with a guard. A cordon of agents surrounded the building, then Henry and five other armed men walked through the front door. Simultaneously, six more entered by way of the back. The downstairs bar contained only three customers and an elderly barman, all of whom, with one look at the semiautomatic weapons, sat stock still, hatred in their eyes. The back door gave on to an empty kitchen. Two men took up station there; the others crept forward through a passageway, meeting their counterparts at the foot of a flight of stairs. As at the rear, two men remained in the bar. Eight more men outside would dissuade any further trade at Mason's.

A murmur of voices coming from the first floor indicated the next move. Henry, machine pistol at the ready, led the way up, gesturing with one hand for two men to check the rooms from which there was no sound: two more were dispatched to the top floor. Satisfied that everyone was in position, Henry opened the door of what was, he was amused to see from a small plaque, the "Committee Room."

"God bless all here present," he said politely.

LaDonna lay, totally at peace, in the curve of Grayson's arm, her cheek nestled against his shoulder, one arm across his chest, a smile of utter bliss on her lips. Their lovemaking had been just that—an expression of love rather than of passion. Not that passion had been lacking, but it was a means, not an end in itself. For a man so slender, Dan was surprisingly well built, she thought contentedly. Not that it would have mattered had he proved otherwise: she loved the man, not the performance, although that had been an additional delight. I'm so happy, she thought, that I'm afraid something might spoil it all. She brushed the idea aside; nothing could take this moment away.

Grayson was asleep, hardly surprising after all he'd had to do in the last few days. He, in his turn, had remained slightly bewildered by the mere fact that LaDonna should be attracted to him, of all people, a man nearing middle age, with thinning hair and (in his own mind) not much personality. Certainly, he didn't question her honesty, he knew her too well for that. No, it just seemed too, too...well, too improbable. For a brief moment he remembered Janet and a flash of—not guilt, something more like closeness—came to him. *I always loved you, Janet, and I always will, but this is different and I hope you'll understand and be happy for us.* It was then that he dozed.

Henry rang. The sound of the telephone shattered the stillness of the bedroom and, for a moment, disoriented Grayson. Reluctantly, he picked up the receiver. "Grayson," he managed.

There was a momentary pause before Henry, who realized at once what the circumstances must be, spoke apologetically. "Sorry again to break in on you, Dan, but you really ought to know this. We've got 'em, the Committee, I mean. Nearly thirty of them, all together in one place. I can hardly believe that Riordan was so careless, but I suppose he's even more exhausted than you are, after the last week or so, and he's been under huge stress. Whatever the reason, he led us to 'em, and we've netted the lot. Oh, there may be a handful who weren't at the meeting, but we'll nail them or they'll fade away. Main point is, the Committee is now defunct, and whatever their main agenda may have been, it's defunct too as of tonight."

Grayson, now fully awake, said: "Henry, that's the best wake-up tonic I could imagine." Here, LaDonna made a suggestive motion, and Grayson's amused smile could be heard in his voice. "Well, almost the best." Henry understood. "I'll come over to Belfast early in the week, and we can have a little chat with these naughty fellows."

"There are half a dozen women," Henry told him.

"Are there, now? Let's put a little pressure on them, shall we? Sometimes they're even harder than the men, but sometimes not. Either way, we have a bit of time, now. Before I come over, though, there's a nasty bit of business I have to take care of here. That'll be tomorrow, so I'll probably see you on, say, Wednesday. As a matter of interest, how did Riordan take it?"

"Total surprise at first, of course, then anger—I expect with himself—and finally a sort of resignation. It may be that he's really a bit relieved to have the whole thing off his back. In any case, he won't have any responsibilities for the next several years."

"Except for staying alive if anyone finds out that he grassed on them to the Yanks."

"We'll keep that to ourselves, but there's bound to be speculation. We'll just have to see to it that he's kept apart from his associates."

"Which would be tantamount to telling them he's the source of their problem. No, let him take his chances. He's earned them."

"Take your point. Well, that's a bit down the road, anyway. 'Kay, that's all I've got for now, so I'll let you get back to sleep." With a muffled snigger, he was gone.

Grayson did not get back to sleep immediately, of course.

In Belfast, the questioning began. At the same time, the home of each of the Committee members was searched, and some interesting items came to light.

❖   ❖   ❖

Ever cautious, Youssef did not go directly to his rendezvous with the leader of the Council. He surveyed the neighborhood, close to the city's waterfront, for any possible danger point. Empty buildings were always subject to suspicion, but there was none to be seen: this was a busy and clearly quite prosperous area, and there were many holidaymakers, to whom numerous establishments catered. The Uri Buri restaurant where the meeting was to take place had umbrellas over the terrace tables, and there was a pleasant view of the waterfront. The place appeared immaculate, and trade seemed to be brisk, so Youssef decided to seat himself at one of the tables to be sure that they weren't all taken before the Chairman arrived. He checked the time: slightly more than an hour to go. He selected a table, and opened the English-language newspaper he had bought along the way here. More Israeli incursions in Gaza, more car bombs in Baghdad, more unrest in Cairo, more bloodshed in North Waziristan, Libya, Syria and Yemen, more accusations and counter-accusations starting the American election process—an election still over a year away—more trouble for the coalition in Britain, more grisly reports from several parts of the globe. *The world doesn't change much*, he mused. *I wonder if our own efforts will really make any difference.* His mood improved as a waiter approached and, seeing the paper, addressed him in English.

Youssef ordered a glass of red wine and a cup of black coffee. "I'm waiting for a friend," he told the waiter. "We'll order something to eat when he gets here." The waiter departed, soon returning with the wine and coffee, and Youssef went back to the paper. His mind, however, was really on how he was going to break the news to his superior. His apprehension was, on the other hand, considerably mitigated by the memory of the bleating confession of the slime he had erased in Jordan.

As Riordan had realized, Youssef was of a sadistic nature. It had been a major factor in his deliberate decision to become an enforcer for the Council, but not the sole reason. The merciless rape and death of his mother before his eyes as a child had given him a cause to pursue and an outlet for his hidden tendencies. It had been the smallest of steps to graduate from personal pleasure to dedicated operative, but the personal aspect had never been fully suppressed. In Amman, the sight of that remorseless face had re-ignited a flame which had never been totally quenched. Youssef felt a surge of hatred uncommon for him. Murder was his business, albeit with a larger objective in mind. This, however, would be satisfaction. Slow, painful, extended, relentless, excruciating and, finally, to the point when death would be welcome. Except that Youssef did not intend to kill. He would leave that shattered body to find its own release. And he would watch.

But it was not thus that Suleiman Razak left this world.

They chose the conference room, it being larger than the individual offices, even that of the Director General. Grayson arrived first with LaDonna, who would be taking notes. Next, the DG came in, slightly unkempt as usual, accompanied by his own secretary and a new Basset hound puppy. The DG was known to be fond of dogs. Ted Garvey appeared a few minutes later, looking slightly nervous, LaDonna thought. Then Jacko Perkins, fit and bronzed from his holiday in Ibiza, followed by John Bloom and Colin Trent. A minute or so later, Peter Ngami made his appearance. When everyone was seated, the DG, his renowned eyebrows in full intimidation mode, began.

"Ladies and gentlemen, I've called you together to discuss an unusual development. As you know, we've had a joint investigation with the Americans concerning a possible attempt by Irish malcontents to obtain large sums of money from an oil company in Oklahoma. Frankly, if it hadn't been by sheer accident of nature, a major tornado, the plan would probably have succeeded. I'm going to turn this over to Dan Grayson, here, to put you more fully in the picture, and outline our intentions to deal with the threat. Dan?"

Grayson did not stand up. He appeared distracted for a moment by a paper on the table in front of him. "Morning, director, thank you. You all know each other, I think, but just for the record, Miss Chauduri will make the notes. John Bloom, from the SNP/Plaid Cymru section"—Bloom nodded—"who used to be with my department. Ted Garvey of the Irish desk; Colin Trent of Middle East, who has an interest in these proceedings; and Jacko Perkins, head of the Irish desk. Peter Ngami, some of you may know, has done some good work for me, as well as for Jacko. I'll expect you'd agree, wouldn't you, Jacko?" Grayson turned over the paper in front of him, so that it lay face up. "Or should I call you Greyhound?"

On the table was the enlarged picture of Rachel Taylor's sunglasses.

❖ ❖ ❖

"Sorry to disturb you on a Sunday, Zee," Grayson had said, "but there've been some developments," and he went on to describe the events of the previous evening.

"So you've hauled in the bastards: that's great news, Dan."

"It's certainly answered a lot of questions, although some do still remain. Still, the committee of the PFRI is now out of business."

"The who?"

"PFRI. The Patriotic Front for the Reunification of Ireland, that's what they called themselves. They've got it in Erse, as well, but I can't pronounce that. We found all sorts of interesting stuff when we got a really thorough search going. My goodness, these people knew how to keep things hidden. We uncovered a complete workshop for forging documents—run, incidentally, by Maire Riley, Bernadette's sister—several caches of arms, and a number of computers which we're sure will help us wrap up the whole nasty organization. That's one thing."

"So your idea of letting Riordan get away worked out?"

"Better than we could possibly have hoped. Now, there's something else."

"Yeah?"

"We now know for certain who Greyhound is."

"Ye Gods! Dan, you guys have really been hustling."

Grayson was suitably modest. "Yes, well, things have actually gone quite well, I must admit. Thing is, you see, our chaps have possibly rather more experience in breaking codes than the very competent experts in Missouri, and they've performed their magic on the documents we got out of Taylor's computer. What's more, we inaugurated a search of Greyhound's home, once he'd been pretty much identified, and that produced so much information that it'll take us several days to sift it all. What is certain, though, is that we now have a line on the Council itself. And in that respect, I have a little favor to ask you."

"Ask away."

"It would be extremely helpful if you'd send an e-mail for me."

"Sure. Give me the details, will you?"

"If you don't mind, I'd rather send them on the secure fax line at your office. I know it's asking a lot to drag you away from Carol, but this may prove crucial."

"Carol knows what a cop's life is like."

"Thank you, and thank her for me, too, if you will."

"She'll be glad to hear about the progress."

"Right. Well, I'll get this sent shortly."

By the time Ziplich arrived at his office, the fax was waiting. The message it contained was addressed to a name unknown to him, and it appeared totally innocuous, but he understood that it had been encrypted. He had been wondering why Grayson didn't send it direct himself, but a brief notation made it clear. "This is going to be forwarded, and it needs an American point of origin." To show its authenticity, of course. Ziplich lit up his computer, and, using the standard untraceable address, sent the message exactly as it had been presented to him. Then, wondering where all this was leading, he went home to Carol.

At precisely four o'clock, the Chairman arrived, accompanied by the expected phalanx of bodyguards. Youssef had watched them as they spread out, checking the people crowding the café and its immediate surroundings. *Now,* he thought, still elated by his success in having eliminated the last of his mother's killers, but aware that he was on very thin ice, *we come to the moment of truth.* Razak had groveled, pleaded, confessed, implicated a dozen others, screamed into an unsympathetic cellar, and finally died. Youssef sniggered inwardly at the memory. His real regret was that his younger brother, now in England, could not be contacted to tell him of the outcome of that chance encounter.

To Youssef's surprise, the leader, as soon as he saw him, lit up his face with a broad smile. Youssef rose, and the Chairman clasped him in a warm embrace, kissing him on both cheeks.

"My brother," he exclaimed, and Youssef genuinely felt a moment of kinship, "A triumph! The news came not fifteen minutes ago, and I have not yet had time to communicate with the other members: that can wait a little longer. Waiter! Champagne." The waiter's face displayed excitement at serving such a well-known patron. Youssef hoped that his own face betrayed no bewilderment.

The Chairman sat, and the sunglasses-bedecked minders spread out in a protective shield some yards away.

"The Irishwoman," the leader continued, "sent her coded message to Belfast. It was intercepted by the...by our contact in Britain," he corrected himself, "who forwarded it at once to me. The Ferguson money will be transferred and in our hands by the end of the week. In another two weeks, our shipments will begin. By December, everything will be in place. What a Christmas present this will be to our enemies. They don't believe in Christmas anyway. The Irish will, of course, get nothing or next to nothing. That will not please them, but they're such stupid oafs that they're unlikely to cause us any serious concern. They'll make threatening noises, I have no doubt, but they're not in any position to do very much about it. We must be prepared, naturally, for a few minor losses, but that's the nature of the situation. Our London connection told me that most of the Irish organization has been captured by the British. That's unfortunate for them, but very convenient for us, particularly since there is nothing to link the two groups. It's all ours, now, and it's only a matter of time—a short time—before our total success."

Youssef's mind was racing: Bernadette must have persuaded the Americans that she was what she had claimed to be, an IRS official. How she had done that he had no idea, but it didn't really matter. His own incompetence had not been uncovered, and he drew a breath of relief. The champagne arrived.

"Now," the Chairman resumed, sipping at his glass, "what about the man, Malone?"

"I have to confess, I don't really know. I never actually saw him in Oklahoma, so I can't truthfully say whether he was there or not. It seems to me unlikely that the woman, whom I did see, was allowed to be there on her own, so I feel that he was somewhere in the background. I would really like to put an end to him," he added, shrugging, "but that's just a personal thing, and it can wait a little longer. For the time being, I'll just enjoy a bit of relaxation here. Haifa's always been one of my favorite holiday spots." What he did not think it necessary to add was that he had selected the city when Razak had screamed out the name of the fifth man who had been in the group that had killed his mother. The scream had sunk to a low moan when The Chameleon relaxed the torture of the man's genitals for a brief moment.

"Where is he ? If you want the pain to stop, tell me the exact address." Razak gasped the location of a street in Haifa, and Youssef kept his word about the pain. He had killed Razak without further delay. After the meeting with the Leader, he had another appointment to arrange.

❖　❖　❖

Perkins gave an amused smile. "Greyhound? You think I've been betting on the dogs?"

"No, Jacko, I think—I know—that you've been living a double life. Make that a triple life. Which is why you took the name Greyhound, the street that runs outside this building. You might just as well have selected the Colton Arms. Or maybe it's just close enough to my name to amuse you." There was a contemptuous snort from Perkins. "Anyway, let's start with why you were taking snaps of Michael Nolan, Jimmy Riordan and Rachel Taylor." He gestured at the picture on the table.

Perkins waved an indolent hand. "Just people I met on a beach."

"Yet, as a member of the Irish desk, you knew who they were, and you recognize the names."

"Names only. I had no idea what they looked like."

"Tut, tut, Jacko. Their pictures are all in your files." Grayson drew several photos from a briefcase beside his chair. "Any of these look familiar?"

"One sees so many faces."

"One does, indeed. Very well, so you don't, or at any rate didn't, know who these three people were back in 1995, when these pictures were taken. Oh, yes, we've been able to establish that. Ibiza, one of your favorite holiday spots." He used the same term that Youssef had in Haifa. " But what about this one?" Grayson stood up, dropping other pictures on the table, "or this, or this?"

At the last one, Perkins blenched.

"Colin, you're head of the Middle East desk. Do you recognize anyone in this photo?"

"Beniamin Meier.

"And with him?"

Colin Trent sighed. "Jacko Perkins."

"Of the extremist 'JUA' faction? Meier, I mean."

"Yes."

"What do the letters JUA stand for, Colin?"

"Juden Uber Arabien."

"German, not Hebrew? Strange, after the Holocaust."

"There are enormous numbers of Israelis who are German immigrants or of German extraction, among them many of extreme views. Some even regard Palestinians as some sort of sub-species. Meier seems to be one of them, judging by his continual inflammatory speeches. History repeating itself I suppose. Nobody takes them very seriously."

"We do now," the DG interposed

"That photo was taken at a consular function," Perkins said. "Heaven knows how many are taken at parties like that. Dan, this is all nonsense and you know it."

"Except," Grayson countered, "for this." And, from his briefcase, he pulled a laptop. "Yours, Jacko, hidden in a compartment under the eaves above your bathroom window. Who put that bit of carpentry in? Michael Nolan, perhaps? Care to comment?"

"Never seen it before."

"Well, that's a bit of a surprise, because Colin and his searchers found it at your flat and it's got your fingerprints all over it."

"It's been planted."

"And, I suppose, the DNA from your 'dabs' was planted as well? You'd probably have got away with hiding it except for a new modern miracle of science, the MRI. They're portable now, you know, and can be tuned to find all manner of concealed things. So the space above your bathroom window became, as it were, an open book. And when we *did* open that book, we found all your naughty secrets. You are," Grayson smiled blandly, "nailed, old son. This computer contains enough evidence—and don't think you can arrange its destruction by some means, because we have extracted the information—enough evidence to have you put away for life. We have, for example, several of the messages Rachel Taylor sent to Michael Nolan. We haven't yet found how you managed to intercept them, but we will, though we *have* discovered that you sent them on to the JUA Council, the clandestine, violence-loving arm of the Party. We also found communications of interest from you to the US, ostensibly official contacts from our department; deliberate attempts to keep the American federal authorities from taking a hand in all this. Afraid they'd put two and two together, but that the police in Oklahoma wouldn't be bright enough even though I was on hand with our department's backing?

"You," Grayson went on, staring into Perkins's impassive face, "are guilty of treason, if only by association with a violent Irish extremist organization, let alone the Middle East aspects. I just hope you have to share a cell with Jimmy Riordan. We even know that your handsome suntan is due less to the beaches of the Balearics than the farmland of the Beka'a Valley." He turned away as if in disgust, but added over his shoulder: "Oh, by the way, we forwarded an email message from the Irishwoman—sent to Nolan's successor and apparently intercepted by you—on to the Chairman of the Council."

Perkins had so far retained his composure, but now he was clearly shaken. "You did what?"

"Ah, a surprise to you? We found Rachel Taylor's computer, too, in America. Like yours, it was full of fascinating news, such as your initial contact with her after she complained to a cousin in Tel Aviv about Ferguson's sympathy for the average Palestinian. Those complaints of hers were brought to the attention of the Council, who already knew about you because it had been instrumental in getting you your British education and hence the position at the Irish desk. There she was not, as you claimed, a name without a face, since you are now shown to have been with her in '95. Fact is, Jacko, you were working with Riordan and Nolan from the outset, and that's one of the reasons we failed to penetrate the PFRI. You, at the Irish Desk, kept us out. Taylor's job, at first, was to find out as much as she could about Fergoil's finances, and pass that on to Nolan. He then transmitted it to the leaders in Belfast. A cumbersome arrangement, but it provided a cutout. That's to say, it would have but for your own ability to intercept Taylor's communications. We don't yet know who made that possible, but I suspect that'll come out of all the material we picked up in Belfast on Saturday."

"These are all fairy tales, Dan." Perkins had regained his composure, regarding the others in the room with an air of amused tolerance.

Grayson ignored him. "By then, you were firmly in the pocket of the Council and yes, we've found your operational bank accounts. You suborned Taylor as well—easy enough, I imagine, given her background. She it was who put the Irish in touch with the Council by way of Nolan. That promised to be a fruitful partnership for both sides, each side thinking, of course, that it was merely making use of the other. Where were the arms to come from, Jacko, Russia?" Perkins remained silent. "Well, it doesn't really matter in this case, although we know anyway, because the money has been cut off.

" Mr. Perkins may not see the humor in this," said Grayson to the others, "but it really is rather funny. The message to the Chairman of the JUA Council—Beniamin Meier—was to the effect that the Ferguson money had been successfully obtained. Very soon the Chairman will gather the Council to let its members know, and each member will have an assigned task. We don't know who all those members are, at this point, but he'll lead us to them. I say 'us,' but that really means the Israeli authorities, with whom we've been in touch.

"Touchy is probably the right word for that situation, since even the highest echelons of the government and military are now known to have been infiltrated by JUA sympathizers—even Mossad is not thought to be immune. So they'll have to be very careful, especially with the volatility of the political situation there. Heaven knows what complications that has yet to produce. Hamas has been infiltrated so effectively that it continues to fire its feeble rockets at Israel, a cynical ploy by the JUA to arouse public hostility against the Palestinians, and a very successful one. The weaponry they intended to buy from a renegade Russian source was to go to Palestinian extremists, who would have provided the ideal excuse for a complete takeover of Gaza and, quite possibly, the West Bank, or 'Judea/Samaria' as the JUA like to say. They're fond of biblical terms; those have a nice emotional ring.

"But why stop there? There's a lot of oil in the Middle East, but none of it in Israel. Wouldn't it be nice to lay hands on some of that, too? After all, Iran is the sworn enemy of Israel, and it has lots of oil. So has Libya, and look what's going on there. It's not by accident, you realize. The ramifications are appalling. I suppose it's almost too obvious by now that Hezbollah, Islamic Jihad, even the Muslim Brotherhood have been infiltrated equally thoroughly, not to mention factions in almost every Middle East country.

"Why, Jacko? " Again there was no reply. "Well, that doesn't really matter much either, now." Grayson sat down. "That more or less concludes the reason for this meeting. There are a few loose ends, naturally, but we'll take care of most of 'em before too long. DG?"

The Director General was hard-faced. "This has been a very sad and unpleasant business for the entire department, but I must commend Dan Grayson for his work."

"I could never have got this far but for Miss Chauduri," Dan put in, "she's been a marvel. And, of course, our American cousins.

"They all have my deepest thanks, too. Garvey, you are now the de facto head of Irish." Garvey, who had been looking bewildered, smiled briefly but without much delight. He realized that a reputation he had for saying the wrong thing occasionally had kept him out of the loop.

"Bloom, I'm assigning you back to Dan's section. There's going to be a lot of work needing to be done, and the Scots and Welsh seem pacific enough at the moment. Ngami? You know the unfortunate reason you're here."

Ngami did, and he led Jacko Perkins firmly away. Over his shoulder Perkins snarled: "All those stinking Arabs will pay one day for what they did to my mother. My brother will see to that. 'Behold, the whirlwind of the Lord goeth forth with fury'..." His words trailed off behind the closing door.

"Book of Jeremiah," observed the Director General. "We'd better look much more closely into Perkins's antecedents, find out what drove him to such action. He was recruited while still up at Cambridge, so clearly something was seriously lacking in his vetting process. That'll be your responsibility, Garvey. And find out about his brother. Did we even know he had one? Some heads may need to roll.

" Now," he turned to Grayson, "Dan, I think you've earned yourself a spot of leave. Why don't you take yourself off somewhere nice for a week or two?" The DG smiled slyly towards LaDonna. "Take a friend. Ibiza, perhaps."

Grayson smiled too. "If it's all the same to you, sir, I'd like to finish this business off. After that, though, I'd appreciate a break. But not Spain—somewhere cool."

Chapter 16
July 2011

Newspapers and television were full of stories about the rolling up of two extremist networks and, although they had no firm corroborative evidence, strove to make a connection between the operations. Speculation was rife as to whether the initiative had come from Britain, Israel or—since such speculation always included it—the CIA. The usual "reliable sources" seemed to be of little assistance in this. The Israelis issued a terse statement to the effect that "disaffected elements" had intended to launch an all-out attack on Palestine, with the intention of placing it under total Israeli occupation and control, but Israeli intelligence services had identified the main figures in the plot, and they had been arrested. Trials would be forthcoming at a later date, after investigations had been completed. The British announcement was couched in similar terms regarding a plot to form a United Ireland by force of arms. Here, too, trials were to be held at some unspecified time in the future. The CIA, quietly furious at having been deliberately excluded from the affair, denied all knowledge of either conspiracy but, as usual, virtually no-one believed them. One of the few exceptions was Youssef, who remembered only too well that he had warned the Council of the danger of underestimating the British.

He had watched with dismay as the principals of his organization were rounded up, even his own brother, if he had interpreted correctly the veiled references to a mole in the British Intelligence Service. Even he had been amazed by the depth of penetration of government, military and Arabic organizations that JUA had achieved. Under the leadership of Meier, the JUA had infiltrated not only the Israeli military, giving it a strong chain of command when the conflict it was to precipitate actually broke out, but several of the Palestinian militant groups as well.

Thus it was that the rocket attacks on Israel, pinpricks though they were, had continued to keep the Israeli populace incensed. The woman suicide bomber in Haifa had been a JUA catspaw, intended to stir up further Israeli sentiment against Palestine and Arabs in general. Then there were the Israeli 'Settlements" in the Occupied Territories; many had been given to groups dedicated to the Council's way of thinking. The proceeds of the Ferguson episode were to have furnished them with quantities of weaponry, sufficient to overwhelm an inadequate Palestinian resistance.At the same time, operatives in Egypt would take over the tunnels currently used to supply Hamas and other radicals in Gaza, and thus secure that territory as well. Unrest in Egypt itself, as well as other neighboring states, was already being used to foment further turmoil in which Israeli forces, now under JUA control, could then intervene without too much international clamor..

A "domino effect," that had been the plan, but Youssef now realized that his work over many years had proved, in the end, totally worthless. His sole satisfaction had been the elimination of the remaining two of his mother's murderers. He would never get money from the Irish, but he was still a wealthy man as a result of his previous assignments, and he decided to take advantage of that fact before his own real identity became known. The British were sure to be working on that, particularly since it appeared that his brother's past activities would now be under the most rigorous scrutiny. Consequently, using a typically circuitous route, he arrived back in Geneva; there he consulted a surgeon about his injured knee and awaited events.

While Youssef was fretting at the enforced inactivity, his brain continued to pick at the reasons he had found himself in this position at all. With the occasional help of distant, impoverished relatives, he had managed to cope and to bring his little brother a measure of stability. Together they had gained the techniques of first, mere survival and then later, as they grew, development. Both were innately intelligent, perhaps a legacy of their father, who had died young but had shown the beginnings of a successful career in teaching. His two sons had learned rapidly how to turn adversity to their own advantage, ruthlessly making use of everybody and everything life presented to them. Among those opportunities was the school to which their uncle had directed them a few years before.

They had some good fortune: a young teacher at the "specialized" school recognized their extraordinary potential, nurtured it, and eventually put them on the road to university. There, he had told them, they would be able to develop the social skills to complement the physical, practical and ideological training they had received here. And it was at university, amid student idealism and the turmoil of the times, that they learned how to direct their hatred while keeping their newly-acquired skills veiled.

The colleges they went to were totally diverse. Youssef was fiercely independent, and would accept no perceived favors. His younger brother had actively sought help, and had been adopted at the age of nine by a middle-aged and well-meaning British couple who had come on a tour of the Holy Land. The boy had no illusions: his new "parents" were a means to an end. Youssef worked his own way through the American University in Beirut, and became an expert in foreign languages. He went to New York to study international disputes, and there took a course in theatrical make-up at The Parsons School of Design. By now he had irrevocably determined the course he would take. It was at about that time that Joseph approached a nascent organization and became Youssef, while Yakob, now known as Jacob (eventually to become Jacko to his friends up at Cambridge), had long since taken the name of his adoptive parents: Perkins.

Jacko's dedication was no less than that of his brother and he worked studiously to ensure that he would be noticed by the British security services. Unlike Grayson, Perkins was by no means surprised to be approached by a recruiter, though he feigned reluctance for a short period before accepting. Once in the midst of the twilight world he would be able to help shape events. His secondment to the Irish Desk had been fortuitous, but any other position would have served his purposes nearly as well.

For both he and his brother had fallen under the spell of the man they considered to be almost a Messiah. That Beniamin Meier had started his lucrative career as a forger, helping Nazi fugitives escape from Israeli agents who sought them in Brazil, Bolivia, Chile and other Latin American nations, was never public knowledge. Certainly Joseph and Jacob didn't know. Meier's parents—he had changed the name upon arrival in Israel—were Ewa and Kurt Mayer, Jewish refugees from Hitler's Germany, who would have probably denounced their own son had they known of his activities. He, in his turn, actually felt some remorse and finally determined to make amends by destroying those other enemies of the Jews—the Arabs.

❖　❖　❖

Bernadette Riley finally came unraveled after Malcolm arranged for her to read the newspapers. She admitted, after considerable plea bargaining, that she had tried to siphon money out of Fergoil, using her cover as an IRS official, while never conceding her connection with the PFRI, and was sentenced to ten-to-twenty years. She would probably be out in five.

"We can put that chapter behind us now," Malcolm said to his wife, Ziplich and Carol over an after-dinner drink at The Polo Grill, where the cooking was almost as good as Carol's, "and get on with the serious business of life."

Carol wanted to know if he didn't consider kidnapping, multiple murders and grand larceny, not to mention armed insurrection—even open warfare—serious business. She sipped delicately at a glass of Chablis. "That Youssef is still out there somewhere," she observed, "and as long as he's at large, he's a danger."

"I doubt that he'll trouble us again," was Malcolm's opinion. "There's no money for him to collect now, since that has been made completely secure with the restructuring of Fergoil. I have to say that Jenna Grant has shown herself to be an absolute master at her craft. Fergoil is going to be a major player in tomorrow's petroleum world, even without that illegal well. It's about the only advantage I can imagine stemming from the whole sorry business, although Fergoil was lucky not to be indicted for fraud and Heaven knows what else. Too late to nail Ferguson for that, though."

"I wasn't thinking about the money," Carol rejoined. "Didn't you say, Paul, that Youssef had killed that man in London, what's his name?—Nolan, that's it—for revenge? What makes you believe he hasn't got an even stronger reason for revenge now?"

Ziplich was thoughtful. "That's a very good point, Honey. He has a lot of people he'll want to blame for his present position. Us, of course, Benny, Jenna, even the guys in Missouri. Then there's the whole British contingent, particularly Dan Grayson. I think Carol's right, Lieutenant, don't you?"

Malcolm tasted his brandy and conceded: "I hadn't looked at it like that but, yes, I guess I agree. I wonder if the Brits share that concern?"

"I'll call Dan in the morning and mention it to him," Ziplich said. "It'll be good just to talk with him a little. Wonder how his romance is doing."

"Oh, I do hope it's going well," Carol exclaimed. "He's such a sweet man, and he deserves some happiness after losing his wife and child. That was very bitter for him."

"I'll ask about that, too," Ziplich promised. "Discreetly."

As it turned out, Grayson's romance was going very well indeed. He and LaDonna had decided not to move in together, although they spent almost all their free time with each other, since they both felt that marriage was something special and setting up a home was what Grayson described as a "turning point."

"Somehow I feel it might spoil the sense of a new beginning. I know I'm not expressing this very well, but I hope you know what I mean, 'Donna," he'd said, and she agreed. So LaDonna stayed in her flat, and Grayson started to make plans to sell his house. London property prices were astronomical despite the economic downturn, even in Willesden, and he stood to make a large profit. "Then we can get a small place a bit farther out," he suggested to LaDonna. "Somewhere nice for kids to grow up. Besides..." he trailed off.

"Besides, Janet would always be a presence. It's all right, darling, I do understand, truly I do."

And that is how matters stood when Ziplich rang to express his concerns about Youssef.

"Yes, we've thought about him quite a lot," Grayson said, a cup of tea in one hand and a copy of the latest Daily Telegraph's parliamentary scandal revelations peering at him from the desk, "but the bloody man seems to have disappeared off the face of the earth. We're looking as hard as we can, but we have simply no idea where he is, what name he's using or even, frankly, if he's still alive. What's more, we never know what he's going to look like, judging from past experience—the man's a bloody chameleon—so he could be here in London, for all we know, just waiting for the right moment."

Ziplich feared that might be true. "So, what precautions are you taking?"

"I've been issued with a firearm, and I practice quite often in our basement range here. 'Donna doesn't like it, but she admits it's probably a sensible measure. Now, it's my turn to ask if you're pretty much doing the same thing." Once again, Grayson forbore to mention just how skillful he was as a marksman.

"From today, yeah. We hadn't thought about it a lot until Carol mentioned it to Stan Malcolm and me last evening. Trouble is, the guy has so many potential targets. 'Course, the one he really wants is Riordan, but he's out of the loop, I guess."

"Ah."

"Dan, what does 'ah' mean?"

"Well, I hate to tell you this, but Riordan's got away again."

"You're kidding me."

"Alas, not so." He still talks like that, Ziplich thought, but said nothing. "Last night, it seems—I've only just heard this, may I add— he walked out of prison into the dark. Without our connivance this time."

"And straight home, I suppose."

"No doubt he's learned his lesson about that. No, he's just disappeared. Not before crippling a guard with some sort of karate chop or similar."

Ziplich was more than exasperated, he was angry: "How the hell could you let that happen, Dan? Wasn't he in maximum security?"

"Not maximum enough, it would seem. Look on the bright side, Zee."

"If there is one," Ziplich growled.

"Well, yes, I think there is."

"And that would be?"

"Riordan wants Youssef even more than we do. For us, it's business. For Riordan, it's personal. Riordan won't come after us: certainly, we're the enemy, but Riordan isn't a casual killer. In fact, I'm not aware that he's ever killed anybody, even though he may sometimes have been complicit. But Youssef murdered his former girlfriend and two other friends in cold blood. Youssef isn't the only one out for vengeance. My hope is that one of them will lead us to the other."

"Some hope," Ziplich said wearily.

"It's the best we've got just now," Grayson told him. "Have you any better ideas?"

Ziplich had to admit that he had not.

Riordan slipped across the porous border into the Republic without difficulty and without challenge. He hoped he hadn't seriously harmed the prison guard, who was only doing his job, but it had been some time since he'd had the chance to practice his skills and he was afraid he might have used too much force. He'd hitched a lift on a lorry, whose driver asked no questions: a sympathizer, Riordan deduced, and he asked no questions either. His immediate destination was Dublin, where he was sure of a friendly reception at a house near the harbor. A hot bath—God, he could use that—a change of clothes, a night's rest, and the next day he'd be on the Dun Laoghaire ferry to Holyhead. Train to London, lie up at that flat in Hampstead—not Kilburn, not any more, after Michael—then, as Youssef had also decided, wait.

The media moved on to other, more current news, most of it, especially financial, bad. Happy stories don't sell newspapers or increase viewing figures, unless your side is winning a sporting event or a war. Still, small items do occasionally appear on the inside pages. Thus it was that both Riordan and Youssef read: "Senior Civil Service Officer to Wed." There was a short column of sententious praise for a man who had done, so far as the article made clear, nothing worthy of note. There was also a blurred picture of Daniel Grayson.

For Youssef, this was an opening. He recognized Grayson immediately, elderly though the photograph had been: one of those who had caught him, if only briefly, in Missouri. Here was an opportunity to settle at least part of the score.

Riordan's reasoning was different. He knew it had been largely due to Grayson that he had been arrested, yet he held no bitterness for that; it was how the game was played. On the other hand, he thought, the "psychopathic scum" he despised probably would be less complacent and would go after Grayson, one of the people who had destroyed his organization. Youssef had killed Colum, Michael and Rachel—Riordan had no knowledge of his former lover's double-dealing—and his own life was, therefore, forfeit.

Both men began their planning.

Over a drink in The Bear at Long Melford—a pint of bitter for Grayson, Sauvignon Blanc for LaDonna—they discussed the cottage.

"Isn't it a bit far out?" LaDonna had asked. "I mean, whatever time would we have to leave to get in by nine?"

"We could drive over to the station at, say, Bury St. Edmunds or Sutton, and take the train in. Hour, maybe, one and a half at the most."

"Assuming no delays."

"You can never assume that, what with our railways, but the rest of the staff have to put up with the same problems, those who live out of town. Look at the DG, for goodness' sake: his place is in Dorset."

"He's also got a chauffeur-driven Bentley and a flat in Mayfair," LaDonna rejoined. "Not strictly comparable."

"All right, all right, if you're not happy..."

"Oh, but I am. Deliriously." She kissed him with enthusiasm. "And the cottage is perfect. Just think: what a lovely place to raise a family. Finish your drink, darling, and let's go back to the estate agent before someone else snaps it up."

"Look at 'em," beamed the barmaid as they left. "Have you ever seen two people so madly in love?"

"I dunno," responded the sole customer at the bar morosely. "Never been too sure about the outcome of these mixed marriages meself."

"Tell that to the American president!" came the tart rejoinder.

Chapter 17
August 2012

They met in The Wells in Hampstead. Riordan had made a discreet phone call to a Hendon number from a call box in King's Cross. The conversation was unexceptional to any potential eavesdropper, of whom there were none, and the rendezvous was quickly arranged. Riordan's main problem was that he was now almost without funds, and he certainly couldn't go seeking help from Social Security. On the other hand, although the organization was now defunct, there was no shortage of expatriates who would help where they could, and Riordan had finally managed to dredge a long-forgotten name and number from his memory.

"'Tis like this, y'see," he said over a pint of Guinness, "the bastard who dragged us all into the shit, the filthy scum who killed Michael and Colum and Rachel, will be coming to London at the end of October, and 'tis my intention to make him pay."

"How can ye be sure he'll be here at all, Jimmy?" Padraig Costello was a burly man who made his living as a builder, a fact to which his hands gave witness. He had never been directly involved in the workings of the Committee, but he'd had some peripheral dealings as a go-between for Michael Nolan.

"There's a wedding coming up in a few weeks, and the groom is the man who frustrated his intentions. Now, this is a vicious, evil bastard that I'm talking about, me boy, one who enjoys killing and inflicting pain. He's been a paid assassin in the past, that I know for certain, but this will be personal; he'll be after the one who made him look stupid and incompetent. I'm betting that he's some kind of egomaniac. At all events, I know, I just know, that he's going to try something, and the most obvious time would be at the wedding. There'll be lots of people about—that'll help him, just melting into the crowd."

"Suppose it's a small wedding in the country?"

"It isn't: 'tis at St. James's in Piccadilly. Just think of the jams of people there always are down there. That'll be the place, I know it. There's another thing: he'd like to get me, too, so I've to change me appearance."

"That'll be why you've not shaved, then."

"It will. Now, I'm going to need money. And a weapon. Now, is it not true that Michael had a hidden account? Not part of the main organization, I mean, but a kind of emergency fund?"

"'Tis so, Jimmy, but you're not supposed to know about it: no one is."

"Ach, Paddy, for God's sake, the man's dead, the organization's rolled up, the Committee's all in prison. Several people have lost their lives and the whole operation's gone to hell—all because of this one focking foreign murderer. I need that money." Riordan paused long enough to order two Bushmills, then returned to his theme, his words masked to all but Costello by the hubbub of a busy local pub.

"I tell ye, I need that money to deal with this man, and I intend to have it. Now, will youse help, or shall it be the hard way?"

Padraig Costello was not a stupid man.

In Geneva there was no problem regarding money, since Youssef had been accumulating it for many years, and a great deal had been advantageously invested. The news item in the Daily Telegraph had enraged him. That effete, damnable Englishman had been a large part of the reason for his failure with the Ferguson business, and now his own organization had been completely destroyed as a direct result. The English "civil servant" had allowed himself to be identified by name, and also by place on his wedding day. *I shall,* Youssef thought, *allow him his moment of pleasure. Let him marry his bitch: then he'll die.*

A thought struck him; maybe some of those Yankees would be present. Now, that would be a real bonus. He had more or less decided to make another trip to Tulsa in order to exact his revenge on the—to him—nameless Ziplich and Benny, not to mention those two women, but maybe that wouldn't be necessary. He hobbled to a public phone

and started to make his bookings. Fly to Paris. Eurostar to London—
different identities for each segment, naturally—and a room at the
Meridien. Another discreet call gave him an address in Hounslow
where—for a figure—suitable equipment could be purchased. Since
the London Underground attacks, security had been tightened considerably, and the price of weaponry had shot up. Youssef didn't care.
He *would* have satisfaction.

Grayson haunted Savile Row and Jermyn Street, seeking the
exact clothes for his wedding. It had to be a morning suit, of course,
and the obvious choice was to hire one, but somehow Moss Bros. just
didn't seem appropriate. LaDonna was worthy of better than that, so
he eventually settled on Huntsman and spent nearly three month's
income for a single occasion. Maybe I can sell it later on eBay, he
reasoned. Except the expensive cufflinks, which he really liked and
of which the Chameleon himself would have approved. LaDonna utterly refused to disclose what she intended to wear or where it would
come from. The two of them did manage to agree on dresses for the
two bridesmaids, they being the Director General's granddaughters.
Fortunately the DG, and possibly the basset hound, had approved.

On the day, LaDonna was stunning in the simplest dress of pure
white, with just a touch of blue edging at the scalloped neckline. She
told nobody that it came from Selfridge's.

There arose the question of security. Ted Garvey, mollified now
by his promotion, mentioned to Grayson that it had been unwise to
allow his wedding announcement and picture to appear in the press.
Grayson agreed.

"It wasn't my idea," he said, "but the company had put out a release before anyone even knew about it. I went to the DG and told
him what I thought, and he was of the same opinion, but the damage
had already been done. Some over-zealous twit in Communications
seemingly took it upon himself to let the world know that he was actually earning his salary. He certainly hadn't made his mark up until
then, and now, of course, he isn't earning that salary any more."

"Let's hope he keeps his mouth shut from now on."

"Oh, he will, I promise you," Grayson told him with almost fe-rocious certainty, and Garvey made no further comment.

Grayson was now practicing daily at the firing range in the com-pany's basement. He had become so proficient with such a variety of small arms that the instructor, a former SAS sergeant, took him to one side after a session on a Wednesday morning a few weeks before the wedding.

"I can't teach you anything more, sir," he said to a Grayson who was still not accustomed to the deference his new position as Deputy Director General gave him. "You've reached a level of ability that I've seldom seen. Unless, that is, you want to try for RPGs and mortars." This suggestion Grayson politely declined. He did choose, however to exchange the Walther he had been issued earlier for a Glock, a weapon he found he preferred. His true preference would be for no firearm at all, but a certain sense of reality told him that would be, at the very least, unwise.

A week before his wedding day his decision proved to have been the right one.

The Luxemburg police had arrested a man in possession of a British passport on suspicion of drug trafficking, but had agreed to his blustering demand to see a British consular official, a decision they rapidly came to regret. Instead of taking him in their own ve-hicle, they ill-advisedly allowed him to be accompanied to the em-bassy in his rented car. As they climbed from his vehicle outside the legation, the man snatched a pistol from under the front passenger seat. He held it firmly under the senior officer's ear and forced the two other policemen to precede him into the building, where he also drove the armed security officer and the receptionist before him to an inner room. There, where he found four more people to add to his captives, he made his demands. He was to be allowed to leave, the receptionist as his hostage, and not to be followed. If he discovered he was under observation, he would shoot the girl, first to injure and finally, if he was still being followed, to kill.

He was out of luck. One of the men in the inner room was Gray-son, on a mission concerning another British National's questionable activities. He shot the gun from the trafficker's hand as it was pressed against the young woman's neck, and followed up with a bullet to the man's left leg. The girl, unhurt, fainted; the dealer fell, the security man grabbed him, and the incident was over. And Grayson had proven to his own satisfaction that his marksmanship was proficient, should it ever be needed again.

Praise from the Luxemburgers was turned aside with a "You caught him, so he's yours." Grayson wanted no questions as to what he was doing in a friendly EU country with an undisclosed firearm, even on what was technically British soil. In their turn, the authorities were quite ready to report the capture of a dangerous criminal. The British Ambassador, alerted by Grayson, agreed that the security camera tapes would remain confidential, since Grayson's reason for being there was even more confidential. So everyone was happy. Except the drug dealer, of course.

Chapter 18
October 2012

For Youssef, it was a dream come true. He peered down the telescopic sight from his sixth floor room at the Hotel Meridien, chosen for its clear view of St. James's courtyard over the placards on the church's railings. He focussed first on Grayson, then the black woman who'd trapped him, the American detective, the bitch who had smashed his knee, and that big Redskin. All of them: he could scarcely believe his luck. A leather-clad biker loitering among many on the sidewalk near the courtyard entrance received not a second glance.

Youssef knew he probably shouldn't have been surprised that the Americans were present, but he had mentally more or less consigned them to a separate occasion. Finish this, he said to himself, and then retire. The pain in his leg, instead of diminishing, had grown steadily worse over the last several months.

"The damage," his Swiss doctor had told him, "is irreversible. That leg should have been immobilized the moment the injury occurred. Your only two choices now are take it easy or end up a cripple." Youssef, while having no urge to be a cripple, could not even consider leaving business unfinished. His only regrets—for very different reasons—as he checked the range yet again and tightened the rifle's silencer an unnecessary fourth time, were that both his brother and Malone were in prison.

Jimmy Riordan was not the Malone that Youssef would have recognized. Taking a leaf from The Chameleon's own book, he had totally altered his appearance by shaving his head, growing the beard that Bernadette had suggested over a year ago in the Tulsa motel, and donning motorcycle leathers. A crash helmet dangled from his left hand, leather gauntlets inside it concealing a Beretta nine-millimeter.

He was like a coiled spring, which the sight of Youssef would release. He *knew* this was to be his day.

The groom's wedding party entered St. James's church, and Youssef could faintly hear organ music through the roar of traffic in Piccadilly. Half an hour, he thought, an hour at the most. His escape plan was complete. In the moments of panic following the shooting, he would jettison the rifle and leave the room, pocket the surgical gloves for disposal later in any convenient waste bin, and take the lift to the ground floor. Leaving the building, he would turn right and walk—never run away from an incident, he reminded himself, it attracts attention—towards Green Park, where he would take the Tube to Heath Row. He already had his airline ticket. He'd be back in Geneva in time to catch the evening news.

❖ ❖ ❖

"...as long as you both shall live?"

"I do."

As the bride and groom kissed, Grayson being careful not to press the shoulder holster against LaDonna, there was a spontaneous round of applause from the congregation. Benny was wiping his eyes surreptitiously, Carol and Millie were openly weeping. The Director General—eyebrows in "indulgent good humor" mode—was beaming. Three weeks previously, he had been pleased to inform Grayson—to the latter's delighted surprise—of his elevation to DDG.

Ziplich was swallowing a lump in his throat, while Trent, Garvey and Ngami pumped one another's hands. Henry, Sean Smethwick and a dozen others automatically swept their eyes around the church. Stan Malcolm, his head still slightly fuzzy after last night—Grayson had fulfilled his promise to show his American colleagues a pub, and had chosen his bachelor evening to extend that invitation to include several of them—was mentally rehearsing his reception speech. He had found that the "bitter," apparently so prized by his host, was a beer that tasted flat, sour and warm. Even Budweiser seemingly came in two versions in Britain, one subtitled "Budwar," and he was not thrilled by that either.

Survival had depended on the discovery of readily available Jack Daniel's. He was now regretting that discovery, which had been repeated in The French House, The Flask, The Spaniards, The Gatehouse, The Colton Arms (of course), Ye Old Cheshire Cheese, The Lamb and Flag and others whose names were now indistinct. *It was a good thing,* he reflected muzzily, *that Grayson had rented a chauffeured coach for the occasion, which had lasted a good twelve hours.* Of course, the news of Grayson's promotion had been further reason for celebration.

Jenna Grant, her new-found position as head of Fergoil having given her a sense of authority, was poised and elegant. Even Grayson's rather reclusive brother, Neville, put in a rare, if typically disheveled, appearance, seemingly none the worse for the bachelor revels.

The organ pealed Mendelssohn's triumphant Wedding March, and the joyous couple, accompanied by the two smiling bridesmaids, walked up the aisle and into the crisp autumn sunlight.

Riordan, standing on the sidewalk close to the church gate, saw it: the fleeting glint of metal from a sixth floor window of the Meridien, and a faint wisp of vapor. It was too late already, he understood at once, to prevent what he'd feared, but not too late to catch that murderous bastard. Ignoring the blast of car horns and the shouted words of abuse, he dashed through the congested Piccadilly traffic to reach the door of the hotel.

As Youssef fired, Grayson swept a radiant LaDonna into the air in exultation. An ugly red stain appeared on the back of her white gown. He felt her body stiffen, then go limp. For a moment he thought she'd fainted, then he felt the blood on his hands, smelt its metallic tang. Benny was writhing on the ground, silent but clearly in agony. Jenna was in a crumpled heap on the flagstones, motionless. Ziplich was clutching his chest, blood foaming on his lips. Of the others, Grayson saw nothing before he was himself on the ground, tears streaming down his face over the body of his bride.

And an Asprey's gold locket, with two small portraits and intertwined initials, stayed in its little presentation box in his coat pocket.

Youssef stepped calmly out of the hotel main door, and turned right, angry with himself for having hit the woman instead of Grayson, but showing no trace of it on his bland face. He had changed his appearance yet again, now seeming to be a City businessman, complete with mustache, briefcase and bowler, and Riordan failed to recognize him until a scream came to his ears through the din of traffic. It was Carol, who had caught a glimpse of the profile imprinted on her memory during her hostage ordeal.

"Him! Him! The limping one! Oh, my God!"

Riordan glanced across at the sound of Carol's voice, and at once took in the carnage. His experienced eye registered instantly that only Grayson's bride was beyond earthly help, and he said a silent prayer for her soul. Now his fury was recharged, and he closed on his quarry, one hand groping into the crash helmet.

"Hello, Youssef," he hissed, and shot him in the left leg. Youssef fell to the ground, terrified pedestrians scattering in all directions. "That was for Rachel." Another shot, this time to the damaged right knee. "That one's for Colum." He fired a third time, at Youssef's right hand, which was scrabbling for the knife taped to his shattered leg. "That's for the bride, you filth." Another bullet ("That's for Michael") smashed Youssef's left arm.

"Finally," Riordan grinned wolfishly into the Chameleon's malevolent eyes, "this is for me," and he put his fifth and sixth rounds into Youssef's stomach. "Wouldn't want you to die too easily."

He straightened up, throwing his weapon to the ground and turned to face the sprinting—and very obviously armed—Henry, Smethwick and Ngami. With empty hands held clearly out in front of him, Riordan nodded his head toward the twitching, blood-drenched figure on the pavement.

"Trying to resist arrest," he explained brightly.

14811518R00163

Made in the USA
Charleston, SC
02 October 2012